EAST OF SUEZ

THE ARGOSY™ LIBRARY

EAST OF SUEZ

THEODORE ROSCOE

ILLUSTRATED BY
**SAMUEL CAHAN
DOUGLAS HILLIKER
ROGER B. MORRISON**

COVER BY
PAUL STAHR

POPULAR PUBLICATIONS · 2022

PUBLISHING HISTORY

"The Gold God Laughs" originally appeared in the February 23, 1929 issue of *Argosy* magazine (Vol. 201, No. 5). Copyright © 1929 by The Frank A. Munsey Company. Copyright renewed © 1956 and assigned to Steeger Properties, LLC. All rights reserved.

"Two Daggers" originally appeared in the July 13, 1929 issue of *Argosy* magazine (Vol. 205, No. 1). Copyright © 1929 by The Frank A. Munsey Company. Copyright renewed © 1956 and assigned to Steeger Properties, LLC. All rights reserved.

"Blood of the Rose" originally appeared in the September 7, 1929 issue of *Argosy* magazine (Vol. 206, No. 3). Copyright © 1929 by The Frank A. Munsey Company. Copyright renewed © 1956 and assigned to Steeger Properties, LLC. All rights reserved.

"The Death Song of Absinthe Devolle" originally appeared in the January 11, 1930 issue of *Argosy* magazine (Vol. 209, No. 3). Copyright © 1930 by The Frank A. Munsey Company. Copyright renewed © 1957 and assigned to Steeger Properties, LLC. All rights reserved.

"Checked Retribution" originally appeared in the September 13, 1930 issue of *Argosy* magazine (Vol. 215, No. 2). Copyright © 1930 by The Frank A. Munsey Company. Copyright renewed © 1957 and assigned to Steeger Properties, LLC. All rights reserved.

"Bentfinger" originally appeared in the May 23–June 13, 1931 issues of *Argosy* magazine (Vol. 221, Nos. 2–5). Copyright © 1931 by The Frank A. Munsey Company. Copyright renewed © 1958 and assigned to Steeger Properties, LLC. All rights reserved.

"Dirge of the Nancy D" originally appeared in the August 22, 1931 issue of *Argosy* magazine (Vol. 223, No. 3). Copyright © 1931 by The Frank A. Munsey Company. Copyright renewed © 1958 and assigned to Steeger Properties, LLC. All rights reserved.

"Animal Man" originally appeared in the March 2, 1935 issue of *Argosy* magazine (Vol. 253, No. 6). Copyright © 1935 by The Frank A. Munsey Company. Copyright renewed © 1962 and assigned to Steeger Properties, LLC. All rights reserved.

"On Evil Beach" originally appeared in the April 23, 1938 issue of *Argosy* magazine (Vol. 281, No. 2). Copyright © 1938 by The Frank A. Munsey Company. Copyright renewed © 1965 and assigned to Steeger Properties, LLC. All rights reserved.

Visit argosymagazine.com for more books like this.

TABLE OF CONTENTS

THE GOLD GOD LAUGHS

*When a wise young gunman from Chi goes
blundering among the ancient beliefs and
customs of India, trouble is not far off*

"Brave not the eye in Siva's head,
Or the Gold God will laugh and strike you dead—"

LEAN AND BROWN and tired of most things was Lynn Hagedorn. Now, as he idled on the sun-blistered upper deck of the Lady Marguerita and watched the burnished water slip by abeam, he felt himself bored to an extinction that rivaled the Nirvana of Putai Ho-Shang.

It was hot on that upper deck. The wind off the mainland was like the breath from a furnace door. But it was hotter on the foredeck below him, and rank with the odor of the natives who milled like corralled cattle. And the cabins were unbearable.

The gaunt American sighed—an effort that brought a flow of sweat to his cheeks. He mopped the sticky water away. He was used to heat; he had just finished a tough engineering job around the corner from Singapore, one of the hottest little nooks, at certain seasons, in the whole world. But he never could get used to poky water voyages on a dumpy, smoky tub jammed to the bows with yellow men and giving over its hind quarters to anæmic missionaries, green-faced colonial planters bent double with curry-and-rice livers, sickly tourists with rubber necks, and naturalists hunting heaven knows what.

Hagedorn glared through a headache at the Mergui

Islands. Jewels cradled in a mirror of sea. He had seen them
too often to appreciate their beauty. He mopped his face,
and decided to brave his cabin for a stengah.

"Say, those islands look swell. Sort of green and cool."

The engineer did not want to turn around, but he did. He
was too hot to be civil to some yawping tourist from Corning, New York, or Fitchburg, Utah, and that was exactly
what this speaker appeared to be. A tourist; not from
Corning or Fitchburg, though—more likely from some
big city. He had that aggressive big-city face. Sharp eyes
and a sharp mouth and a quick, nervous way. The stranger
wiped his face with a linen handkerchief, and said, again:

"Nice-looking, these islands around here. What place
is that?"

"Mergui," replied Hagedorn bluntly. He eyed the man
before him. Good Lord, even as a tourist, the fellow was
green as grass. He owned all the tourist junk—a sun-helmet glaringly new, a Kodak-case slung under arm, a cane
just out of some bazaar, a fancy duck suit, and a neck flaming with fresh sunburn. But like the worst novice he wore a
blue shirt with pink stripes and a green tie. Garments that
would sop up perspiration like a blotter. Already the green
tie had acquired pink and blue stripes and the shirt-collar
resembled an artist's pen-wiper.

"Say," he chuckled, noting Hagedorn's eye on his shirt.
"I'm a mess, ain't I? About all I been doing since I left old
Chi was waltz into a laundry for clean duds. This travel
racket ain't all it says in them Cook Tour booklets. Some of
these places are the berries, though, at that. Take Penang.
I got on this boat back there at Penang. The hotels there,

some of 'em, ain't so bad. Say, doc, I could tell with a glass eye that you was an old hand in these parts."

Hagedorn grunted. "Out here eighteen years. Grubbing around the Orient ever since I was twenty. All except three years I spent with Allenby chasing Turks in Mespot." He resented his speech the moment it was out of his mouth. Now this green Yankee would be hanging on his arm like a Kelantan leech and asking about tigers and dancing girls and all the things tourists expect to see in the East.

He heard the chap exclaiming: "Eighteen years. Well, I'm a sucker. You sure don't look no thirty-eight years old. Say, pal, where are you goin'? Are there any good places in this country to go? Any good places?"

THERE WAS ONE good place to send all green tourists who bothered him, the engineer reflected sourly. He stared dismally at the shimmering water, and mumbled the information that he was going to India. More immediately, however, he was going to his cabin.

Nodding with false cordiality, he left the rail and started to descend the companion ladder leading down to the open foredeck. Once he was off the heights of the upper bridge the stench of the milling natives smacked him in the face. Malays and Chinamen and squat Burmese women with babies crowded in a sticky mess at the foot of the ladder. The sun smote down a savage glare, and the rails of the ladder were scorching to the hand. The foredeck reeked.

A bulky coolie with a face ugly and fat blocked Hagedorn's progress at the ladder bottom. Ill-humoredly, Hagedorn ordered him out of the way. Adamant as a hunk of butter, the big Malay grunted, breathing a staggering gust of alcohol. His eyes were bright from native liquor. Hagedorn gave him a rough elbow, and shoved him aside.

The next second that Malay's hand was in the air, fingers closed around the hilt of a gleaming parang. The jam of natives screamed, and Hagedorn tried to jump aside. The wicked blade swept out in a blow that would have clipped the American's head from his neck. But the blow never fell.

Wham! From the deck above a sudden, roaring shot. The parang clattered to the deck. The Malay's hand spouted blood as he bent double screaming. Hagedorn dealt him a kick that flung him spinning into the milling; press, and vaulted up the companion ladder.

At the top of the ladder stood the tourist from old Chi. His Chicago face was bright with a sprightly grin. In his fist glinted an automatic that smoked languidly at the muzzle. He nodded cheerfully at Hagedorn, and indicated the prostrate Malay on the deck below.

"That Malay now," he chuckled. "And that knife! No way to go after a fellow. He'd have bumped you off with a good rod." He tapped his automatic, grinning. "What they need out here in the East is a sense of humor and a little Yankee ingenuity."

And that was how Lynn Hagedorn came to know Rip Conray from Chicago. Rip Conray, tourist. Or, as he himself explained it: "Little Rip Conray from Chi. The smartest pistol-shot in the game; an' tourin' one year for his health, or, at least until they railroaded in a new district attorney back in the big town."

Little Rip Conray from Chi was not the most moral of men, nor was he an ideal traveling companion. In the first place he suffered rather an exalted opinion of little Rip Conray from Chi, and was never slow in admitting it.

And he was troublesome in other ways. For example, the big Dutch planter coming up from Java happened to admit to a company in the dining saloon that he possessed a little Javanese urn of beaten gold. Before the steamer panted into Martaban, the Dutchman was squalling to high heaven that his precious urn had been stolen. Lost it? *Ach!* Could he have lost it when it was at the very bottom of his bag? A thief had taken that urn and the ship must be turned outside in to find it. The Javanese urn was not found.

Again, a pearl buyer from Singapore had displayed a diamond ring that glimmered like sunshine on the sea. The pearl buyer was accustomed to stifling cabins on torrid nights, and slept like a log. During one of these sleeps the diamond had vanished from his finger. Once more the Lady Marguerita was scoured from stern to stem. Neither diamond nor robber turned up in the shuffle. The dozen white passengers glared at one another with suspicion and distaste augmented by the ordinary run of tropic discomforts. Unpleasantries developed.

Somehow Lynn Hagedorn conceived the notion that Rip Conray knew what had become of those stolen goods. Perhaps it was because the gentleman from Chicago was so sympathetic to the losers; volunteered so eagerly to lead the search.

THEN THERE WAS the poker game in which Conray plucked clean the purses of a Scotch diamond merchant, a British consulate attaché, and an Australian army officer. The game took place just before they sighted Moulmein. The plucked victims denounced Mr. Conray as a gambling sharp. Rip Conray did not deny the accusation, spending his breath in bravely calling them all sorts of sons. The quarrel ended with Rip Conray walking from the cabin, gun in hand, pound-notes in pocket.

And two hours out of Rangoon a furious hullabaloo broke out on the foredeck of the vessel. Once more, Rip Conray. He had insulted an aged Buddhist monk by spitting at the old chap's foot. The monk had a gang of disciples around him in a jiffy, and Conray found himself the nucleus of a cyclonic riot. Hagedorn and the second mate had rescued him before he could get his automatic in action, but not before his aggressive face had been scratched by tooth and nail.

Whereby it became apparent to Hagedorn that Rip Conray was something different, all things considered. Ordinary tourists, even from Chicago, did not carry automatics on their hips and call them "rods." Nor could an ordinary tourist shoot a knife from a Malay's hand, or ream the pocketbooks of colonial poker players. The engineer was indebted to the Chicago man, rather liked him, but there was no denying the fellow was proving difficult.

"Look here," he warned, taking Conray aside. "Go easy, old man. You can't go flashing that gun all the time, you know. It isn't done. After all, you *are* East of Suez. The folks out here are apt to have frazzled nerves and resent things like that. Some of them are mighty smart shots, too. And then you won too much money in that card game. Those boys are pretty mad. I happen to know Peacham, that consulate fellow. He says you drew your aces too often. Liable to make trouble for you. Maybe you can laugh down all that. But whatever you do, don't rile the Orientals. You can't kid a native. It isn't the thing. That Buddhist monk, for example. He's holy to these folks. You're lucky to have got out of that racket with your neck. Leave 'em alone, Conray. Leave them and their things alone."

Conray shrugged. "Say, they're all a mob of bum sports. What if I did trim them poker players? They'd trim me if they could have. An' that old yella-face was just a crab, see? It's like I been sayin'. All they need out in this country is a little Yankee ingenuity. An' a sense of humor." He shrugged again. "All this Orient stuff is the bunk. It's like I said."

Hagedorn shook his head. "Leave 'em alone," he warned. "Leave them an' their things alone, or you'll be going back to Chicago in a pine box."

SHADOWS OF DEEP violet—cobalt blue when caught in the narrow defiles—slanted down the valley as the sun burrowed into the westward Himalayas. Twilight did not cool the floor of that valley. Coming dark was breathless, suffocating, and only served further to terrify the crowd of natives scrambling wildly for the pass. Urging their skinny legs to the utmost, they made for the valley's neck like a startled bevy of outlandish birds, running and stumbling and filling the shadows with clamor. A plume of fine dust settled on the sand behind them.

The steep cliffs on either side of this long-emptied river bed caught their outcry and tossed it echoing among the rocks. Squads of monkeys fled away across the bowlder-strewn slopes, swearing. The crowd of natives gained the narrow pass just as the sun went out. They took their disturbance with them, leaving in the valley behind a silence as vast and utter as the impermeable blackness that plunged from the sunless sky.

A scatter of white stars began to wink in the black dome that spanned the valley; and finally a timid moon, sickle-shaped and silver, became apparent as it crept from behind a lofty ridge. Its wan ray could not dispel the deeper shadows in the valley. But a faint luminescence washed down the open slopes, and, though shedding an even blacker gloom in certain defiles, sought out nooks and crannies, and filled them with silvery light. And as the moon ventured higher its cold ray fell across the door of a little shrine that stood backed against an upshoot of cliff wall that rose at one end of the valley. The ridge of cliffs, the breathless slopes, the rocks, the very sands of the valley, seemed old as the moon, old as Time itself. And the shrine might have been fashioned with its surroundings.

The stone roof sagged. The rock walls were cracked and polished by wind-blown sand. Even the tiny bell above the door might have been cast by the Vedic gods who molded the valley and the moon and the shrine. Stirred by ghostly hands—for no one could have said there was a wind in that forgotten oven-corner of the world—it voiced a senile *clong* that was quieter than silence. The three human skulls that lay in a row beside the shrine door, though yellow and thin as paper, were by contrast young.

The straying moonray was not the only light to find the door of the shrine. A dim, lambent glow, eerie as the light of phosphorus, stole from the mysterious interior. And five little pairs of lights crept around a corner of an outer wall. Eyes. Jackal eyes.

The five jackals scurried like thieves into the moonlight. A moment they quarreled together. Then as if by common consent they broke into a wailing chorus and lamented the moon. In keeping with their dead surroundings, the mourning cries melted into the silent valley walls. A somber note whispered from the shrine bell, and the jackals sped with guilty stealth into the house of worship.

Once over the threshold, the pack stopped short for a furtive survey. Fearfully they glared at the ugly image squatting against the back wall. Menacingly, the image glared back at them. Its monstrous face, contorted, decadent as only the countenance of a Hindu god could be, glowered from a halo of light cast by the tiny flame held in the palm of a golden hand. The hand was raised chest high so that the fire illuminated little more than the face; the remainder of the image sitting cross-legged on a pedestal was lost in kindly shadow.

The guttering flame fell full on that criminal visage, burnishing the golden cheeks, polishing the lobes of the ears and lighting up the yawning mouth, for the god sat as if yearning to take a huge bite of the fire that disclosed his depraved features.

And in the middle of the forehead, most wondrous of all—a live eye! Set loosely in a shallow socket, it winked and glimmered and glowed like a fanned coal. Red as blood, it snatched a lively glint from the open flame in the upturned palm, and blinked and twinkled, and spattered crimson darts of fire into dark crannies of the shrine.

Unlearned men might have called that marvelous eye a ruby, and as large as had ever been seen! But all learned men and Hindus knew it for an eye, the power of which passed mortal understanding. For its owner was the great god, Siva—Siva, the Powerful, Siva, the All-Seeing. Had Siva not, with a spark from that central eye, reduced such mighty deities as Vishnu and Brahma to cinders? Could he not destroy the lowly human who so much as dared to look into that eye?

Testimony to the awful power of the eye was given by the three skulls going to dust beside the shrine door. Other skulls had lain there and faded into the sand. And just now a more than potent testimonial lay spraddled on the floor before the mouthing image. The thing that had sent the crowd of pilgrims yowling back across the valley. The thing that had beckoned hither the band of vagrant jackals.

Moonlight creeping into the shrine fell across the recumbent figure and disclosed it as a native. The body lay doubled in an incredible twist, legs and arms splayed out like the appendages of a crushed spider. The feet stretched toward the idol. The head lay in a pool of moonlight near the door. Only it was never a head. It was something shrivelled, gone, black, faceless. A dried fig. A *thing*. As if the demon-faced image had, indeed, hurled a spark from its glowing eye to blast the head from this body.

The jackals saw; rushed forward, fighting. The massive image yawped its ghastly, yawning grin. The flame in its palm fluttered, and the eye in its forehead twinkled merrily. In the long-dead, breathless outside, hot and petrified, the shrine bell voiced a noiseless *clong*.

EXCITEMENT BROUGHT A shrill note to Conray's voice. He grabbed at Hagedorn's arm. "Look, pal! Those Hindus are makin' a real whoopee. I thought they were full of red-eye, but when you dodged in after your pipe an old Irish fellow came along an' told me they was all fussed up about some god of theirs just gone on a rampage. What's it all about, anyhow?"

Hagedorn shook his head, watching the jabbering throng clustered beneath the low balcony. Waving hands and bobbing turbans threw bobbing, waving shadows across the walls that hemmed in the bazaar. A gabble of voices rose in a clatter like that of a startled henhouse. Dust rose like smoke under the shuffle of bare heels.

Those natives were certainly upset about something. Hearing the racket, Hagedorn had darted from his room, fearful that his companion had started it, or that the natives were protesting against the presence of white men in the *serai*. There were times when it was not politic for a European, a *Feringi*, to show his face in one of those God-lost frontier towns of the Northwest Province.

The engineer lit his pipe and studied the faces tagging in and out of lamplight below. "I haven't the foggiest idea what they're clamoring about. It isn't us, that's sure. Here comes old McCrailey back again. You say he told you it was

some sort of religious gathering? He's the commissioner or
something here. Been stationed in this hole for years. He
knows the natives like he was one of them. Better find out
what the rumpus means. We've got to clear out of here in
an hour, and we don't want to run into any mess." Hagedorn pointed out a white sun-helmet weaving up the lane.
"There he comes."

"That's the guy," Conray said. "Ask him again."

Hagedorn leaned over the balcony rail; called. McCrailey answered from below, and a moment later walked on to
the balcony. He was a heavy man and short, with jutting
gray whiskers, a face of seamed leather, and squirrel-like
eyes that lampooned the world from the shadow of his
helmet. Hagedorn poured him a spot of whisky, and he
drank, with his eyes on the street. To Hagedorn's query he
replied in a brogue-soft voice.

"What's the trouble down there? Nothing serious. Those
boys are just panicky because one of their pet demons has
knocked one of 'em dead. Happens every so often." He
turned on Hagedorn. "You remember when you was out
here before and took that east trail that runs along a valley
rim for a few miles? The same road you'll be takin' out of
here to-night when you go. Well, down in the valley there's
a shrine. It's a devil of a place. I've been down that valley
a couple of times. Hotter than hell, an' so still it's spooky.
Well, there's a shrine down there, an' the Hindus make
pilgrimages out there on certain days. You must of heard
about the place when you was up here before."

"You mean," asked Hagedorn, "the shrine of Siva?
Where there's an image with an eye that kills the man

who looks at it? That's the story as I recall it; big legend about the place. If you look at this eye you're a dead man."

Conray chuckled. The Irishman turned a slow smile on him. " 'Tis queer," he murmured. "Mighty strange. You see, stranger, once in awhile a native or somebody goes in there an' never comes out alive. It's a Hindu legend, all right, an' cooked up with a lot of hokum an' rigmarole. Only, like a good many of their ghost stories, it works. There's funny doings in the East, my friend, an' it don't do to laugh too hard at 'em. This is one of them cases—about the eye of this damned idol. The story seems to hold. Ain't a Hindu a thousand miles from here dares look at the eye. They go to the shrine to kiss the feet of the image, an' leave money an' food. But they don't stare at the idol's eye. You bet your life they don't! Save every once in awhile. Somebody goes into that shrine and is found a jackal-eaten remains later on. Don't know what happens to 'em, but they certainly get it right. One of those things has just happened. My house boy tells me a gang of pilgrims marched out there this afternoon, and found a corpse with a burned head lying at the Siva's feet. They remembered the legend about a spark from this eye striking an unbeliever dead, and hiked back here fast as they could get. Don't ask me about it. The place is deserted save for an old priest who goes there about once a week to tend a candle in the idol's fist. But the old devil has been in town for the last three days, an', besides, he couldn't kill a soul. His arms are withered. An' the shrine is deserted as hell. I know."

CONRAY'S EXPRESSION WAS one of unbelief and interest. He looked at Hagedorn; stared at McCrailey. "Say, chief, it's a swell story, but you don't believe it, do you?

Fairies an' witches ain't in style these days. You ain't tellin'
me a look at an idol's eye is goin' to drop me dead in my
tracks, are you? Say!"

The Irishman sipped another whisky and said soberly:
"I told you the story. I don't know what's behind it. Only
every once in awhile this idol gets a fellow. Got one to-day,
you see. Of course a stare at the idol's eye don't kill you.
I've stared at the thing myself. From a good distance. I got
curious about three years ago. Lynn Hagedorn, here, was up
in the hills engineerin' a railroad, weren't you, Lynn? And
havin' a tough time too, what with the natives stealin' all his
truck. Well, just about that time this idol got goin' again.
Far as I can recall, it hadn't killed anybody for a number
of months. Then it got three in succession, an' one was a
Britisher who'd adventured through here. They carted him
out of that valley, his coolies did, an' he wasn't worth a four
anna bit, what with the heat an' all. You couldn't have told
what had done him in.

"But I got curious, an' nosed up there for a look-see. I
hadn't been up that valley before. It wasn't a nice place, an'
furnace hot all the time. Lord, but it's hot! An' I packed up
there an' found th' shrine, all right. It's a little stone place,
an' I looked around mighty cautious before I went messin'
in there. Wasn't a livin' soul within miles.

"It's a rotten place, that valley. Made me nervous as a
singed cat, I can tell you that. Blessed Saint Boniface, it
was so quiet it wasn't nice!"

The commissioner paused to mop his face; and his two
listeners leaned forward so as not to miss the telling. Hagedorn's mien expressed a grave interest. On Conray's tight
lips, however, there was the faintest suggestion of a smirk.

"I looked around," McCrailey repeated, "and right over the shrine door, engraved in the stone, was a legend. Roughly translated it read something like this: 'Brave not the eye in Siva's head, or the gold god will laugh and strike you dead.' Holy Saint Andrew! Three men had been knocked dead there to my knowledge, an' McCrailey is one who believes in a warning. It took a little nerve to stick my skull through that door, but I did it. An' it was worth it. There was that damned idol. An ugly one, you bet! Five feet tall, an' solid gold, or I'm a liar. It held a tiny light in its palm, but that was just to show its scurvy face an' put a glow in its eye. It had an eye, my friends. Arrah, that it had. Right in the center of its forehead. Big as an egg, an' redder than hell. By the saints; it was the biggest ruby I ever seen in all my life!"

"*Ruby!*" Rip Conray barked out the word. "Ruby, you say!"

Hagedorn exclaimed: "By George, McCrailey, that's a great yarn!"

"Ruby!" Conray barked again. "You mean to say that idol was solid gold, an' there was a ruby in its nut big as a hen's egg?"

McCrailey crossed himself, and nodded. "I've been from Peking to Aden across the Orient, an' seen some great gems in my day. But that there ruby was the biggest I'd ever seen."

"An' what," panted Conray, "did you do then?"

"Do?" The Irish commissioner grunted, grabbing at his beard. "I got out of there as fast as these old boots would get me. I'd looked at the eye, an' that was plenty, you believe. I just poked my nose into that door an' yanked it out again, an' beat it. I wasn't goin' to stick around an' be carried out rotten. No, sir! That Siva had a pretty mean face. He'd laid three victims in the dust, an' there was that sign over the door tellin' you not to look too long. I didn't; an' here I am." Tilting his helmet with a leathery hand, he poured down another drink, then nodded at Hagedorn. "I've got to get back to my bungalow. You'll be ridin' off soon, eh? Good luck with your huntin', then, an' a easy trip. I'll see you goin' out."

HAGEDORN TURNED FROM bidding the old commissioner good-by to see Conray leaning over the balcony, fists tight on the rail. From the street rose the mumble-bumble of the excited throng. An enervating breath of wind sighed through the bazaar. Overhead a slim sickle of moon rode high in a sky of ebony, shedding magic light on balcony and minaret and arabesqued wall. Old McCrailey had left behind him a faint odor of whisky and a strange story; and the tall engineer experienced a curious malease.

He rather wished McCrailey had kept his story to himself. It had been a relief to learn the natives were unconcerned about the advent of himself and Conray. He wanted to get himself and Conray out of there without any misadventure. Conray had come with him all the way from Rangoon, clear across India, to get in some shooting in the mountains. So far Hagedorn had managed to pilot him along without mishap. The gentleman taking an enforced leave of absence from Chicago had a penchant for making trouble that tried one's patience. He was the sort who knew it all, steeped in smart Americanisms and bluff. Hagedorn was not a moralist, but had Conray not saved his life on that Malayan steamer, the engineer would not have tolerated him for a minute. And Hagedorn expected what was coming when Conray flung around from the rail.

"Say, Hagedorn! You heard that old codger's yarn. Wow! A idol of solid gold with a ruby stickin' in its brow, an' nothin' to protect it save an old priest without no arms, who never goes near it. Listen to me, chief! That old harp was either lyin' or a damned fool!"

"He was neither!" snapped Hagedorn, incensed at the glitter in his companion's eye. "And forget this idol business! Forget it, and come along. We got to saddle up, an' get our boys ready to start. Come along, Conray, and quit glaring like a blithering jackass."

"But a ruby!" Conray brushed a sleeve across his face. "Say, didn't th' harp say our trail would take us right by there? An' you say he wasn't lyin'! Well, I'll be damned!"

"Forget it!" the engineer snarled, grabbing Conray's arm. "Or you will be damned. And our trail isn't going nowheres near that shrine; we aren't going by that road. Now come on we've got to pack up. An' for heaven's sake, don't be a fool!"

"All right," said the gentleman from Chicago meekly. But as he followed Hagedorn into the *serai* room he turned to bestow a jolly wink at the moon. And, being an unimaginative person, he no doubt failed to note that moon's similarity to a curved steel blade.

DIGGING HIS HEELS into his pony's belly, Hagedorn, low in saddle cursed and urged his mount to greater speed. After all he told itself again and again, he was a spicy idiot not to have expected this. A seedless raisin would have had brains enough to guess that a man like Rip Conray would be fired by a legend about a tremendous ruby, and light out after it the second one's back was turned.

Hagedorn had left Conray with the saddled ponies behind the *serai,* and gone back into the inn to hustle up the coolies. He had fooled around inside for about half an hour, quarreling about the bill with the old buzzard who ran the place. Returning to the courtyard he had found nothing more than his Punjabi boy, Mardo, and one mount.

The gentleman from Chicago and his pony were glaringly absent.

Where was the white *sahib* and the pony? The Punjabi boy, Mardo, could only shake his inflammable whiskers and point a bony finger at the archway that opened on a night-hung back of beyond. Here was no guessing game for the engineer. His effervescent friend Conray had dashed off to find the shrine. Hagedorn became at once conscious of the fact that Conray would drop into some wayside pitfall, lose himself, or prove easy rations for a roving tiger.

"Which," he reflected aloud, as he raced down the trail, "would be a good riddance. Only the beggar saved my life an' I couldn't let him lose himself on these God-forsaken sands an' have any peace of mind afterward. That crazy maniac! He must think this desert is all mapped out with roads an drinking fountains placed along the way. Good Lord!"

Darkness spelled difficulty. The moon seemed disinclined to help; confused instead of clarifying. Marked out plainly enough in daylight the road at night was impossible. Ninety horsemen, nine, or none might be riding through the puzzling shadows up ahead.

Here a sandy slope showed white as a drift of snow. Here the ridges were veiled in shades of blue, violet, black. There a wandering cañon was flooded in a darkness opaque as ink. There was a valley wall painted with silver. Was that a rider up the trail? Or a puff of wind-blown dust? Or only a banshee?

At the mouth of the narrow valley, Hagedorn drew rein. No use dismounting to hunt for tracks. He wished to Heaven he was a man-hunter in an adventure story—the sort who could bounce from a saddle, snatch up a broken limestone pebble and immediately announce that a horse-man with red hair and a bulbous nose had passed that way two hours before, heading northeast by north. A Wazir tribesman might have done it, but Hagedorn was a tired and disgusted engineer. Sitting his saddle, he glared at the sweeping vale; strove to listen.

The silence, as McCrailey, the commissioner, had expressed it, was not nice. Moonlight and shadow in the valley. Jagged cliff walls mounting on either side. Dust and bowlders rolled there by the playful gods. A heat that sucked perspiration to one's cheeks. A jackal that sped over the rocks like a shadow chased by honest thoughts. And nothing more. Save ghosts.

This, thought Hagedorn, must be the place where the souls of the warriors of Jenghiz Khan had vanished with the passing of the Golden Horde. The jumping-off place of the world. He had ridden down the rim of the valley several times before, always in company.

Never had he noticed it as desolate, as brooding, as forbidding. Perhaps it was the moonlight; perhaps his imagination had been roused by the old Irishman's yarn. He felt that once he rode his horse into that gully of gloom and moonray he would become a wraith. He looked at the moon, and noted its resemblance to a curved steel blade.

The moon was not going to last long. Once it melted away the valley would be blacker than tar, and his chance of finding Conray gone to nothing. A hopeless job at best. That a man from Chicago—a chap who could keep repeating of Asia: "What they need out here is a sense of humor and a little Yankee ingenuity"—could be found in such a locale seemed utterly improbable. Hagedorn himself, with something of the Orient burned into his Western skin, knew he did not belong there.

Even his Indian pony was growing uneasy and restive. The sturdy little beast bucked and shied repeatedly as Hagedorn turned its head to start it up the road.

"If Conray didn't find his way in here, he's lost for good," the engineer told himself. "It can't be four miles to the valley end, an' the shrine is there. McCrailey told directions pretty well, though. If Conray did find his road in here, he's safe. Goin' hell-bent for a place where angels fear to tread. Might have known—"

HIS PONY GALLOPED along, but the echoes of road-pounding hoofs were short lived. Up and down the sanded slopes; skirting bulgy rocks; across a stony wash-bathed blue in pallid moonshine; past a row of white bowl-ders that marched silently along the parched valley bed. Hagedorn bent his trail straight for the shrine. If Conray was not there the engineer would wait on chance. If Conray was there—

Hagedorn sweated at the thought. Long before McCrailey had spun his story about the place Hagedorn had heard about the shrine. This home of the golden Siva had a reputation evil as a witch's curse. And Hagedorn had known the British adventurer who had fallen victim to the idol's wrath. A stupid braggart of a man, newly come to the East. What had happened to him? What had killed the others? Certainly it was no mystery to bungle into.

"A ruby for an eye, eh? Never heard of that before. But *something* there has been pickin' 'em off. An' a bird like Conray is just the sort to catch it. 'What Asia needs is a sense of humor! Yankee ingenuity!' Th' fool! When I showed him that Malay irrigation wheel he laughed. An' when I show him the smile on the face of that little jade Buddha, he sneers. Lord! This road isn't so hard to follow at that. Hope to Heaven he hasn't found th' shrine already! If he's there—"

He was.

Lynn Hagedorn spurred over a low ridge, and saw at once the hobbled pony standing a pace from the little stone house. The engineer yanked to a halt. Moonlight flooded down the sheer face of cliff that loomed above, shrouded the shrine with wan ray, lay in a silver lake before the little door. The silence here was carved in stone. The bell above the arch, uttering a small echo, failed to disturb the soundless pall. Silence. It rained down from the heated sky, whispered from the bowlders, and poured from the shrine door. Hagedorn promptly sweated, and could feel perspiration dripping from his chin.

His cheeks leaked. Carefully he swung from the saddle. So overpowering was the quiet one scarcely dared interrupt. He felt as if he must go on tiptoe, or the atmosphere would crash. That little door. It was silent as a grave. And silent as the grave were the three skulls, bleached and cracking, that stared with mournful eyes from their roosts in the sand beside the door.

It was with a whispered oath that Hagedorn discovered and translated the legend carved in the stone below the bell arch. McCrailey was right. "Brave Not the Eye in Siva's Head, or the Gold God Will Laugh and Strike You Dead."

Warning enough! And there were those hollow-eyed death heads; the haunted, nerve-draining silence.

Hagedorn rushed to the shrine door; gained a fleeting picture of a boxlike room, dark from the obscured light of a tiny flame flowering in a golden palm; a bulk of gold hunched atop a stone pedestal; an unholy golden face aglow with light that gleamed on the bloated cheeks, cast a shadow in the gaping maw of mouth, and kindled a blaze in the giant ruby flaming in the forehead.

Yet another image lay there before the large one. Conray. His hands were fastened on the pedestal; eyes pinned on the scintillating gem. His back was toward the engineer in the doorway. He stood as if petrified, unable to draw his gaze from that lustrous, fabulous jewel.

Hagedorn took a step forward, and kicked into a little heap of human bones.

Escaping his lips, Hagedorn's gasp of repulsion brought Conray flinging around like a jumping toy. Stiff in his tracks, Hagedorn managed to find a voice somewhere in his tight throat.

"Conray! Come on! Get out! We got to get out of here—"

Words lost on the gentleman from old Chi. He stood rocking slightly on his toes, veins snaking across his forehead gone crimson, cheeks bright with a flush of anger. His lips stammered, hunting words.

"Clear out!" he screamed suddenly. "Clear out, Hagedorn. That gem is gonna be mine, see? Mine! I know you didn't want me to beat your time out here after that little sparkler. Worth a fortune, that stone is, an' it's all mine. Believe me, you ain't goin' to get it!"

With the final snarled warning Conray struck out furiously; his automatic barrel, drawn under cover of his speech, smashed hard against Hagedorn's jaw. *Thwack!* The tall engineer spilled over like a drunken sailor; stared stupidly from a sitting posture near the door. Conray chuckled, an avid glitter greening his eyes.

"There. Sorry I had to do that, old man. But you just set there nice, an' all will be dandy." Dodging down, he whipped Hagedorn's pistol from its holster; tossed it out through the open door.

"Now!" Laughing shrilly, Conray darted back to the idol, clambered on the pedestal, flung a grabbing hand at the ruby above his head. Lusting talons, his fingers snatched the gem.

All Hagedorn saw was a burst of white-hot, roaring, blasting flame that lapped like a tongue of lightning from the Siva's yawning mouth. A screaming, devastating breath of fire and heat that forked from that idol's golden throat, blazed, flickered, and vanished. For half an instant the shrine was the bowel of a smelter furnace. Then the blast was over.

A terrible, rancid odor at once stung the gloom; and there on the floor, smoldering and awful, huddled what was left of Rip Conray, stricken dead by a bolt of fire before a split minute could tick away.

Half blinded, scorched, choking, Hagedorn sat with a stomach of cold iron nailing him down, and strove to make muscles in his legs behave. The flame in the Siva's golden palm fluttered and made the shadows dance. The blood-red ruby eye, safe in its forehead socket, twinkled its cheerful wink. The blotted mouth of the image yawned its mocking grimace. Outside, quieting the silence, the shrine bell tolled an echo from a vanished yesterday. *Clong!*

AFTERWARD HAGEDORN DID not regret it, though the giant ruby must have been worth a fortune. Obeying his first impulse, the soul-shocked engineer caught up Conray's fallen automatic and sent a bullet to smash that crimson eye into a million fragments. A terrific thunderclap in that narrow shrine, the explosion of the shot shivered the quietude, brought down age-lain dust, sent a hundred echoes caroming down the arid cañon, and quite clapped Hagedorn to his senses.

Thereafter certain unpleasant duties he performed. Such as doing the right thing by the gentleman from Chicago. An extremely unhappy business, but Hagedorn went through with it. Asia, the engineer, had learned, as elsewhere, often provided miserable situations; only in Asia one could not grab a street car and run away from them. So Hagedorn had schooled himself to do things he did not want to do.

He did the right thing by Rip Conray. Incidentally, on going through the dead man's pockets and pack he found letters in which Conray had signed himself Connery, Conway, Coles, Crandall, and Crisp. Also Hagedorn found in the pack such articles as a marked deck of playing cards, a little Javanese urn of beaten gold, a diamond ring that glimmered like sunshine on the sea. Hagedorn put the loot, the aliases, and the gentleman from old Chi side by side in the warm, forgiving sand. It might have been lonely for him there among the slant-eyed ghosts of the Golden Horde, had not Conray been in the company of Connery, Conway, and Coles and Crandall and Crisp.

When he had finished piling the mound of stones, Hagedorn strolled through the moonless dark, propelling and compelling his feet back to the shrine. The blinded image could not see him now.

Hagedorn took the tallow torch from the golden palm, and bravely studied the god. Feeling like a circus clown with his head in a lion's mouth, he peered into the yawning gullet; examined the socket where the eye had been. And in that orbless socket the engineer discovered something he was mighty careful not to touch—a little metal hook that grew from a hole in the idol's brain.

Through sheer luck and a careless elbow he discovered the image could be swung on its stone base; and swing it he did with a curse and a will. The golden monster turned around with a loud moan. Hagedorn held high his light; swore. Had he uncovered the foolish brain that fashioned the universe he could not have been more surprised. Siva's secret was thus easily exposed.

The metal hook in the socket was fastened to the ruby eye. When a lusting hand, ignoring the warnings of legendry, snatched at the gem, it naturally yanked the hook. At one time, Hagedorn guessed, a pull on the wire released a flood of gas that escaped from a fissure in the cliff wall against which the image was backed. The rush of gas poured out of the idol's throat, was ignited to bursting flame by the fire in the upturned palm. And the thief, whose face would be on a level with the open mouth, would thus be hurried to an unbeliever's Gehenna.

However, the natural gas had apparently given out with the passing centuries; and the power of the eye had been revived by a huge, high-pressure blow torch—a metal torpedo of compressed gas, fastened to the idol's spine. Hagedorn, staring in wonder, guessed it might have been stolen by priestly hands from his own engineering crew when they were building a trestle in these hills!

Here it made a terrible engine of destruction. The hook in the eye pulled a hair-trigger on the torch handle; released a compression blast that could melt a steel bolt to liquid. That idol's mouth would laugh a flame which could blow a human head into a cinder.

Sense of humor! Good Lord! And Hagedorn glared at the gas torch with sweat bubbling down his forehead. There was the final phrase of Conray's pet declaration. Stamped in the metal band around the neck of the welding torch were the famous words: "Made in America."

TWO DAGGERS

Seeking one thing and one only, stoker Jukes
drifted from ship to ship on the seven seas,
forever on the trail of a man he had never seen

ALWAYS JUKES CARRIED the dagger. Razor-sharp and ready, the lean blade waited in its leather sheath, worn limey fashion in his belt with the handle scratching the small of his back. A sinister sort of weapon it was, long enough to stab clean through a thin man, and possessed of a unique green sheen to its metal and an evil, blue snake-headed handle with three hilt-guards around which fingers could be curled.

"An' you'll stab it up to the guards in 'im, won't you, Jukes?" his mother had made him promise. A gaunt, shabby woman was Jukes's mother, with long, flat cheeks slanting up to pale eyes that were tired beneath a forlorn nest of colorless hair. A woman as gray and sooty as the funnels of ships at Albert Dock.

Jukes remembered her best as she was when she lay that day, like the corpse she was soon to be, on her ragged cot, and called him to her side. He was only ten years old then, but elderly; and he never forgot. "You'll stab it up to the hilt in 'im, Jukes," his mother had panted, drawing the weapon from her shawl and pressing it into his hot fist. Her pale eyes were flickering so queerly.

"You'll stab 'im with it, lad. Just like 'e stabbed your father. You won't fail me, Jukes? You promise me, Jukes. That's—that's the lad. And never lose that dagger, Jukes.

'Is name was Parks, but 'e's changed it now most likely. An' like I told you, 'e's a stoker. A stoker like your father, Jukes. Like your father was afore 'e stabbed 'im. An' never lose this dagger. I don't remember Parks so well, but—but I had this 'ere blade made to match the one I seen on '*im*. That's how you'll know 'im, Jukes. 'Is dagger is exactly like this-un— same color, an' handle, an' all, an' you'll see it—"

Unfortunately, she had suffered a lung hemorrhage at that point, and made haste to depart this vale of woe. But her son had promised to avenge her husband's murder; the last mortal sight she saw was the boy, tearful and appalled, kneeling beside her with that long, lean dagger gleaming in his hand; and she knew he would not forget.

He did not. He remembered. He remembered her every word. And always he cherished the dagger and the memory of his promise. Always he watched for the man who had murdered his father—a stoker who would be carrying a green steel dagger with a blue handle wrought in the fashion of a snake's head and crossed by three hilt-guards. A dagger exactly like his.

JUKES WAS A coal-passer; labored in the livid fire-rooms of the ships that tramped the seven seas. Impossible to identify him with any one vessel, for he never remained with a crew longer than a single run. Sometimes he would sign on and jump the ship the same day. He had been on dozens of steamers. By his twentieth year he had sailed most of the navigable waters of the world. His penchant for jumping ship had won him a small notoriety in the circles of the maritime. Because he was known to have left one vessel after another, gone deliberately from a good

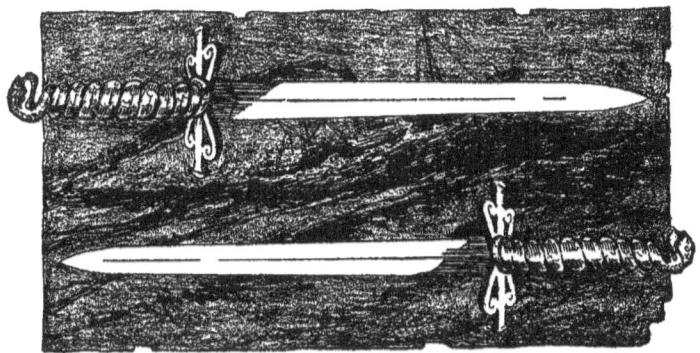

outfit into a shunned "starvation" line, there were those who thought him daft.

"There's that loon, Jukes," the keeper of the famous Waterfront Willy's Starboard Light Rum Palace in Penang might say. "In port 'ere again. Bobbin' up from somewheres or other. Left a good berth most likely, an' waitin' to sign on a bad one outa 'ere. That bloke 'as shipped on every bleedin' craft between 'ere an' 'ell. 'Im, there. 'E's nuts."

But east of Suez, harbor towns are always full of strange, irrational folk. So nobody would give Jukes more than a hasty stare.

He deserved more than a hasty stare. He was slim as a willow, and tough as the meat you could eat at Waterfront Willy's. Eight years at passing coal in the torrid stoke-holes of scorbutic tramps had built slabs of muscle across his rangy shoulders and down his arms. There was a firm set to his chin that told it had been punched at by life, and withstood. His gray eyes saw and were unafraid. They watched; sought.

For Jukes, the coal-passer, was hunting. Always watching for men who carried daggers. Always seeking sight of a dagger that would match in every detail his own. Hunting a stoker who had on him a dagger with a blade of green steel and a snake-head handle crossed by three guards. "I don't remember Parks so well, but—but I had this 'ere blade made to match the one I seen on 'im. That's how you'll know 'im, Jukes. 'Is dagger is exactly like this-un—same color, an' handle, an' all, an' you'll see it—"

But he did not see it. Many men he saw who carried daggers on them, yes. Stokers, firemen, sailors, engineers, longshoremen he saw with daggers. All manner of men he saw thus armed, for he moved in a world where such things often came in handy, and a glint in the shadows was apt as not to be edged steel.

And he saw, with his seeking gray eyes, daggers a-plenty. He saw daggers of iron that smelled of fish and had cost a bob, and daggers of silver that smelled of treachery and had cost twenty lives. He saw stubby Dutch dirks, heavy and stolid as their wielders. He saw thin French poniards, lightning-sharp, Portuguese stilettos pointed like needles, ugly Arab daggers curved like the moon of Allah the Merciful; wicked knives from the Emerald Isle; evil Chinese short swords, wavy and slim; and strange Persian blades that had stabbed home the religions of Mani and Zoroaster with a flash of fire.

From Rangoon to Rio, Yoko to New York he had gone. But nowhere had he found the knife that matched his own. Nowhere had he seen a man who carried a dagger with a greenish blade and a handle like the head of a snake with three hilt-guards across.

Sometimes Jukes wondered. It never occurred to him the man he hunted might be dead. Somehow Jukes knew the man lived. But suppose he had given away this dagger his mother had seen! Suppose that the dagger had been lost? Still, his mother had seemed so certain, so sure. So positive Jukes could find the murderer and know him by the dagger that was exactly like the one she gave him. If only she could have lived to give Jukes a bit more of a description. Yet, it ought to be easy to recognize the other dagger.

And sometimes Jukes wondered just what he would do when he did find the one he sought. Provoke a fight? The other might battle and escape. Knife him in the back? An unclean business. But he would go through with it. A hundred times a day he practised speeding his right hand behind him, snatching the long blade from its sheath. Often when alone he would slip out the weapon, and run a careful thumb down the glinting edge. A splendid piece of steel. A streak of flame when he dodged it through a shaft of sunlight. Keen as pain.

But this other dagger—it, too, would be a sharp flame. And driven by an older hand, more practised. Jukes would study the drop of blood his weapon would draw on his thumb. A mean business, this. A bloody business, for certain. But the man had murdered his father. And Jukes had promised his mother as she died. Yes, if he ever found the man with the dagger that matched his, he would go through with it.

WATERFRONT WILLY LEANED across the bar to slap at a fly, and asked: "When'd you blow in, Jukes? On the beach fer a bit, or shippin' right out? What boat you come in on?"

Jukes looked up from his virgin (vermouth and gin), and brushed sweat from his forehead with an impatient gesture. "Come in on the City of Tonkin. I'm leavin' 'er 'ere an' gettin' any craft comes along. May 'ave to wait a spell. They ain't so many coal-burners out 'ere as there was last time I was in. Wouldn't mind goin' into the Western Ocean, maybe."

"Leavin' the City of Tonkin!" Waterfront Willy's Chinese-Egyptian-Cockney face registered incredulity. He missed the fly. "Look 'ere, Jukes. Wot's the bleedin' idea? You gonna really jump that big Romney Line freighter? W'y, blimy if 'alf the bloody sailors in the world wouldn't give their legs to get aboard 'er. Best feedin' boat out 'ere, an' good orficers. You must be daft!"

The boy grinned faintly and dropped his yellow head over his glass. A voice behind him, hoarse as a rusty saw, demanded: "Did I 'ear you tell you was jumpin' the City of Tonkin, sailor? Say, I'd like to get on 'er, meself. Just dropped hook in 'ere this mornin', an' if I c'n git away from the bloody rotten craft I'm wiv now, I'd give me eyes."

"Don't look," chuckled Waterfront Willy, "as if yuh had such fine eyes to give, pal. Not so good, neither."

Jukes turned around. The man behind him was a scarecrow in worthless dungarees, distinguished from other drifters down the wave, however, by a pair of puffy black eyes that gave evidence of someone's triumphant fists.

"Just come off the Queen of Asia," he snarled, scowling painfully. "An' I'd like to quit 'er fer keeps. A lousy bleedin' 'ell-ship, if yuh arsks me. A fi' thousand ton hunk o' 'ell wiv pig-sty food an' most o' the crew Malay yella. If they's a berth in this 'ere City of Tonkin fer a man goin' below I'm takin' hit!"

"You just come in on the Queen of Asia?" Jukes asked. "She's burnin' coal? An' you're gonna jump 'er 'ere?"

"Jump 'er I am! An' does she burn coal? Bet yer bleedin'

eyes she do! Runnin' short-handed below, an' she's got a
stoke-'ole that's plain 'ell! Standin' four on an' four off in
that fire-room is nothin' but burnin' yer bloody self alive.
She hits 'er up 'ot, believe me! An' work! 'Ow that craft eats
coal! Wot's more, her stoke-'ole is bossed by a bleedin' devil,
that's all. 'Im as give me these 'ere smashed peepers. Stokin'
alongside 'im most broke me back, an' then 'e slams me fer
slowin' up. Meanest blighter on the sea, 'im. Knifer Alf,
they calls 'im, an' even the Ol' Man ain't rilin' that chappie
none. Knifer Alf—"

"What's 'is name, fella? Knifer Alf? Totes a dagger, does
'e?"

"Dagger? 'E's 'andiest devil wiv a stabber I ever seen. Cut
a Malay all up, 'e did, an' I wouldn't stand a watch wiv 'im
for fifty quid. Plain bad, this 'ere Knifer Alf. Come aboard
the Queen of Asia at Calcutta, an' is bossin' the stoke-'ole
'fore we're a hour out. She's goin' to Bangkok, an' I 'opes
this Knifer Alf goes to 'ell wiv 'er!"

"You tellin' me straight? This bloke's aboard the Queen
of Asia? All right, friend. Go over to the City of Tonkin
an' get my berth. Guess I'll give the Queen of Asia a try.
Wouldn't mind seein' a stoker name of Knifer Alf." And
leaving his vermouth and gin to the throat of the stranger.
Jukes hurried from the bar.

"That fellow Jukes," puzzled Waterfront Willy, "must
be plain daft!"

IF SHE EVER had owned royal blood, the Queen of Asia
had surely followed evil ways and slipped long since into
utter decadence. Only the caprice of Neptune keeps such
craft afloat. A slut she was, lolling there in the slip with
black smoke pouring from her skinny funnel and hang-

ing low over her forecastle head as if to hide her festering hull from the betraying sun. Huge blotches of red rust ate into the plates of her beams and prow. Chinese seamen could not have left her deep well-decks in greater disarray. Unpainted deckbooms, tangled with gear, cluttered her aft and fore decks. An unshipped anchor and lengths of chain jammed her bows. And the smashed kindling of a wave-splintered lifeboat clung in the davits on her starboard quarter.

Swinging up a staggery gangway, Jukes made his way aft towards a cluster of Malays who squatted cheerfully indifferent to their unseamanlike surroundings. A tousled head poked out of a companion hatch and accosted Jukes.

"Wot you doin', there!"

"Signed on ashore," he informed the sailor. "Goin' below. I'm just comin' aft to report."

"Holy hell! Ya don't mean to say as you deliberately went an' signed to go below on this craft! Well, I'm a son of a camel! You don't know this vessel, lad. 'Specially her stoke-hole! Worst ship afloat, she be. Me an' the skipper, an' the *serang*, an' engineer, an' a stoker is the only whites aboard. An' I reckon you won't be thinkin' that stoker's white. A mean cuss an' good to steer clear of! An' ye're a goin' below, eh? Well, we're movin' in fi' minutes, pal. Soon as I c'n wake the Ol' Man outa a drunk an' git my *serang* sober enough to kick them niggers inta haulin' in them hawsers. Reckon you'll go below fer the next watch. Sorry. Good luck, pal."

Good luck! Had it come at last? He would see this chap called Knifer Alf. But, assigned the dog watch below, it was not until eight bells that he caught a glimpse of Knifer Alf. The Queen of Asia had staggered out of the harbor into a walloping head sea. The Malay crew had slipped back into betel-nut chewing and indolence. The Old Man had succumbed to alcohol, and the engineer was finishing his gin when the bells sent Jukes to the stokehole. On his way to the fire-room he had encountered the tousle-headed mate.

"I s'y," Jukes had asked. "Which stoker is this 'ere Knifer Alf?"

"Port fire-door," the mate had told him. "Big cuss. You'll hear him bawlin' at his coal-passer, most likely. A quarrelsome bloke, an' mighty wicked. Was I the engineer I'd boot him out in a minute. Only maybe the ol' engineer ain't got the nerve. This here Knifer Alf would stick a blighter he didn't go without another thought, I reckon."

With a stiff hand waiting to flash behind him, Jukes picked his way to the fire-room hatch, stood at the top of the iron ladder dropping into the fire-pit. A blast of hot air smote his face as he stepped in from the alleyway, and wrung tears to his eyes as he stared at the iron floor below. The man in Waterfront Willy's had made no mistake when he described the stoke-hole of the Queen of Asia as plain hell.

Open furnace doors shed a white hot blaze at the slaving black gang. Panted oaths sounded above the monotone roar of eating flame, the scrape of heavy shovels, the clangor of stoking irons. There were five men laboring at those shouting fire-doors, but Jukes could never have told which one of them was white. All were made of wet coal.

Naked but for cut-off dungarees, they danced from black shadows into a lambent, crimson glow, now flinging fuel at the blasting throat, now prodding into the roaring tonsils with long black irons that came out white. The infernos fed, they dodged back into shadow once again, to reappear bearing laden shovels. Shoulders gleamed like wet tar in the fireglow. Glistening muscles ran ink. No men of flesh, these, but devils, and that iron, torrid, clangorous hole a pit in hell.

FROM THE HEAT-ASSAILED height of the ladder-top, Jukes peered at the crimson and black fire and iron and coal phantasy, peered at the Vulcan who labored at the port fire-door. The stoker's massive shoulders, stooped under the blasty glare, glistened. His dripping face, with pale slits where eyes and mouth would have been, was cut from ebony, and his torso was black marble.

Inked by sweat and bituminous dust from crown to toe, he flaunted his mighty frame at the furnace maw. Rhythmically his tireless shovel whipped black rocks at the flashing blaze. Rhythmically his stoking rod jabbed and jammed and came out on fire. A cinder scattering blue darts of flame dropped from the fire-door. With naked foot he kicked the brand away.

So his name was Knifer Alf! Carefully Jukes clambered down the hot rungs of the ladder to the fire-floor. A well of heat, that fire-floor, from which there was no recoil. Gasping, Jukes crossed to the port bunkers, picked up a shovel. The Malay he relieved slipped away. Jukes loaded his scoop and flung it at the stoker. The Malay relieving this Knifer Alf was coming down the ladder. Knifer Alf turned on the coal-passer behind him. His inky face gleamed and his blacked chest heaved and glistened, reflecting the fierce firelight. His damp, coal-dusted hair tossed.

"New hand, eh?" he snarled. "Well, if you was workin' wi'

me you'd age, kid. I eats little boys." White teeth sneered.
"An' if you go usin' a stokin' iron, don't knock down any rods
an' cripple my crate, or I'll cripple *you* an' fling you out the
ash chute. Don't never forget *that!*" With the word "that,"
he tossed his shovel. The heavy scoop would have smashed
Jukes's foot to a vegetable if he had not made a frantic skip
to one side and let it go ringing against the iron floor. As
it was, the handle banged his shin, and he voiced a stifled
howl.

"Try that again," raged Jukes, "an' I'll cut yer heart out
for ya!"

The provocative threat brought the desired result. "Cut
out my heart, eh?" A laugh shouted from the white teeth,
shook the glistening, inky chest. Slapping his sweaty thigh,
the big stoker jerked to light a dagger. "Don't make me
laugh, bucko. Don't make Knifer Alfie laugh!"

DISAPPOINTMENT IT WAS, and not fear, that brought
a twist to Jukes's mouth. Once more he had failed. Once
more he had been unable to locate the man who killed his
father. And why should he have expected to come to the
end of his search just because a bloke was a stoker and some
fool had named him Knifer Alf?

Knifer Alf had a knife, all right. But it was short and
broad and single-edged with a bone handle. Nothing like
the dagger with a blade that glinted green and three cross-
guards on the snake's-head handle of blue.

"Put up yer knife," Jukes growled sullenly, bending to
rub his shin. "You could cut me up all right. 'Ave it yer own
way. But don't go flingin' shovels around, neither. I got a
blade o' my own."

"Got a blade o' yer own, 'ave you? Well, any time you wanna match it ag'in' this weapon o' mine, yer free to try.

"Say, they don't call me Knifer Alfie fer nothin', kid. I done some cuttin' in my day, an' any bloke as wants to try 'is bleedin' steel ag'in' mine can allus find me ready fer a bit o' sport. This 'ere little blade 'as been doin' my knife-play ever since I was ole enough to cuss." He let go of another throaty laugh, returned the dirk to its sheath on his hip, wiped a black, wet arm across his wet, black face. "Maybe some day, kid, you can try a knife ag'in' me—if you ever get big enough to carry one!"

Jukes turned to his coal bunker, shovel in fist. Bloody luck, this! He would jump this rotten Queen of Asia at Singapore, and try again. He shoveled angrily, gasping in the stifling heat, his skin beginning to go wet and black.

He cursed as he wiped his face. Would he ever find the man who carried a dagger that matched his own? Maybe out of Singapore—

But Jukes was destined never to get to Singapore. That is, not on the Queen of Asia.

IT WAS A unique mutiny in its way, for mutinies are not often hatched in the stoke-hole and led by one of the black gang. However, Knifer Alf was a unique man. As was evidenced in the sanguine way he sauntered up out of the fire-room, strolled forward along the deck to the Old Man's cabin, and cut the skipper's gin-fumed, drunken throat.

Leaving the Old Man, then, he climbed to the bridge, sneaked up behind the mate, standing at the binnacle, and stabbed him deader than a chuck. By this time he had the Malays docile as school children at his heels, and it was a simple matter to post one of them at the wheel to keep the ship on her course, walk aft, and cut a few veins on the helpless *serang*.

The Queen of Asia was placidly plodding down the Straits of Malacca, spouting black smoke at a round, canary-yellow moon, and it was Knifer Alf's sincere intention to run her over to a little Sumatra port he knew, sell her to a one-eyed, unspiritual Dutchman who bought such things, and spend his remaining days in righteous calm. He furthered this plan by putting the Australian engineer into his bunk and his knife into the Australian engineer.

By now the Malays worshiped him with deadly fear in their hearts, and would do his bidding with alacrity. The Malay mate promised with a thousand strong metaphors to navigate the boat as instructed. The Malay second engineer swore to keep the teakettles boiling at any cost.

Knifer Alf walked across the deck in the moonlight. A tenuous ribbon of black coastline showed off the port beam. A mile or so to the starboard there bobbed the running lights of a schooner. Schooners and coastlines were not interested in dowdy tramps like the Queen of Asia. Secure in his exalted rating as master, Knifer Alf lounged into the skipper's cabin.

Here he helped himself to cigars and gin and a glance in the speckled mirror.

This last displeased his ego. He was black as tar and his hands were cardinal red. What he needed, decided Knifer Alf, was the luxury of a bath.

The Old Man's bath boasted of an overhead hot water faucet, and Knifer Alf bellowed cheerily under the plunging steam. The novelty pleased him, for most of the world's big-muscled boys enjoy seeing the physiques once in a while. Knifer Alf shook his huge frame under the smoking water.

A week's accumulation of sweat and coal dust washed from his muscled-slabbed limbs. Black enamel went like stage paint from his face, and his countenance appeared grinning and bronzed and porcine with tiny sea-boils glowing atop each high cheekbone. The sluicing water washed ink from his arms and shoulders and torso and found the hide brass.

Blowing like a porpoise, he turned off the water, stepped his dripping and newly-laundered frame into the cabin. Moonlight gleamed pleasantly on his clean person and he looked with approval at the ropes of muscle rippling on his forearms. Then he was conscious of a shadow in the cabin door, looked up. A smile of huge tolerance exposed his crooked teeth.

"Well, now, if it ain't the new coal-passer signed on at Penang. Blimy if I didn't ferget him complete! Hello, little bucko. Meet the new skipper. An' yer just goin' below on yer watch, eh? Well, now. *I'm* the new boss o' this vessel, kid. Surprise yuh, heh? Well, don't let yer eyes pop outa yer bleedin' 'ead! It's just—"

Knifer Alf never finished his announcement. The coal-passer in the door had been glaring; pressing a fist against his mouth. Cords were jumping out on his jaw and forehead, and a strange twist had come to his sooty face. With a sudden gesture he had dropped a hand behind him, and jerked to light a long, lean blade that glimmered green in the moonray. A blade that flashed like a heated wire as it dodged through a slanting shaft of pale beams. A blade as

keen as pain, cutting as the voice that strained from the
coal-passer's colorless lips.

"An' to think I almost missed 'im!" the white lips said:
"*You!* The man who murdered my father! 'Ello, you! 'Ello!
'Ello, Mister Parks!"

A scarlet oath blew from the stoker's teeth. His own
stubby blade with the bone handle lay on the table with his
dungarees. He squalled for the Malays; jumped for his dirk.
Too late! Green flame zaffed out in the moonlight. Zug!

CALM AS THE violet star hanging close to the sea in the
tropic night, Jukes walked from the cabin. Calm as the
moonlight on the Straits, he climbed the port rail, looked
once at the strip of distant shore, inhaled, and plunged.
The Malays did not raise a hand to stop him. Not they! For
the Malay may be brave, but he is superstitious. And those
Malay sailors crowded at the door of the captain's cabin on
the Queen of Asia were too frightened to stir their feet.
Too terror-ridden. Too fascinated.

For face up on the cabin floor spraddled the corpse of
Knifer Alf. ("An' you'll stab it up to the guards in 'im, won't
you, Jukes?" his mother had made him promise. And he
had tried. But the blade was long.) Moonlight glistened
on the muscles bulging down the wet and naked white
stoker's frame; found a greenish glint in the blade of the
still-quivering dagger that, driven through the corpse's
neck, nailed it to the floor.

The Malays stared at that quivering green-steel dagger
with the snake-head handle crossed by three hilt-guards,
and prickles scampered down their spines. And they stared.
They stared at that dagger and they stared at the corpse

and they stared at the dagger tattooed on the chest of that corpse.

And they tell to this day of the man who could snatch from another man's chest the dagger tattooed thereon, and stab him with it.

BLOOD OF THE ROSE

*Scion of a staid old American family, Ronald
Swain barges blindly into the intrigues and
mystic spells of wise and wicked old India*

THIS IS THE queerest, maddest story I know.

To "get" this story you must understand what an absolute, dyed-in-the-wool, hundred per cent American Ronald Swain was. And what a dyed-in-the-beard, unsanitary, glitteringly thousand per cent Oriental place was Nagarabad. And about Gulabi.

There was Swain. In the first place he had a lot of money. That, and his Saxon blue eyes, his ambition and corn-colored hair had come down to him through three generations of Swains—good Nordic Swains—who had made their home in the young republic. I believe his great-grandfather had stuffed thirteen or eighteen children and a musket into an ox-cart, pioneered out of Maine, and built the second flour-mill or something in Rochester, N. Y. For the next century the Swains had stuck it out there and flourished with the town. One of those "old families." Swains in the Legislature, Swains expiring on Southern bayonets, Swains voting civic improvement and the Erie Canal, Swains running for the Senate and up San Juan Hill; that sort of thing.

When I abandoned the town to go out East, Ronald Swain was growing in wisdom and stature in one of those block-square, roomy brick mansions with a hideous cupola sitting like a dowdy hat atop the roof, and a sweep of

As she danced, one forgot the hideous music, the
stale breath of the crowd, everything

elm-shadowed lawn guarded by a rusty iron mastiff. Behind
those eminently respectable walls his mother (D.A.R.) had
schooled him to say "thank you," wash behind the ears,
and never tell a lie; while his father had been turning the
barns into a three-car garage, and an apartment house had
popped up across the corner.

Later he had gone to "Y" camps and a private school that
"instilled manhood and responsibility in your boy." Then
he had done rather well at calculus, football and fraternity
in some intolerant and minute-big New England college
redundant with ivy and traditions. After which he had
gone into advanced engineering.

Now you know him at twenty-seven years. A husky,
heavy-shouldered chap, American as the verse of Long-
fellow, with his red-cheeked, groomed face genial behind
horn-rimmed glasses, his easy smile, his indulgent
good-fellowship. Carefully reared. Honest. Always bathed.

Comfortably endowed with the ability to work hard. Faintly proud of his democracy and instinctive morals, and—though he would never have admitted it—his "old family."

I happened to be in the States, making a brief visit in Rochester at the time Ronald Swain had just completed his engineering courses. The Swains took me in tow, and Ronald, home at the time, ventured to show me the town and the changes made since I had left. He drove me about in his glossy roadster—a guerdon won by the achievement of the diploma—pointing out the new court house, county hospital, golf club, conservatory of music.

I was not surprised to learn that Swains were behind each of those goodly endeavors, for the Swains and the town were practically the same thing. Old Harlan Swain had coughed up for the hospital and designed the court house. The Ephraim Swains had built the club, Junius B. had erected the conservatory of music. Ronald Swain was a little uncomfortable and proud about it, and he would get away from it to ask me about what he termed my "East of Suez adventurings that must be damned interesting."

LATER, THE WHOLE family bundled me into their sedan—a private Pullman, I should have called it—and we rolled out into the park to see the statue, recently erected by the city, of Junius B. Swain. The Swains male chuckled a lot about it, told me to "wait till you see the darned thing"; but the female Swains were openly indignant. It seemed the statue had been mangled and done in bad taste. And ridiculous, too.

The sedan purred to a halt along a boulevard curving through the park, and there was the statue of Junius B. To

this day I can see that bronze piece as I saw it that afternoon rearing in the mellow sunshine. Ronald Swain, at the
wheel, waved at it, and laughed.

"Behold our good Uncle Junius. Creator of the music
conservatory. I say, it's mighty rotten taste, isn't it? And isn't
it a mighty rotten statue?"

Certainly it was bad taste, glaringly out of place in that
perfumed park garden. I could feel the Swain pride pricked
into squirming about me. But it was not a rotten statue.
It was a mighty good one. The artist who fashioned that
bronze had wrought well. No doubt about its itching the
family Swains, though, to have one of their blood marching
down on an azalea bed in the nakedness of a public park,
marching without a shirt on. For civic romance had wanted
to remember Junius B. Swain, builder of its music conservatory, as the brave young drummer-boy he had been in
the Civil War. And the commissioned sculptor had made
the drummer-boy again. And made with masterful hands.

That Civil War drummer-boy lived in bronze. The youthful face was staring wide-eyed at advancing Confederate
lines, quivering at the fearful tune of smashing canister and
grape and minie ball. Naked to the waist, a rag bound about
his forehead, he drubbed the clumsy marching-drum that
swung at his belt with all the fury of fear. And—here is the
marvel of it—despite the unnatural expression the artist
had caught on the bronze face, despite its round youth, its
wide eyes, its fright-grinning mouth, that face was Swain.
Junius B. as a drummer-boy, pouncing and scared. Marvel-
ously Junius B. No wonder the family resented it, though
perhaps they did not see it as I saw it that afternoon.

Moreover, not only was family resemblance there;

but the face on that graceless statue was Ronald Swain! Whereas it might have mirrored the young Junius B., it *was* Ronald, naked to the belt, thumping a deep drum, features twisted in unhappy fear, mouth dropping oaths. A truly amazing likeness.

I almost laughed as the sedan swung along the road and away. It was like catching the Swains off guard, as it were. Like seeing a Swain—how proper they always were—wearing a green tie at a dinner party, making a voluble disturbance in the church vestry on Easter. The Swains of Rochester. And there was that uncle, who had built a conservatory of music, raising hell in the quiet park another uncle had built. Thumping a drum and cursing with fright!

I laughed about that horrible statue on the boat to Bombay. I chuckled about it all the way to the Northwest Frontier Province where I lived. Then I forgot the image and my Rochester friends and Ronald Swain until I received a letter from Ronald a year later.

He was coming up on the Afghan border to build some manner of dam for the International Construction Companies, Ltd. He hoped I would be around to show him the works. Fortunate to be located at the spot where I was working. Dam was a big proposition. We'd get in some shooting together. Going to stay three years and marry when he went back home. Had always wanted to see the Orient. Great fun. Getting into Bombay on such and such a steamer—

And so he came to Nagarabad, bringing a picture of his mother, sixteen cartons of cigarettes, an un-thumbed Bible, a photograph of his Rochester fiancée, his Rochester traditions and altruisms and the Rochester God.

NAGARABAD! NAGARABAD DID not believe in God. Nagarabad believed in Allah—*Mohammed an rasool Allah!* It believed with devotion, intolerance and fury. Its beards and prayers were colorful, long and frequent. Mullahs, preaching of the Prophet, crowded its dusty corners. Muezzins chanted from its minarets. And three generations? A century? A century meant nothing but accumulated dust to this town where shaving was forbidden, bathing done with circumspection and never behind the ears.

Legionnaires of the mighty Jenghiz Khan had bloodied Nagarabad streets and found them old. Sabaktigin and the Brahmin King of Lahore had charged their cavalries across Nagarabad squares and the horses had stumbled in ruts left by the war elephants of that Persian Darius who came before Alexander. And Nagarabad was older than that—and older than that—and had been old when the Saraswati joined waters with the Indus, and the Vedas were being penned.

Its name, of course, had been as different as its faith in those dawn days, but its encircling hills remained unchanged, its blazing afternoons and metal nights and fetid smells were for eternity.

The temples erected to Rama and Vishnu were still there. The walls of shrines to Buddha and Zoroaster still baked in the sun though Moslem scimitars had won the city's soul to Allah.

Its civic pride? Never in good-fellowship and public morals. Pride in marksmanship, gold, women, ability at theft; for its old families banded to slay, and virtue meant starving until the Ramadan sunset gun or shooting a fatal bullet at an unwary spine. Perhaps bullet-holes pocked the city's blank wall face less often since the advent of the British Raj, but steel glinted in the most innocent of belts; groans could throb out of dark, steamy shadows; and the local vultures did not go unfed.

No parks and conservatories of music for Nagarabad. Rather, a marketplace where turbans could bob, beards could wag and curse, caravan cameleers could squabble and fight and drink, Shinwari beggars could scrabble, Mahsud and Wazir and Gurkha and Sikh could barter and scrap, and holy-men fleece. Rather, the Lane of the Charas Smokers where pictures could grow with the poisoned resin-smoke of little pipes. Smoke that brought coughing and delicious dreams and lust and leprosy and death. Rather, the arching Gate of the Camels and Bulls, built when Haroun-al-Raschid was a boy, through which the caravans and tribesmen from the hills could come and go. Rather, the Street of a Thousand Delights, where *tam-tams* thumped, stomach-rotting *bhang* was drunk, and vermilion-painted toes and fingers danced behind blue doors.

By day an oven-hot, stinking rabbit-warren sprawling in the dust. By night a fairy city of silver spires and minarets, magic shadows, mystic lights—a silver city peopled with kobolds and ghosts and jinn. For the sunset, cupped in the westward Suleiman crags, wrought an alchemy of fire and blood. When the moon rose clear in that enchanted sky the market-place became a legend, ragged Shinwaris and wolf-faced Wazirs were warriors from the Arabian Nights. When the moon was high the painted hussies in the Street of a Thousand Delights became houris loosed from their hollow pearls in Paradise. The wretches in the Lane of the Charas Smokers were Knights from Haroun-al-Raschid's court. The Gate of the Camels and Bulls an entry to a Never-Never Land.

Nagarabad—now dust and silver, now decay and gold. Ancient, uninhabited Nagarabad. Drop a Ronald Swain from Rochester on your seething, lusting, leprous, perfumed, enigmatic Oriental bosom, and anything queer might happen!

TWILIGHT SLANTING DOWN the twisty lane lay in crimson pools on the flagstones; enameled red the arabesqued wall across the way; draped kindly shadows to hide ragbag and scab and littered gutter. Enervating breath of heat and odor still clung low on the flat rooftops. But the blasting sun had flamed down the west; soon the sky would cool.

We sat on the balcony of Abdullah ben Brahim's coffee house, Swain, Fletcher and I. Those who see in the foreign missionary a quinine-soaked fanatic, pallid with a curry-and-rice liver and trying to cram a recondite religion down heathen necks, should have known Fletcher. Quinine-soaked, yes. But never a pallid sky-pilot attempting to clothe naked urchins and give Moslem devils a Yankee or British deity. Not Fletcher.

The man owned a horrent black beard, a penchant for gaseous cigars, and the ability to speak only forty Asian tongues along with good round Western profanity when need be. He preached with a medicine case; won souls to sanitation and soap. His little English church, standing in a brave plot of grass near the Gate of the Camels and Bulls, did not defy the epileptic Apostle of Islam, but strove to work with him.

"You can't preach Christianity to the Orient," he was saying that evening to Swain, over his coffee glass. "It's got to be demonstrated; and the way Europe misbehaves and the U. S. squabbles, it's getting difficult. Besides, you can't change these Orientals, anyhow. Not their souls. You can wash their necks, but you can't change their blood corpuscles. They want to die Moslem. Why not? Old Mohammed promised them a pretty nice berth if they'd make Paradise. All the wine they can drink. Jewels. Beautiful ladies who dwell in big hollow pearls." He chuckled. "I've got to go some to beat that."

Swain chuckled too. I think he was a little surprised at the missionary's commentary on Paradise. He had asked Fletcher how the mission was going, and I suppose he expected a vivid discourse on the "good work." He drank his coffee; smiled at us through his moon-round spectacles.

"Things are different out here than I expected," he offered. "I think I'm going to like it here, first. Way the talk was back home I expected to get cobra-bite or cholera or be stabbed by a mad dervish the minute I stepped into Asia. Been in the Orient over a month, now, and haven't seen a snake." He grinned; scrubbed a fist down his sunburned nose. "I'm disappointed. Here I sit in a wicker chair drinking the best coffee I ever tasted. My foreman up at the dam speaks English with an Oxford accent and the coolies are dirty devils, but—"

"Your Bombay hotel wasn't the Orient," Fletcher reminded. "And you've only been up here a few days. Think you'll like it, eh? I'm not the one to throw water on enthusiasm. Nights like the one coming are beautiful. But wait till you can't get water to bathe and the thermometer marches up to a hundred thirty. Wait till your Moslems strike in the middle of a hard stretch. Wait till you've heard me yap the same jokes a thousand times, and Henry, here, repeats himself on the latest specimen he unearthed from the rocks, and the drinking well gets full of wigglers. Then you'll know you're away from home."

Swain laughed and fingered his new sun-helmet; started to speak, and stopped. Fletcher turned around, and I heard it, too. We listened. Worming its way up out of the murmurous mumble of the bazaar stole the chill, thin *toodle-oodle-dee* of a *zef,* timed to the muffled, pulsing throb of a *tam-tam.* Twisting, coiling, the plaintive minor bit through the mauve dusk; the drums beating dull undertone, tuneless, rhythmic, weird. Distant, but approaching.

SWAIN SAT UP. "Wow, that sound is creepy." He brushed a kerchief across his chin. "I'd know I was in the Orient, now. Sounds like it's coming this way. What is it, fellows?"

"Show," Fletcher informed. "Traveling show. Comes through here about every two months. Magicians. Snake-charmer. A trick bear an' a contortionist who'd loosen your back teeth. And dancing girls." He turned to me. "You remember 'em, Henry, we saw them a couple of times. That circus run by that scurvy Eurasian blighter called Elmer Hamid? They're a rotten bunch of thieves and pickpockets, Swain, but they put on a good show. Have the natives pop-eyed. Got one dancer with 'em who isn't so dusty. Hell, no. Henry remembers her. Girl called Gulabi—means rose."

The missionary nudged me, and brought a flush to my cheek. Yes, I remembered this show and this dancing girl called Gulabi. I had been a little whiskied the first time I had seen the outfit, and the girl had gone to my head, I suppose. No doubt I had made a few idiotic comments on her beauty, and the missionary had never ceased twitting me about it.

"It's a rum bunch," I told Swain. "But this Gulabi, their star performer, can dance all right. She's—well—good-looking. Circassian or Eurasian or something. But they're a good gang to steer clear of."

Swain had clapped on his helmet; gone to the edge of the balcony. Now he leaned out over the lane. I could catch the sheen of his glasses in the purpling dusk. "I say," he exclaimed. "They're coming right down this lane. Gee, they make a picture. Here comes the circus parade, fellows. Just like home. Look!"

A circus parade, but never just like home. Flotsam that had crawled below the coffee-merchant's balcony now seeped up the cobbles toward the moving torchlights and sound. Two bent old mendicants scurried around the corner and hastened up the lane. Ghosts and shadows and a *charas*-doped muleteer were the only live things left below the balcony. Like water the crowd ran up the lane, moved back down it like gray molasses. Clustering about the circus.

And Swain had been right in proclaiming it a picture. That circus of Elmer Hamid's! I wish you could see it as we saw it in Nagarabad that evening when the sun had gone and a dollar-round, orange moon cruised low, beginning its subtle magic behind the minarets and the Gate.

First came torchlights—crimson flower-flames blossoming on the tips of long poles. Little blazing fires that bobbed and ducked, illuminating random faces and feet, picking out cubes and triangles of wall and hanging balcony, shedding flickering shadows far down the cobbles.

Torches carried by wretched urchins with the faces of jinn and monstrous splay feet.

Pompous behind them marched the master of the outfit, the Eurasian, Elmer Hamid. I had seen and marked this creature a ruffian before, but never had I noted him as poisonous. For the torchlight that made his corpulent body a billowing shadow was merciless on his face. The flickery glow made a mask of that face bobbing in front of the thrown-back burnoose hood, tipped with crimson the bulbous nose, glistened on the sweat-wet, bloated cheeks, rimmed with red the porcine little eyes.

As he strolled into view a yawn opened his pulpy lips, revealed his mouth a pink cave with every tooth missing from the left side and every tooth golden on the right. And now I noticed he was cross-eyed, and spied the tiny boil glowing in the center of his forehead. An unlovely creature, Elmer Hamid, mingling the worst of the Orient with the worst of the West.

BEHIND HIM CAME the moribund *zef*-player, cheeks pouting on the tip of his squealing lute, fingers fluttering on the stem, bare feet shuffling in the dust. The *zef*-player's face was a skull under a huge turban, scurrile with a wispy beard-growth sprouting on the jaw. At his heels marched the skeleton who could twist his spine into a sailor's knot; a skeleton leading a lugubrious, moth-eaten black bear—a bear that had escaped from a furrier's window after most of the sawdust had leaked from its mangy flanks.

The skeleton and the bear were followed by another skeleton. A wraith of skin and bones, wearing yards of turban and baggy Moslem breeches and clots of rag on its feet. The face was sick and sunken and doped, beardless save for straggling hairs and the betel-nut juice dribbling down the chin. Its hands were made into fists and pounded cadently on the head of the bottle-shaped drum swung at its hip.

Roum-bubba-roum! Roum-bubba-roum! A throbbing beat that timed the squeals of the *zef* up ahead, and the flashing feet of the dancer who wove a tortuous path behind. The dancer called Gulabi—which means rose.

Now this Gulabi. Circassian or Eurasian, perhaps. Whatever she was, she was beautiful. Whatever she was, she could dance. I had seen her before, and I did not fail to see her this time.

A torch and the street crowd moved slowly behind her, a cloud about a smoky star. Head thrown back, her laughing face caught the torch-glow, her sinuous body misted in shadow, her weaving, braceleted wrists and ankles twinkled as she spun.

"She was built!" American slang would have said; I can find no other expression. Never buxom and not slim. "Built" I believe is the word. And her face! What witchery laughed in her smile and pale green eyes, shone in the gloss of her tossing, wavy dark hair!

Oriental? Yes! And Irish! Oriental Irish. That was it. Lord, how the little lady could dance!

The procession passed right under the balcony of Abdullah ben Brahim's coffee house. The torches, the scabrous Elmer Hamid, the dead *zef*-player, the skeleton and stuffed bear, the decaying *tam-tam* beater, Gulabi of the Irish eyes and Orient soul, the final torch-bearer and the dust-raising crowd. The *toodle-oodle-dee* and the rhythmic *roum-bubba-roum*. The patches of crimson light and grotesque shadow. Right under our balcony.

Swain stood at the rail, his eyes round behind the horn-rims, his hands twisting on the brim of his sun-helmet. "Say!" he said, to himself as much as anybody. "She—she was wonderful! I'm going to see this show! I'm going to see this show!"

WE WENT TO the show, Swain, Fletcher and I. The hubbub had congealed in the marketplace where a caravan from Bokhara or Kohkand had anchored for the night. Camels knelt there in the dust of the open compound. Absurd, long-necked dromedaries, grunting under humping bales of carpets and silks, leather and brass goods and merchandise smuggled from hell and concealed from the British eye. Camel-drivers, their faces hidden under peaked hoods, slipped in and out of shadow-like shrouded dead. Sheeted tribesmen and what appeared to be the major population of the town jammed the center of the square where the circus of Elmer Hamid was holding forth.

Fletcher led us, pushing a path through the pack. Brown faces scowled, a few shaggy beards spat pointed epithets at the *feringi,* but the missionary was a power among the local folk and our progress went unhindered. I was behind Swain; could not see him. Still, I had conceived a sense of uneasiness about our seeing the show. Swain had insisted. His face had been too flushed. But, after all, to a newcomer the East must have been vastly exciting; and the circus might be a break in the monotony of the young engineer's first days. As long as Fletcher thought it was all right—

We brought up on the inside rim of the crowd. The wide circle of gray, shadowy burnooses was lined off by the torchlights jabbed into the ground. Elmer Hamid and his entourage had erected a small tent backed to a mud watering-trough that was used by local muleteers. Carpets spread in the dust made a stage for the weak antics of the starving bear which cavorted under the impelling slashes of a whip in the contortionist's fist. We could see the other actors crouching in the tent; and Elmer Hamid squatting like a toad on a ragged pillow, grinning, waving his hands, haranguing the saturnine faces of the onlookers.

Then the bear was yanked away, and the corpse that had played the *zef* skipped out of the tent, a little pot of earth in his hands. Kneeling on a carpet, he faced the crowd; placed the pot in front of him. His gaunt fingers dug a hole in the earth; planted a seed. The mango trick! The rascal worked it cleverly. Covering the pot with a rag, he waved his hands at the stars, spat an incantation—and before our eyes grew the mango tree. Fletcher chuckled. But Ronald Swain was quiet as a mummy. I looked at him. He was not watching the masterful legerdemain. His eye was on the tent.

A murmur of applause stirred from the crowd as the magician and his flower pot ducked from the stage. However, the applause was not for the magic. That mango trick is humdrum to the East. The applause was for the girl who had slipped from the tent to skip out into the crimson torch-glow and pirouette across the carpets. The corpse was at his *zef,* again. The decaying drummer stepped into the light, knuckles pounding the head of his bottle-shaped drum. *Toodle-oodle-dee. Roum-bubba-roum!*

Gulabi! No Oriental dancing girl of the ordinary run. I had seen a lot of them in Asia, and not one of them could dance as did the Rose. Compared to her, the others were galumphing dummies, insulting rhythm and decency and beauty. But this girl of Elmer Hamid's shabby circus was something different.

Poetry in motion is a stale term for her. She was lovely and quaint and—those pale green eyes, that sea of lustrous hair, slim hands, graceful as the dive of a bird. Impossible to describe the girl, for she was dancing that night as I had never seen her dance before. One forgot the hideous music, the stale breath of the crowd, the dust, the pungent smoke of the lamps. One caught a whisper of the Orient; a queer tingle that might pulse in one's veins at the hearing of a rare and beautiful symphonic chord; a—

But her dance had stopped. The *zef* and the *tam-tam* had choked quiet. The girl darted over to a gaunt Moslem on the edge of the crowd; clasped his hand, gazed down at his palm, murmured. Telling fortunes. Another hand. Another. Quickly. Until she stood before none other than Ronald Swain.

I FELT HIM stiffen as she reached for his palm. Standing next to him, I was aware of the faint perfume of her hair, the sheen of her arched throat, the warm glow of her strangely Irish eyes as they met and held his startled gaze. Then—as if it was not the most improbable thing in the world—she said softly: "I—talk—English. You nice Englishman. Saw you on balcony. I do my dance for you, yes? For you." (The grace of Asia! The winsome beauty of the Emerald Isle! Can you understand? An Oriental, and an Irish lass fresh from the hills—at the same time? Lord!)

Ronald Swain was of wood. I know Fletcher was lost behind his beard. I could not have twitched the least of my fingers. And this dancer called Gulabi did not move to go. Just stood there smiling into Swain's eyes. And stood. And stood.

A dozen minutes—a dozen years—must have ticked away. The girl looking into Swain's eyes. The impossible crowd of hooded ghosts, staring, shuffling sandals, staring. The torchlights wiggling aloft, scattering strange shadows. The night growing taut with waiting. Waiting. Waiting for something queer, something Asian, something strange to happen.

And it did. I imagine the thirteenth minute ticked, as it did. Then the bloated, cursing face of Elmer Hamid came looping across the carpets. The Eurasian's doughy cheeks were crimson in the torch-glow. The boil in his forehead made a third eye above the two that were hugging his nose below. He got a hand out of his burnoose; trapped it with a loud slap on the girl's wrist; spun her to her knees; kicked.

A fury-choked American yell, and a furious American fist whipping five knuckles up from Swain's belt, flying like a projectile through a patch of red light and landing smash in that bloated face of dough. *Crack!* Swain's sun-helmet flying from his yellow head and swooping to roll across the carpets. Swain's fist again. The face of Elmer Hamid, gone wet scarlet, reeling and weaving and howling.

Instant turmoil, as the fat Eurasian whirled backward, staggered over the stakes pinning one edge of the tent and splashed into the water-trough. A crazy tumble of hoods and turbans and bare arms, woven into patch-work quilting by the flaring lights. Riot, as the Moslem crowd tumbled like breaking surf to flood over the carpets, circus-tent, compound.

For the first time since coming East, I had out my automatic. I heard Fletcher yelling like a maniac; saw him go bobbing and fighting into the chaos. Dust smoked under tramping, tripping feet. One by one the torchlights toppled under jarring bodies. Then the crowd was shoving in a crazy half-darkness; pushing, hedging, wallowing, fighting and scarcely knowing why, only wanting to get claws on the *feringi* who had struck a Moslem.

Lord knows where that *feringi* had gone. At the first mad rush Swain had been drowned, enveloped. Now, in the treachery of moonlight, shadow, dust, tangling arms and wigs and hoods, Fletcher and I, fighting elbow to elbow, could not locate the engineer. Floundering, calling out Swain's name, we struggled in the whirlpool of bodies; found ourselves locked in the very middle of the jam. And to be locked in the vortex of a hostile mob of Mussulmans is no entertainment.

Fletcher alone was the man to unravel things. The stalwart missionary with the black beard shouted and punched; named a familiar face or two, and soon had a cordon of friendly Nagarabad townsmen around us.

Gradually the crowd fell apart; extricated itself. Little by little the mob dispersed. Finally the center of the market place was visible. I had feared to see a trampled, bleeding Swain—perhaps dead—spraddled where the rush had met; but the engineer was nowhere to be seen. Too, the circus seemed to have been swept away. A few scattered carpets lay crumpled in the dust. The tent sprawled empty and flat, and the gaunt bear was calmly drinking from the water-trough. Dust languidly settled in puddles of moonlight.

"HE'S BEEN CARRIED off!" panted Fletcher. "That confounded Elmer Hamid and his gang have mobbed him and carried him off! We've got to find him, Henry; no telling what those scoundrels will do to him. We'll get a few of these boys to help us. Hey, Mohamet! You, Abdesalem! Achmed!—We'll foot it after the crowd going down that lane. Scout around."

We scouted around—up one lane and down another, peering into huddled crowds, poking into jabbering clusters of tribesmen on this corner and that. We scouted around, all right, half the night. Questioning. Demanding. Hunting in desperation for a clew. But of Ronald Swain, the white engineer, we could find no trace. That boy might as well have been gathered to the stars.

"He's gone, Henry," Fletcher finally gasped admission. "Only one place we haven't looked. That's your bungalow where he's been staying with you. We might see if he's there by any chance. Maybe he's found his way up there."

He had. We found Ronald Swain in my bungalow. He had the lamps going, and the room was full of bugs and cigarette smoke. He was sitting calmly at the table, and talking. Talking to the girl curled up in the chair in the corner. Talking in English and French, and telling her about America, and Rochester, and the Swains!

"Gulabi is here," he said quietly, seeing us framed in the door. He did not even rise from his chair. "She's not going back to the circus, you know. She wants to do this; I'm going to send her to an English school in the mountains."

"YOU REALLY WOULDN'T know the girl," I told Fletcher, when I came back with Swain to Nagarabad after a visit in Nani Tal. "Twelve months in that school has done marvels. Marvels. I swear, she might have just stepped over from London. Her clothes, manners, and all. There must be an

English background somewhere. Her speech is almost flawless. She is beautiful. I don't wonder Swain fell head over heels in love with her when he saw her seven months ago. Don't really see what we can say about it, now. His experiment, if you want to call it that, seems to have won out. Why, she's the loveliest little lady—"

"And his family?" grunted the missionary. "This marriage?"

"There were a few letters, I believe. I'm not just sure he's told them all about it. They'd never guess anything to see her."

Fletcher shook his head. "My ideas are still the same," he admitted. "There's no use talking to Swain any more, of course. But I still believe what I told him. She was a dancing-girl. She's Oriental. Eurasian, perhaps, but Oriental to the core. Oriental as these Nagarabad walls. You can paint 'em over, maybe, but the heart is still there. I'll admit she's remarkable. Her dancing was beautiful. How she kept above the usual trash is more than I know. Far ahead of that crowd of skunks she traveled with, and all that. But she's Asian, Henry. Won't change. Blood. You can't alter it."

"She's more than remarkable," I insisted. "No one disapproved the engagement more than I did at first. I thought Swain was mad. Thought the sun or the moon had got him. But now I can't say a thing. Why, think of her knowing that smattering of French and English even when she was with that bum show. Picked it up—"

"Yes. Who did she learn it from? A dancing-girl. It's all wrong, I think, Henry. She's Oriental, Asian. But what the hell, I suppose. The boy was stubborn as steel from the first." Fletcher sighed.

A *mina* was calling its strident song without the window. The hot afternoon droned in the savage sunlight. The smart rapping of a hammer carried my eye to the new bungalow nestling against the dun-colored hill. From where I sat I could see Swain, braving the heat, busy nailing shingles on the veranda roof. A cheerful whistle pierced from beneath the brim of his broad sun-helmet. Hours he did not spend at his engineering job he gave to the bungalow. Everything money could obtain in the East had gone into that little house. Fresh paint on its walls. A little ice plant all the way from London. Glass blinds in the casements. Cedar finishings. Everything to make comfortable the cottage for his bride.

"It's almost done," observed Fletcher. "He's surely worked hard on it. Beautiful little place. I certainly hope things go off all right. I say, Henry." The missionary's eyes narrowed. "Hamid and his gang were here while you two were away. Stayed their usual week. I ran into the lousy beggar in front of the mosque. And he snarled out his threat, again, Henry. But we won't tell Swain. No use worrying him, and I'm sure that Hamid skunk won't try any knife-play or gunnery. I warned him, same way you did. He growled out the same threat."

The Eurasian, again! A second threat! This time I *was* uneasy. The first time I had paid it scant attention. But now that Swain had decided to bring the girl to Nagarabad with him—Fletcher was going to marry them the day she arrived—it might be different. That scoundrel Elmer Hamid. What plan had he generated in his leprous mind?

Three months after Swain had sent Gulabi to Nani Tal I had chanced to encounter the Eurasian and his circus crawling down a road in the hills. The caravan blocked my path, and I had been forced to pull up my horse at the roadside. Elmer Hamid had recognized me; shuffled over to drop a hand on my saddle and shove his leering countenance up at mine. His crossed eyes had glared weirdly from their rheumy sockets beneath a black scowl; flickered up at me. His pulpy lips had twisted out the hoarse words:

"Don't worry none, me bleedin' friend. I got me eye on 'er. An' I'll get 'er back. I'll get 'er back!"

I had raised my whip and warned the scurvy devil that any move on his part would have him dangling on the end of a rope in the government gallows. Just let him raise a hand, and the British police would fix him for good.

His eyes had flickered like lizards' tongues. "I'll git 'er, so I will. I'll git 'er from that accursed engineer *sahib*. I'll get 'er back!"

I DOUBT IF I will forget the day and the wedding when I die. The sun toiled up in the east and speared the land with a blasting, fiery ray. By noon Nagarabad radiated heat like an oven. By one o'clock I was a panting rag, red-eyed from nerves and perhaps too many whisky-pegs and because Fletcher had come to my bungalow that morning to tell me that Elmer Hamid's circus had sprouted with the dawn in the market place. He had passed the market place on his early way to a sickbed; glimpsed the tent and the mangy bear. The Eurasian must have come during the night.

We said nothing about it to Swain. The boy was as nervous as any lad about to be married; spent the morning bathing, fidgeting in and out of his new bungalow, glaring at his wrist-dial, cursing because the motor bringing Gulabi from Nani Tal had not arrived. A thousand times

I rejoiced that the market place and the circus were at the other end of town, and Swain knew nothing of Elmer Hamid's arrival. Myself, it made me sweat to think of it. Undoubtedly word of the wedding had been slipped by spies to the vagabond. Impossible to keep such an event secret in a Moslem community, where every crack and keyhole is a telephone receiver. As well try to hide a divorcee in a ladies' sewing circle.

But what did the rascal have up his scorbutic sleeve? I was on the point of charging down to the market place and ordering him out of town, but I could not get away from Swain, and by the time I had framed an excuse to escape, Gulabi had arrived with the school officials.

Then we were collected in Fletcher's bungalow behind his little church, to meet the bride-to-be and await the ceremony. As Swain's best man, I was occupied with forty nervous details. No wedding in the States could have caused greater commotion and preparation. Fletcher's little chapel, standing in the shadow of the arching Gate of the Camels and Bulls, wore hill flowers and bunting. The missionary, Swain and I were decked out in freshly laundered drill, smart in spite of perspiration. Fletcher's Afghani boy bustled about with grins and wine decanters for the guests. And Gulabi—even Fletcher showed surprise. A white rose in her simple satin dress, sheer stockings, dainty white satin slippers. The bouquet at her waist could not match the flush of her cheek. Smiling eyes and hair spun of black gold. Low, careful voice. This girl had but come from the drawing-rooms of London!

Then the church with its warm shadows and a violet shaft of light slanting from the stained glass Fletcher had battled to put behind the altar. The little arched door flooded with brilliant afternoon sunshine. The crimson *pugrees* of two stiff-chinned native policeman—and I was glad to see them there—guarding the door.

Now Swain and I strolled down the aisle. The bride was smiling, white hand on the arm of one of the skinny school officials. Fletcher, large in the tinted shadows of the altar, intoned solemn words through his beard. Swain was nodding, a drop of perspiration gleaming on his forehead, his smile tight-lipped. The bride, pale eyes radiant. Sweat stung on my lashes and catching tight the collar around my throat. The church was quiet, somnolent, warm.

FLETCHER'S VOICE, AGAIN: "To join together this man and this woman in matrimony; which is an honorable estate… therefore is not by any to be entered into unadvisedly, but reverently, discreetly and in the fear of God. Into which holy estate these two persons present come now to be joined. Therefore, if any can show just cause why they may not lawfully be joined together, let him now speak or else hereafter forever hold his peace—"

The ministerial pause. The chapel quiet as a tomb. Nagarabad murmurous in the blatant sunshine outside. And then I was brittle with nerves and the palms of my hands were numb. Certainly I heard it, then. Twisting through the door with the sunbeams, a tenuous coil of sound. The chill, thin wail of a *zef* timed to the pulsing echo of a drum. *Toodle-oodle-dee. Roum-bubba-roum.* Faint. Faint. But approaching.

Fletcher chanting loudly, again. Swain mumbling. The girl softly: "I will." Their voices reciting in unison. "… And thereto I plight thee my faith—" A thin squeal winding through the sunshine in the door. The throb of a *tam-tam*, barbarous, insistent. *Toodle-oodle-dee! Roum-bubba-roum!* Nearer and nearer.

Fletcher's voice went hoarse, and Swain darted a nervous glance over his shoulder. The girl stood staring vacantly as I fumbled the ring and Swain juggled with stiff hands to put it on her finger.

Toodle-oodle-dee! Roum-bubba-roum! That horrible, hideous clamor. Dust drifting like smoke through the chapel door. Fletcher shouting: "I pronounce that they are husband and wife together, in the name of—"

And there they were, filing past the doorway, wraiths in the sunshine and dust.

The bloated figure of Elmer Hamid. The corpse with lips pouting on the squealing *zef*, fingers fluttering on the stem. The skeleton leading the scrawny, snuffling bear. The urchins weighted with bundles and unlighted torch-sticks. The dead *tam-tam* player, fists pounding, red juice leaking from his chin to drop on the booming drumhead. Filing slowly, like a moving camera-film, past the chapel door. Leaving in their wake a whirl of dust and a taunting echo. *Toodle-oodle-dee! Roum-bubba-roum!* Profaning with its echo the dusk-hidden beams overhead.

Elmer Hamid, the Eurasian, had found in his sardonic brain a masterful gesture!

I heard a queer, dry laugh. I saw Gulabi slither from Swain's hand; twist into the aisle. I saw one small satin slipper go one way. I saw its mate go twisting the other. I saw her head arch back, her hair toss, her hands glide. She laughed, poised on her stockinged toes for a brief moment, then went spinning and pirouetting down the aisle and out of the door.

You could have heard molecules moving in an iron bar during the petrified silence that ensued. I could only be conscious of a sweat-tear tantalizing the tip of my nose; conscious of a futile effort to lift a hand to brush it away. Then the stone-quiet was smashed by an insane shout; and Swain was pounding down the aisle, out of the door.

I caught him under the span of the Gate of the Camels and Bulls. Elmer Hamid and his circus had just dusted out of sight around the bend in the red highway to the hills. Swain struck me on the jaw. With dazed, half-conscious eyes I saw his feet thudding quickly up the road, vanishing around the bend.

EIGHT MONTHS HAD gone, and I was on my way down to Allahabad to ease nerves worn raw by the sight of the monkeys scampering about the empty bungalow on the hill, the bungalow peopled with ghosts that were cobwebs—and the letters, letters, letters. Letters from Rochester in America. Letters I answered with lies and lies. Eight months of it.

I rode in the saddle out of Nagarabad with Fletcher; was picked up by a friend and his motor on the border of the province.

We were bearing southward through a village one evening, when I saw the torchlights, the press of onlookers, the marching procession. I was out of that car in a second, and running; elbowing into the crowd, shouting hoarse, short cries.

The creature drubbing the *tam-tam* stood stock-still, eyes wide with fright; his mouth—wet and crimson with betel-nut juice—dropped oaths and grinning fear. He was naked to the waist. His knotted fists pounded the head of the drum swung at his belt. I know I stood in my tracks and yawped idiotically when I saw the drum! There was even the rag of cloth bound around his head. Swain! Swain thumping that heathenish drum. And—you can see it, of course—the Swain of that statue in the park a billion miles away in his home.

I saw him there and I saw the statue—and the whole business was a horror, you may well believe. It was even more horrible when he grinned at me; came close; chuckled. The ribs were showing in his chest and he was unbathed and had not shaved. He poked that frightened face at me, and chuckled. His voice coughed and sawed. What do you think he said?

"I like the life," he said.

"Swain!" I panted. "The devil! You can't be—"

"But she's gone," he snarled drunkenly. "Gulabi is gone. She left me five months ago. Ran off with an American who wanted to take her to the States. Gone."

"We've been hunting all over for you!" I shouted, tearing at his arm. "Swain! Ronald Swain! You hear me?"

"She's gone," he panted. "Gulabi—gone off to the States." He hiccoughed. A tear wiggled down his cheek. Suddenly he wrenched from my clasp, and melted in the shadows of the crowd.

I could not find him.

He had stolen from my pocket my watch.

WHEN I TOLD my house-boy to answer the unexpected knock on my door and he ushered in Fletcher and the lady, I knew at once she must be one of the Swains. She was. Fletcher nodded somberly in the lamplight as she removed her veil.

I gasped. "You!"

"Yes," she said quietly. "I have come back. I have been in America, Dancing. It was one night when I was on tour that—You see, I had been dancing in a fine conservatory. I do not remember where it was, what city. But I danced that evening in a fine conservatory, and later my managers were motoring me through a park. The moon was fine and the gardens made me think of India. And then—then I saw *him*. I saw him there with my own eyes! I saw him as I had last seen him when I left him. And he was there in the park—with his drum—the little *pugree* on his forehead."

She had talked quickly, whispering, and it took me a moment to recover my scattered brain and unravel her words. Dancing in a conservatory? Saw *him* in the park? Why, she had danced in the conservatory of music built by Junius B.! Had seen that statue!

"I saw him there in that park so far away, and I knew I could not leave him. So I—I've come to find him. I know I can. I've come to find him and take him back."

THE DEATH SONG OF
ABSINTHE DEVOLLE

*All the East knew that China Coast Charley's
dance hall was a curious place—but no one, least
of all Prefect of Police Achille Bouvard, guessed
what a curious drama was to be staged there*

THIS IS THE amazing story of Absinthe Devolle, the little flame-haired piano-player down at China Coast Charley's in Saigon. It happened out there in that Orient-smitten corner of Cochin-China. But it's a French story, you will understand. As French—and surprising—as a glass of absinthe or the astonishing little lady named after it. As French as her throbbing song that sobbed out its astounding climax.

And it should have been played out in Paris. Still, Saigon was near enough. Do not certain tourist catalogues pronounce Saigon the "Paris of the East"? Though just what part of Paris they refer to, this writer cannot imagine. (He can, but he won't for publication.)

A MIGHTY QUEER quirk in a mighty queer story, that it should be Achille Bouvard, Saigon's Prefect of Police, who first introduced her to me. He left his ricksha standing at my gate that night, came up to the veranda, and yanked me out of a doze with:

"Milford! You have been begging for an excitement to break this tropic monotony and ease your Yankee soul. You deplore the place and say there is nothing of interest in Saigon since you came to the consulate here. Come, then. Something of interest has appeared. But yes. Name of a

name! Come with me to-night. I will show you something
to shock your interest, indeed!"

The flurried trip of Bouvard's voice sat me up in my chair,
surprised. Obviously my friend was unusually distraught.
He loomed a lean, uneasy shadow against a background
of night-hung *kaladang* and lime trees, and a shaft of
moonlight stealing through the heat painted pallid his
gaunt cheeks. He stood juggling his sun helmet in trembly fingers, and his shoulders were jerking; and I noticed
with a start that peculiar, far-away expression in his eyes.
He must have stumbled across something exciting, at that.

"Be right with you," I told him; grabbing up my helmet
and stick. "We're off. What's up, anyway? You look as if
you'd seen ghosts."

He said nothing until we were seated in the ricksha and
had started to lurch off through the scented shadows that
make every tropical night so impossible. Then he swung on
me nervously. *"Nom de Dieu!"* he snapped. "I do not know
why I should be unstrung. But it seemed to get me by the
stomach. I swear you will be surprised when you see and
hear. Hear, you understand!" He bit off his voice sharply.
"You will see and hear and be surprised. But yes. Aunt of
the devil, what a woman!"

A woman! I eyed him, more surprised than ever. Sitting
taut as a cat, he poked a cigarette into the tan-colored beard
masking the lower part of his face; puffed jerkily. He would
explain no farther.

Now, Achille Bouvard had been in Saigon ten years and
I had known him as a friend for five, so I knew him as well
as any man in our white colony. On first acquaintance I had
guessed him an artist. Yes, he had been an artist. Saigon

That fantastic crowd swayed to her voice

knew little of his history, save that he had appeared on Rue Catinat the year after the war, and that he had been an artist with those game little French seventy-fives that had done so much to crack Von Kluck in '14.

Bouvard, gallant artillery veteran, had fled East to forget the holocaust. But smashing guns and hirpeling steel hadn't let him forget. His mind hadn't ever erased those visions of blood and iron, those echoes of screeching men and shells. Every so often he would smell the blood and hear the screams; and when that happened, his mind would lose a mite of control, his shoulders toss, his hands dance, his eyes stare vaguely at pictures no human should have seen. The war had hit him pretty badly. A queer case of shell-shock, aggravated by any untoward excitement.

"Strange case," one of his *gendarmes* had explained to me. "When Bouvard is wrought up, it happens. His brain is clear, but it is not. For example, when we were fighting those Annamite raiders on the Hue railway, Bouvard did splendid work. It was on the strength of that clean-up he was made head of our police. But the excitement did things to his nerves, to that shell-shock left him by the war. At times he would forget his name; forget who he was. His eyes would stare so queerly—"

Opiate of life in the Oriental tropics was doing much to heal this neurosis. It would only recur when he was tremendously upset, I knew. As our ricksha scuttled toward the waterside through the perfumed dusk, I wondered who this woman was that she should set my friend "off" again.

Achille Bouvard was no simpering, silly roué such as popular fiction loves to paint the average French gentleman. He was a true gentleman, and almost notorious for paying the ladies of the colony strict inattention. Then who was the woman we were going to see? Perhaps she had some connection with a certain Lucien the Scorpion, a renegade whom Bouvard had been trying to run down in Saigon recently.

"BUT HERE WE are," Bouvard exclaimed.

I looked up from reverie. Our vehicle had wiggled away from the pseudo-French boulevard into a region more indigenous to Oriental towns. Under the shadowy foreheads of modern oil tanks, our lane wove its way through a native scramble, escaped respectability down by the river, and scrambled off into fetid-smelling water front dusks. The ricksha had halted under a *casuarina* tree in a court filled with sour darkness. A rickety frame building backed this courtyard, and a little pink door in the frame blared noisy clamor and the stench of powerful liquors. The door bammed open. Yellow light and a uniformed trio of drunken Annamite Tirailleurs staggered out into the court.

I recognized the place at once, without reading the lurid sign over the door. China. Coast Charley's Café de la Guenon Pourpre. As we clambered from the ricksha, I wondered. This was one of the most notorious, unsavoriest dens in the country, this Café de la Guenon Pourpre. *Guenon Pourpre* means—Well, look it up in your French dictionary.

Anyway, China Coast Charley's resembled one.

When I followed Bouvard's jerking shoulders through the little pink door I was glad to note the automatic strapped to make a bulge under his tunic. The place was no church, and my companion was often given to wandering into such dens unarmed. A recklessness that won respect from his enemies, but concerned his friends.

Bouvard swung the little door and a wave of smoke and smell slapped into our faces. The café was crammed. Ropes of smoke coiled down the low ceiling, making the only halo that would ever adorn the heads of that crowd. The tables were jammed with coolies and sailors, soldiers from the barracks, beach combers, beggars, tramps—the usual China Coast jetsam.

The room clattered and jabbered, tinkled and swore. At one end a faked American bar rushed trade. At the other end stood a low, narrow platform giving eminence to a piano that must have floated ashore from a shipwreck. Near the entrance where we stood a gaunt stairway clambered "heavenward"; and across the room a row of screened doors led off to opium bunks and gambling dens. Drinks went flickering about on trays borne by sweating Tonkinese waiters; and nobody in the establishment was busy reading the Bible.

Smiling dourly, Bouvard led the way through the welter with all the authority of a policeman; and we dislodged a drunken sailor from a table near the platform.

"She will come to play the piano soon," Bouvard shouted to me as we sat down. He had to shout to make himself heard above the clamor. "And then you will see, my friend, and hear. Her name is Absinthe. Absinthe Devolle. That is what they call her in here, at any rate. She drinks that absinthe like water. When you see her you will be as astonished as I was when I first encountered her in here last night.

"I came down seeking this Lucien the Scorpion for whom I hold arrest warrants. And I found this strange woman. After you, too, have seen her I will tell you her story. You will be surprised, I think. *C'est ça!*"

He was mopping his face, and his eyes were strange again. I noticed they were glaring at the ruffianly piano on the platform. I glared, too. Here was an instrument to make Beethoven cry out in his grave. A wine cask served it for a left front leg; another cask for a stool.

Once it had, indeed, been a grand piano; for its sounding board was intricately carved, and the board backing the keys was of delicate wood lace-work. But it was a harridan, now, spotted and worm-eaten. Damp heats and abuse had rotted its teeth; and its body was carved with the names of sailormen and other oddities. And I could only imagine the sort of lady who would come to play on such an instrument.

However, I failed to imagine her. Suddenly the mob in the place went stone quiet, as if the café had been a cheap phonograph on which a blatant record had abruptly smashed. The room emptied of sound, I say, and every face turned to the stairway near the entry.

Bouvard kicked my shin. His cheeks were gray.

"Here she comes, Milford," he gnarled. "Here comes this Absinthe Devolle."

I AM NOT quite sure what manner of woman I expected to see at the top of those dowdy stairs. After all, China Coast Charley's was a dive in an Oriental town. My tongue may certainly be forgiven for hanging out when I saw, framed in a nimbus of smoke on the top step, a slim figure in white, with fair white arms and a face of porcelain lit by sea-blue eyes, crowned by a wavy toss of maroon hair. Unexpected! By me, at any rate.

But China Coast Charley's had evidently been awaiting her arrival. The mob in the place watched her as it might have watched an angel strolling down from the Golden Gates. She was an angel, in that place. Only the top of that stairway was no Golden Gate. It was a smoke-hung, rickety balcony in China Coast Charley's café. I must have stared like a yokel.

Bouvard was staring, too, and jerking his shoulders. She walked down those steps with the grace of a queen, mantled in a silence chiseled out of blue smoke. And when her little foot—shod in white satin, by all the gods!—touched the floor, that jam in the café set up a squall.

"Ahee! *Holà!* It is Absinthe!"—"Our Absinthe! Queen of the Song!"—"Bravo, Absinthe! Sing 'Madelon' for us!"—"Give for us 'La Casquette de Père Bugeaud!'"—"Play for us! Sing for us! Absinthe!"—*"Holà!"*

Can you see that pale oval under a flaming blaze of hair move through that sea of bloated, scabrous countenances?

Can you hear the hoarse bawl of applause as she steps to her platform and, smiling, seats herself at that wretched piano?

No maestro was ever accorded more enthusiastic, and certainly no louder, acclaim on entering a Paris salon. And the contrast here! This beauty in a den of beasts. This rose in a bramble patch. A white rose, yes. Thus she looked, in that roaring, smoking Saigon alcohol-garden poisonous with the reek of opiates and sour sweat. Bouvard had been right about her. She was a shock.

Now the din was stilled; so quiet one could almost hear the movement of the coiling smoke-fog. Every eye was on the platform where Absinthe Devolle sat with hands motionless on the piano keys. A leprous little rogue came bustling forward from the bar. This was China Coast Charley, himself. He elbowed his way to the platform, grinning majestically, and placed a slim black bottle in Absinthe's white hand. Head thrown back, Absinthe drank. Believe me, a lady who could quaff a third bottle of absinthe at one draft, deserved that title.

The liquor brought a glow to her cheeks. Setting aside the bottle, she turned on her stool, clasped her hands, and surveyed her audience. From face to face her blue eyes traveled in level scrutiny. And when she sighted Bouvard and me at our near-by table a smile came to her lips.

Bouvard dropped a curse from his rusty beard. I thought he shivered as he muttered: "Always she does that. Looks over her crowd. Now she will sing. Imagine a lady like her in this place. When she is done I will tell you why. Uncle of Satan! Good. She begins—"

With a lithe gesture she had turned on the piano;

dropped fingers to keys. The next instant China Coast Charley's rocked under a torrent of sound. A cheer went up as she struck into the virile marching song "Madelon." Promptly the café roared out the famous war song, chanting with a vim that brought a shower of lizards and dust down from the walls.

"—Madelon! Madelon! Madelon!"

The song ended with three vibrant crashes. Without waiting to give her audience breathing space, Absinthe plunged them into another melody, and the mob sang with delight. When she had given the café opportunity to bawl out its lungs she drove it quiet by smashing out a basso chord from the keys. Then she played! And sang!

I swear she made a Steinway out of that battered, yellow-toothed, tin-tongued infamy on which her fingers raced. Never in my life had I heard such playing. And sing? I did not know the song she gave us, but I did know her voice was witchery rarely heard.

Chin lifted, her storm of hair tossing pure fire, her white fingers working magic on that piece of junk before her, she sang in a manner that had me wiping drops from my chin and sitting like a blob. When her voice laughed, the room laughed. When her voice sobbed, the room sobbed. If you've ever heard a Frenchwoman's deep-toned, mourning love song, you'll know. And when she had finished, the café was stunned; and the vagabond faces of the crowd were bright and altered with memories.

BOUVARD WAS MOPPING his face, and his hands were quivering. A hurricane of applause finally stormed from the mob; yelling for more. But the amazing Absinthe danced to her feet, blew a kiss at every one, and was off the platform. A moment later she stood at Bouvard's elbow, and I saw her fingers on the shoulders of his tunic. Mockingly, from dry lips, her voice came low:

"So? The good *préfet de police* calls once again to see the peace of noble Saigon remains undisturbed! Splendid! No cause for you to bother to-night, eh? I looked carefully among the mob, but *he* was not here. Call tomorrow."

With a light finger-snap and a sneered, "So long," she was off to the stairway and gone. Bouvard turned on me with a bitter oath. His face had gone the color of old paper. War-harried nerves were yanking at his hands. His eyes were very strange.

"You were right, Bouvard," I heard myself saying. "She did break the monotony; she was a shock. What the devil is she doing here? Where—"

"The good Lord alone knows where she comes from," he whispered in reply. "But last night she told me why she is here. *Sapristi!* I saw her then for the first time, I say. I came here to hunt this Lucien renegade. A spy told me the dog sometimes comes here. I sat where we sit now. This incredible woman came to the piano. She played; sang. Her voice tore the heart from me like it ripped the hearts of this filthy mob to-night.

"When she had done she passed my table. She must have come on the mail boat Saturday, but she had signed no police-entry record. So I stopped her as she passed, told her who I was, and asked about the record. She peered into my face a long time. I thought she was frightened. Then she said with a sneer: 'So you are the Law in Saigon, eh? Then I can tell you something of interest. I came here to commit a murder. How do you like that, M. the Law?'

"Something in her tone showed me she did not jest. She startled me, I can tell you. 'You can commit no crime, here,' I warned. 'I am the head of the police.' She laughed, and said: 'Bah, my brave one. I fear no *gendarme*. Listen. I hunt a scoundrel who deserted me. I expect him to visit here. He will put his ugly head in this café. I will sing for him a little song he knows, pull a little gun and shoot him dead. *Oui!* This husband who left me. I know he will appear in this café. And when he comes, I sing to him his death song. And kill him with a bullet!'"

I BECAME ACQUAINTED with Absinthe Devolle. When a chap is buried alive in some god-lost "Paris of the East" he must keep amused or rot. So I made a habit of dropping in on China Coast Charley's café. He served the best beer in the Orient. And there was Absinthe Devolle.

Amusement? Lord! The little lady was melodrama. Past belief. Imagine her—a *lady*, understand!—entertaining at piano in an Asian drink den, because she thought she could find there a husband who had deserted her three days after the wedding—could find and kill him. One night I sent her a note asking her to share a bottle with me after her performance. Bouvard had left early, and she came to my table. I guess she wanted to talk to somebody. And she told me fragments of the story.

She had married the man, one Justin LeLong, in Marseilles just before the war. Three days after her wedding he had vanished from their honeymoon hotel, without a warning word, and never to return. The young bride, left thus ingloriously, had waited. And waited. Waited throughout weeks, months of stunned wonderment. While friends back in Paris had gossiped. While relatives wagged tongues. While yellow journals lied. Finally had come belief that the scoundrel had made the gesture to insult her, and fled to a hidden past. With the belief had bloomed hatred. And then the aching desire to find the man and kill.

"Yes, I will find and kill him. He left me that first war year, you comprehend, and every hour since I have hunted and hunted. I set detectives on his trail. But no trace of my dear Justin LeLong could be found. Oh, the horror of those days. The talk! How I yearned to murder him. But for ten, twelve years there was no word. And then one day came a letter from an agent. He had traced a man answering my husband's description to the Orient, Saigon. The letter had been years coming in the disrupted mails. Now, when it reached me, I had no funds. But I saved, begged, saved and fought to make my way out here. Only a few months ago could I take passage. But here I am. I feel that he is here, too. I will find and kill him. I know. I know."

"But how," I had marveled, "do you know he will come *here?*"

"To this place? But I know. I stay here. I play for this China Coast Charley, bring him a crowd, make my food and board. I am not molested. Save for my evening performance I live quietly, locked in my room. The mob hears of me and visits. *He* will hear, too, and come. I have advertised my story; told every one. So he will learn the gossip and be curious. Full of bravado, he will want to see what I shall do. One night he will call. I will sing for him a little song we used to sing together. Afterward I will shoot him dead. He will understand."

She hummed for me the song she was going to sing to this man she wanted to kill. Never will I forget the little tune. It was one of those plaintive, minor-keyed ballads so dear to France, and it ended on a queer, tremulous high note. The highest "C" on the piano, Absinthe told me.

"And when I sing it for him it is going to be echoed by the sound of a shot!" How her eyes had blazed when she told me that!

LOOKING BACK I find the threads of that melodrama a little hard to unravel. But what a story! You understand how this French lady had followed a trail of vengeance to Saigon, how she was nightly setting her stage in that preposterous waterside café, and why she was doing so? Then imagine Achille Bouvard, that unfortunate shell-shocked Saigon police officer, becoming tangled in the affair. Wandering into China Coast Charley's to find a renegade, he had stumbled on a woman bent on playing out a murder, boasting her homicidal intent, literally thumbing her nose at the law.

"She will not carry out this plan! Not while I represent the law in this city! She is mad. And I must prevent her from murder!"

And to prevent the murder, Achille Bouvard must needs appear in the café every evening while Absinthe Devolle set the stage. Every evening the harried prefect went down there to watch her act. Every evening for three months. And every evening did she carry out her performance, playing and singing her songs after studying her audience, then mocking him as she quit the stage.

I could guess why she mocked him. He was Law; the only possible obstacle, to her mind, that would obstruct her terrific will for retribution. A shell-shocked police-man with a cinnamon beard trying to stop her? Absurd!

When her time came she would ignore this *gendarme* as if he were a roach.

"I go to watch her every night!" Bouvard promised me. "I watch to see where she carries her revolver. So far she has produced no gun. I cannot arrest her, then. But always I warn her. I tell her if her trap does succeed, if she persists in her vengeance, it will mean death for her—the guillotine. Each time I see her, I warn. If she carries out her boast and kills a man in Saigon, she will die!"

The shell-shock had grabbed hold of Bouvard when he told me that. And one evening later he admitted: "I have been begging her to quit Saigon. Last night I asked her to go away; forget her accursed revenge. I appealed to her pride, her wasting beauty. I coaxed. *Dieu!* Listen! Somehow, I, too, believe this Justin LeLong will turn up. Her psychology is right. Fiendishly right. If there be such a man in Saigon—living under another name, perhaps—he will hear of her and blunder into her trap. Men are like that. He will want to call her bluff.

"And she is so certain he is here. Women feel such things. Intuition. And if he does turn up she will kill him. She will kill! For she is mad. She has brooded and brooded and planned this revenge for years. Once, no doubt, she loved this man. Now she hates. Madly, too, Love and hate—synonyms for madness always. But such a hate. It is in her eyes. A terrible fire. She will kill, all right. And so I have begged her to go away. For if this man walks into the café and she sees him and sings for him and draws a gun and shoots him dead, I—I will be forced to arrest and convict her. Send her to the guillotine. To cut off her head."

Cut off her head! The night Bouvard spoke those words

to me I saw something that made me sweat. Heaven knows why I hadn't sighted it before. Perhaps those nights I had sat in the café with him I had been more interested in Absinthe Devolle. But I saw it at last. Poor Bouvard! What a fearful and incredible tangle.

For the Frenchman, as police head, had sworn on honor to defend and enforce law in Saigon, deal unequivocal justice and follow the stony path of duty. Duty! The word was a trumpet call to a gentleman of Bouvard's caliber. His religion. As much his religion as her hunt for revenge had become religion to Absinthe Devolle.

She had vowed to find and kill the husband who had betrayed her. Bouvard had sworn to deal out justice. And if Absinthe Devolle carried out her revenge in Saigon, Bouvard's stony path of duty was going to cut him like knives. No wonder he had begged her to leave Saigon. No wonder he didn't want to send her to the guillotine. Cut off her head! Poor old Bouvard. He would never cherish his duty to do that. He had fallen in love with Absinthe Devolle!

I FELT SORRY and sick about it. Bouvard was my friend, and it wasn't pleasant to watch the hurt of an already-wounded man. Heaven knows he didn't realize his love. Men never do, at first. He thought he was making this nightly visit to the café in the interest of law. He was. But I knew it wasn't shell-shock alone that made the weird stare in his eye and disturbed the peace of his warrior shoulders whenever he saw Absinthe.

As the days inched along he began to wear a heart on his sleeve whenever she sang her songs of old France—how I feared I would hear that other ballad!—or whenever she made magic on that scorbutic piano. To see her in that rotten café, to know her deadly mission, to watch and wait and bear her raillery every night, must have been agony to the shell-shocked veteran.

So the strangest of dramas continued. Each night the revenge-mad woman setting her stage for murder in the café. Each night Bouvard dropping shaky and betrayed of heart into an unwanted front row seat, determined to play his role in the tragic last act of the play. Each night the crowd fattening as dusk brought promise of a final climax.

Three nights a week I managed to go with Bouvard, hoping, in spite of myself, to be "in" on any last act.

And because it was expected, it happened very unexpectedly, indeed!

BOUVARD AND I were late that evening, because the Friday mail packet was tardy. Bouvard had been in the habit of dropping down to the Messageries Maritimes wharf when boats came in, and watching disembarkers. A passenger list might divulge a Justin LeLong.

After a fruitless wait, that night, we hurried back to the café. Bouvard spoke on how queer it was he could never see Absinthe carrying any manner of gun. He was getting, he said, vastly tired of the whole affair. But he was going to see it through. Sitting tight-nerved in the ricksha, he was more neurotic than ever, I noticed.

Quite unthinking, I had started to whistle the tune Absinthe had hummed through a fierce grin for me on the evening she told me her story. Believe me, the plaintive melody ending so weirdly on high "C" had often run through my mind. As I started to whistle it, then, Bouvard glared and whacked his knees with nervous hands. "Stop it, will you! To-night I am all nerves. I hate whistling!"

Poor fellow, his shell-shock had been aggravated of late. He had taken to forgetting things again. And his shoulders were twisting uneasily when we stood at the door of China Coast Charley's and heard the singing, which had commenced before our arrival.

Bouvard opened the door and we stood in the blast. Like masks could be seen the smoke-wreathed faces of the song-roaring mob. Absinthe was a vague white figure on her platform, her hair tossing flame, her inspired hands wrenching music from that piano. Bouvard tilted his helmet in a curt nod at China Coast Charley, who smirked behind the bar, and we started for our customary table near the platform.

Suddenly Bouvard halted. His hand crushed my wrist as he pointed a shaking finger.

"Name of a name! Look, Milford! The man sitting next to our table. He of the thick black beard. The devil! We must be fast!"

Bouvard pointed at a fat hulk who squatted at a table alone. The man's eyes were on the platform, and I remember them as they were when I saw them later—poisonous raisins set in bulgy pools of sour milk. His big dirty hands were strumming time to the music on the table-top. His mouth was a pink, noisy cave in his whiskers; bellowing in chorus with the crowd. A diadem of sweat beads ringed his bald head.

"Uncle of Satan!" Bouvard panted. "I had quite forgotten him. Ho-ho! So he has come at last. The renegade. Lucien the Scorpion!"

He had out his squat automatic in a minute; and a minute later was poking its snout into the renegade's unwary neck nape. I was close on Bouvard's heels. Like my friend, I, too, had forgotten the original object of the law's visit to the Café de la Guenon Pourpre.

"Take it softly, my Lucien," Bouvard was warning. "Perhaps you have forgotten you are wanted for murder here. That little killing you worked four years ago. Bold, eh? Then come quietly with me."

What happened then I didn't quite apprehend. I only know the surprised criminal sprang up fast as light. The table whirled over as he whipped to his feet, lashing out fists. Flung off balance, Bouvard went to one knee; fired a bullet into the floor; lost his gun. A savage fist stung my jaw and a kick bent me wailing over a torn shin.

The café's song changed to a wild, frantic yell. Lucien the Scorpion floundered over my head. Bouvard, scrabbling to retrieve his lost gun, got a hand on the renegade's ankle. Then they were fastened together in fierce conflict, body to body, arms twined and flailing, feet stumbling in mad dance.

It all happened so suddenly, happened while I was corkscrewed with pain on the floor. I could see little but red shadows and white hands. Then steel made a wicked flash in the gloom; and there was a knife in the renegade's fist.

Bouvard struggled desperately as the savage blade slashed. *Zaff!* And *zaff!* Once the steel gashed across Bouvard's bearded chin and drew a streak of shiny blood down his jaw. Again the blade daggered into the cloth over his ribs; brought a crimson smear welling down the breast of his tunic. Staggering, he crashed over backward;

sprawled atop the low platform directly behind the keg that made a piano stool.

I glimpsed Absinthe Devolle's face, marble-white with shock as she spun about from the piano. I heard her thrilling scream as the Scorpion, spitting oaths and waving his blade, sprang like a gorilla to the platform. As the raging criminal stooped over Bouvard's recumbent, bloodied frame, she rocked back against the piano. The Scorpion's knife was high, waiting to plummet into Bouvard's throat.

It never fell. There was a smart shot. *Wham!* It might have come from anywhere, but I could smell the powder smoke, not distant. The smashing echo silenced the frenzied room; sent Lucien the Scorpion waltzing backward on sudden heels. His fists flew open. The knife dropped onto the floor of the platform. His legs became rubber; bowed humorously as he teetered back and forth on unsteady feet. Slowly, heavily the dark lids came down over his bulgy eyes. Then he sighed, a crimson fount squirted from his throat, and he was down.

Somehow I found feet; battled in the sweat-smelling mob that charged the platform. I wanted to get to Bouvard. A billion stupid arms blocked me. I could hear a feminine voice raging in shrill French:

"Keep back, swine! Get away. Are you pigs in a sty? Give him room to breathe. Can none of you fools call a doctor? He is badly hurt."

When I finally gained the platform it was to see Absinthe Devolle on her knees, her face bright with anger and tears, Bouvard's bleeding head caught to rest against her bosom.

WEARY ON HIS cane, Achille Bouvard moved to the edge

of his veranda and stared off into the shadows gathered early in the cycas trees. The man was a wraith in the dusk. Hospital pallor made waxen his thinned cheeks. His eyes lay deep in dark hollows. Though the wound in his ribs had healed well, he would wear a limp for some time to come. And there was the jagged, ugly scar crawling down the side of his jaw.

How different he looked since the doctors had shaved his beard! I hadn't noticed it so much while he was in the hospital. Now it occurred to me he looked another man. Beardless, he was an old young man. Before he had been elderly but young. The face was entirely altered, as if a mask had been removed to reveal a strong, tired mouth and competent chin.

"I suppose, Milford," he said, eyes on the dark trees, "that you heard at the consulate about my resignation. I am through and not sorry. *Dieu!* what a mess I made of arresting that stupid renegade. Deserved the stabbing I got. So there will be another *Préfet de Police* in Saigon tomorrow. I leave tomorrow morning on the Albert Durande. Back to France. Paris!"

His low voice trailed off. I promised him I was desolate at seeing him go. He said: "I am glad to get away. Lately the job had been—getting on my nerves. I had been inadequate; not well. Now I go. It will be nice to see France. It is strange, my friend. You know, I have forgotten what France is like. Quite, quite forgotten. Paris I do not recall. It will be like seeing it the first time. And I am glad to go."

I noted vast relief in his tone. He was glad to quit his job as prefect. I knew why. He admitted with a tremulous smile as he turned to face me:

"Absinthe Devolle—no longer will I be forced to warn her off, spy on her, watch to see she does not carry her promised gun. That gun she threatens to murder with. I say, Milford—are you *positive* it was not she who shot dead the Scorpion that night?"

"That's the queerest part of it," I confessed. "I'd have sworn she fired that bullet into the bandit. He faced her and the bullet got him in the throat. Powder smoke hung about the platform. But she had no gun in her hands. No sign of one anywhere. Queerest part of the whole affair."

But it wasn't the queerest part of the whole affair after all. I wondered what Bouvard would have thought if I'd told him about Absinthe Devolle's caressing his unconscious head; if I'd told him Absinthe loved him.

"Eh bien," he sighed. "I had hoped the girl had ended her act by killing this Scorpion cur. But you say she still sings in the café each nightfall? Come then!" He smiled wryly. "Let us pay her a call to say good-by. I should like to hear her sing and play once again. I want to pay China Coast Charley's a last visit. It will be amusing. Now that I have done with the affair I hope the little lady gets her man. Come along, Milford. A farewell visit. Let us call a ricksha."

KNOWING MORE ABOUT Bouvard's heart than the man himself knew, I didn't want to go down there. Besides, his hospital experience had not eased his nerves. The sickness seemed to have got into his bones as we rattled off in the ricksha; and his teeth were clicking as we stepped into the café for that last call.

The place was stuffed with the usual clamorous mob. We were only in time to watch Absinthe seat herself at her piano. As we picked our way to a vacant table near her platform she made her scrutiny of the audience. I saw her eyes rest on us as we sat down. Me, she recognized at once. But I believe she failed to recognize Bouvard, at first.

He was glaring at her with that weird-eyed expression. She frowned as she stared at him. Then her blue eyes widened into the strangest glare. She stared and stared and caught at her throat with a white hand. Well, Bouvard did look like the devil, so thin and white. And certainly her agitation at seeing him thus proved she loved him. But, Lord, was she going to faint?

And all this time the room was smoking and roaring about us.

"Sing for us, Absinthe!" "Give us a song!" "We want 'Madelon'!" And, as usual, China Coast Charley came grunting forward with the bottle; pushed it into her fingers; lost himself in the smoke.

The café cheered. But Absinthe did not drink. With slow hand she placed the bottle on the piano, untouched. Then she stepped from the platform, and, in a sudden quiet, moved to our table. I saw her hand on Bouvard's sleeve, like a carving of chalk. Her voice came as an echo as she said to my companion:

"*Bien.* I am glad to see you out of the hospital. I am told you have given up the police post. You are leaving us? Leaving Saigon? Come, then. Let us have a farewell celebration. Let us sing a good-by." She raised her voice to the crowd. "The good *préfet* is leaving us. I will sing for him!"

The café applauded. It had come to know Bouvard well. He managed a bow. Then somehow or other he was on the patform. Absinthe stood him at her right elbow beside her, held him there with her eyes. Bouvard was smiling. But I wasn't smiling. Alone at the table I could do nothing but glare and feel the little hooks grabbing at my stomach.

Now the café was hushed in a silence that seemed to sweat. Absinthe Devolle touched fingers to the yellowed keys before her and began to sing. Fingers and voice wrought low, plaintive melody. The audience sighed in rapt delight. Voice and piano grew louder.

Absinthe was playing and singing as she never had before. Her hair tossed lambent fire at the wooden, white-faced man beside her. A transparent tint came to her marble cheeks. Never before had I seen her as strange and beautiful. Never before had I heard her play and sing like that. But, good God! What was the woman singing? That song!

It was a century before the idea worked into my brain, and when I did finally grasp it I couldn't believe. I couldn't believe, I say. Like a straw dummy I sprawled in my chair, pinned motionless by a hundred-weight stone in my stomach, listening and glaring pop-eyed. Yes, she was singing the sorrowful, minor-keyed ballad she had hummed for me that night. The song ended on high "C." The high "C" that was to be echoed, she had promised, by a shot. True; she was singing that plaintive French love song, and singing it to Achille Bouvard!

I wanted to get out of my chair and yell then, but the muscles had atrophied in my legs. I could open my mouth, but could make no sound. And I did not believe my senses! Absinthe had no weapon on her person, and what possible chance could connect poor old shell-shocked Bouvard—

I guessed it then. Like an explosion in the back of

my head. Of course! Bouvard without his beard was not Bouvard. And the gun. I never knew how I got out of that chair, booted aside the table and took a drunkard's step forward. That song was almost ended, almost ready for that last fatal note—that high "C." Why couldn't I scream at Bouvard!

I saw it, yes. Absinthe never finished the song. She flung about from the piano, and the next minute had Bouvard by the knees. Her wet face shone up at his and her voice came like an echo from a vanished yesterday. "Justin!"—I guess *that* didn't smack the wind out of me! "Justin! I cannot go through with it! I love you!"

And Bouvard? He got a palsied hand up into the smoky air and held it high. His lips panted strange words.

"Althea! Althea! Name of God! What—what in heaven can all this mean! And—Althea? That song? We used to sing that song. I—I—the devil! You were waiting for me down at the—the hotel! I had left to buy some wine down at the corner. They—they arrested me in the café. That seems so—so long, long ago. Arrested me. Flung me back into the Legion. Three months on the front. Cannons! But I had not deserted. It was a mistake. I—I tried to send word. Then—the shells smashing into my head! But at last. *That song!*"

His hand came down out of the smoke; struck by sheerest chance a smashing blow on the keyboard of the old piano. That high "C"! A gunshot crashed out. A tongue of flame flickered through the lacework of wood backing the keyboard, and a bullet spun into the fleshy part of Bouvard's shoulder.

LAST ACT. I saw Achille Bouvard and his wife off on the

boat for France. Only, of course, he wasn't Achille Bouvard. Relieved of his beard, snapped from shell-shock amnesia by his wife's love song, he was once again the bridegroom of three days—the man he had been when, arrested by accident as a Legion deserter, he had been stolen from her and thrown into the battle that had robbed his memory. And how lucky the renegade's knife had slashed his jaw, allowing the doctors to remove his beard.

Or his wife might never have recognized him. After all those years, you know, and his voice and eyes so different from shell-shock.

Strange story, was it not? How he fell in love with his wife, and his wife, failing to recognize him, fell in love with him again. What a shock it must have given her when he strolled into the café "unmasked" that night. Bravely she strove to carry out her vow to kill him. That gun concealed in the piano was an ingenious device, all right.

If Bouvard had been standing where first she had planted him he would have got it the way the Scorpion got it when she fired the gun. Swung by levers attached to the foot pedals, it had ample range for him. The trigger, you comprehend, was touched off by the high "C" string.

But after all her years of brooding, she had been unable to see it through. Love had stayed her hand.

She was a woman at the end. A Frenchwoman.

So this is a French story, you will understand, and it should have been played out in Paris. Still, Saigon was near enough. Do not certain tourist catalogues pronounce Saigon the "Paris of the East"? Though just what part of Paris they refer to, this writer cannot imagine. (He can, but he won't for publication.)

CHECKERED RETRIBUTION

*The big Dutch naturalist Van Deventer
trampled on the weaker Jackling, and
laughed—but no man in that Cambodian
jungle-town laughed at what came after*

1

THE FEUD

"Hatred is self-punishment"
—Ballou's sermons

IT HAPPENED LONG ago, but to this day shaving is an ordeal that has me sweating in the barber chair distraught. The unexpected sight of a blade still cuts away the cobwebs darkening memory.

Once again I am a lad shivering in a dank doorway—it was hot enough, Lord knows!-—with one hand anchored for safety in father's fist, the shadowy jungle night whispering evil incantations behind my back, and before me, bloody on the mat of light thrown by our lantern, that awful, meaty *thing!*

Once again I can hear my missionary father's stern: "My God!" Nor was it prayer. And once again I can see, coming out of gloom into the reach of amber lantern-glow, a monstrous face that grins with huge approval on the razor which had wrought the deed.

The razor gleams wickedly in the murderer's agile fist; showers ruby drops. Already a stray quartet of flies has buzzed out of the tepid darkness to find that thing, with

"That you, Jackling?" boomed big Checkers contemptuously

its severed throat and butchered face. Then a soft, terror-choked voice speaks, to tell the story.

Small wonder that of all the stories my boyhood in Asia stored in memory that story is outstanding. That story of an Asia-smitten land where the heat and fever and rain could spoil man's brain to sponge, and make easy the doing of scarlet deeds. That story of Jackling and Big Checkers Van Deventer. That story of a strange love and a savage hate, a miracle and a murder.

JACKLING HATED VAN DEVENTER and had threatened to kill him. That was funny. Like the mouse menacing the lion. For the English naturalist stood no more than five and a half feet of undernourished skin and bones, and his soul was a veritable well of frustrations.

Weakness. One saw it in the hesitation of Jackling's hands, his scuffly feet, the cringe of his stooped shoulders,

the harassment written on his pinched face with its inef-fectual chin. One read it in the uneasy shift of his pallid gaze; heard it in the uncertain quaver of his voice. A weak man, Jackling was. A man whom Life had bent. A mouse.

Van Deventer was the lion. Big as a monument and strong, the Dutchman had grabbed at Life with his massive hands and bent it to his own uses.

Power. One saw it in the muscles cording down his mast-thick arms, in the tendons of his crimson bull neck, in the tremendous chest. One read power in the patroniz-ing wink of his little Teuton eyes, in the truculent thrust of his battleship jaw, in his condescending grin that showed strong teeth.

He boasted it with a crass, bawly voice of command and by adorning his muscle-slabbed back with a cotton shirt that shouted with huge black and red checks. There wasn't

another shirt like that one East of Suez. The Dutch naturalist always wore it, you understand. It was his trade-mark.
By that black and red checkered shirt he was recognized
and known from Sellore to the Boto Islands.

"There's 'Big Checkers' Van Deventer," men would say
with deference. "Finest naturalist out East. He's the guy
who once fought a tiger with nothin' but a old LePage
smooth-bore single-shot an'a jackknife. Killed his cat, too.
With the knife." Big Checkers, yes, he was a lion.

And he was the man whom Jackling hated and had
threatened to kill! I imagine that enmity had been meat
on the local tongue for quite some time before father first
took me up there to that steaming Cuachaven backwater,
in a portion of Cambodian jungle that was little less than
the bowels of Asia. How avidly the white colony must have
gossiped and fed on the tale!

But the first I heard of it was on the river boat, where
a diamond trader, whom I recall as nothing but a burst of
black whiskers, was discussing the affair with father.

I was just turned thirteen years, then, and I recall how I
stood on the blunt bow of the river boat and ignored a new
land of wonders to listen to the story of the feud.

Our boat was waddling toward a town lying trapped
where the river swung, burbling and green, into a hilly
jungle-land as mysterious as midnight. There was the tin
wharf plastered with lurid posters. There were the native
huts, blobs of thatch set high on poles, for all the world like
queer four-legged birds stalking over the mud flats. There
was the Chinese quarter rambling inland, and farther back,
on a slope spotted by pandanus groves, a cluster of European bungalows.

Crazy native craft came scooting across the water, and the river boat slid close by a bank where a little Buddhist *wat* stood among lime trees with its temple bells tinkling. The sound stole through the poisoned tropic heat like the tinkle of ice in a slim glass.

I had just come from an academy in Bombay. Bombay was civilization and here was hinterland jungle to make a boy's eyes pop from his head. But these novelties were not for me; I was listening, all attention, to the diamond trader.

"SOME CLAIMS," THE trader was saying, "that Jackling really will try to kill Big Checkers one o' these days. Every time he gets drunk, Jackling starts rantin' and ravin' against Big Checkers. But Big Checkers just stretches his muscles an' laughs. I guess he ain't afraid o' Jackling. He's broke Jackling so far, I reckon, an' could finish him with a flick o' his thumbs. But I guess as how he's kinda amused by Jackling's rage. Gives him somethin' to play with, eh? Van Deventer's that bully type, you know. An' he's certain that Jackling'll never hit back. Time for Jackling to hit back was when the Dutchman started puttin' it over on him. Certainly he should 'a' done it when Big Checkers run off an' married his girl."

"So there's still bad blood between the two naturalists?" my father asked with a sigh. "I thought maybe while I was away—"

"It's worse'n ever. Since you went to fetch your lad, here, Big Checkers has bought up the notes on Jackling's paddy fields. Guess if he grabs up them rice lands like he's grabbed most everything else of Jackling's, the little Englishman will hate him proper. As it is, Big Checkers ain't left Jackling much besides a piece of paddy field, a shack, an' that ape.

"They do say Big Checkers has offered right generous to buy that orang-utan, but Jackling won't sell. No, sir! He still refuses to sell. He can't have no use fer it neither, now he's lost his Jardin des Plantes contract. The French got sick of him, you know. But he just won't sell. Not to Big Checkers, anyhow. He hates Big Checkers all right. Lord, how he hates him! An' you' can't blame him, since the Dutchman's rode over him so."

And I can remember my father getting a stern finger pointed skyward in that Jehovan manner of his, and rumbling: "The quarrel will bring them to no good end, my friend. No good end. Love is the mightiest of virtues, my friend. And hatred is self-punishment."

And the diamond trader was nodding agreement the way every one must nod agreement before the local cure-of-souls; then he was beside me at the rail, pointing a thumb.

"There's Big Checkers, now, standing by them fish crates, there."

An exciting little shiver trickled down my spine as I caught sight of the monumental figure under the lofty sun helmet, the giant shoulders clad in checks of black and red. The man who had stretched his muscles and laughed when some other man had threatened to kill him.

"Where," I had asked, bravely breaking father's rule that children should be seen but not heard, "is the— other man? The man who was going to kill him?"

Whereupon father had dug fingers into my arm, and pronounced:

"This is not for you, boy. Jackling lives across the compound from us, but you will not go near his bungalow. The man is ill, an illness of the soul. His house is a sink of hatred."

2

FACE TO FACE

A THIN SCREEN of lime trees fenced our mission compound from the ragged grounds surrounding Jackling's place. Father had issued strict orders commanding me to keep away from there; named the place a sink of hatred. Naturally I didn't keep away.

Already, I fear, I had begun to manifest the rebel spirit supposedly common to ministers' sons. And I'm forced to confess the shabby gray shack with its attendant shed, gloomy, sequestered, vastly foreboding with jungle shadows slanting down its saggy roof proved far more entertaining than the triple-dry readings of father's austere library.

"Ballou's Sermons," "Brigg's Studies of Holy Scripture," "Works of Dwight L. Moody" and the "Systematic Theology of John Miley, D.D." were by no means as intriguing to a lonely, quinine-nerved, thirteen-year-old boy as a sink of hatred.

I'll never forget the memorable evening I ventured to call on Jackling and his ape. Many a time I had sneaked into the lime trees to peer at the "sink of hatred" before I dared such audacious adventure.

I had learned how the withered English naturalist sat out the fetid tropic twilights on his shabby veranda in

company with the big orang-utan. Spying from behind the
screen of limes I would see them there, strange ghosts in
the dusk; stranger companions. Jackling would be sprawled
in a cane chair. The ape would squat beside him. Sometimes
I could hear him talking to the animal.

Always the skinny little man would stare out through
the *kaladangs* fronting his place; stare and stare, until the
swift dark tumbled down from the hills and he retired to
lock his ape in the shed behind the shack and bury himself
behind drawn blinds.

How this weird neighbor fired my youthful imagination!
Especially when I learned more of the story from the town:
how Jackling and Van Deventer had once been friends,
how their rivalry had turned to enmity, how the big man
had crushed the little one.

I was not too young to sense the drama of that bitter
feud. Those two naturalists locked there in the heart of the
jungle. The big, strong Dutchman forging a path to success,
despising his weaker rival. The little, inefficient Englishman had been the greatest naturalist on the river. Now he
was reduced to a shanty down by the mud flats, while his
rival could live in a spacious white bungalow far up the
slope among the *pandanus* groves, and wear a noisy black
and red checkered shirt to boast his power and successes.

A muddy road crawled past Jackling's compound gate,
climbed through the Chinese quarter of the town and
mounted the hill where Van Deventer's white bungalow
stood. On clear evenings, I discovered, you could plainly
see that bungalow there atop the hill.

Once I had seen the Dutchman up there, a red and
black flag moving among his trees. Then I knew why Jack-

ling stared from his veranda; knew he was watching the white bungalow; knew he was gazing at the man who had reached the top of the road down which he, Jackling, had fallen.

And Jackling had threatened to kill the big man up there—because the big man had won too much. He had even won Jackling's girl. She had been a beautiful girl, father's house-boy told me; the daughter of the French agent. But Big Checkers had snatched her away from the futile Englishman; carried her off to the white bungalow where she had died of cholera six weeks after the wedding. Jackling had hated his rival more than ever, after that.

So the beaten man, reduced by poverty and drink to the company of an ape, sat out the brief evenings on his veranda and watched his enemy on the hill across the town—while I flagrantly deserted my studies (father had determined me for a missionary) to watch this melodrama next door.

It was more of a three-ring circus to me, perhaps. I had known a score of monkeys in India, but never before, and never since, had I seen an anthropoid as huge and tame as the orang-utan housed in the shed under the giant *mohor* tree behind Jackling's shanty.

Eyes popping, I would spy at the wretched man and the great ape sitting together on their veranda. I would fancy Jackling crouching there with a gun in his fist waiting to get a chance shot at the man on the distant hill. Once I thought I saw a gun. I was scorched with curiosity. I would just take a little stroll past Jackling's veranda and see for myself.

FATHER HAD GONE to spend a week with a mission

conference at Eua Penh, where he hoped to gain himself a new and adequate bungalow in the European quarter of our town. With no chance of parental interruption, I skirted our compound and scuffled into the road, intent on braving a walk past the "sink of hatred."

Expecting the sunset light to knock me dead for disobedience to father's commands, I did walk by Jackling's gate. I wanted like anything to get a better view of the forbidden man and his weird comrade; wanted to see if the thing I had seen flashing in Jackling's fist was a gun.

It wasn't a gun. It was a bottle. And he caught sight of me lurking in the roadway. To my fearful consternation, he hailed me.

"Halloo, there, lad. Come up a minute."

"I can't," I quavered; and opened his gate in spite of myself.

The sun, low behind a bank of tumbly black cloud, was shafting sullen streaks of red at the oncoming darkness. The *kaladangs* by the road became suddenly agitated in a breath of oppressive air. Already the jungles hedging the river were blue in dusk and the slope behind me was hung in a queer orange half-light. In three minutes it would be night. My legs wanted to run. But they didn't. The man on the veranda creaked to his feet and gestured a bony hand.

"Come up a bit, lad. Don't be scared of Bobo," he patted the ape's flat forehead. "He wouldn't harm nobody. Come on up, an' say hello to old Jackling. You're the *padre's* kid, eh? Come up."

His cracked voice was kind enough, and I moved through the gate and inched up the path. This was heresy of the worst order; but father was away and the house-boy asleep, no doubt.

"You won't tell my father?"

The skinny man chuckled. He had pale lips and they twisted in a wry smile.

"So your old—so the *padre* didn't want you to call on me, eh? Well, sonny, I reckon he thinks I'm a wicked sort and all. Afraid I don't get over to his services often as I ought…" He fumbled fingers over his chin. "But I wouldn't hurt you, old chap. Guess if you can't call on a neighbor, why—. But come on up."

Looking back, I can see how lonely the man must have been. Since Big Checkers Van Deventer had gained a position of prominence in the little community, Jackling had become something of a recluse. The Dutchman had all the friends. Men respect success. The town pitied the broken Englishman; but men despise those whom they pity.

So Jackling was lonely. He wanted some one to talk to. He welcomed my timid visit; stammering and fumbling with enthusiasm, he urged me into his shanty.

What an Aladdin's cave the naturalist's mean shanty was! The squalid little room was stuffed with all manner of interesting trash. Crates of queer fossils. Wormy pieces of taxidermy. Mounted cats, gavial skins, bottled lizards, pickled snakes.

Jackling sat me in a corner, exhibited his specimens with trembly hands, talked. He had wanted to talk for a long time. His gaunt cheeks flushed as he told me stories. Stories of tiger hunts, of strange animals, of his former work in the Zoological Gardens at Cologne and Munich, the London Museum, the Jardin des Plantes in Paris. Scurrying back and forth across the room he delivered a lecture on natural history while I sat in a world of wonders, forgetting my wickedness.

THE BIG ORANG-UTAN trailed about after Jackling like a servant. Walking on its knuckles and long-toed feet, it moved after its master, grinning and mouthing, obedient as a child, for all the world like a moronic old man.

Jackling put an arm around the brute; told me he had captured it in Borneo and trained it himself.

"Knows more than plenty of men," he praised, smiling down at the ape's quarter-human grin. "Raised him by myself. We're pals, boy, pals. I wouldn't sell Bobo for ten thousand pounds. Here, Bobo—shake hands with the lad."

Plucking at the mat of cinnamon hair tangled down its powerful chest, the ape waddled over to my corner. If you know how similar to a chill wet glove is an ape's hand, you can understand how I quivered when the orang's lank fingers coiled about mine.

I wanted to go back to father's brightly-lighted library after that, but Jackling wouldn't let me. Outside it had started to rain. Swift darkness had come, and buckets of water flailed down on the roof overhead. Jackling lit a match, handed it to the ape, and the animal started a lantern.

I stood up to go, apprehensive of my run home through the black rain. The downpour had hung a misty sheet across the doorway. Water had begun to leak in black, wiggly ribbons down the ceiling. Jackling fumbled in a cupboard; produced a red bottle.

"I'm not honored with guests very often," he chuckled, he handed the bottle and three dirty glasses to the ape. The orang carefully filled each glass. "Better have a spot of wine before you go, sonny. A little drink with Bobo and me. Just don't tell the *padre* and it 'll be all right, eh?"

I reached a cautious hand for the glass. Certainly I would not tell father. If he ever found out I'd spent an evening with this neighbor I'd win an old-fashioned thrashing I'd remember. Enjoying a delighted feeling of guilt, I took the glass. Then I set it down with a start of fear. Footsteps stamped on the veranda outside. If it was father—

It wasn't. A giant figure loomed in the rain-swept doorway. I saw a black and red checkered shirt, an enormous grin gleaming under the visor of a drenched sun helmet. A big hand yanked off the helmet; flung a shower across the floor.

"Well," boomed the visitor, "everybody home? That you, Jackling? It's me. *Ja.* Big Checkers Van Deventer!"

THE MAN AND his voice jammed the little room. Little in my corner, I saw him a giant in the feeble lamplight. Me he dismissed with a glance, fastening his bright eyes on Jackling.

"Well, Jackling," he announced, "I haff come on business. Let's get us right down on the point, eh? *Ja.* Now to-day I get a letter from the Hagenbecker Brothers of Rotterdam. They want the biggest orang-utan I can find. The order came to-day and I leave for Holland in four months. But I want the ape as soon as possible. *Ja.* They want the finest of specimens, that is so. This one of yours is the finest I haff ever seen. Always I haff asked to buy it. Now I want it badly. Here is the money. A hundred pounds for you, Jackling. A generous offer not to be refused. *Ja?*"

For more than a minute the only sound in the room was

Jackling's breath coining in steamy gasps out of his twisty smile. When he finally spoke, his voice was low, hoarse.

"Bobo," he ordered the ape at his side, "go to your house. Quick!"

Obediently the animal swaggered to the back door, opened it, crept out into the rain. A moment later we could hear the door of the shed under the *mohor* tree slam shut. Then Jackling flung about on his visitor, his voice coming in a series of difficult sobs.

"Get outa this bungalow, you. Clear out. Listen, Big Checkers! I won't sell my orang for a million, and I wouldn't sell him to you if I ever did, see? You're wasting your time coming down here. Get outa here. Less I see of you the better for both of us, you Dutch beach comber. Get out!"

"Wait a minute. Wait a minute." Big Checkers's voice made me, lost in my corner, shiver. It was oily and drawly and outwardly genial. But there was menace in it, too.

He pushed his red and black checkered shirtfront at Jackling. His grin was tremendous, friendly. Too friendly.

"*Ja,* wait. Now I want your orang, Jackling, my boy. I want your orang. Me. I get what I want. Always. But I pay for it, too. Look now: you haff no use for that big brute of yours, *hein?* You haff much use for some money. I know. You are penniless. Soon you be on the beach. Now I hold notes on your rice land by the river. So. It's worth something, maybe. Tell you what. Sell me the orang and I let the note on the paddy field run. If you do not sell, I take the land to-morrow. See? That is fair. I haff here the money for the orang. A hundred pounds. I am generous."

The money must have looked a fortune to the shabby Englishman. But his eyes blazed and he shouted:

"Robber! You've beaten me always, you have. But you can't get the orang. No! You bloody leech, you! I helped you at first. Then you stepped on me. Got away my contracts. Got the girl, too. With lies. But now—get the heck out of here. Dutchman, if you force those notes on me to-morrow, I'll—I'll go up to your bloody bungalow to-morrow night and shoot you. I'll shoot you! I'll kill you, I will. You can't tramp on me any longer. Get out!"

His voice had lifted to a screech. His eyes were points of phosphorous in his head. His spidery hands shook under the Dutchman's massive chin.

"Get out!"

"You haff always threatened to shoot me because I haff bettered your business deals, my friend," Big Checkers grinned. "But so. I take your rice fields to-morrow. And I get the ape some time, too, I wager. So!"

A gust of rain spattered in as the Dutchman lunged out of the door. He was gone, leaving a puddle of water where his wet boots had stood and a hoarse and hearty guffaw ringing in the choked room. A guffaw that lingered under the ceiling; echoed like the rattle of nails in a can to conjure a vision of a bullying grin and a black and red checked shirt.

Jackling, gasping, wild-eyed, stood against the wall, his thin lips twisting out needle-pointed oaths. It was his eyes that frightened me. Like the eyes of a cat, they were. Cat eyes burning in the dark. And his hoarse voice was croaking: "I'll kill him, so I will. Kill him. Kill him—"

Unnoticed, I fled out into the watery night.

3

THE MARCH UP THE HILL

THE WHOLE TOWN seemed to be congealed on Jackling's compound—a wedge of gray figures murmurous in the slanting rain. Lanterns floated through the soggy mists picking out a glistening face there, a bare arm here, a pair of muddy boots restless in a patch of lighted mire.

Natives and whites jostled the Englishman's front step, crowding the veranda. From my hiding place in the lime trees I could hear above the rain and the excited hammering of my heart and the slosh of boots, snatches of flurried conversation.

"He'll never dare do it. I bet he never pokes his nose outa the shack."

"Said he was gonna shoot Big Checkers to-night if Big Checkers grabbed up his rice land. Big Checkers foreclosed this morning."

"Big Checkers was laughin' all over the place about it. Dared Jackling to come up and try."

"Fightin' over that orang again. Jackling won't never sell it for love nor money."

"He won't dare raise a hand against the Dutchman, either. He's threatened before. He was gonna shoot him when he walked off with the girl."

"*Sacré nom,* but he hates Big Checkers. Remember how they would curse each other out down at the trader's? But he will never try to kill him as he threatens."

"The big fellow could crush him with a thumb. He's a mouse, Jackling is. Never had a chance to compete against Big Checkers. He'll never make good his threat."

Then the crowd's buzz went quiet and the rain became a roar. From where I hid I could see the door of the shanty fling open to let a faint yellow glow wander vaguely out across the soaked compound. There was Jackling on the veranda, and to me—a frightened and fascinated boy—the rifle in his fists looked a mile long. Hatless, coatless, glaring, he moved across the veranda and stumbled off through the bucketing rain.

The crowd fell away and let him pass through; closed in, morbidly expectant, behind him. Then the pack was striding up the muddy hill road, and I, choked with the suspense and horror of it all, skipped along on its outer fringe, glad father was not in town to give me a hiding.

Somehow or other I found myself behind the diamond trader I had met on the river boat. I remember him saying to a companion: "Stop him? Why should we stop him? If he does get his crack at Big Checkers it's only fair. The Dutchman's rode him for the last ten years an' practically robbed him of his property. But Jackling won't do anything, you see. Too spineless. This 'll be a joke. Good comedy."

Comedy? Perhaps it was. Tragic enough to be comedy. Looking back into that dark past I can see Jackling's wretched march up that hill to shoot the man who had always won from him as symbolic of Failure striking back at Success. Failure revenging itself. Failure driven desperado by hatred; spurred to action by drink.

Comedy or tragedy, it was drama at all events. And the mob on Jackling's heels loved it. The natives paddled through the rain, bright-eyed. The Europeans sloshed along, whispering, intent on the figure in the lead.

THE RAIN SLUICED down and made of the roadway a bubbling creek. Every man in the pack—and a certain scared boy—might be victim of fever from this tramp, but no one there was willing to abandon the play.

I don't know whether Jackling realized a thrill at thus exciting the interest of men who had heretofore ignored him. Possibly he enjoyed his leading role in the melodrama. But I rather believe he was conscious of nothing but a terrible determination to carry out this threat against a tormentor who had laughed at him, dominated him, contemptuously double-dared him. Fast ahead of us he marched; and he had left us a good way behind when he gained Big Checkers's gate at the hilltop.

Then he was moving across the compound, up the gravel path to the white veranda, while his audience waited on the compound fence like a row of gallery fools. A stir animated the watchers when they heard his hail.

"All right, Big Checkers. It's me— Jackling. Come out if you dare, an' I'll blow your damned head off your neck!"

Jackling paused on the veranda-step, and when the door opened it shed a patch of brilliant yellow on his hunched and dripping frame. Then Big Checkers stood in the doorway. We could see the gay shirt; the joyous, jolly grin that split the Dutchman's cherry-red face as his twinkling eyes found his visitor. Abruptly a tremendous laugh exploded from his teeth. Fists on hips he eyed the gray figure before him, shouted lusty guffaws, rocking back on his heels with the mirth of it.

"Ho-ho-ho! A thousand laughs. So it is my old friend Jackling!"

Slowly the barrel of Jackling's rifle lifted until the muzzle pointed squarely at that laugh-roaring, checkered chest. That rifle could have weighed half a ton. We, at the fence, could almost hear Jackling pant as he struggled to point it. We panted, too, as the Englishman's voice fought out the words:

"You beat me before, Van Deventer. Robbed me. Shoved me on the beach, you did. Now—now I come to kill you. You can die—"

"So?" Van Deventer's lips leaked oil. "You know, I thought you haff come up here to sell me your ape, my friend. But no, you say. It is to shoot me you haff come. Then shoot, I say. Haff it over with. *Shoot!*"

Two minutes ticked away and timed two hundred years. Jackling pointing his rifle. Big Checkers squirming with suppressed laughter, his face rosy with amusement, never moving fist or foot, a monument on his threshold.

The Englishman could not do it! He could not. His back seemed to sag. The strength seemed to trickle out of his skinny arms. Slowly the barrel of his rifle came down, wavering, lower and lower.

THE SUSPENSE SNAPPED. The Dutchman lunged from his doorway with a rush. Out lashed a hand to snatch the gun from Jackling's white fist.

There was a brittle *crack!* I saw that, or I'd never have believed: that Dutchman rammed the stock of the captured rifle across an uplifted knee, and it splintered to match-wood at one smash. The broken weapon he hurled as far as the fence where the yawping audience stared. Then he fastened a five-fingered trap on Jackling's throat.

"Coward! You come up to my house to shoot *me*, eh? Ho-ho! Well, come again some time, but come on business! Come again, to sell me the big orang and get some money to keep your skinny hide from starving. Not a hundred pounds I offer for the ape now. *Nein!* Fifty pounds I give you now, because for me you haff made much nonsense. And so good-by, Jackling. Next time you come, you do better."

Thud!

Everybody heard the smash of the big Dutchman's fist driven hard against the nape of Jackling's neck. Jackling came spinning down the path like a trick toy, skidded on the wet gravel, buckled at the middle and sprawled into wet spear-grass to lie sodden in the beating rain. The Dutch-man's guffaw was cut short as he slammed his door behind him.

From the spear-grass came the sound of hysteric sobbing. This had not been comic. Somehow ashamed, the crowd on the fence drifted away from there, slipping off in the dark downpour, anxious to escape the unpleas-ant. Myself, I was a sick kid when I sneaked guiltily into bed a short time later.

Next morning father returned; and I woke to hear his voice on the veranda. Through a crack in the window-screen I saw him greeting the French doctor from the government hospital down river. Then the doctor told father something—something about Jackling. He had

ridden past Jackling's gate early that morning, and discovered the man lying under the *kaladangs*, half-drowned in
the rain.

Jackling had been mumbling like a drunkard:

"I'll kill him. I'll kill now for sure. I'll kill him, so I will."

The French doctor went on to tell father that Jackling
would never kill anybody. Jackling's hands were paralyzed.

4

IN JACKLING'S CUPBOARD

RAIN. I HAVE good reason never to forget those following four months of weather that plagued our God-lost jungle town with mists and mud and water and smoke-gray gloom. Weeks of semi-darkness and logy air; sunless days under skies that scowled and wept; warm, oppressive nights soggy with pattering drops. Showers. Cloudbursts. Drizzle.

The jungles going rotten with fast-growing vine. Lush green vegetal things born, sprouted fat and spoiled in an hour. The river aflood, surfaced with slime. Every road and footpath a simmering gutter. Every compound a miniature swamp. Everywhere leeches and mold and snakes. The town a sopping, dank huddle under the mourning clouds. Four months of tropic rain.

Years later I was to meet in America an eminent psychiatrist who was making a study of the effect of rainy days on the minds of men—the influence of rain on Wall Street fluctuations, business depression, that sort of thing.

Something of this story I told him; and it was his opinion that the rainy season bringing its shroud of gloom had much to do with the astounding miracle that climaxed—with a climax all Nature's own—the somber doings of those somber days.

For something queer was fomenting in Jackling's desolate shack.

I suspected it; but the rest of the community did not. Every white and native in the jungle-bound, rain-eaten town knew about the wretched Englishman's disaster the morning after that dismal episode at Van Deventer's bungalow.

The isolated community buzzed with the story. Gossip tongues were a-wag. It was reported that Big Checkers Van Deventer had paralyzed his mouse-like enemy with one punch. It was reported that the Dutchman had laughed himself tearful on hearing how his one punch had stricken his rival. It was reported that Jackling would die.

The town stole through the rain to have a peek. It saw Jackling's shanty sullen with drawn blinds and fastened doors. It saw the French doctor make a third visit and come away with sweat-beads on his jaw and his lips reciting a vow to never go near the place again.

"Nom de Dieu! He is like a madman, that one. Just sits in a chair mouthing how he will some day kill the big Dutchman—'kill him, kill him, kill him'; over and over again. But yet, his hands are indeed paralyzed. They lie like dead things in his lap as he snarls. And that huge orang, that monster ape stands at his shoulder like the devil's right-hand man, grinning and patting his head. I am one *salopard* if ever I go there again."

Too, the doctor confessed himself puzzled. This paralysis that had rendered useless Jackling's hands he could not understand. The Dutchman's blow must have broken some nerve from the brain; or it might have been the Englishman's condition of decay from drink, fever, the tropics.

Well, there was the end of Jackling; the town could see that. Week days buried behind the forbidding door of his shanty, alone with the enormous orang-utan and his bitter thoughts.

Jackling would appear briefly on Sunday at the trader's store. Like a ghost out of the past, he was only made human by the spending of his failing resources to buy quinine and a meager supply of food.

I saw Jackling at the trader's store once. The man had gone emaciated as a mummy, his face turned the color of parchment. It was awful to see those thin, blue hands dangling helpless at his belt; but he was clever at catching up his bundles between his wrists, though the trader was obliged to dig into Jackling's ragged pocket himself for the money.

"The last of your coins, Jackling," the trader had said. "Now—now as how you can't work at all, why'n heck don't you sell Big Checkers that ape as he wants so bad to buy? He'll give you a small fortune fer th'beast, an'seein'as how the animal ain't no good to you anyhow—"

Jackling had spat a curse, and waved a hand that was like an empty white glove. He stumbled away snarling. "The only thing I'll ever do for that Dutchman is kill him!"

BUT A MAN without hands is less than half a man. And no half man, the town knew, would ever kill the Dutchman who had slain a tiger with a knife. Jackling was through. Back to hide himself in his dreary shanty where he could sit with his ape and glare at his dead fingers and listen to the rain pound the shingles over his head.

The town, then, could soon forget the man, but his next door neighbor's boy could not, with more than his share of imagination. It made my flesh crawl to see the little shanty through the limes and think of the creatures it housed so secretly.

To me that gray shanty was a place of haunts and mystery and intrigue. Father's ban made it doubly so. Boys of my age with healthier outlets for youthful enthusiasm, in America, were staring goggle-eyed at delightful horrors in Barnum's circus; was it unnatural that I should have spied at that neighboring house in those friendless jungles, where I could see a freak sideshow, menagerie and mystery story all in one?

Father had laid down an eleventh commandment: "Keep away from there!"

So every chance I had, I would hide my fusty lesson books, dodge across the compound, and enjoy a set of shivers, peeking at the forbidden.

There wasn't much to see. Each morning Jackling would go to the shed behind his shanty; get the ape. Together they would vanish behind the shuttered shanty windows. Every nightfall, stumbling through the rain, he would return the animal to its shed beneath the *mohor*. Save for those daily trips between shack and shed and his occasional journey to the trader's, the crippled man remained behind locked doors. A recluse with his ape.

But how did the man and the animal wear out the long, glooming days? Neck-nape prickling, I crept one afternoon up to the blinded shanty, bent on finding out. I'll bet money my eye was bigger than a glass marble when I fastened it to a crack at one of the shanty windows and saw what was doing within.

The jaundiced light that stole from a shuddery candle

to illumine the room was mean and dim, but I could see well enough. For all the world like one of his moldy dried specimens, Jackling was there in a corner, sitting. His eyes were fixed on the death-blue hands immobile in his lap. Only the lips in his yellow face were alive.

Their faint speech animated a shadow hunched darkly in the opposite corner; and I saw that big cinnamon ape come waddling across the floor with a pail and a spoon in its fist. My eye was bigger than a marble, now. That orang-utan was feeding its master!

Spellbound I watched as the enormous anthropoid, solicitous as a nurse with a patient, dipped spoon into pail and conveyed dripping mouthfuls to the helpless man.

That frowsty room, that animal ministering to that mummy-like man, was a scene from a tale by the Brothers Grimm. I wanted to get my eye away from that window, but I couldn't. Fascinated, I watched the ape and the ghostly Jackling share the contents of the pail.

Jackling's white mouth murmured. Once the ape put an arm around his shoulder and the man rested his head on the chest of the grinning brute. I think Jackling's affection for that creature was the only human attribute left him. I could just catch the mumbled words:

"You're my hands now, Bobo. *My hands.*"

What a strange affinity! Jackling had lost the use of his hands, only to win another pair—a vicarious pair of hands. I tell you, no circus animal was ever trained as that big orang was trained. I watched it feed its master, busy itself at odd tasks about the room, pour him wine from a bottle, clumsily light and start for him a black cheroot.

FOR PERHAPS TWENTY minutes I crouched there in the

rain and spied at that astonishing and gruesome exhibi-
tion. Then something occurred that almost popped my eye
out of its socket.

Jackling had finished his strange feast; now he lurched to
his feet and gestured an elbow at a tall cupboard standing
at the room's end among crates of stuffed specimens. The
ape had its back toward me; waddled with arms swinging.
Something glinted in the beast's fist. A key? I didn't know.
But I saw the ape reach out and open the cupboard door;
then I was glaring with the chills racing from neck to heels.

The room was dark and shadowy, you understand, and
my view was partially obscured by the shoulders of the
orang-utan. But I saw something in that cupboard to make
my hair stand up.

Some one was standing there in that coffin-tall box.

The face I was unable to see. The figure was a blur. But I
heard the ape growl in its shaggy throat, and I heard Jackling's voice command: "Get him out, Bobo. Work on him!"

At that very moment there sounded a sharp knock on
the door of the shanty. Things happened. Jackling sprang to
slam shut with an elbow the door of that awful cupboard.
The ape scurried into a corner, plucking at the hair under
its chin. The Englishman wheeled, darted to the shanty
door, threw the bolt with a clumsy wrist. And it was my
father who stepped unexpectedly on to that ghastly stage.

Thoughts spun through my fear-addled head. So this
was the place my father had been making afternoon calls.
Of late he had been in the habit of going out at teatime, and
I had thought him visiting the natives. I couldn't understand then, but I can see the how of it now. At last the idea
that misses so many in the service of the Lord had come

to my father—the idea that the native heathen weren't the only "sinners" in need of spiritual help, and missionary work could lie closer to home. Father had included Jackling in his round-up of the "lost sheep."

But I never wanted to see him in that room, and I watched in cold terror as he dropped his soaked broad-brim on a chair, stood nodding pleasantly at the cringing naturalist, and tugged from his pocket a Testament.

I wanted to scream as I heard him utter a quiet greeting and say without further preamble: "Jackling, have you been thinking over what I told you yesterday? The Book says, 'Love your enemies.' Do you still hate Van Deventer, my friend? Do you still wish to slay him? Remember what I've been telling you—this hatred means death to the soul. Hatred is the despoiler of the human heart. Hatred is self-punishment."

Jackling had shambled to the corner to stand beside his ape. His face was turned toward that horrid cupboard, and father could not see his eyes; but I, at the window, could. Cat's eyes in the dark.

"Do you still hate your enemy?" my father's quiet voice persisted.

Jackling mumbled: "Look here, *padre*. You been comin' here every day for a week to ask me that. I—I been thinkin' over your proposition. Maybe—maybe I don't hate the man no more. Maybe—"

"Then you'll sell him this ape of yours, Jackling? Remember, it will give you money enough to go away. You can go home. You'll follow my suggestion? He wants to buy, Jackling. To-day he sailed for Borneo on the mail packet to try to find another ape—"

"Van Deventer? Sailed for Borneo to-day?"

Jackling snapped the words shrill. His head came up, startled. And I was startled, too.

"DON'T WORRY," FATHER said. "He will be back at the end of the rainy season. He comes back here to catch the Messageries boat for France, you see. He'll not find such an animal as this one, that I know. Let me handle the deal for you, Jackling. He'll only be here again for a day or so, and you must seize that chance to sell. Then you can return to England on the money. You can forget this dreadful hatred, and make peace with your God!"

"You're sure he'll be back here? You sure?"

Now what was father saying?

"I saw him off on the mail boat this morning. Talked with him. He desperately wants to buy your animal. Calls it the best specimen he ever saw. He'll be back to see about it."

"Padre!" Jackling's voice drifted so low I could scarcely hear it above the tattoo beat by the unending rain. *"Padre,* I guess maybe you won me over. I don't want to kill him no more. When—when Big Checkers comes back to town, you come over an' tell me. Then I'll—I'll take my orang up there an' sell him. I'll forget th' rest, I will. I'll—"

I knew that jubilant note in father's voice. It came to him when, for example, he felt a sermon was winning an audience. Queer background for prayer; but there they were—father on his knees near the door, Jackling on his knees near that cupboard; father's voice invoking the blessings of the Almighty on this soul so hardly won to grace.

But it was not only rain-water that dampened my face as I fled through the lime trees for home. For the sick candle-glow that had found such kind calmness on father's upturned face had also caught a lethal gleam on the grinning teeth of the ape that had crouched in its corner. A lethal gleam that had matched for ferocity the glitter of Jackling's eyes.

Those eyes had remained as the eyes of a cat in the dark, and had suited not at all the eyes of a man who petitioned his Heaven. Nor had they looked heavenward. They had stared at that loathsome corner-cupboard in which I had glimpsed a blurred figure. And though I had snatched but a glimpse, I had seen enough.

For that figure in the cupboard had worn a shirt. A black-and-red checkered shirt!

HOW COULD I ask my father? How could I find out about the thing I had seen in Jackling's cupboard? How could I warn father to stay away from that room with its awful contents?

A hundred times during the following weeks I opened my mouth to speak. Guilt and fear nailed silent my tongue. I was a thirteen-year-old boy, and my father the sternest of men. To tell him what I had seen I must make confession; admit I had broken his commandment, shirked my lessons, disobeyed.

No. I could only sneak around, mum, conscience-smitten, tortured with fear every time I saw father leave the house, and, from my hideout in the limes, watched him enter Jackling's shanty on his afternoon call. And father called regularly.

Wild horses couldn't have dragged me to peek through that window again; but my imagination, working long overtime, could picture him in there with the crippled man whose eyes were never on heaven. And there would be the grinning ape; and the coffin-like cupboard hiding something that wore a checkered shirt.

I could hear Jackling's words: "Get him out, Bobo. Work on him!" But father and the town thought Big Checkers had sailed for Borneo on the monthly mail packet.

The affair became an obsession. I knew I ought to tell. I dared not. Nights I dreamed; days I waited alone in father's library, haunted by the sound of ceaseless rain pattering down the rattan blinds, fighting in agonies of apprehension to unravel the nightmare.

It did not unravel. There was rumor in the town that my father had converted Jackling. Things like that get around. Jackling still preferred to keep to the solitude of his shack; my father was the only man who saw him daily. But I heard it told that the Englishman was going to make up with the Dutchman when Van Deventer should return. Perhaps Van Deventer *had* sailed off on his Borneo visit. Perhaps I had only imagined seeing a red-and-black shirted figure in that cupboard.

And then there came a morning when the rain whipped down like a loosened flood, and I awoke with a start to hear the hoot of a boat siren out on the river. I ate no breakfast that morning. I got down to the wharf as fast as the mud on my heels would let me. Father and the whole town— save Jackling—were there ahead of me.

I arrived just in time to see Big Checkers Van Deventer, black and red shirt and all, swagger down the gangway, bawl greetings, and start off large as life for his bungalow up the hill.

THAT WAS A most amazing day. All morning and afternoon the world was dark wider lowering clouds. An inky downpour squalled. Indoors was like a hothouse.

A coolie came from the mail packet with a note from father. He was spending the day with a friend aboard the steamer. I was commanded to spend the day at my studies with the concession that I might, if the rain lessened, go to the wharf that evening to watch the arrival of the big Messageries liner that would dock in for the night and start its journey for France next morning early.

My studies! I sat in the hot, damp library with a book titled: "Franklin's Review of Wesleyan Perfection"; and for Franklin or any kind of perfection I had no mind at all. By noon I had read the first sentence. At five in the afternoon I had finished the second.

One sentence I did know: "What's happening next door? What's happening next door?"

I listened to those words run through my brain over and over again, and I listened to the pounding rain. What would happen next door? Somewhere a clock tolled six. The chimes echoed softly. I could stand it no longer. I dodged out on the veranda. A pair of ghosts were moving up the road that led to the top of the hill across the rainswept town. Ghosts. Jackling and his orang-utan.

His face was like white paper drawn tight over bone; chin on chest so that the rain water streamed from his nose. Slowly he moved through the lancing sheets of water, feet slogging in the soupy mire of the roadbed. The soldiers retreating from Moscow must have moved like that, might have carried wounded hands in that same odd way—dangling limp and white and crooked like queer, helpless vegetables appended to the wrists.

Swinging long, strong arms, waddling with a sailor's roll on its bow legs, the ape followed, for all the world like some monster goblin of folklore. Up that dark, weeping roadway they started to climb.

I could not help it. My legs moved in spite of me. Dodging, creeping, puddle-jumping, keeping in blue shadow, choking with heart in throat, I followed.

The town was on the wharf; it was not there to follow this second mad march of Jackling's up that mounting, washed-out pike. That road was a million miles long, then. An exhausting road. Jackling did not walk fast. The rain on his chest seemed to hold him back. How that water came down!

I seemed to be swimming along in the rear of that strange processional. The white bungalow atop the hill seemed to float there, suspended. Nearer and nearer. The man and the ape had almost reached the compound fence. Jackling was elbowing open the Dutchman's gate.

Suddenly I was sick. Sick! It was as if a bomb had burst in the back of my head! I wanted to cry out. I wanted to run. Like a flash of gunfire the whole thing had come clear, the puzzle of the thing in the cupboard solved itself; I had guessed enough, and the ice-beads leaked out on my face.

But I was too far behind. I was too late. Jackling was calling out, and through the gate and up the gravel path and the ape was after him. The door of the white bungalow bammed open, and there was Big Checkers Van Deventer grinning and confident and monumental on his threshold. Little did he guess…

And then it happened! A simple thing, and amazing: the rain stopped!

That four-month downpour quit as if the last drop of
water in heaven had squeezed itself out and the sky had
dried at one breath. The rain quit falling and the air went
clear. A sudden warm breeze ripped the clouds apart and a
shaft of mellow gold sunbeams tumbled through where the
evening sky showed old rose high at the top of the world.
In the *pandanus* grove behind the white bungalow a bird
blew a bugle note clear as a bell. And Jackling stood dripping on that gravel path with his feet in a pool of sunshine.

Then the wonder of it was this: Big Checkers Van
Deventer called out, but Jackling only looked at the rose
in the sky. And the Dutchman called again: "Ho-ho! This
is splendid. The *padre* told me you would bring the ape to
sell me in time for me to take it back on the boat. Come
up, Jackling. Ja. Bring the orang here. I haff ready for you
the money."

The black and red shirt vanished from the doorway. The
Dutchman had dodged back inside to get that money. He
could not hear Jackling's reply.

"No, no!" the Englishman called. "I can't do it, Van
Deventer. I must keep the ape. You shan't touch him—"

Wheeling in the path, Jackling drove the animal before
him and started fast down the hill, astonishing in the
sunset light.

I could not believe it. I could not! He passed within three
feet of the brush where I crouched hiding, and I saw his
hands fluttering like white wings. He was holding them
in front of him and staring at them wide-eyed and panting at the ape.

"I can move 'em, Bobo. Oh, dear God, I can move 'em
now. They *move!*"

5

STRANGE JUSTICE

THE LORD WORKS in a mysterious way His wonders to perform. That is one of the theological pronouncements remaining to be believed. For example, the sky can rain for weeks and the sun, unquenched, can dry out the clouds and suddenly shine gold again. Then there's that pathological phenomenon known to medical science as an "ictus."

Queer thing, the ictus, not easily understood. Small wonder that our inept French doctor in that backwater jungle town had failed to fathom or recognize it. Cure it? Possibly Christian Science would touch the thing when medicines and physical treatment might not. For in some cases it may be a morbid malady induced by the mind, though the common dictionary defines it, "a stroke or a blow, attack or fit." It is more. A subtle relief by nature. Whereas sudden fear or fury can strike one momentarily helpless, the long nursing of a violent emotion such as hatred may render one more definitely stricken.

It was so with the case of the man who had buried himself in his shanty, brooded through the long, black days, stoking his hate to a pitch where the mind could stand it no longer and made reprisal by numbing the nerves of his hands.

Here lay more mental phenomenon than miracle. That the sun should have shone when it did was the miracle.

You can see how it must have been for Jackling. On the very moment of his chance for revenge, the world had brightened, the sun shone, a bird called song. Like coming out of a cave, it must have been. It is simple for me to understand it now. You may murder a man at the end of a foul, dark alley, but it would be impossible for you to do it in a rose garden.

Or, perhaps, father's daily sermons had burrowed deeper into Jackling's consciousness than Jackling had guessed. At any rate, the coming of sunshine and summer at one abrupt burst had scattered his plot as it had scattered the rain. And with the weakening of his hate-lust, the man had been released.

He could not understand it. None of us could, that evening. Father and our house-boy and Jackling and I were there on Jackling's veranda. In the west the sky flew gold and scarlet banners. High overhead a young star flashed in the clear indigo. The clean-washed jungle trees were emerald green in the dusk.

I recall how the dusk went mauve, then cobalt, then blue-black; and a thin slice of moon showed overhead and the lime trees were like those in a Japanese print, and the breeze was almost hot. From the direction of the river drifted the throaty call of a steamer siren—the Messageries boat which would head for Europe in the dawn to come.

Our house-boy brought a lantern, and the lambent amber light showed patches of color in Jackling's cheeks. In his eyes there showed a reverence seldom seen in the eyes of men, and he kept them fixed on the hands that moved

so oddly on his knees. He just sat there smiling and smiling and moving his hands and talking, and the world was
a queer place for one small boy, you may believe.

"I *had* planned to kill him," Jackling was whispering
to father. "I'd planned all along. Seems as if the idea had
eaten into me. Seemed to be the only thing kept me alive—
trying to figure out some way to do for that man, Van
Deventer. And when my hands went crippled on me, I
hated him more than ever. But—when I got up there and
the sun came out so sudden and all, I—I just couldn't do
it, that's all. It wasn't that I was scared, *padre*. It was different. That bright sunshine—well, I suddenly didn't want
to do it. I could have finished him. Nobody could have
hung anything on me for doing it, that way. But there
was the sunshine. And when I found I didn't—didn't hate
him; when I turned around to bring the ape back here an'
lock him up in his shed—why, it seemed I could move my
hands, again. Like I'd been cured of something. Like—"

There was a soul-curdling scream. It spiraled up into the
peaceful night and strung it with horror and alarm. It came
from the shed under the *mohor* behind Jackling's shanty.

ONCE AGAIN I can hear my father's stern: "My God!"
Nor was it prayer. And once again I can see, coming out of
gloom into the reach of amber lantern-glow, a monstrous
face that grins with huge approval on the razor which had
wrought the deed.

The razor gleams wickedly in the murderer's agile fist;
showers ruby drops. Already a stray quartet of flies has
buzzed out of the tepid darkness to find that *thing* asprawl
on a mat of blood, with its severed throat and butchered
face. Then a lemon-cheeked China lad, recognized as Van

Deventer's house-boy, slips out of the shadows and struggles to speak.

"Ahee! He come down here and break into little house. He want capture ape and take him waterside to hide on boat sailing for west in morning. He want ape bad. Take ape to France and sell much money. He bring me down here to help take away ape—"

Fingers of blood creep and fatten, reaching from under the black and red checkered chest that hugs the dirt so tightly.

When Jackling can finally speak his voice seems to echo from the bottom of a deep-sunk well.

"That's it—that's it, *padre!* I swear I never thought— never thought to take that razor off that orang. You see what's happened, *padre?* That was how I was going to kill Big Checkers. I—I trained the ape to carry a razor, in a blade-case fastened under the hair on his chest. Taught him to draw and slash out with the blade, I did."

Jackling mops dry the pores of his face with a shaky hand. (So I had guessed his secret, after all!) His voice echoes on:

"See how it was? All the time I was shut up in my shanty I spent teaching the ape. Worked with a paint brush in my teeth, and fixed up a shirt, I did. I—I rigged the shirt on an old mummy I keep in a cupboard in the shack. Hung the shirt on this mummy, an' trained Bobo to stab his razor at it. It was a red and black checked shirt! So if the ape ever saw Van Deventer... And now, when the Dutchman sneaked down here to steal the ape—"

BENTFINGER

Striking with cobra-like deadliness, the mad killer who concealed his identity so cleverly had left a trail of victims in many countries when Benson, of the American consulate at Pahang, encountered him on a lantern-lit street

1

THE ASSASSIN!

BENTFINGER! AND FROM the very first there was, to me, something queerly sinister about the name. Bentfinger. A christening of the sort hinting at genius. A sly kind of cognomen, calculated to make one think of an aged servant with a squinty eye, a crooked claw poked through a purple curtain, or a hooked talon waiting to grab. Bentfinger. It gave me a creep the first time I read it.

A battered copy of the New York *Times*, dated the year before, carried the item. "Police again baffled. Once more the mysterious shadow has crossed Times Square and foiled the best of New York's Finest. The safe was emptied; the diamonds gone. Only the typed card remained to mock, gibing the sleuths with the unknown's trademark, 'Bentfinger.'"

Next time it was a bit nearer. The January *Morning Post* from London: "This time the Yard is at its wits' end. There is the gutted shop on Regent Street. The ruby tiara gone. The dead watchman with the bullet in his temple. And exactly a half hour later the body of Inspector Cushing found on Ludgate Circus, the bullet also in the temple.

"At first there was no connection made between the Regent Street killing and the murder of Inspector Cushing. Then it was ascertained that the Inspector had been near the Regent Street address at the time of the murder, and apparently followed in his own motor a suspect. The car was found abandoned on London Bridge. Apparently the killer had headed for the docks in that quarter.

"Man or woman? The police do not know. But the trademark was found. On moving the body of the Regent Street watchman a blood-stained card was found beneath the shoulder blades. A similar card was found tucked in the Inspector's waistcoat. Each card bore the typed name: 'Bentfinger.'"

In April the European press dispatches carried a blazing story. "Marseilles, France. Minister of Finance Doumeron's wife found dead in her hotel room, shot through the temple. No sound had been heard by the hotel staff. There was no sign of a struggle. But the Doumeron strongbox containing the famous Moreaux string of black pearls, which Mme. Doumeron had planned to wear to Count Fallicet's ball the following night, was missing. And stuck in the frame of a picture of 'Mona Lisa,' above the unfortunate Mme. Doumeron's bed, where all could see, was a typed card. Again the name that is striking its terror across the Continent. 'Bentfinger.'"

IN MAY IT was the Cairo *Crescent*. "Police and government operatives of four countries are to-night combing the city in as desperate a crime hunt as Egypt has ever experienced. French, British, Greek, and Egyptian authorities are turning up the city from end to end. Shops are locked and under guard. A spell of terror envelops native and white quarters alike, the streets being patrolled by armed constabulary. In his palatial residence on Rue de la Treizième Lune, Prince

*Benson screeched like a
banshee as he struck out*

Hamid Jahl, his guest, Eleutherios Poulogos the famous
diamond merchant, Mme. Poulogos and Addadud Ahmed,
the prince's secretary, were shot dead in the most daring
and coldblooded murder and robbery known in the annals
of the Cairo police.

"It was known that the diamond merchant had in his
possession the Kizam Star, but none thought he would
carry the illustrious ninety-carat gem on his person.
However, his agents informed the police he had decided
to brave the risk; a gesture that led himself and three others
to an ugly end. Prince Hamid's residence is isolated in
a gorgeous ten-acre garden. The doors were locked. It
appears the killer entered, unobserved, by an open window.
Servants heard four shots and broke in the drawing-room
doors.

"The dead lay in a row. An empty jewel case was found
in the hand of the prince's secretary. In a poinsettia bed

beneath the open window the police discovered a woman's shoe of expensive Parisian make. To further the mystery, a half hour before the crime Abdallah ben Brahim, a policeman of the Cairo force, saw a crippled beggar lurking under the street wall of the prince's garden.

"A traffic accident on the opposite kerb called the policeman's attention for a moment, during which the beggar—a down and out Arab dragoman by the looks of his ragged cloak—disappeared. The policeman thought the beggar had slunk off in the accident crowd. However, he may have vaulted the wall. Thus again the authorities are stupefied. A woman's shoe. A crippled beggar. Man or woman, at any rate the fiend left his mark on his handiwork. Once again a fortune in precious stones is gone. The victims shot through the temple. The little typed card on the breast of Prince Hamid, stamped with the name of the untrackable menace, 'Bentfinger.'"

THE BOMBAY *INDIAN UMPIRE* came through in June with the somber headlines: "Dirigbijah Singh, Rajah of Malangore, slain at *talookdar's* ball. Sir Ian Havelstock, K.C.S.I., and Lady Stokes dying. Menace to society strikes again. Attacks native prince and guests in hotel garden. While the ballroom of the Asian Queen Hotel resounded with festive merrymaking, the master criminal of the era struck like a thunderbolt among the rhododendrons of the famous Asian Queen terrace. Once more the fiend's uncanny marksmanship felled his victim, Rajah Singh, who strolled with his friends, Sir Ian and Lady Stokes, in the garden. Evidence that Sir Ian and Lady Stokes gave fight.

"Sir Ian lies close to death with bullet lodged beneath

ear. Lady Stokes's skull crushed by blow from gun-butt. The fabulous Islamahad Ruby gone from rajah's turban. Frantic police searching every quarter of city. Special detail on Bund. Authorities all over India to lend every effort in tracking of international criminal. Hotel guests grilled. Unknown woman cannot be located after slaying; but may have been Roumanian princess attending ball with consort, incognito. Scotland Yard on scene. Man's bowler hat, unclaimed by guests and wearing band of Bond Street hatter, found in trampled death-garden. Police believe fiend to be leaving confusion of clews. Brutality of crimes enrages authorities. Typed card left in turban of slain rajah. Once more the dreaded unknown, the murderous Bent-finger, has come and gone—"

In July I grew sick and tired of my room at the Colony Club with its broken electric fan, its profane parrot, its uninspired typewriter, its host of empty bottles; sick of waiting for phone calls from the consulate, and sick of reading month-old newspapers crammed with far-away excursions and alarms; so I left the club for a stroll.

Some parts of Pahang I had not yet visited, and I swung my Malacca stick down a street that was dark enough to be entertaining. A mild tropic rain had dimmed the night, and the rickshas pattered by with a sound that was almost cool. A boat siren mourned among the mists of the water front; and I stopped at the mouth of a twisty lane I didn't recognize. At the end of the lane a Chinese lantern floated aloft in the gloom. A patch of pale yellow light suspended there, with a frail and fierce black dragon intriguing over a doorway.

A Chinese lantern—two cents' worth of moist, painted paper and a stub of candle—got me into this!

MYSTERIOUS EAST, CRIMES in newspapers, adventure, love—you never expect them to "happen" to you. The spell of Asia? Bah. I'd lived there seven months, hadn't I? Seven months right in Pahang. The first two weeks were all right when you swanked about in a nice new sun helmet, tried a *stengah* or two, bought a Tibetan rug that was probably loomed in New Jersey, purchased a parrot and saw Haroun al Raschid or Lao Tse in every amber face that went by.

Then the faces turned brown, the sun got too hot, you'd seen better jugglers on the stage at the Hippodrome. The spell of the East became the smell of the East. You looked for it and you didn't see it. It was a ghost, like things in newspapers, adventure and love. Everybody talked about it, as they say, but nobody'd seen it. Dangerous to walk down that alley? Pshaw! If things did happen (which they didn't) they happened in Chicago and not in a place like Pahang.

Still that Chinese lantern was a lure; a real piece of Asian atmosphere. In spite of my worldly cynicism I sighted the dim yellow glow with something like a thrill. The lane was deserted and hung by a wraith-like mist. A wet mud wall reflected the feeble gleam. There was the paper lantern winkering at its dim end, and beyond that the faintest suggestion of a dark river. Hopefully I turned down the lane, bent on discovering an adventure. Probably nothing but a shack full of sing-song girls down there, but if anything happened in the Orient it should happen in a setting like that.

The trouble was, it did! I knew, of course, it wouldn't. And it did! It happened so suddenly I didn't believe it and it was unreal and I wasn't prepared and it took the stomach right out of me and it happened with a bang! You see, the mysterious East, crimes in newspapers, adventure and love are likely to be "real" after all. I ran into all of them beneath a Chinese lantern at the end of a Pahang lane. The maddest, most astonishing adventure a man could hope to have. Believe me, if it hadn't been for the wisdom, the penetrating sagacity, the steady hand, keen eye and, most of all, high courage of a certain brave Englishman from Scotland Yard, this story would never be told—

SOMETHING WAS DOING. I had thought the muffled echo of scuffling came from the river; then I traced it to the doorway beneath the lonely lantern. It seemed as if the shadows there had come into sudden activity. A stealthy noise came from the animated darkness, as if a pair of wraiths had bumped together in ghostly conflict. A scraping, heaving, and whispering. A stifled gurgle. A soughing of labored breath. A thick, *"Aaaaah!"* Then a smack, for all the world like a fist against flesh, and a human cough.

Now that prickles were on my neck-nape, I didn't fancy them there. Adventures are all right until you find yourself into one, and my feet stood within ten paces of that troubled doorway where certainly a terrific struggle of some kind was taking place. Having no mind for a wharf-rat broil, I was on the point of beating a discreet retreat when the shadows plunged out of the doorway and swirled across the mud of the lane.

The puny light from the pale lantern caught a pair of dodging heads, flailing arms, fists, teeth. Locked in conflict, the battling couple danced a macabre waltz through the mire. Puddle-water scattered under trampling boots. The

dank air was alive with furious gaspings. Then I glimpsed
the glitter of metal in a yellow fist; and came away from
the wall with upraised cane. I must have yelled; for the shot
was simultaneous with my charge.

Crash! A snake's-tongue of scarlet flame bit through the
murk. A tortured scream ripped out.

Numb with the horror of it, I watched a sagging figure
buckle at the knees, flop backward like a tripped baby, go
sprawling. I was conscious that his face had been smeared
with red; that his hands had grabbed at the air and failed
to catch hold. All this in an eye-flicker; and in another
wink I had whirled on a black ghost that seemed to be all
cloak and yellow hands. I shall not soon forget those awful
hands as I saw them first that night. Dandelion yellow
hands with loose, floppy, jointless fingers. And one of them
closed about a pistol.

Of the face in the black hood I had only a glimpse. Eyes
like savage embers fanned to blaze. Streaming hair. A face
so wrinkled with hatred that it seemed to be old. A mouth
contorted with fury; the lips sucked in to give an impression that the jaws lacked teeth. Damp and punky-color
in the feeble illumination from the overhead Chinese toy.

The shrouding cloak billowed and tossed like the wings
of a bat as the phantasm launched itself at me. Black cloth
masked the face and the goblin yellow hands snatched
about as if jerked on strings. I tell you that pistol-muzzle
looked like the mouth of a Krupp cannon; and I screeched
like a banshee as I struck out with my Malacca stick. Thank
God for me that I managed to hit that gun. The cane splintered to matchwood. The chunk of grim metal went flying.
I heard a sharp shriek, and saw one of those impossible

yellow hands go flopping through the air like a moth. A second I was tangled in the folds of a cloak, strangling, kicking, lashing out frantic fists. Yanking my head free, I lunged at my assailant with pounding fists; tripped on an inert arm and went spraddling in the mud.

Kicking like an overturned beetle, I bounced to my feet in time to see that cloud of dark cloth go swirling around the twist of the lane. Three objects lay in the roiled mire at my feet: A Webley pistol. A yellow cloth glove. A dying man.

He was dressed in the uniform of a French sailor, a tight-fitting navy jacket, blue-and-white striped jersey showing beneath the throat, the little sea-hat with the white band jammed on his head with its fuzzy tassel red as the blood which enameled his lips. The rays of the Chinese lantern fell across his pain-wrung face; and I saw his eyes rolling while his mouth struggled desperately for speech. Panting, sick, I dropped to my knees in time to catch the word. Just one word, and then he was through. And there I knelt, something foolish carved from ice.

Beyond the bend of the lane sounded the thump of fleeing boots, and then the echo of a mordant laugh that trailed back through the unfestive gloom, evil and taunting as the curse of a hag. A laugh of joy in evil. A mocking guffaw. The laugh of a murderer. It yanked me, snarling, to my feet, and brought hot rage to my face. Catching up the pistol and the yellow glove, I spun on heel and raced after that heinous laugh. Sweat bubbled on my forehead, too, and for a good reason.

The sailor's dying breath had voiced a name. "Bentfinger—"

NOW, I'VE NO more courage than the average fellow who gets up in the morning and goes to bed at night and tries to beat bill collectors out of the back door. If I'd stopped to think about it I might not have dashed so readily in pursuit through that gloomy *cul-de-sac* Pahang water front. No time for thinking though, and I'd have given a hand to drop a bullet in the brain of that killer who had laughed mockery while his victim lay dying in the mud.

Every time I thought of that poor French sailor's face I lifted my heels faster; and we were running like antelopes when we reached a string of waterside godowns. The assassin was going like a ghost, the long cape flagging in the wind. Feet pounding the muddy road. Dodging up a lane. Down an alley. Through a bamboo fence.

Boots hammering, clenched teeth jarring in my jaw, I hung on. Once I almost had that cape in my fingers. The gun clicked in my fist. Jammed! Clawing at the accursed weapon, I raced faster than ever. A mongrel dog launched itself from somewhere and fastened teeth in my left ankle. I stumbled; slugged with my gun-barrel. The dog sped off howling.

But the thing in a cape had gained a turn; raced through a reeking maze of empty alleys, crooked archways, deserted lanes where balconies of rotted wood hung overhead and mud walls reared suddenly in one's path.

Rain started; a nasty drizzle that thickened the dark to black soup. I was chasing nothing but footsteps now. Chasing footsteps down the rim of the River Styx. The river was there, all right. A dank smell of river water lurked in the mist, and somewhere a boat was hooting. I'd have given plenty for a light in that locale. Even a Chinese lantern.

I hadn't been able to eject the jammed cartridge from my pistol, and I sprinted along with my fingers closed over the gun-barrel, armed only with a chunk of iron and expecting any minute to be led blind into a death-trap. I knew I was somewhere on the Pahang dock front, but it was darker than Hades and silent as two graves. Those who had lived there seemed to have turned out all lights and traveled ten thousand miles away. Running boots scarcely echoed in the sodden rain.

Then a tiny cone of light pricked the gloom, and I saw the reach of a long wooden pier; yellow, dim reflections in wet wood and a sense of gummy water and the stench of rotten weeds beneath. The rain fell in good earnest, silver lances slanting out of the night and bouncing showers of twinkly water on the faintly luminous timber underfoot. The light moved in a slow arc through the blackness veiling the river, and a dim point of green hove into view. A boat was out there, wheeling in the current. The pier seemed a mile long with those faint gleams far at its end; and a black shadow sped ahead of me, going like a wind down that dim-lit jetty.

It was queer, I can tell you. The shadow sped straight for that cone of yellow light, and I, chasing after, followed the silhouette of a cloak that billowed in the rain. I gained on the cloak and the cloak gained on the point of light. The point of light grew larger as we neared it, appeared as an amber mushroom blossoming in the murk—a ship's lantern lighting the taffrail of a vessel that turned in midstream.

The light grew larger as we neared it, I say, but the figure I chased seemed to dwindle in size. Running in a half crouch, the assassin was doubling up in a hunchbacked sort of knot. The creature I had battled beneath the Chinese lantern had been man-sized in stature. Now as I chased it up the long pier in the rain it seemed to have diminished, hunched and doubled over with shoulders contracted and head awry, no larger than a girl.

Imagination, of course. The rain, the shadows, the cloak, the weird effect of light seeping through dank night mist. But I swear it looked nothing so much as a bat, that fleeing assassin, when it gained the end of the pier and flung through the mists, cape aflutter, to hit black water with a splash.

I WAS CHASING no fairy-tale bat, however. I heard the plash of arms whipping water, and I dived hard after with a yell. If you think I made a fancy dive, you are wrong. An old-fashioned belly-whacker took the skin off my middle, and I thrashed like a porpoise to catch the foaming swirl ahead.

It was no funny race, that Olympic swim down the middle of a tropic river. The hull of a steamer loomed gigantic in the darkness; the taffrail light glowed bright behind thick-lensed glass; a ship's screw churned frothy foam and the swell of a cutwater swamped my head. When I came clear again, the light glowed far above me, slanting down a bulge of dark wet iron. Water swished in burbling whirlpools. I was within a pace of that perilous propeller. I caught a glimpse of a rope that dangled from a high rail and dragged in the boiling ink. A figure in dripping black cloth swung hand over hand up the rope.

With a frantic lunge I grabbed that hawser; dragged myself clear of the river. My boots skidded on metal plating. For a second I hung, gasping; then fought inch by inch up the ship's side, after an eternity got elbows hooked over a stanchion, swung up with a shoulder-wrenching twist and slid through a rail.

The afterdeck was deserted to a slamming rain. Water burbled and hissed down the scuppers, and grease on winches gleamed. I had an eye-wink vision of hatch covers, a high bridge, a smoke-spouting funnel, a brown ventilator. Then I saw a shadow go dodging for an open companion; saw the wet cloak shimmer and vanish; and went shin-banging after.

The companionway was lighted, and my charge took me tumbling down a ladder to a fusty-smelling deck where battered luggage lay heaped in disarray. A trail of foot-tracks skirted the mound of trunks and dropped down a second hatch. I plunged in hot pursuit; came upright in a dim-lit hold reeking with the stench of engine oil, bilge and bad food. Gear and ropes, fire hose and cans of red lead were stowed in every corner; by the contour of the room I judged I was in a store-hold, perhaps behind the engine house.

I banged against a fastened bulkhead, and could not get through. Tracks led to the metal door, and I knew the assassin had slipped through and locked the bulkhead after him. Good Lord, I couldn't stand staring like a fool. Racing topside, I stood in the rain-whipped hatchway, glaring at the deck, and for the first time realized that a ship was actually trembling under my boots. Suddenly I was voicing a string of oaths.

I was on a steamship. Outward bound. A passenger boat, by the looks. And somewhere aboard was a demon killer, an international criminal, a master assassin (the newspa-

per phrases tumbled lurid, through my addled head), jewel
thief and murderer who had dealt brutal death and baffled
the police of three continents. A fiend who had slain a man
under my very nose and japed at the deed with a laugh. (I
thought about it now, I can tell you!) Bentfinger! I had been
chasing Bentfinger! Bentfinger was aboard this boat—

I stepped out of the hatchway and opened my mouth
to yell. I was going to bawl an alarm that would turn that
ship topside from stem to stern. But the yell never came.

Something whipped out of the darkness and crashed
down hard on my head.

2

DEATH IN THE DARK

"DO WIV 'IM?" the far-away voice came dimly through a painful red fog. "Wot'll we do wiv'im? Put th'blighter to work on deck, I say. I been short'anded all along, an' wot with them bleedin'Malays workin'th'way they do—bloody lascars!—I can make good use of an extry'and. Don't go sendin' 'im to th'galley. Give 'im to me. Soon's 'e comes outa that belt on th'knob, I'll set'im to work in th'fo'c's'le."

"You didn't need to slug him so hard, bos'. Might have killed the fellow. He's been unconscious an hour and a half."

"Didn't th' Old Man tell me?" answered the cockney whine. "If any more these stowaways comes aboard,'e says, give'em what for. Maybe I belted'im a bit'eavy, sir, but any bloke as swims that channel full o'sharks to board a ship th'way'e done, sir, must be a tough'un. I sees'im sneak over th'port rail an'dodge down th'companion. Minute later'e's back on deck, an' I lets'im 'ave it."

"Well," came the second voice, "take him along, then, and set him to work. A dashed odd-looking fellow to be sneaking a passage, but he'll have to work it out. We'll drop him when we make port in Shanghai. Send him to the bridge when he comes out of it. He'll probably make a fuss and say it's a mistake and want to go ashore. You can tell him we're out of sight of land—"

Out of sight of land! A firecracker exploded in the back of my aching head, and I sat up with a jump, wide-eyed. A crazy cabin and a dozen faces revolved slowly about me amidst a twinkle of lights. Then the patchwork merged to take form, and I was sitting on the edge of a mussy bunk in a mussy cabin, staring at a little, horny-faced cockney with big ears and a bald head.

A second face appeared behind the Eastham caricature; a moon-round, grizzled Scotch countenance with a rakish white officer's cap pushed back on a tousled gray thatch. The sea-cap wore gold braid and twined anchors over the visor, the insignia reading: "First Mate." The blue Scotch eyes bored at me, and I addressed them with a yelp.

"Out of sight of land—"

"With Pahang 'most two hours behind," the mate growled. "You got yourself a sailor's job, fellow. We don't land stowaways, you know. We make 'em work. You'll have to explain to the authorities at Shanghai; meantime you go to th' fo'c's'le. This is Crammer, the bos'n. He'll detail you a watch and you'll take orders from him—"

"Listen!" I yelled, bouncing off the bunk. "I—you've got to take me to the captain. At once!" I guess I had the mate's arm. "Quick! Take me to the captain. I've got to see the captain—"

"Don't worry," the mate snapped; grimly. "You'll see him—"

"You don't understand," I shouted. "I've got to see him right away. Now! He'll have to know. Quick! I'm not a stowaway! I'm with the American consulate at Pahang! I—

there's—there's a criminal aboard this ship. A murderer! I chased him here—"

If my words didn't sound insane I must certainly have looked it. Dancing and yelling and waving my arms, my duck suit clinging in soppy patches, a bump like an ostrich egg bulging out of my brown hair. The bos'n backed off, a club suddenly sprouting in his upraised hand; but the big Scotch mate stared, and took me sternly by the arm.

"Come along, then, and don't try any tricks on Andrew Hague. Captain Lane will be wanting to see you, anyway. If your yarn is true—"

TRUE! WITH THAT knob on my crown, my brains spinning like a squirrel-cage, river-water in my stomach and a headache blasting my skull, I wasn't too sure of anything's veracity. But there was the ship's deck swept by dark rain; ventilators and boat davits leaning out of shadows, a dim funnel reared against the night, a ghostly white bridge. Metal plates trembled underfoot to the jar of deep-bellied marine engines.

Somewhere forward five bells clanged off and a lookout's voice hailed. The deck tilted to the wash of lifting seas. Salt wind smarted on my cheeks; and I was being led forward where loading booms loomed above a battened hatch.

We passed a cabin where light streamed faintly through curtained ports and voices sounded muffled behind a closed door. A steward with a big nose that dripped raindrops, tray balanced in his hand, clattered down a ladder and reeled by, offering a brief: "Bit thick to-night, sor."

I was conducted down an alleyway under the bridge and stopped before a dim screen door. The Scotchman put a hand to the knob; then hesitated. Voices came strident from within. The voice of a man raised in altercation. A woman's flurried speech.

"I told you never to come aboard," the gruff voice was reproving. "You shouldn't have done it, girl—"

I thought I heard the word "trouble"; then the sound of a feminine voice close to tears: "But I wanted to see. I've always wanted to. This ship—and the China Sea—and all. I'm not afraid—of trouble. It was—was fun. My cabin was—"

"Make trouble, I tell you!" the gruff voice rumbled. "I can't do it! Not allowed. You never should have started. Why in the name of heaven at this time—don't you understand? The authorities will get after—"

The Scotch mate's hand closed on my arm. "Passenger in there with the captain. Complaints, I suppose. We'll have to wait. Go to my cabin and you can give me the whole story, there. Come along, and—"

But the screen door suddenly swished open, spilling a blaze of white light. A girl in a raincape stepped over the threshold and slipped past us, hurrying away down the tilting deck. I'd been on the point of charging into the cabin on my own accord; and shaking free of the Scotchman's hand, I did so. Every second counted. Every second we were farther seaward on that steamer, and if I knew anything about it that ship's wireless should have been yelling for the police right then.

The captain was on his feet, standing against a mahogany, book-littered desk. I got an impression of a gray sort of figure, middle-aged, with round stomach straining the gold buttons of a shiny, threadbare coat, white duck trousers baggy at the knees, a saggy, faded face crowned by wisps of thin hair, eyes sunk in an embroidery of fine wrinkles, a worried frown creasing his forehead. The picture of a man who had dedicated his life to the sea, to ships, bad food, quarrelsome passengers, sullen men. His frown on me darkened to an angry scowl.

"What now!"

The Scotch mate began: "Captain Lane—"

Then I heard my voice spouting the wild story. My name. Pahang. "I'm an American!" Walk on water front. Chinese lantern. Murder. Yellow hands. A French sailor—

Somewhere the captain raised a hand to stop me, muttered a word, and the Scotch mate withdrew, closing the screen and a door on top of that. Captain Lane had slumped into a chair. I was spouting again: The shot. The French sailor killed under my eyes. My wild chase. The cloaked assassin racing down the pier. The plunge in the river; race for the boat.

NOW I WAS stopped. Stopped by the look on the captain's face. His head stuck forward on his heavy neck. His flabby hands gripped the arms of his chair. His body was rigid, but his hands and face had gone flabby as paste. The color had drained from his aging cheeks, leaving the skin a queer robin's-egg blue. Sweat glistened on his forehead.

"A sailor!" He was panting. "A French sailor. You saw him—saw him shot dead on the water front. I—and the—the murderer fled for this ship? God! I can't believe it! I should have—But go on. In heaven's name, go on—"

The room was sweltering and there was a smell of lamp-oil and paint. My head was swimming.

"And the murderer climbed a rope!" I blurted. "There

was a rope dangling in the river. I followed. Up the rope. Chased down a companion. Down to a deck below. The tracks led to a bulkhead. The killer had got through and locked it. I ran topside fast as I could. I was going to yell an alarm. But your bos'n thought I was a stowaway, and slugged me over the head. When I came to—it was just a few minutes ago. The mate brought me here. But that killer is aboard this ship, captain. Somewhere down below. Right now. I swear to heaven! And—and you've seen the newspapers? It's been in all the papers! Wanted everywhere. International criminal. Murdered a man right under my eyes, I tell you. The dying sailor told me the name. It's *Bentfinger*—"

A thick oath blew from the captain's sucked-in cheeks. He looked like one struck from behind; with his hands striving to crush the wood arms of the chair, sweat-like beads of hot candle-wax on his upper lip. His boots scuffled for a foothold as he stiffened his elbows and wobbled up out of his chair. "Bentfinger!" he whispered. "Again?"

And suddenly a dark fire came to his sunken eyes. I don't know why I thought so, but it sounded to me like the voice of a judge pronouncing his own death sentence:

"Mr. Benson! As you value your life and the safety of the passengers aboard this—this ship, do as I say. A desperate criminal is on my boat. A fiend. This—this fiend will stop at nothing. Murder—a pastime. Naturally the—the wind is out of my sails. I'll wireless a call to police, of course. But we must be careful. Terribly careful. You know the record of this assassin. A monster of whom nothing is known—save that valuable gems have been the incentive. And shooting to kill. A master-shot. Victims drilled through the temple.

And that fiendish little typed card. And this fiend is now aboard my ship—"

He sponged his forehead with a sleeve. "You must do as I say, Mr. Benson. Change into some of my dry clothes. I've a suit of drill here. Get cleaned up. Later I'll fix things with my steward who also acts as purser—this isn't much of a ship, you understand. Bound for Shanghai, but we'll put in before that. You'll be sent back to Pahang, all right. But for now we'll have to act fast."

He glared at a watch on his wrist. "It's just ten thirty now. This line serves the passengers an evening meal when the boat sails at night. They'll all be in the saloon. Get cleaned up and I'll have the mate take you down there. Join the luncheon. Pretend you're a planter or something. You got aboard this morning at Pahang and have been in your cabin. Headache. Bumped your head. Anything. But for God's sake don't let on. Act as if nothing had happened. Don't tell anything. You'll be all right. Have a whisky. Quick, get started. Understand? I'll be coming down to the saloon." He gulped the drink he had poured for me. "I've—I've something important—terribly important to— tell the passengers, and—" His shaky voice faltered. *"Everything'll be all right, by eleven o'clock…"*

By eleven o'clock!

THE ARCTURUS WAS one of those second-class, six-thousand-ton ocean boats, American owned under British registry, that roll the seas long after they should have been scrapped, tramping from world's end to world's end, carrying freight cargoes and accommodating a chance handful of passengers who can't afford anything better. A framed document above the desk in the captain's cabin told me the ship had been reconditioned in Liverpool, 1906, and was operated by the Champion Line.

Nothing so champion about the ship itself, I found time to observe, rocking aft in the captain's clumsy-fitting drill. Rolling awkwardly in the heavy sea-swell, its decks shuddered to the chug of straining engines, blocks and stanchions creaked out above the thud of waves against the bow. No pleasure yacht, by any manner of means.

The passenger cabins, I noticed, were forward on the main deck. Twelve cabins in all; six doors opening on either side of a fusty corridor that ran lengthwise with the ship and was littered with fire-buckets and life-preservers, and floored with a carpet of brick-colored paint in decidedly ugly contrast to the dirty white woodwork. An electric fan hinted at air in a way to make one wish there was more. I got a glimpse of a deserted smoking room that looked uncomfortable. The dining room was on the deck below, far enough aft to acquire less air and more smells.

I won't forget the dining saloon of the steamship Arcturus. Not that it impressed me just then—my mind was jangling with too many other things. It was a room no better nor worse than the saloon of the average tramp steamer; stuffy and a little seedy with old-fashioned trass lamps depended from the ceiling, a shoddy sideboard near a closed serving-window, a long table of the boarding-house-reach type made maritime by the racks that ran around the table-edge to keep things from spilling in bad weather. A red and white checkered cloth covered the table, and it was lined by rows of swivel chairs like lunch-counter stools, bolted to the floor.

Evidently the passengers of the Arcturus were making

the most of the evening luncheon served by the line. The steward with the big nose was dodging from place to place, pouring tea, and there were plates of sandwiches. Even in the Orient your Englishman must have his "snack."

The scattering of travelers sat about in various attitudes under a buzz of talk as I sauntered into the saloon on the heels of the Scotch mate. I wanted to appear casual, and felt about as casual as a gawk with a lighted bomb in his pocket. As a matter of fact I had a bomb on the tip of my tongue. Somewhere about this ship there skulked a murderous criminal, and here were these passengers gossiping over Bovril on bread. The Scotch ship's officer introduced me around and I nodded a wooden head and said things with a dry tongue.

YOU RUN ACROSS some odd numbers on boats that tramp down the Oriental seas; and the passenger list of the Arcturus was no exception. There was the Dutchman, De Stroon, with close-clipped blond hair crowning a flushed Dutch face, eyes that suggested bouts with the bottle, a cotton coat showing sweat on his shoulders, a striped tie and a melting bat-wing collar rimming a scarlet neck. He was waving a half-consumed sandwich in emphatic argument:

"I live in Baltimore twenty years once, yes! But why should I become American citizen? I told you many times before. You think an American who goes to live in Amsterdam becomes Dutch citizen? Not so!"

He gave me a brief nod on the mate's introduction; then plunged back into his discussion with a Reverend Norwood, a gaunt-faced missionary who sat back on his chair, fingers interlocked on threadbare vest, sun helmet on back of head, deep in contemplation of his traveling-companion's heresy. The reverend had the face of a theologian; and I didn't like him.

No better did I like the looks of the British Army officer, Major Phillipots. Just coming back from a year's furlough, most likely, a devilish grouch with his men. A heavy-shouldered, heavy-handed man with a voice used to bullying command, small eyes in a beefy, unhealthy face, and a mannerism of snorting through his nose. His wife sat across the table from him; and you could tell they quarreled violently about once an hour.

The woman was pompous and bulgy in an unbecoming, beaded gown, wore cheap rings on a fat-wristed hand, had a saggy chin and a discontented mouth and whiny eyes. The brown dye had faded about the roots of her hair; and she would have been a snob if she could have controlled a tendency to drop her "h's." The usual army-life couple stationed in an Asiatic treaty port and living only to grab a pension.

A man named Gorn sat at the place next to Phillipots, his nose buried in a newspaper. He turned as I passed, and I won a brief impression of a swarthy face, unusually dark, with a tight-lipped mouth and bead-quick eyes beneath bushing, wiry eyebrows. His eyes met mine in a rapid, piercing flicker; shifted quickly back to his journal. Gorn. A sullen, unpleasant face one would be likely to remember.

"Silk buyer," the mate informed me with a whisper. "Bound for Japan."

Perhaps the strangest-looking of all was one Dr. Ernest Wonger Smartbeck, who insisted on his full name, and sat munching Bovril sandwiches opposite the silk buyer,

Gorn. Where such creatures come from and go, the good Lord only knows. What do they do on second-class boats in the East?

It was almost as if the man had dressed for a character part in an obvious play. A frock coat that had gone out of style about the time of McKinley's administration. How he must have been sweltering in the thing! A fussy shirt-front ruined by a spot of egg. Nervous hands that fingered chunks of sandwich, rolled the bread into little balls and popped the little balls into a colorless mouth. Eyes like white raisins behind pince-nez glasses that gleamed in an angular face. And a great burst of gray hair that stood out fuzzy on his head, so that Dr. Ernest Wonger Smartbeck, thin and nervous-faced with a skinny body, looked not unlike a dandelion with a blossom that was ready to blow away.

IN FACT, THE only normally decent-looking couple in the saloon of the Arcturus was the one at the table's end. The chap introduced as Stephen Blair looked like a hundred other planters I'd seen heading far East. Dressed in neat English drill. A face that might have been thirty or forty. Clean-shaved, quiet-voiced, a companionable pipe in a lean hand, eyes that could be amused.

He was chuckling to the girl and helping her to a fresh cup of tea as I came up. They looked up curiously, and I suppose I stared back at the girl. Brown, her name was. A Miss Brown. I suddenly remembered the conversation overheard in the captain's cabin. But the girl looked way above all right.

Her hair was a dark curly bob—"shingled" I believe they call it—giving an independent set to a nicely molded head. Gray eyes and short British nose. A cool white frock that could look decent and expensive in that shabby background. A frank mouth that quirked in the quick smiles. Her eyes were quizzical on my loose-fitting costume; and the chap, Blair, dealt me a searching glance.

The fact is, I must have been something of a sight, for the bump was still there on my head, a nice scratch forked down my cheek, and I know I was pale. Believe me, I was on tenterhooks as I slumped into the chair at a vacant place between the girl and the elongated Dr. Smartbeck. Every nerve in me was yanking with apprehension; I could not keep uneasy eyes off the door that made entrance to the saloon; and I wanted to keep a hand on the pistol which I'd remembered to transfer to the pocket of my dry drill coat. Thank heaven I'd transferred my pipe, also. The trusty brier had dried out and it gave me something to fiddle with.

The steward with the big nose cat-footed behind me with a cup of tea, gave me an obsequious cockney smile, and slipped out of the saloon. The chap named Blair, noticing my pipe, proffered a friendly tobacco pouch. Dr. Ernest Wonger Smartbeck removed his pince-nez, polished the lenses on the shiny cuff of his frock coat with a fussy gesture, the while he fixed me with a pale fishy eye, as if expecting me to make an overture that would explain my late appearance aboard ship. Mrs. Major Phillipots craned her neck so that her head appeared around the corner of his shoulder.

"You'd better not smoke, Mr. Benson, if you've been seasick. I tell Major Phillipots that the smell of his tobacco is enough to—"

"I haven't been," I denied. "Just a trifle headachy.

Bumped my head when I came aboard at Pahang this morning—"

I saw the newspaper lowered in the hands of the man named Gorn. His fingers moved a loose sheet to one side and the black eyes beneath the bushy brows gave me a stealthy scrutiny. It wasn't that glance which made the prickles sting on the back of my neck. It was the news-sheet the man had been reading. Quickly he lifted the paper, but not before I had caught a glimpse of the head-lines. An old copy of the Bombay *Empire* it was, and stark across the top of the page a black headline. "Ghost Killer Terrorizes City"—

"But the ceilings of the cabins are so dreadfully low, no wonder." Dr. Smartbeck's voice was a fluty treble. Flirting a handkerchief from his cuff he blew a blast on his thin nose. "Dear me, I hope you'll like the ship, though heaven knows it isn't too carefully appointed. I knew I should have taken an Indo-China Line boat, but the agents assured me this one was a splendid vehicle. The food isn't too frightful—"

"It's beastly!" Major Phillipots's head turned on its doughy neck and he delivered the lean dandelion a sneer of undisguised contempt. His voice was crass. "Worst meals I've ever been served in my life. Too much curry. Stale meat. Wine like dishwater. Humph!"

"I *like* the ship." It was the girl's voice. "It's been fun. I was just telling Mr. Blair—"

Mr. Blair laughed pleasantly and said: "Righto, Miss Brown," in a London accent. At the other end of the table, the Reverend Norwood leaned across the checkered cloth, and in the tone of a sermon offered: "When I was going to China for the first time, I took a P. and O. to Calcutta, and—" Something or other; and the Dutchman, De Stroon, evidently satisfied with the outcome of his argument on citizenship, said nothing, but grinned a mouthful of gold teeth, drank loudly from his teacup, wiped a crumb from his chin and reached for another sandwich.

BY THIS TIME I was ready to fly to pieces like a smashed alarm clock. Pictures conjured in my brain, making the bread in my mouth taste like chalk. The face of a French sailor, bloodied with death. Yellow hands clawing out of darkness. A mouth so twisted as to seem toothless, cackling mockery. A phantasmal shadow flickering down a long pier with a glim at its end. A blowing cape. A weird amorphous figure that might have been dreamed, might have been man or woman or animal. Newspaper headlines. Gunflame in gloom. Bentfinger.

Intoning voices swam the air about me. I was conscious of an automatic nodding, of making dull response to the clicking, useless chatter. But there was that pistol so heavy in my pocket, and the floor beneath me, throbbing to ship's engines, drummed a faint repetend. Somewhere below. Somewhere below. Somewhere below.

And where the devil was Captain Lane? The Scotch mate, standing in the saloon doorway, kept looking uneasily up the companion leading topside. It gave me a measure of comfort to see the big Scotchman there. There was a competence about his Highland jaw and blue eye good to see. A capable man in emergency, this First Mate Hague.

But what was the captain doing? No doubt the wireless operator was busy at the radio, sparking the news to shore. Probably the ship's crew was armed and combing the decks below, engine room and hold. My ear was out stiff as tin ready to catch the first sound of commotion. There was only the undertone of thudding water and chugging turbines. But something off the books hung in the air. Captain Lane's face had gone strange up there in his cabin. He hadn't looked right. An undercurrent somewhere in the man. What had he known? What was he going to tell?

Suddenly the captain was there in the saloon doorway. It had scarcely been twenty minutes since I'd left him in his cabin; on my word he seemed older by forty years. He stood swaying with the tilt of the ship, his cap over his eyes, one hand in a weighted pocket. And I got a shock! His mouth was half open and his face wore the expression of a man paralyzed. The mate looked startled; and the captain walked slowly to a chair at the head of the table, leaned on his palms for a moment—you could hear him breathing—sat down.

The passengers were startled, too. Captain Lane sat at that end with the girl on one hand and the chap, Blair, on the other. He was facing the length of the board; every eye in the saloon turned on him. The girl uttered a stifled exclamation, and Blair made a move as if to rise. I saw Gorn drop his newspaper to the cloth, and the Dutchman, De Stroon, staring above the rim of his halted teacup. I heard the Reverend Norwood whisper something; Dr. Smartbeck reared nervously; the major's wife dropped a spoon that rang like a gong; Major Phillipots turned in his chair.

"I—" Captain Lane had trouble working his tongue. Once more he was gripping the arms of his chair with hands that seemed to be made of bread-dough. "As passengers of the Arcturus, you—Being captain, I—I'm—You must listen. There's—something—I've got to tell you—"

Sweat glittered on his struggling face. "I've got to tell you—"

But Captain Lane never told. At that very instant the saloon was plunged into Stygian darkness. There followed a deafening *smash!* A spurt of red flame tore the black. Screams and a smell of burned powder. A voice shrieked: *"The lights!"* The electric lamps glowed their blatant glare, and the room burst afresh on our vision.

I shall never forget that tableau. Never! The girl standing with wax hands pressed tight against her mouth. The Scotch mate, a queer carving in the doorway. The major's wife contracting her bulges somehow and fainting, collapsed like an emptied balloon. Still, the movement did not break the picture, nor the thump on the floor break the silence. All the others were stiff on their feet. All, that is, save Captain Lane.

Captain Lane still sat, hands gripping the arms of his chair. But his head had dropped, chin on chest, and his eyes stared, unmoving, at a card on the tablecloth before him. A rag of gray smoke drifted over the card, and a cold breeze from somewhere came to blow the smoke away. A scarlet brook ran from a puncture above the captain's left eye; streamed into the collar on his throat. Blood wiggled from the captain's left sleeve and seeped across the crystal of the watch that ticked loud on his wrist. It was eleven o'clock.

3

UNEXPECTED IDENTITIES!

"**DON'T ANY OF** you try to leave this room!" The voice of the Scotch mate knifed through the quiet. A blue-steel Luger automatic nested in his hand; made him gigantic in the doorway. His mouth had gone to a thin white line. His jutting jaw quivered. "Stay right where you are—"

His speech brought a reality to the scene that had not been there before. A number of things happened, then. I recall the sound of footsteps running across the decks above; faint calls. Wind whipping from an open porthole and freezing the moisture on my cheeks. Dr. Smartbeck gnawing his knuckles. The Dutchman marble-eyed, with his mouth open and gold teeth shining. Blair wiping his throat with a handkerchief. The Reverend Norwood gasping: "God's mercy! God's mercy!" Major Phillipots clawing to loosen the collar under his chin and wetting his lips with a pink tongue. Gorn, balancing with hands in coat pockets, his face gone to dark stone, black eyes riveted on the captain. The girl smitten motionless, stunned by horror, all color drained from her cheeks.

As for me, I could only take my eyes from that dreadful little card on the tablecloth to glare from face to face, nearer to stark panic than I'd ever been in my life. That was the second brief picture; then it blew into a hump-ty-dumpty scene as feelings were relieved by a torrent of words, hand-wavings, yells.

The Dutchman's gold mouth blattering: "Who turned out those lights?"

The missionary's hoarse: "He's dead!"

The major bawling: "It came from over there, I tell you. The shot came from *there!*"

Dr. Smartbeck shrilling jargon.

Gorn snatching up the little white card, pocketing it with an oath, shaking Blair by the arm. "Do something!"

Major Phillipots grabbing across the table at Smartbeck. "Help! You're a doctor—"

Smartbeck's hysterical: "Doctor? I'm a Doctor of Philosophy. I'm an epistemologist. I'm going to my cabin and—"

Bobbing hands. Faces working as if yanked by strings. Fingers pointing. The saloon deafening with a swelling whirl of words, hoarse, shrill, wild. Until lights and shadows danced together in jabberwock confusion; the tilting, stifling room fairly rang; and I was dimly conscious, through the turmoil, of seeing the girl, Miss Brown, go down on her knees beside that chair of death, catch at the inert captain with butterfly hands, crying: "Oh, no. No. No. Please, no!"

THANK HEAVEN FOR men like First Mate Hague, for his voice had never stopped. Men from outside came into the saloon, and the captain was better with a kindly cloth over his face and gone. And the Scotchman was thundering: "Quiet, all of you. Quiet!" Searing every one of us with a white-hot eye and ordering us in a row against the sideboard behind the table. "I'm in command now. What I say

Benson groped through the smoke toward the girl's cabin

is' law." His gun covered us where we stood in line. "I'll kill the first one of you to make a false move. I saw that card on the table. I saw where that shot came from, too. It came from somewhere at that table. *Some one of you fired that—*"

"I didn't fire it!" Major Phillipots bellowed from a purple face. "It came from the other side of the table. From that end—"

"It did not!" Dr. Smartbeck shrieked. "It came from your side! It came from down there at that end where—"

"That's a lie." The voice of the Dutchman, De Stroon, shook with fear and anger, and he stabbed a glance of hate at the fuzzy-headed Smartbeck. "Could I have fired that shot without a gun? I haff no gun. Herr Gott! You all look at me! I am looking at this man, this missionary. This Reverend Norwood. *Ja.* He has a gun. I saw him loading it in his cabin last night. The door was open—"

"That isn't true!" the missionary panted. "This Dutchman's insane! Why should I—a man of God—carry arms? Why should I have slain the good Captain Lane? How could I? I tell you that shot came from down there by that man—" He pointed toward Blair.

"But it didn't!" Blair rasped. "I'll prove it. It didn't come from this end—not from me. Good heavens, I can't tell where—"

"It seemed to come from the *middle* of the table," the man named Gorn snarled. I thought he glanced at me; then he was glaring boldly at First Mate Hague. "Any one here could have fired that shot, yes. Grabbed out a concealed gun, leaned across the table in the pitch dark; fired. Any of us could have done it. Any of us. You're an army man, Phillipots. Used to guns. You, De Stroon. And Blair, here. Planters. Mean to say you never carry arms? The women, too. And the missionary. All of us. This man, Benson, had a gun on him when he came into the saloon to-night. I saw the lump in his pocket. Hold us up, Hague. Give us a search—"

"I think," Blair growled, interrupting Gorn's unexpected speech, "that a gun-hunt will do no good. The lights went out. The shot. Then you see that open porthole? That's where the gun went. The killer threw it out of that port. I heard you, Smartbeck, ask the steward to open that port—"

"For air!" Dr. Smartbeck screamed. "You fiends are plotting against me. You murderers!" He rocked back and forth on his heels, his face twisting beneath the dandelion blossom. "I am an epistemologist. A student of theories on cognition. A college professor—"

"Who turned out the lights?" Norwood raised his yell. "That's the killer. Find out who—"

"*Ja!*" De Stroon squalled. "And if any one could do the shooting, how about this woman on the floor under the table? So! The wife of this army major. *Ja!* How about her, too, so—"

Faster and faster went the voices. Faster and faster spun the room. Hints. Accusations. Denials. I remember how the Scotch ship's officer waited, like rock, immobile, grim, purposeful in the din, his gun unswerving to catch the first break. I remember how Mrs. Major Phillipots crawled out from under the table, stood tottering with breast aheave and cheap jewels glittering, gave one wild stare at the captain's empty chair and fainted, again. I remember how the girl stood at the end of the line, motionless, her face in her white hands. How the rest of us jigged in line like so many lunatics, waiting for more to happen.

MORE HAPPENED, ALL right. Vaguely I was aware that the doorway behind the Scotch mate had become crowded with armed sailors who watched us down the barrels of leveled Winchesters. A man with a black beard and an officer's cap wearing the insignia of second mate dodged across the floor at a word from his superior, and stepped down the line of us, patting pockets. All but two of us were guiltless of firearms. But the hip pocket of the silk buyer, Gorn, divulged a 9-mm. Luger automatic that had not been fired. From me, you understand, he filched a Webley that had been jammed. The two guns clattered on the checkered cloth.

"No others armed, sir."

And then, because things happen without rime or reason, a red-headed young Britisher, the ship's third officer, burst through the wedge guarding the saloon doorway, and flung words and gestures at the mate:

"The radio, sir! Cabin's empty! Sparks ain't there, sir! He's

gone. Can't find him nowheres. Bos' says he seen him last
at two bells off duty an' headin' for a scoff up in the mess
room. Then—it was just before all them lights went out
aboard us, sir—the bos' says he seen Captain Lane headin'
for the radio room in a hurry. Whether Sparks was on
deck then or not, the bos' don't know. But Sparks ain't to
be found. I've had the whole watch out huntin', but there
ain't no trace of that operator. But his cabin's open, sir. And
the radio instruments are *smashed*—"

A hundred times I'd opened my mouth and nothing
had come out. Now the words came like a torrent; I heard
myself blurting the mad story of my own part in this
jabberwocky—the chase back in Pahang, my boarding
of the Arcturus, the yellow hands, the queer assassin, the
murder of the French sailor, my talk with Captain Lane.

A weird concerted cry went up when I bawled out the
name: "Bentfinger!" And my listeners yelled when I stammered the climax:

"Captain Lane was going to wireless the police. And
he was coming down here to tell us something important. Terribly important, he said. Perhaps he knew who—
who Bentfinger was. Perhaps he was going to tell! And it's
Bentfinger who killed him. Bentfinger! Right here in this
saloon! Bentfinger—"

Everybody yelled, then. The Phillipots woman, just
balanced on her feet, went down for the third time. The
Scotch officer glared at the jammed gun which had come
from my pocket; and the dark-faced Gorn suddenly
stepped out of line, tossed on the checkered cloth the typed
card, snarling:

"There it is. There's the name. A typed card. And the

captain drilled through the temple. The devil is among us—"

"*That girl!*" The missionary, Norwood, was pointing a shaky hand. "Where did *she* come from? She's been on the boat with the rest of us since we left Bombay." His voice quavered to a high key. "That Bentfinger murder was in Bombay the night this boat sailed. You remember the papers? It might have been a woman! And you remember? There was a murder in Cairo when our ship was there—"

"*Ja!*" De Stroon's gold teeth glowed. "And when we were laid up on this devil's craft in Marseilles there was also a slaying. Pearls were stolen from a hotel. So. You recall, Herr Major, the papers? You were on the boat, too, Herr Blair. And it was Dr. Smartbeck, *ja,* who came up the gangway just as we sailed, with the dreadful news and terror-stricken because he had stayed that day in the Grand Hôtel! And so when we were in London and Marseilles and Cairo and Bombay, there were these Bentfinger killings! *Ja!* But this girl came on that night at Bombay and hid in her cabin— it was next to mine—and I heard her bribe the steward to tell nobody she was aboard until we were out at sea—"

"And I," snarled Phillipots, "heard her quarreling with the captain to-night. I'd stepped on deck for a breath of air. Even in the rain it's better on deck than inside this hell-ship. There was a light in the skipper's cabin. They were quarreling, I tell you. Distinctly I heard this woman's voice. Then I came down to the saloon and she turned up a few minutes later; looked all upset"

A WRY SMILE twisted across the lips of the silk buyer, Gorn. His black eyes fixed on the girl.

"So you *were* in that hotel ballroom in Bombay, Miss

Brown." His words clipped out short, metallic. "I thought
I saw you there that night. I passed the door just after
the murders in the garden and saw you dodging away to
a motor on the avenue. I came aboard the Arcturus at
Bombay, too. And I asked you in the smoking room that
night if you'd been at the *talookdar's* ball and you denied
it. But you can't deny that you ran past my cabin door in
soaking wet clothes, drenched from head to toe, about the
time this man Benson says this cloaked assassin—and *you*
had on a cloak—boarded this ship. You weren't to be seen
around at sailing time. I know because I looked for you—"

"But none of us were around then, Gorn," Blair interrupted. "When the Arcturus cleared Pahang it was pouring rain, and—"

And then the girl's hands were down from her face,
and she was staring. Staring at us, wide-eyed. Her cheeks
the color of snow. Dark hair gleaming against a forehead
drawn with pain. Bravely she faced the row of passengers,
the commanding Scotchman with the massive gun, the
crowding sailors on guard. Her voice was so low it could
scarcely be heard above the creak of the swinging ship and
faraway grinding of engines.

"I would give my life to find the—the one who killed
Captain Lane," she said quietly. "I did not do it. Captain
Lane was my father—"

"Good God!" The exclamation came from Blair. The
young British planter seemed the only one left of us with
any wits about him. Sympathy in his face, he stepped
toward the girl, reaching to take her by the hand. In crossing the floor he kicked something that had been lying in
shadow under his chair. The object slithered into view; lay

limp on the floor at my very feet. It had been lying, under Blair's chair, you understand, and by accident he kicked it into light. A glove, it was. A floppy, large-size, yellow cotton glove. A glove to match the one I'd picked up in that Pahang alley and given to Captain Lane.

I stared at the thing in horror. The Scotch mate barked a sharp oath. Stooping quickly, he grabbed up the yellow glove and tossed it on the table. "It was under your chair, Blair," he snarled harshly. "Stand back, there, and put up your hands—"

"Righto." Blair stepped against the table with hands aloft. I saw him glare at the glove, intently. Then he turned on First Mate Hague, stern-mouthed.

"I'm afraid you've forced me to it," he declared grimly. "And I'm beginning to take some stock in this fellow Benson's story. I've got a few things to go on, now. Didn't want to show anything till I did have. But you'll find the papers in my pocket, Hague. *Captain* Hague, it is from now on, I suppose. Well, you've done very well so far, Captain Hague. Put up your gun and I'll take over the job from now on. My name's Blair, but I'm not a planter. The notes in my pocket will tell you who I am. I'm from Scotland Yard."

4

LITTLE WHITE LIES!

WE SAT—A GROTESQUE group of passengers, I can tell you—in the smoking room; and I, for one, was relieved. I was relieved to get out of that dining saloon, and relieved to see among us a man who could flourish the credentials of Scotland Yard.

"You'd best get busy running the ship," Inspector Blair had instructed the Scotch first officer. "I'll handle the murder investigation. Send a hand down to the engineer and try to find if some one below threw that lighting system out of gear. Get a line on our radio operator, too. We've got to try and repair those wireless instruments. I'm afraid I should have jumped on the case at the start. But I didn't want it known there was a headquarters man aboard at first. Wanted to let everybody talk and act freely."

He turned on the passengers. "You're all under arrest. Every one on this ship is under arrest. But you who were here in the saloon when Captain Lane was shot will have special attention. I'm certain that shot came from the table. Then the gun was flung through that open port. Bentfinger and one of you are one and the same. I'm going to get you, Bentfinger. Before God, I'm going to. Captain Hague, we'll march these people into the smoking room. I want a steward to search their cabins for arms. I'll talk to these suspects right now—"

He stood in the smoking room door, facing us. The smoking room of the Arcturus was dreary; a scatter of hard-backed funereal chairs, a bare table showing wine-stains, a loud-creaking floor, a wall dull with two pictures of sailing ships, a card of lifeboat instructions, a photograph of the Sleeping Buddha of Hakai. Brass gaboons jangling against a bench and a decaying rubber plant flopping limp in a corner. But the smoking room was on the deck above the dining saloon—not quite far enough above to be Paradise, yet a vast lungful of improvement just the same.

It was hard to believe, once away from that fatal dining saloon, that any murder had happened. It was harder to believe that one of the number about me was the terrible assassin whose name meant a scourge in ports half around the world. Harder still to believe that the face of the demon I had chased across Pahang could have been owned by one of these passengers.

De Stroon with his gold teeth? And yet the lips in the face of the assassin had been sucked in—perhaps to hide such betraying marks. The Reverend Norwood with his long flat cheeks and blue nose and wry mouth? Major Phillipots with his red jowls? Bulgy Mrs. Phillipots with the moons stained under her eyes? The pale, gray-eyed girl? The fuzzy-wigged, chittering Dr. Smartbeck? Gorn, swarthy and somber and narrow-eyed?

But the light from that damned Chinese lantern had been dismally bad. My whole brain had focused on those ghastly yellow hands. I was forced to confess that I could no more recall the exact look of that demonlike assas-

sin-face than I could recall the details of a nightmare; and
I glared at the group about me in mounting apprehension. The assassin might have been anybody. And evidence
proved it was one of them. The hair kept rising on my head
at the question: "Which one?"

IF YOU THINK the little grouping in the smoking room
was a festive meeting you are wrong. My fellow passengers (but one of them was surely faking) were every bit as
wild-brained as I was. Major Phillipots blustered, glared,
made fists and threats.

"So one of you is this bloody killer, eh? Well, I'm watching all of yuh! Keep an eye on these birds, inspector! I'd feel
better if I could have my gun—

De Stroon wiped his face and lapsed into a chatter of
Dutch while his eyes never stopped a scared roving.

Mrs. Phillipots sat on the edge of her chair, panting.
"If you keep me here one more minute I shall scream. I'll
faint. I'll die. I've a bad heart, and I can't stand this. Not
another minute—"

The missionary was sunk in his chair like an empty suit
of clothes, frightened to a faint whispering.

The girl (she sat next to me, and suddenly, out of all my
mental rioting, I was conscious of lovely brown hair) was
quiet, marble-white, twisting a bit of lace in pale fingers.

Dr. Ernest Wonger Smartbeck told who he was at
least forty times in the voice of a piccolo, bit his fingers,
announced he expected to be shot to sponge any minute,
and called on Heaven, Inspector Blair, the United States
and Aristotle to save an innocent man from undeserved
death.

Gorn sat back in his chair and studied the room through narrowed eyelids.

Blair sponged his face with a handkerchief. "None of you are going to be shot. There's not a gun among you and our new captain is behind me, armed and ready to kill at a sign of alarm. One of you before me is a killer. I'm not fool enough to expect an easy discovery of that one. Bentfinger. Well, Bentfinger, whoever you are I've got you right here.

"You, Norwood, De Stroon, Major and Mrs. Phillipots, and Smartbeck, you've been on the Arcturus ever since it left London River. So have I. The Arcturus made port in Marseilles, Cairo and Bombay. In Marseilles, Cairo and Bombay this Bentfinger played red-handed while the Arcturus lay loading in the harbor. I, a Scotland Yard operator detailed to watch another party on this ship, made no connection between the Bentfinger case and the itinerary of the Arcturus. Headquarters hadn't assigned me that case—yet.

"I was only to stay on this tramp steamer until we made Shanghai. But I was not too unawake to the curious coincidence of the Arcturus leaving port on the day this Bentfinger had struck that same port. In Bombay, you, Miss Brown, and you, Gorn, came aboard. You, Benson, boarded us in Pahang. Your extraordinary story will bear inspection. Close inspection. Yet—I received a cable from London when we docked in Pahang this morning. A cable that set me on the Bentfinger case. Scotland Yard had now decided that the killer was aboard this ship. I'm now certain that Bentfinger sat with us at the table to-night when Captain Lane came to tell a secret that would have betrayed the assassin. Whoever you are, Bentfinger, you worked well. I'll get you—and I'll get you to-night—"

"THREATS!" AN UNEXPECTED sneer came from Gorn. "You can't bullyrag us this way, Blair, until you establish the right authority. You've arrested us here without any warrants. We're all under his majesty the—"

"See for yourself, Mr. Gorn," Blair said evenly, extending a sheaf of documents. "Scotland Yard needs no warrant in this case—"

The silk buyer glared at the papers. I thought I caught a most curious expression on his face—an expression I was, later, to remember. "Full authority, all right," Gorn muttered. "There's the seal of headquarters. Cabled authority from chief inspector to Inspector Blair. But—All right, you can do as you please with the lot of us."

"You seem," Blair snapped, "to know something of Scotland Yard, Mr. Gorn. I gave you a look at my papers to see if you did."

"I had business with the Yard once before," Gorn countered quietly. "Business in Tokio. I—"

"What business did you have in Bombay, the day of the Bentfinger murders there, Mr. Gorn?"

"The business of waiting for a cheap passage to Japan," Gorn growled. "I'd spent a week there. Lived at Crown Hotel. My home is in England. Bedford, England. I'm a silk buyer for Hilton and Curtis, Ltd."

"Hilton and Curtis of London? Good. Then, of course, you'll have letters, papers, something to identify your affiliation with them?" Blair drew from his pocket a little blue leather notebook and jotted an item. "Can you show something of that order? And your passport?"

"Naturally. There are some letters on the shelf in my cabin." Gorn fumbled in his coat. "My passport—"

Blair glanced over the little booklet bearing the seal of Great Britain; returned it with a cheerless smile. "You were in Bombay the night of the killing by Bentfinger. Below in the saloon you told Miss Brown you'd seen her at the ball in the Asian Queen Hotel. What were you doing in that vicinity?"

Gorn moved in his chair. "An affair like that would be of local interest, wouldn't it? I saw the crowd in the hotel foyer, and hung about. Curiosity. Might see some of the celebrities. All the big bugs were supposed to be there. I was standing around looking on when this girl, here, came hustling through the crowd. She had such a—a sort of frightened expression on her face I was curious. Minute later the word got around of the murder on the terrace. The place was in an infernal uproar, and I got down to the Bund. I'd booked passage on the Arcturus that same morning. But my letters will tell who I am, all right—"

Blair seemed to be satisfied. I thought an expression of relief crossed his face. He scribbled in his book a moment; turned on the officer behind him. "Mr. Hague, will you please go to Mr. Gorn's cabin and look for the letters on the shelf? Righto. One thing more, Mr. Gorn. Bentfinger struck in Cairo, Marseilles, London. And first in New York, America. Can you have been in those cities during those episodes?"

Gorn nodded approvingly. "I was waiting for that. Of course my alibi's established. I've never been in those cities, Mr. Blair. I sailed straight from London to Bombay on the Chelidra."

BLAIR SWUNG ON De Stroon. "Jan De Stroon, you're on
the books as a planter bound for Shanghai. You've been
with us on this craft ever since she left London. Of course
you went ashore in Marseilles when we were held up there.
Cairo and Bombay and Pahang, too. Unhappily for me this
whole crowd who sailed out of London seems to have gone
ashore at those fatal ports. But were you in New York at
the time of the Bentfinger diamond robberies?"

"No!" De Stroon wiped his face and gurgled. "I haff
never been in New York City, Herr Inspector—"

"When in the States you lived in Baltimore?"

Ja. And when I sail to England I sail from Baltimore,
and—"

"You're lying, De Stroon," Blair asserted icily. "Our first
night out from London I overheard you, right here in this
smoking room, tell Major Phillipots you'd sailed from
America on the Atlantic Transport liner, Minnekhada.
Permit me to remind you that the Minnekhada is famous
for making its slow run only between New York and
London. So you *have* been in New York."

"Only for one day," De Stroon blurted desperately. "I
was—"

"Herr De Stroon, your record for truth-telling is shaky. I
want facts. Now, then, one night at dinner on the Red Sea
did you not show Captain Lane a medal you'd won some
years before in the Dutch Colonial army? Yes. A medal for
sharpshooting, it was. A medal for winning a pistol-shoot-
ing championship. You are, then, a crack pistol shot, De
Stroon. And the man who shot Captain Lane through the
temple to-night, the killer who slays always with a bullet
through the temple, is a master marksman, too." His eyes

were steel points, stabbing the Dutchman. "I'm noting these facts, De Stroon—"

"I'm no assassin!" the Dutchman yelled. "With this devils affair I haff nothing to do—"

"That," growled Blair sternly, "remains to be seen. Major Phillipots, it would be better if *you* told the strict truth. You showed me your passport once before. You're returning to join a Shanghai regiment after a year's leave, I believe. I take it you're no bungler with weapons. Now you and your wife were ashore in all the ports under suspicion, save, perhaps, New York. Tell me, major, did you and your wife chance to travel in America during this year of leave?"

The army officer stiffened in his chair; played at his collar with nervous fingers. "In—in New York? Why, no. The wi—Mrs. Phillipots and me, sir, can prove our innocence easily. You're wasting your time on us, sir. Ridiculous to believe me—or her—capable of being criminals. I've been in the colonial service for twenty years. My record, sir—"

"Can be easily established," Blair admitted. "But every one who sat at that dining table is under suspicion, major. But then, of course, if you've never been in New York that lets you out of it. Mrs. Phillipots, you back your husband up in these statements?"

Mrs. Phillipots appeared capable of backing her husband up in nothing. Hands on her stormy and voluminous bosom, she strangled out a stream of words calculated to assure the world that her husband, though nothing to brag about, was not quite an assassin, and that she, herself, was the acme of respectability, though God knew she'd be in a madhouse if the killer in their midst wasn't captured within five minutes. Just as she was ending her plea with a histrionic account of her ailing nervous system, Dr. Smartbeck jumped out of his chair.

"THAT MAN!" HE shrieked, pointing at Major Phillipots. "I've been trying all along to remember. Listen. Our boat lay in at Alexandria and everybody spent the week in Cairo. The very day of our sailing—that afternoon—the Bentfinger murders—my God, there were four people slain!—took place. The ship sailed at midnight. I was near the gangway. All the passengers were in the smoking room talking about the murder. All but that major, there. He was not yet aboard. Just as they drew up the gangway he came aboard ship. It was dark, but I saw his face. There was a red smear on his right cheek. It looked like blood. He hurried down the deck brushing it away. It *was* blood—fresh blood—" Dr. Smartbeck shrilled in excitement. "I remember, now. Blood—"

The major shot to his feet. The major's wife slithered out of her chair and bumped the floor with a thud. "Let her lie," the army officer snorted ungraciously. "She'll be throwing faints all over the place. Besides, she needn't hear what I've got to say. In the first place this fuzzy-haired professor is a blithering jackass. Look here, it's nobody's damned business and I won't go into it. But this fool of a Soviet spy or whatever he is with his piano-player's wig happened to see rouge on my cheek. Lip rouge. There was a—a lady—a friend of mine came down to see me off. And as for you, Smartbeck, didn't *you* stay at the Grand Hôtel in Marseilles? The very place where Bentfinger killed that French official's wife and stole her string of black pearls? I don't think," the major sat down with a snort, "you'd have nerve to stick a pin in a wax dummy. But you never can tell," he added savagely.

"But I have never been in New York or fired a gun in my life," the learned one screeched, imploring hands stretched toward Blair. "I'm Doctor Ernest Wonger Smartbeck, of the Philosophy Department at Williams College. Taking a sabbatical year for my health. I wanted a slow boat to tour the world on. I'm to study the oriental philosophers in their pristine environment and I'm writing my last volume on the theory of cognition. I'm an epistemologist: study the grounds for the validity of—"

"Great Lord!" Major Phillipots snarled. "Must we hear all that again?"

"Study the validity of human knowledge," Dr. Smartbeck went on. "I'm writing my book with Professor Burl of Columbia University. Many an hour I've spent with the famous professor who wrote the only answer to Kant's—"

"You've worked in coöperation with the Columbia philosopher?" Blair snapped. "Spent hours with him—"

"And all you'll have to do to absolutely establish my identity," Dr. Smartbeck declared with a triumphant gesture, "is cable him. I was well along in my work, too, until that dreadful murder in the Grand Hôtel. I haven't been able to concentrate since. Fearful. Was just leaving the hotel when the ghastly alarm was given, and—"

"And you've never been in New York," Blair clipped out, "yet you've spent hours at Columbia University, there, with a famous professor. One lie hints at a whole framework of them, Dr. Smartbeck. From now on I'll believe nothing of you save the fact that you *might* be a dead pistol shot, a connoisseur of precious gems and an artist at fabrication."

He wrote at length in his notebook, while Dr. Smartbeck wriggled and sweated on the edge of his seat, gasping: "But Professor Burl came up to Williamstown—"

MEANTIME NORWOOD AND Major Phillipots had propped Mrs. Phillipots once more in her chair. She was thanking Norwood with feeble nods when Blair called on the missionary.

"You've been in New York City, Norwood?"

"I sailed from there," he said in a toneless voice. "My home in the States is Elkhart, Indiana. I am sent to China by the Free Methodist Church, my dear sir. Here is a testament presented to me by the Lovers of the Lord Society of Elkhart—a fine, upstanding group of ladies they are, too—on the eve of my departure." He drew from his pocket the little book. "It will serve to identify me in place of the passport which I can't seem to find anywhere in my—"

"You've lost your passport?"

"I fear so, inspector. Just yesterday when we were docked in Pahang I looked for it and it was gone. Misplaced, no doubt—"

"Tell me," Blair interjected. "How does it happen a missionary is seen loading a revolver in his cabin? Back in the dining saloon, De Stroon mentioned the fact that he had seen you servicing your gun." The Englishman motioned with a hand. "You denied that you owned such a gun."

"But I *saw* it!" De Stroon announced firmly.

The Reverend Norwood twisted in his chair with a passionate grimace. Then he controlled himself with a visible effort. A pious smile replaced the snarl that had started on his lips. "You are mistaken, my dear man. I cannot imag-

ine what you saw. But your eyes deceived you. I carry—or
carried—no weapon. I am a man of peace. Come to heal
the souls of countless heathen, to carry a message—"

"But," Blair interrupted with a show of annoyance, "if
you had no passport, how did you pass the customs and
shore officials at Pahang while the Arcturus lay at dock?"

"Praise the Lord, there is my alibi," the missionary
intoned. "I was not ashore in Pahang, neither was I ashore
in Bombay where the fiendish murder of the rajah took
place. I stayed on the Arcturus. The very hour when the
people were slain in Bombay, the very hour when this assassin dealt death in Pahang, I, of all these other passengers,
was on board ship. The others were somewhere ashore. I
stayed aboard."

"You remained on the Arcturus? Did any one see you
aboard during those times, my man?"

Norwood looked about him with a self-satisfied smile
that was almost a leer on his theological face. "Exactly. I
spent the whole time talking with Mr. Dunlop, the ship's
radio operator."

"And," Blair's voice grated, "insomuch as the ship's radio
operator has totally disappeared it would seem there is no
way of checking your statement." The Englishman sighed.
"It's your turn, Miss Brown," he continued in a kindly tone.
"I'm sorry. This dreadful affair has worn all of us to a beastly
state. It's late. I'll hurry this up so we can go. I'm frightfully
sorry to have to question you, but I'm afraid you're in this,
too. At—in the saloon, below, you said Captain Lane was
your father. Please explain that statement, and tell me all
you can about yourself."

5

A PREMONITION

NOW ALL OF us stared at the girl. She took a deep breath, looked straight at the man before her, and began in a level voice: "Captain Lane was my foster-father. My own parents were Americans. My father was in the embassy at London; died there before I was born. I was born on the boat when my mother was returning to her home in New York. My mother died at my birth. Captain Lane, then first officer of the ship, adopted me. I kept the name, Hope Brown—the name I was to have had. And Captain Lane was the only parent I ever knew. He—he was splendid to me; put me through school in New York. Sometimes I traveled with him. On White Star and Anchor Line ships. Then—about a year ago—he went with the Champion Line.

"He made several South American runs as master of this boat. Then he sailed her to London. I think he'd expected to bring her right back from London, but he cabled me that the ship had been commissioned for a run to the Far East. From a letter I judged that something was not quite right. He seemed uneasy about something. Then I got a letter postmarked Marseilles. It sounded unhappy and—and queer, somehow. He didn't like the boat. He didn't want to go on. It would probably be his last voyage."

The girl shook her head. "It wasn't like father to write that way. I—I was frightened and cabled him that I'd catch him in Cairo if I could. He told me not to try. I caught a fast boat to England, and the Champion offices, there, told me I might catch the Arcturus as it had been tied up in Marseilles with engine trouble.

"In Marseilles I learned the ship had cleared a week before for Egypt, and I managed to get a fast mail boat to Cairo. The Arcturus had just cleared for Bombay. I got passage on a P. and O. liner to Bombay, and my boat passed the Arcturus a few miles out of Suez. I beat the Arcturus to Bombay by three days, and there was a—a man on my ship. A British official. He—he was pleasant company and we—spent some time together. When we got to Bombay he showed me about the town, we went to dinner at several clubs, and he asked me to the *talookdar's* ball at the Asian Queen Hotel.

"I consented to go. Just an hour before he came to take me I learned the Arcturus had been in port several days. I rushed down to the tourist agency in my hotel, booked passage on father's ship, ordered my things made ready. And at the same time I overheard some people in the lobby mention the name of my British friend. And they spoke of his *wife*. I didn't know he had been married. I scarcely knew what to do. But I went to the ball with him, expecting to leave early and give my sudden sailing as an excuse. You see, he had been—been awfully attentive to me before, and—but I went to the party with him.

"He—during the party he asked me to marry him. He was leaving for North India the next morning and asked me to go with him as his wife. It was—dreadful. I was on

the point of demanding an explanation when the terrible—
the terrible news of the killing on the terrace threw the ball
into—into tragedy. He—the man I was with—was a high
official. I knew there would be a police investigation. I fled
away. It was the only thing I could do. My name—his wife's
name—the papers and all."

IT WAS NO time for such a performance, but I remember
that I damned the name of this girl's British "friend" not
quite under my breath, and suddenly found I had reached
over to press her hand.

"Just two more points, Miss Brown," Blair persisted
gently. "You were heard—well, heard talking heatedly with
Captain Lane some minutes in his cabin to-night before
the—the captain was killed. Your father was—"

"I'd hoped to surprise him," the girl explained brokenly.
"He didn't know I was on his boat for several days, you see,
after it left Bombay. When I finally went on the bridge
to see him he was very angry. He was even more alarmed
when I told him about—about Bombay. He seemed terribly frightened, too. And all the time he did not seem
himself. I had an impression something was on his mind.

"He told me his nerves had been troubling him. He said
this was the worst ship he'd ever sailed and that I'd have
to leave her when we got to Shanghai. This evening when
I went to his cabin we talked things over. He reproved me
severely. Poor father!" She put her handkerchief to her eyes.
"I'm certain, now, he had a premonition—"

Blair studied his blue notebook thoughtfully. He looked,
suddenly, very tired. "Captain Lane, your father, told you
he didn't like this ship. Did he tell you why? Did he say

anything about any of the passengers?" He fixed a steady gaze on the girl. "Try to remember."

She shook her head hopelessly. "He just said he disliked the boat. That was all. And that I'd have to leave at Shanghai and go back home."

"And last of all," Blair reminded her, "about your rushing to your cabin soaking wet when we cleared Pahang. Gorn, I believe, claimed he saw you. And you wore a cape."

"I'd been standing by myself on the bow," she whispered. "Alone. It was raining very hard."

The Englishman sighed heavily, delved into a pocket and produced the yellow cotton glove. "Have any of you, besides Mr. Benson, seen a glove like this before?"

They shook their heads. He wrote in his notebook, and turned on me. "You're the key man in this little party, Benson," he promised me. "I suppose you weren't carrying a passport when you started on your evening stroll to-night. But you may have something on you to establish your connection with the consulate at Pahang."

I showed three letters and a pawn ticket. He smiled. "I'm glad to see you are corresponding with people in Los Angeles. Your home?"

"Yes," I was glad to say. "And I sailed the Pacific to get here, thank God."

"This French sailor you saw killed on the Pahang water front. He said one word to you and that was all. 'Bentfinger.'"

"And that was enough," I protested. Blair nodded; writing.

"And then you caught sight of the killer's face. According to your story, you won just a brief glimpse. Now then.

Study the faces of those about you." He spaced his words for emphasis. "Could one of them have been the face you saw?"

THE SCOTLAND YARD man had never taken his eyes from the one he was interrogating. Now he watched me with the gaze of a hawk. Beads of sweat started afresh on my forehead. Unhappily I turned about in my chair and studied the faces grouped about me. Lord knows, I'd been doing nothing else since coming aboard ship. I peered like a half-wit, and, as my glance rested on Mrs. Phillipots she made a sudden and astonishing bounce to her feet.

"This is ridiculous!" she screamed. "This Mr. Benson and his insane story. I'll go mad. How can any of us believe such a story? He says he saw this terrible assassin's face. Yet, he can't tell what kind of a face it was. The face of a woman, even, he says. Do you think I'm going to be stared at like that? Let me go. I'll die. I'm a nervous woman, sick; tortured. I'm going straight to my cabin!"

"Please, then," Blair nodded. "You may leave. We'll all go in a moment." Mrs. Phillipots flounced from the room with a gush of sobs. "Don't try to leave the corridor," Blair warned her. "For your own safety, you know. Besides, the sailors on guard are forbidden to let any one pass as yet. Your husband will be with you straightaway."

Her door slammed like a bomb. "Inspector," I groaned. "I can't possibly say it was any one here. I recognize no resemblance. Yet it *might* have been anybody."

"It was somebody, all right," he declared savagely. "Somebody in that dining saloon. Somebody who tossed that yellow glove under my chair. Somebody who put out those lights, fired lightning-fast with a master eye, tossed the incriminating gun through that port. Somebody who has traveled from America to this spot on the China Seas. Somebody who kills with a laugh; killed Captain Lane, that French seaman, those people in Bombay, Cairo, Marseilles, London. But the start was New York."

He swept the room with an eye that seemed to, falling on me, see straight through my head. "Mr. Benson seems to have an alibi. You, Phillipots, and your wife have never been in America to start with. Your alibi will be good, too. Norwood, you claim yourself a missionary who never carried a gun. That will clear you, if true. And Gorn, you let yourself out at the start if your claim that you've not made the ports along the way holds out. That will leave only you, Miss Brown, and I believe you can clear yourself easily. You, Dr. Smartbeck. And you, De Stroon. But when our wireless is working again I can very easily check up on all of you—"

A sailor stepped through the doorway. "The radio, sir, is pretty hopeless. Can't possibly repair it until to-morrow."

Blair, gave a gesture of resignation. "Work hard at it, then."

The cockney steward with the big nose appeared on the seaman's heels. "I've 'unted over the cabins, sir, like you ordered. 'Ere's the weapons as I found. This Webley pistol from Major Phillipots's cabin first off, sir. This 'ere 'orse pistol from the luggage of Dr. Smartbeck there, sir—"

"It's a curio!" Dr. Smartbeck howled.

The steward went on blandly, holding up a little pearl-handled .22 Colt. "This from Miss Brown's 'and-bag, sir. I'm sorry, Miss Brown. 'Ere's a Belgian automatic from Mr. De Stroon's shelf, sir. An' I didn't find nothing like a gun in Mr. Gorn's cabin. No guns there, sir. But lastly, in the pocket of a Burberry cape 'angin' on the door of Missionary Norwood's cabin, sir, I discovered this 'ere Haenel automatic, sir."

MISSIONARY NORWOOD WENT livid. Blair gave him a thin smile. "So you were armed after all, Reverend Norwood. A lie in your bonnet, too. Lies have a way of coming to the surface even when clerics tell them. Your lie puts you down with the others who try to obstruct justice. Apparently Miss Brown, Major and Mrs. Phillipots and Mr. Gorn are the only ones who haven't troubled to invent fake alibis, and—"

Andrew Hague's Scotch face appeared in the doorway. "I've talked with the chief engineer and the ship's carpenter, Inspector Blair. They've been going over the ship's lighting plant. Can't imagine how those lights were doused. They claim those lights could only be turned out by throwing a switch in the engine room. Nobody below threw that switch. No fuses blown anywhere either. They can't understand it. And here's those letters you wanted from Mr. Gorn's cabin." He held out a packet of envelopes; frowned at the smoking room. "Hurry it up, inspector."

Blair took the sheaf of letters, his eye on the first officer. "Look here, Mr. Hague," he queried. "You were standing in the saloon door when Captain Lane was shot. You had your eye on the whole scene. For perhaps four seconds that room was black as pitch. There was the shot. Just a flash in the dark. Uproar, and then the beastly lights came back on. Now the second the lights went out, all of us sprang to our feet. The killer, no doubt, leaned far down the table—over the table and *away* from the position of his (or her) chair, you understand. Of course, when there's a flash in the dark like that you're blinded and stunned and can't seem to tell where it came from, anyway. The lights flooding on as they did blinded every one, again.

"But Captain Lane, who was looking down the *length* of the table, was struck square in the forehead. Not a glancing shot. Now the open porthole was behind the captain's head. That means that the killer had a straight throw for his gun. A mighty good throwing-eye needed to pitch that gun through that hole in the dark, yes? Even if that shot had come from the saloon doorway—and the flash was somewhere *over* the table—that gun couldn't have been flung halfway across the saloon and sped out through that open port. This seems to exonerate you, Mr. Hague. You stood in the doorway while those lights were out, didn't you?"

"I never moved."

"And if you had leaped across the room, fired as you reached over the table, flung the gun through the port (impossible to do with such speed and accuracy) and sprung back to your place on the threshold, your feet moving across the floor would have been heard. I only explain this to relieve the minds of the innocent members of this group who may have wondered if you, yourself, could be the assassin. I also wanted to know if you stood the whole time right there in the doorway."

"I stood right there, inspector. Stunned, I suppose. When the lights came on and I saw the captain dead I— only then could I reach for my gun. Of course the flash seemed to come—well—it looked to me like it had come from the end of the table nearest Captain Lane. Tell you the truth, I thought Miss Brown or the man next to her had fired that shot."

"A final point. You stood in the doorway. Suppose some one with incredible celerity had darted into the saloon from outside. This is, beyond all possibility, but the whole case is—is impossible. But could such a one have got past you where you stood? You're a large man, Mr. Hague, but—"

"Impossible!" The big Scotchman was emphatic. "Nobody ran past me into that saloon and out again in those three seconds. Nobody went by me at all. I'd have felt it, all right. Captain Lane was shot by somebody right there at that table!"

BLAIR NODDED. "I'M only forestalling some of the more agile minds in this group. I've been waiting for that wild theory to be advanced, and I wanted to save time. Now, then, Mr. Gorn, I'll look at your mail, here, and then we're through for a bit." He shuffled the envelopes in his fingers, opened several, studied the contents. "Business of buying silk for Hilton and Curtis, Ltd., all right," he conceded. "And your Bedford address I'm glad to note. Hello, what's this?"

A little pink ticket had dropped from the batch of papers. I heard a sharp oath crackle from Gorn's lips. Blair grabbed up the stub of cardboard from the smoking room floor; glared. "A ticket on the P. L. and M. Railroad of France. Paris to Saint Raphael, first class. Why, Saint Raphael is the town where that French government official's wife was going to wear her black pearls to Count Fallicet's ball. This ticket is dated April first. And that woman was slain late in April and this ticket is good for a thirty-day stopover in Marseilles. So you *were* on the Continent, perhaps in Marseilles—"

Gorn shrugged. "You haven't done badly so far, inspector," he offered cryptically. "Don't switch off the main track."

For a moment I thought Blair would smite that bland, dark face. Then he scribbled angrily in his blue notebook. "Another liar," he scathed. "And the easy conscience need not lie, remember. All right. Steward, take these guns and lock them up in my cabin.

"Now, then," he waved at us, "you may all go to your cabins. Observe, please, the guards stationed at each end of the corridor. Those guards are instructed to let nobody pass; to challenge any who attempt to leave a cabin; to shoot at sight on any untoward move by any of you. You are all disarmed, which means Bentfinger's front teeth are drawn. In a few hours the wireless will be repaired, I can radio to shore and verify every move made by any of you. Please pass before me into the corridor."

We filed out of the smoking room in a silence laid by staggered nerves and back-breaking fatigue. Blair assigned me the vacant cabin next to his at the corridor's forward end. I heard six bells go somewhere up on deck. Two o'clock. The tolling was inexplicably mournful. For the first time I noticed how the ship was rolling. Water thudded sullenly to the faint sound of a blowing gale; and the deck underfoot was palsied as the ship's screw reared, whirring, for a brief lift clear of the sea. The corridor was full of wind.

I believe the "good-night" Blair and I offered the girl as she stepped through her cabin door was the only bit of etiquette observed on the adjournment of our night's inquisition. She gave a smile in reply that was well worth an effort on our part. The Englishman looked cheered for the first time in the past three hours. I told myself that this poor devil from Scotland Yard was up against a case all the masters of detection in the world could not have solved. The finger of suspicion pointed at every one of those Arcturus passengers who had sat at that fatal table for a fatal evening "snack." Only Major and Mrs. Phillipots seemed, so far, to have established any sort of alibi that was strong—the alibi of not having been in New York.

THEN MAJOR PHILLIPOTS banged open the door of the Phillipots cabin, gave a scowl for the rest of us in the corridor, and stepped inside; and without warning, Blair stepped in after him. Mrs. Phillipots was to be seen at an open porthole. She spun about with a hysterical screech, saw the man behind her husband, and promptly plunged floorward in a heap of beads and cloth. Stooping quickly, Blair grasped her by the wrist. Her hand was closed to a fist. Blair carefully opened the fingers. Bits of colored, glazed paper scattered about.

"Where's your luggage kit? Your bags!" Blair's voice sawed with anger; his eyes impaling the major against a wall. "Your luggage!"

Major Phillipots was green about the jowls. "Right," he gasped thickly. "You don't need to look. The fool had to bungle it. She soaked 'em off the luggage, all right. That's it, inspector. They're baggage posters. She had to paste 'em all over her kit so the blighters in Shanghai could see we'd really stayed at the Astor Hotel on Times Square." He scowled in fury at the offending shards of paper. "Yes. We were in New York. And," defiantly, "we left the very day of the Bentfinger robberies, if you want to know. Now, damn it all, sir, what the devil can you do about that?"

"Remember it," said Blair softly.

And at last I was alone in my cabin. At last I had my shoes off and the door bolted against fear and my weary bones flat on a bed. Faces and facts marched and counter-marched across my humming brain. Bentfinger, the killer who might be either woman or man, master-marksman, jewel thief, cobra-brained, deadly. No clew to the killer but his trail. New York, London, Marseilles, Cairo, Bombay, Pahang, this hell-spot on the South China Sea. Major and Mrs. Phillipots had followed that trail—so had all the others, perhaps, save Gorn.

Had Gorn even been in New York? He claimed to the contrary. But he had lied about being in Marseilles—he could lie about being in New York. The girl had followed the trail. Late. But, perhaps, at the very same time. The Phillipotses, Gorn, Norwood, De Stroon, Dr. Smart-beck had lied. Perhaps the girl lied, too. She had been at the *talookdar's* ball when the murder took place there in Bombay.

Gorn had been there. Had Gorn been in Marseilles? Dr. Smartbeck had stayed in the Grand Hôtel in Marseilles—the very house in which the French woman had been slain. De Stroon owned a sharpshooter's medal. Norwood owned a sharpshooter's pistol and could produce no passport. Major Phillipots had dashed up the gangway in Cairo with a red smear on his cheek. Had it really been rouge? And Mrs. Phillipots had not allowed me to scrutinize her face closely. Always fainting. A stall of some kind? The girl—That girl had told no lie.

I sat up to throw off my coat. Certainly Bentfinger had been in that dining saloon. The yellow glove. But then I could only think of dark hair shaping a finely molded head, clear gray eyes brave in the sight of tragedy (what if she *had* worn a wet cape out of Pahang?) and a certain arched chin not given to quivering. Hope. That was her name. Hope. Thank heaven I could quiet down at long last.

May I state here and now that I thanked the good Lord entirely, too soon? Sighing, I stretched out on the bunk. Next instant I was sitting bolt upright, sweat flooding from every chilled pore. A cry had ripped out of the night. A frantic and terrible cry.

6

SOMEBODY WILL DIE!

"FIRE!" THE CRY stung through the door of my cabin, and was echoed by a bedlam to raise the hair on a mummy. Bells clanged. Feet pounded the deck outside. A confusion of yells was drowned by the wild blast of the steamer's siren.

"Fire!" No lullaby, believe you me! And no peaceful incense was the coiling rope of smoke that curled from under my cabin door and eddied along the wall. Wow! I got off my bunk as if I'd been shot, yanked open the door and slammed full tilt into a marionette in a flannel night-gown. Both of us rolled in a tangle across the corridor and I came upright on top of Dr. Smartbeck.

Dr. Smartbeck had hung a nightgown over his cloth-ing, and he seemed in a desperate hurry to get somewhere. So was I. He shrieked in my face and I hauled him to his feet. Something fell from his clawing hand; and I was never to forget that the object was a little box of safety matches. Smoke wreathed thick in the corridor, and its narrow confines were experiencing a stampede that would have rivalled a charge in a madhouse. Mrs. Phillipots, fully clothed, was able to lead the din, and she wasn't finding time to swoon in that rush.

Major Phillipots, shirtless and barefoot, bawled and

elbowed. De Stroon came out of his cabin like a tornado, hung with lifebelts. I caught a glimpse of Norwood, naked to the waist in the middle of the whirl, and noticed something odd about the missionary. Something so strange that I couldn't fathom what it was until, later, I was told.

Gorn was there, too, calmest of all in the face of threatened panic. I saw him start for the closed door of the girl's cabin; but I was there before him. We banged on the panels, and the door sprung open to reveal the girl in a poppy-colored dressing robe that I'd have remembered through hell and high water.

Somehow her hand seemed to fit in mine, and together, we followed the race for the open deck, darting side by side through the smoke and uproar with Gorn somewhere behind us and the rest of the passenger list whooping up ahead. Chill salted air whipped at us as we floundered across open deck in a blind rush for safety, stumbling like a crowd of football players when the boat rolled. The hatchway we had left was spouting smoke that lingered along the deck and gave an impression that all amidships was on fire. Wind blew the smoke aside to show ghostly sailors in ghostly undershirts dragging a snaky length of hose. Lights winkered aft, and the bos'n darted by like a gnome in oilskins and sou'wester; shouted oaths, and led the hose-crew into the smoke-fogged companion.

The Arcturus, meantime, was shouldering into a goodly gale that filled the night with stinging spindrift, slammed the ship a-rolling with a beam sea and flung green water over the heeling bows. Perhaps you can fancy the situation as it came over me just then. A tramp steamer struggling through the night on a storm-roughed patch of South

China Sea that might have been the end of the world and was, so far as the ship with her useless radio was concerned. The ship's captain lying that very minute in a canvas shroud in his cabin, dead with a murderer's bullet in his temple. The assassin, known to be one of the passengers (yet absolutely unknown), lurking near in a mask of innocence—a demon, a cobra-dangerous killer in our midst.

And now, the ship, itself, was on fire.

The siren brayed; men ran with lanterns, hatchets and hose; the bearded second mate scampered down from the bridge, clad in pink-striped pyjamas and rubber boots; and Mrs. Phillipots finally fainted on Dr. Smartbeck's elbow and tossed him off his footing.

"The cabins!" De Stroon pulled on my arm and yelled in my ear. "Those cabins are burning. *Herr Gott!* My money is in there—"

"And mine!" Gorn shouted; leaped from his place at the rail and lunged into the smoky companion. De Stroon was after him. Major Phillipots yelled something and started to follow, but tripped on his prostrate wife, floundered against Norwood who fought him off shrieking: "Are you trying to kill me?"

Dr. Smartbeck wrung his hands and glared nervously at Hope Brown, as if he thought her to be Bentfinger and ready to take this opportunity for another killing. The girl shivered and a stray gleam of light caught in relief her white face.

"My—my cape is in there. It's going to be dreadfully cold if we're forced to the lifeboats—"

A wooden Indian (which isn't such a bad description of

myself at that time) would have come to life and answered the appeal of those gray eyes.

"I'll get your cape!" I told her with a bravery of voice that didn't go with the feeling in my stomach; and then I was back in that corridor, staggering through the choky fog, making for the girl's cabin.

Shadows darted about me in the smoke, and I caught a gleam from De Stroon's gold teeth; saw Gorn plunge out of a cabin that didn't seem to be the one he had previously occupied; and bumped into a sailor with a hatchet. The crew was jammed at the aft end of the corridor. I could hear the roar of the playing fire-hose. Water swirled across the floor underfoot.

THE SMOKE WAS thick in the girl's cabin, but I managed to find her cape in a cupboard and get back into the corridor. A yelling shadow ran into me; stabbed a gun muzzle into my ribs. It was Blair.

"Get out on the deck, Benson," he snapped at me. "What the devil are you doing in here? Quick, I want to talk with you. You know what this fire means!"

"Are we leaving the ship?" I gasped. "This fire—"

"Fire's nothing!" he shouted. "Nothing but a stall to get the passengers free of their cabins for a minute. Where are the others? Gorn? De Stroon? Did you see them?"

"Outside, on deck!" I yelped. "I just came back for Miss Brown's cape. Where's the captain—Mr. Hague?"

But Andrew Hague was on duty, all right. We found him with his grizzled face stern as granite, his automatic in his fist. He had lined the passengers of the Arcturus against the heaving ship's rail, and he seemed about ready to execute the lot of them. The redheaded third officer

A limp, pale hand reached over the lifeboat's side

stood by with a lantern in upraised fist, and the glimmer-
ing light, the smoke, the tipping deck, the scared faces
and grotesque costumes and incongruous background of
a ship in tropic storm-water was weird as a phantasy from
Halloween.

"They're all here, inspector," he shouted at Blair. "I
caught the lot of 'em huddled right here on this rail. You
all right?"

"I'm all right!" Blair coughed. "But it's like I guessed the
minute I heard that fire siren go when I was talking with
you, there, in the chart room. Minute that siren blew those
sailors stationed to watch the corridor rushed off to their
fire-stations. These people all got out of their cabins. And
somebody broke into *my* cabin, just as I'd feared. Didn't
find the guns, anyway. How about the fire?"

The bearded second officer appeared, stepping from a
gust of smoke. "Fire's under control, Mr. Hague. It was
that last cabin aft on th' starboard side. Steward had piled
a lot of dirty linen in there—that empty cabin, you know.

Th' door was left ajar, an' somebody must 'a' flung a match or cigarette inside. Lots of smoke—"

"Plenty of it!" Blair growled bitterly. "Enough to cover the actions of a killer who wanted to hide his movements behind confusion and get out of a guarded cabin," he flung on the group at the rail. "Nice work, whoever of you is Bentfinger and pulled this trick. But I'll get to the bottom of this if it's the last thing I ever do. You, Gorn. Your cabin is right opposite that cabin used by the steward for linen storage. You could have thrown a cigarette butt or match across that corridor—"

"But of course I did not, inspector. And Smartbeck, here, who was next cabin to mine could have done it easier. The door was ajar on an angle which—"

"That's right!" I abruptly remembered. "Look here, Smartbeck. When I ran into you back there in the smoke you dropped a box of safety matches!"

"I didn't start any fire!" Dr. Smartbeck screeched, running fingers through the fuzzy mop on his head. "I heard the alarm signal and thought we were taking to the boats. There were matches on my table. If we were out on the ocean—in a boat—once I heard of how sailors in a lifeboat wanted matches and—"

"But it wasn't done that way!" Blair snapped. "I see it, now. When I marched the lot of you to your cabins twenty minutes ago some one threw a cigarette into that pile of linen. You had a cigarette in your fingers, De Stroon. I remember. You, too, Major Phillipots. A cigar you were smoking. Tossed it into that cabin and it smoldered for a while—"

Major Phillipots flushed angrily. "That's nonsense. My

cigar had been cold for an hour. The Dutchman had just started a fag."

"The missionary gave it to me!" De Stroon squawked. "He handed me a cigarette and lit one, himself, just as we were leaving that *verdammt* smoke room. You think I start fires on this hell-ship—"

"A missionary of the Free Methodist Church indulging in tobacco?"

BLAIR TURNED; AND the rest of us glared at Norwood. The Reverend Norwood stood against the rail, twisting nervous fingers together, his gaunt face punky yellow in the uncertain light. A cold wind swept the deck, and Norwood shuddered, for he wore no shirt and his naked skin was blue in the chill. And then Blair was pointing an accusing finger; his voice coming harsh as a saw. "What's this, Norwood? You're a missionary, you say, and I'm dashed if you're not tattooed!"

That was it! That was what made the missionary look odd. In the excitement I'd seen it, but the fact hadn't registered. Across the Reverend Norwood's chest a barkentine under full sail bowled down a faint blue wave. Even less ministerial were the three unclad dancing girls etched in green beneath the marine picture. And below the dancers an anchor, a snake, a bleeding heart and the name "Tilly" were artistically entwined.

"It was done before I was converted!" Norwood bawled, striving to hide the tattooing with his arms. "What's that got to do with this fiendish business? You can't prove anything on *me*. I'm not Bentfinger! I'm a servant of the Lord—"

The protest sounded a bit thin in the light of the man's

art-work. He might not be Bentfinger, but he could hardly be a servant of the Lord, thus unspiritually designed. Here was another wry thread in the tangle for Scotland Yard, and I saw Blair wipe a sleeve across a troubled frown. Andrew Hague stepped forward, grim behind his automatic.

"Look here, inspector," he growled. "I've made up my mind. The fire's out and these passengers have got to go back to the cabins and stay under guard. My radio operator is missing. My captain is killed under my nose. Lights go out. The ship is set on fire. I've no wireless. Some one in this crowd is a murderer. I'm not going a mile farther to sea. We're coming about immediately and going back full speed ahead to the nearest port. I'm going to follow your advice. I'll head back for Trengganu!"

"Righto, that's fine!" Blair nodded. "I can hand the ship over to the Federated Malay States authorities, and wire Scotland Yard from Trengganu. We can make it by daylight? Splendid! Trengganu—"

"Trengganu!" The name came like an explosion from the lips of Norwood. In the murky lantern-glow his face had gone from yellow to chlorotic green. "You don't mean—you can't turn the ship around and go back to Trengganu. We've paid our passages! We're passengers on this boat. This man from Scotland Yard hasn't proved anything against me—us—anybody."

"Go back!" The girl at my side caught at Hague's sleeve. I saw she was crying. "Oh, please. Please take us all back to the coast. Don't keep us out here with this—this hidden fiend! Take us back to land. Captain Lane would have turned back, and—"

"Yes! Yes, go back!" Major Phillipots, De Stroon and Dr.

Smartbeck took up the cry. Gorn said nothing. From the corner of my eye I saw him studying the agitated Norwood. A strange, somber, calm face, Gorn's. If I wanted to see anybody locked in a cabin until we made port it was, I suddenly realized, this silk buyer on his way to Japan. And why had Norwood gone to pieces at the mention of Trengganu?

Thank heavens, the Scotch officer had decided to head back to the nearest port. Hell had brewed and smote on this wretched ship; go back, by all means, before it struck again. Bentfinger! Bentfinger! Every revolution of the ship's engines drummed the ghastly name; and solid earth would feel to the feet like heaven.

WE MARCHED BACK into the corridor, watched by Blair's ready gun and steel-sharp eyes. The seamen and the red-headed mate swishing water in the cabin where the steward's linen had burned gave us a suspicious and hostile stare. We stood in the damp and smelly corridor, still dim with smoke, like so many prisoners waiting to be ordered into cells. Two sailors stepped forward, Winchesters under arm.

"You're not to run away this time," Blair ordered grimly. "These passengers stay right here in this corridor until I give the word. Challenge the first cabin door that opens. Those are orders from the bridge, understand? I want you chaps right there until this boat makes Trengganu in the morning."

Mrs. Phillipots sobbed loudly, and the major snorted through his nose. "I expect to be slain any minute by anybody," he snarled, following his spouse into their cabin. "By anybody except the piano-tuner." He sneered at Dr.

Smartbeck. "You can eliminate *him,* inspector. Blokes who wear nightshirts may set fire to towels, but they don't work like Bentfinger does." His door slammed.

Dr. Smartbeck whinnied, "I did not start that fire!" And bobbed into his cabin chattering: "But God knows I expect to be burned alive before I'm done. I swear I'll never travel again. I swear it!"

Quietly, the girl in the poppy-colored robe slipped through her door and I was insane enough to feel a quickened pulse when she turned to thank me for fetching her cape. Meanwhile, Norwood had shut himself in. Gorn, the silk buyer, stood in his cabin doorway, hesitant, his black eyes on Blair. De Stroon's door slammed; Gorn turned about. And then he was back in the corridor, grabbing at Blair's arm.

"Inspector! Take a look at my cabin! Some one's been in there and turned the place upside down. By heaven, it was done during that fire!"

It was true. A cyclone might have struck the silk buyer's stateroom. Bedclothes had been whirled from his bunk. Papers and books were heaped in confusion near the door. Garments lav strewn across the floor and a leather valise had been dumped against a wall, spilling wearing apparel. Cursing, Gorn glared at the mess.

"I thought so, inspector. Somebody tried a bit of robbery. But why in Satan's name they picked on *me* I can't even guess. You're up against it, Inspector Blair. A mighty good thing we're hitting back for port!"

"My cabin was rifled, too," Blair declared. "Easy enough to do it with this alleyway dark with smoke and the ship in an uproar. If you've lost anything, Mr. Gorn, come straight to me. And Mr. Gorn. Don't forget the sailors watching at each end of the corridor. Good night."

I stepped to my own stateroom, and the Englishman slipped past me to his. He looked dead tired, but the metal had not gone from his eye. Myself, I'd have been bouncing insane with that insoluble puzzle on my hands. A puzzle with life and death as the stakes.

"I'll know who Bentfinger is before twenty hours are up," he announced in a low voice, gripping my arm in a hand like a vise. "Don't worry, Benson. Once we get back to Trengganu—"

A sharp peal of thunder cut off the Englishman's speech. The crashing shook the ship from stern to stem. The Arcturus rolled heavily. The corridor took a steep tilt, and I clutched at the wall to hang on. Once again the ship careened, and the thunder muttered like panes of glass smashing down a distant horizon.

"She's coming about," Blair said. "The ship's turning around and catching a bad sea. Let the dashed storm break if it wants to. We're started back for Trengganu. See you in the morning, Benson. I want to go over your story again. But maybe I'll have Bentfinger before then."

BENTFINGER! BENTFINGER! THE name beat up from the flooring at every chug of the straining engines. Once again I was fast in my little stateroom with the door bolted. This time my nerves were keyed to a pitch where I wasn't tired, and I crouched on my bunk, blinking in the bright glow from the overhead bulb, ears assailed by the boom of angry sea and storming sky.

The cabin tipped and tilted, creaking. A shoe banged back and forth across the floor. My coat began to swing on the wall-hook, a thing come to mysterious life. I watched the coat. And then I was on my feet. The pockets of that coat hung inside out. Some one had entered my cabin, too!

I crossed the floor to examine the garment that had been tampered with, and was startled by a rush of water against the thick glass of the stateroom porthole. The cabin screamed out a thousand noises. Rain pounded against the port and there was a flash of brilliant white light followed by a terrific concussion. The sky had fallen on the Arcturus with one detonating crash.

The ship heeled under the shock, putting her starboard beam deep down. Up, up and up tipped the deck; and for one breathless minute filled with the creaking of walls and stanchions and the noise of stumbling gear adrift somewhere on the deck overhead, I thought the craft was going over.

Thunder burst again. Lightning blazed in my porthole, showing a brief picture of the deck outside and a sweep of boiling waves. Then the ship lobbed upright, and I found myself hanging to the bolt on my cabin door. Some one was outside that door, and shouting. I could hear the voice of the Scotch officer, Hague.

"It was tacked on the door of the wheelhouse!" the Scotch voice was bawling. "There it is! See it for yourself! I found it when I went up there not half a minute ago. Stuck on the door with a pin. The mate on the bridge never saw nobody an' th' man at th' wheel didn't, either. But, by heaven, it was put there within th' past ten minutes—"

Blair's voice answered sharply. No need to tell you I opened the door of my cabin and got my own head into the corridor. At the same time De Stroon's door, across the way, swung in and the Dutchman appeared, braced with life-belts. Gorn already stood on his threshold. The girl, too, was in her doorway, wide-eyed, pale, nerved against fresh trouble.

Andrew Hague, shrouded in dripping black oilskins, stood with Blair at the forward end of the corridor. There was something in the Scotchman's massive paw that froze the blood in my heart. I could see it from where I stood, and I gasped. The first officer held it out to Blair. A little card, it was. A little typewritten card.

Blair was glaring; reaching for the card with wooden fingers. "On the door of the wheelhouse? You say you found it on the door of the wheelhouse? Stuck on the outside panel?" His voice was brittle.

"That's where it was, I tell you," the Scotchman snarled. "How the devil it got there I can't fathom. How'd one of these passengers get out of this alley without being seen, I want to know. First thing I did was to ask this sailor on guard here. He says there ain't been a soul in this corridor for th' last quarter hour. But there *must* have been. Look at that damned thing, inspector. Read it! Am I crazy? I tell you I'll kill the devil with my own hands." Sweat glistened on the officer's gray face. His fists waved. "Read it for yourself!"

THUNDER GRUMBLED AND a shiver shook down the length of the heaving ship. I remember that the door of the Phillipots cabin bashed open to allow the major and his wife a view of the scene. Dr. Smartbeck stepped into the corridor, too, gesturing and squeaking dismal opinion that a new tragedy had been enacted.

But Blair was holding the little card to light; reading it aloud hoarsely:

To the Officers of the Arcturus:

Head the ship straight for Cambodia Point. Keep out of the sea lanes and do not attempt signals to other ships. Do not try to disobey this command. I am watching every move. If the ship's course is not altered for Cambodia Point by five minutes of three somebody aboard will die.

Bentfinger.

Blair whirled on the Scotchman. "Good God, man. Signed 'Bentfinger'! And it's typewritten! And—*five minutes of three!*"

"Yes!" The words clipped short through Hague's teeth. "And it's one minute *after* three right now. Turn my ship around? Change the course for Cambodia Point? Stand out to sea, again? Not on your life! No knowing which one of these devils wrote that damned warning—"

"Wait!" Blair's fevered words struck the rest of us to stone. "I—say, a thin man might have got through a port-hole! These are all outside cabins. The ports open on the deck! Open on the deck on port and starboard side, don't they? By heaven, a thin person could have got through! Look! That fellow Norwood—"

"The thinnest chap on the boat!" Gorn cut in with an oath.

"And he didn't want to put back to Trengganu!" Blair shouted. "That missionary—"

"And he owns a typewriter!" The girl spoke hardly above

a whisper, but we heard, all right. "He owns a typewriter. I've heard him using it."

And where was Norwood? Where was this missionary who had carried (and lied about) a sharpshooter's pistol, who wore strange tattooings on his clerical bosom, who feared a return to Trengganu? Where was this Norwood who was thin enough to have squeezed himself out of his stateroom porthole? The Reverend Norwood from Elkhart, Indiana. He owned a typewriter. He could have typed that card, wormed himself out of his cabin, pinned the warning on the wheelhouse. Where was he? His stateroom door was closed and bolted and mute.

I stared at that door, and the sweat sprouted out on my cheeks. I saw Blair motion to the Scotch first officer; mutter instructions. The sailors with their rifles tramped up the swinging, dim corridor to stand, tense, on either hand. Yanking out his automatic, Andrew Hague stepped back; launched at the doorknob a terrific blow. The gun-butt crashed hard against the knob. The door flew open with a *bam!*

A whistly cry blew echoing and away. "Norwood!"

He sat on the floor of his stateroom with his back against a bulkhead, his legs stretched comfortably, hands languid in his lap. The unforgiving glare of the too-bright over-head light played full on his gaunt face; and his face was lacking in piety. When the ship rolled his head moved. But he did not.

Blood bubbled from the hole above his cold left eye, found a channel down the side of his nose and spilled to paint a crimson blot on his picture-gallery chest. A little typewritten card lay on the floor at his feet. We didn't need to read the name. The card in Blair's shaking hand had foretold the story.

"If the ship's course is not altered for Cambodia Point by five minutes of three, somebody aboard will die—"

It was five minutes after three. The Reverend Norwood was dead.

7

WHO WILL BE NEXT?

A SNARE-DRUM FLAM of thunder crackled down the night. The Arcturus leaned on her beam ends. The stuffy corridor quivered and swayed, Blair sprang into the stateroom where the dead man lounged.

"Look!" Blair's white lips barked staccato speech. "The porthole is open! See! The glass pane is cracked!" A spate of dark water showered through the circular casement. The little round pane had been swung inward on its iron hinge. The glass was cracked down the middle. "The murderer did that! Sneaked up on the outside of that porthole. Rapped on the glass with a gun butt; that's what happened. Norwood opened the porthole to see what was up. The killer fired! It was thundering hard and nobody could hear the shot."

I stared at the body against the wall. I thought of the warning pinned on the wheelhouse door. I tell you, the hair stood up stiff as wire on my head. Norwood had been slain within the past ten minutes! Shot through the temple. And trade-marked with a little typed card. My knees wanted to wobble and my vision blurred. A ring of damp, panting faces swam before my eyes. Andrew Hague was yelling at the top of his voice and filling the awful scene with mad words.

"Shot by somebody outside on that deck—how'd anybody get out there? There'll be footmarks—"

Blair's sunken eyes scanned the frantic crowd of faces. "No, Mr. Hague. We'll look, but it's no use. There won't be tracks. Those decks are swept by a flood of water."

He stepped from the dead man's cabin; closed the door; wiped mist from his face. He was old, now. Cords stood out on his British jaw. I knew what was in his mind. Somebody had got out of a stateroom, sped around the dark, rain-whipped decks to pin that dreadful warning on the wheelhouse and carry out the threatened murder.

But how? How? The only possible exits to the staterooms were the doors opening on the corridor and the round portholes opening on the deck. The sailors guarding the ends of the corridor had watched the doors. And those portholes were small. Too small. A skeleton might have wriggled through; but most of us were not skeletons. Not yet, anyway.

There was De Stroon. His fat-slabbed back could hardly get through a narrow door, much less a ship's porthole. Major Phillipots was broad as a barrel around the belt. Mrs. Phillipots? Stout as an opera mezzo. Gorn was short, but thickset and muscular and almost as broad of shoulder as Blair. Angular Dr. Smartbeck—almost as skinny as poor Norwood—might have threaded himself through, and—

The sailor who had stood watch at the aft end of the corridor was yelling protests at Hague. "Ain't I swearin' it's so? None o' these passengers come out into th' corridor. Charley an' me was watchin', wasn't we? We seen 'em all go into them cabins of theirs. This inspector was last to go. They shuts their doors, an' not one of them doors opens up and they ain't a soul in this alleyway till you comes along an' bangs for th' Scotland Yard man to open up. No, we didn't hear nothin', did we, Charley?" The sailor waved excited hands. "I say there weren't nobody in th' corridor. We'd have seen 'em if they was, an' th' devil fly away with me if that ain't God's truth."

Blair sized up the situation with a hopeless gesture. "Then it *was* a porthole! But I'm dashed, Mr. Hague. Those ports are small. Norwood might have been able to get through. But—but it wasn't Norwood. Why, only a boy could wiggle out of a porthole, and—"

"Or a girl might be small enough to get out." The low voice was Gorn's. His black eyes were fastened on the girl in the poppy-hued robe. "And your cabin is right next to Norwood's, young woman—"

SHE SHRANK AGAINST me, clutching my arm, trembling. "That's nonsense!" I was bellowing. "Miss Brown do that—that murder? It's insane! And the gun? Where the devil would she get a gun? Where'd any of us get a gun? Our weapons were taken from us! None of us were—"

"Wait!" Blair yanked his little blue leather notebook from his pocket. "I've got something here. Quiet, all of you. Watch everybody, Mr. Hague. When I was making notes back there in the smoke room, I—"

And then, because the whole stage setting was the stuff of dreams, it acted as dreams do. Thunder bawled and boomed, racking the ship with violent concussion. The flooring slanted as if kicked out from under our feet by the boot of a giant; and the boat's unexpected roll flung every man jack of us in that corridor off balance and down against the wall in a frenzied heap. Down we went like so many ten-pins. Mrs. Phillipots landed on my middle like a falling dry-goods store. Dr. Smartbeck's dandelion blossom of a wig smothered my face. The back of my head banged against De Stroon's gold teeth, and somebody clawed at my ear. Like a tackled football squad we piled up in the corridor. The deck reared under us. Frantic and yelling, we battled to our feet.

And something had happened during that little caprice of the South China Sea! You bet it had. For when the players had picked themselves up and the stage had tipped upright again, Blair was black-faced with rage, shaking a fist at the ceiling, wry-mouthed and furious with a crimson scratch bleeding on his jaw. "It's gone! It was knocked out of my hand! Look for it, you—every one of you! Find that notebook, or by heaven, I'll—You, Major Phillipots! You were on top of me! You snatched that book from my hand, and I'll give you one second to—"

"I did not!" The major clung to the doorknob of his cabin, feet braced for support against the weight of Mrs. Phillipots and the swing of the corridor. "How'd I grab that damned book with that man Gorn choking me and that Benson's feet kicking in my face? How could—"

"Move your feet, all of you. Look on the floor. Get back there, Smartbeck. Down on your knees. Hunt! If that book isn't on this floor—"

He waved his gun, and the rest of us pawed across the corridor with him in mounting desperation. Everybody was chattering nonsense, and it needed a climax, that episode, to prove the whole thing a fizzing nightmare. I got

it, too. I was just wondering how the girl beside me could
have steeled her nerves to be calm in this madhouse hour
(Mrs. Phillipots was wailing hysterically and her husband
was promising to throttle her and De Stroon was gabbling
in Dutch while Blair was rasping: "You'll all be in irons
after this!") when the climax appeared.

It appeared in the guise of two wild and frantic wraiths
who plunged into our midst like a stampede. The cockney bo's'n with the jutting ears and post-bald head. And
the saloon steward with the Pinnochio nose. There was
commotion at the corridor's end. Then the pair were shouting in the center of the insane riddle; the cockney bo's'n
dancing before the stunned Scotchman, Hague, waving
gnarled paws, his Eastham face working like one of those
rubber toys that squeeze into comical shapes.

"*'E seen 'im!*" the cockney screeched. "Johnny Wist, th'
steward 'ere, seen 'im. It was right after that fire was put out.
I'm down in the fo'c's'le, an' th' lads was all harpin' about th'
skipper's murder, they was. Gettin' worked up about it, they
be. They'd 'eared 'ow the Old Man was killed in th' saloon
when the lights all went out. They'd 'eard 'ow 'twas one of th'
passengers as done it, an' they was all for rushin' th' passengers, they was. Then Johnny comes bangin' down th' fo'c's'le
companion blabberin' like 'e's got took wiv th' shakes. 'E
'ides under a bunk, a hollerin', an' I can't pry 'im out until
now." The bo's'n caught at the steward's arm; yanked him
forward. "Tell 'em, Johnny, wot you been tellin' me!"

"I SEEN HIM!" The steward gargled; flung out shivering
hands. The eyes bulged in his head, and his wet face was
silly with fright. A tear of sweat wiggled down his nose.

"Seen him," he whispered. "I'd gone to my fire station

on the deck below, and when the men told me the fire was out I'd started forward. They said the blaze had been in that stateroom where I'd stowed the linen. Thought I'd have to see the bridge about it.

"I'd just come up the starboard companion and—and was rounding that alleyway under the bridge. It was storming hard—dark—water blowing—and—and I had to hold on for a second. There was a flash of lightning—and—and there it was. Right in front of me, it was." His teeth clicked in his loose jaw. "A corpse like, it was. An' wings. I tell you, I couldn't move. All I see is them awful waving wings an' a big black cloak an' clawing hands. Them hands was all shriveled up to bird-claws, I tell you. An' the face was all shriveled up, too, like a dead one. And all sunk in' an' bashed in on one side."

The steward licked at his upper lip; moaned. "It was awful. Awful! An' the mouth was all gone in, and that head twisted like there weren't any neck. I couldn't scream. I couldn't do nothing, I couldn't. It goes pitch dark and then there's more lightning—bright as day—and this— demon—drops off his cape. Then I run—"

The steward's incoherent whisper choked out into dreadful silence. It was quiet as stone in that corridor of the Arcturus right then. Yes, waves sledged the ship's prow, the decks throbbed underfoot, walls and stanchions groaned, off in the night beyond God's thunder boomed and tons of water slammed, but the corridor was still as stone, if you can understand. That corridor was still as stone and peopled with cold stone statues.

It was Blair who finally tried to speak, and whispered: "Shriveled hands! Face sunk in on one side—" He brushed a hand across his lips, struggling for voice with a tongue that stalled in his ivory-white teeth and left him a weird, frightened grimace. "And a cloak? And you—you saw this—this thing on the deck under the bridge? Just after the fire! Why—it—it was while we were all in our cabins. Not—hardly twenty minutes ago. Good God! You ran away. This figure threw off the cloak it wore—"

"And I ran!" The steward blurted wildly. "Ran! I saw, I tell you. It wasn't no passenger, it wasn't. It wasn't nobody—nobody who'd been on this craft before. The lightning was bright as day, and it waved claws and grinned at me! Grinned! And—and the arms were all screwed up like bed-springs. And the legs were twisted like a carrick bend. God save me, it—it's out there somewhere. I saw it. It's out there in the dark! A cripple! The most terrible cripple I ever saw—"

The corridor careened. Lights and shapes whirled as hands grabbed and voices wailed and squalled. The legs almost went out from under me, and I found myself against the wall, holding the girl's hand tightly, trying to work my brain and prove everything unreal. Phantasy. All phantasy. This impossible ship. This swinging, stifling corridor. These scared, babbling people. The whole mad night with its humpty-dumpty of reasonless episodes strung together like events in an idiot's mind.

That fight under a dim Chinese lantern way back in a place called Pahang. That chase to a dark, outward-bound ship. The saloon full of grotesque folk. Guns that fired from the dark. The dead and their unknown assassins. Oaths and questions and lies. Leather notebooks and radio operators that vanished. Storm and fire and death and a girl with

brave gray eyes and unbowed head and something that
made me want to take her hand. In a minute all of this
would be gone. Something would snap in my head and
things would come right. None of it had happened. None
of it was happening.

YET BLAIR WAS speaking and I heard his words, and those
about me heard them, too. "You were wrong then, Hague.
Some one *did* get by you into that saloon. That murderer—
the murderer this man saw out there on the deck—"

And the Scotchman was yelling, the sailors with the
rifles darting to call all hands; Gorn and Dr. Smartbeck
and the girl coming to life and Major Phillipots squawk-
ing: "Give us our guns, inspector. Just let me get my hands
on a pistol, that's all."

De Stroon demanding: "I want mine, too!"

Gorn growling: "I'll not stay in my cabin!"

Dr. Smartbeck crying: "Save us. For the love of God
don't let this fiend get us all!"

The sunflower-eared bo's'n yelping: "I'll warn the engine
room!"

The steward's goat-voice croaking: "All crippled up, it
was. Twisted an' crippled in knots. I *saw* it!"

The girl's white face looking up at me as she whispered:
"I'm terribly frightened. Will you stay near by?" And I, of
course, was a gawk who wanted to do everything and could
seem to do nothing but gulp and try to breathe.

I remember how steeply the ship was rolling to help out
with the confusion, how Andrew Hague shouted things
nobody could hear, how Blair yelled: "I'll arm you all, but
you've got to stay in your staterooms," and rushed down the
corridor and into his cabin at its end. I don't suppose he was

gone two minutes, but I began to want an automatic under my hand and it seemed like forty years. And when he was back in the corridor again it was another forty years before he spoke. White and shaking with excitement, he faced us.

"They're not in the cabin!" he groaned. "I had them locked in my cupboard. They were there when you called me, Mr. Hague, to show me that damned warning. But some one got in there, somehow. The lock's broken. Cupboard's empty! The guns are gone—"

Guns gone! Wow! When would the wild dream end? Who could have stolen those weapons from the cupboard in Blair's cabin while this corridor was jammed with people? Then I realized with a shock that we'd all been glaring at the awful scene in Norwood's cabin and the thief might, at that very time, have slipped into the corridor, unnoticed. This creature that the steward had encountered. This horrible cripple with the cloak that blew like nocturnal wings, the claw-like hands and twisted face.

There was the assassin! The same assassin I had chased across Pahang. The one who had murdered Captain Lane in the saloon, striking through the darkness with the speed of a ghost. How had the killer slipped past Hague in the doorway? Satan only knew. Or was Bentfinger the devil himself, on a Witches' Sabbath holiday?

"I'll scour this hell-ship from stem to stern!" Hague roared at us. "Stay together in here and you'll be safe. You stay with them, inspector. Steward, you're coming with me. I'll—"

"Mr. Hague! Mr. Haaague!" Running boots drummed on the deck outside, beating time to the ghostly hallooing. The Scotchman flung about. Some one raced down the alleyway leading into the corridor; rounded the turn; galloped toward us. A youngster in ragged dungarees, chest and hands and face glistening with grease and sweat. An engineer by the looks of the wisp of rag knotted about his throat. He was waving something at the ship's commander; and I tell you, we yelled like fools. That engineer held in his clutch a little card.

"One of th' firemen found it!" he panted. "Lyin' on th' ladder leading down to th' fire room. On that port-side ladder where th' second landing is. Right near th' ice-water tank. Th' fireman was fetchin' me a drink an' he finds this thing right on th' top step of th' ladder—that one down there. Blimey!"

Blimey was not the half of it. Andrew Hague snatched the card, held it to light, and croaked out the typed legend in the voice of doom:

> To the Officers of the Arcturus:
>
> Head the ship for Cambodia Point. If the command is not obeyed somebody will die sooner than you think. And death will, thereafter, continue to strike until the ship is turned. You failed the first warning. One has died. Who will be next?

Who will be next? Hague stared down the corridor, sweat-beads big as pearls on his seamed forehead, jaw quivering. Then his big fist crushed the card, and his voice rasped fiercely above the booming of near-by thunderclaps. "Turn about? Never, by God! And nobody's going to be next! Found this in the engine room, eh? Outta my way, you bucko! I'm going below. If a man in my crew slips up on me he'll go overside. Found this on th' fire room ladder, eh? Then somebody put it there. And somebody seen it put there! That's the end of this devil's riot, right now! I'll get the dog who wrote this card! I'll get him!"

BUT ANDREW HAGUE never got him. He rushed for the deck outside, and the rest of us rushed out after him. Nobody wanted to remain in that awful corridor. Everybody must trample and yell and stay with everybody else. I got an arm around the girl's trembling shoulder and stumbled along in the frenzied mêlée. De Stroon was on one side of me and Gorn was on the other. Mrs. Phillipots was howling with fright and Dr. Smartbeck wailing a tenor obbligato, and the major brought up the rear with a snarling of good army oaths.

The engine room hatch was amidships, aft of the funnel. Dark? It was dark as a whale hole on that careening deck, with a world of plowing water piling and smashing and blowing beyond the rail. Wind lashed across wet iron. Spray flew and stung like hot salt. Up went the deck, and down; and we hung on and staggered and stumbled, cursing for courage and barking our shins on lifeboat davits, lashed by wind and flying water and fear.

"One has died. Who will be next?" Of that dash for the engine room I can recall little save those ghastly words.

I remember that Blair turned and yelled at us to go back. Gorn and De Stroon and Phillipots shouted. The hell-ship pitched and careened. A whip of brilliant lightning crackled across the sky and stabbed into an ocean of monster black metal waves. And Hague's square shoulders moved on.

At least the hatchway was lighted. Dim, to be sure, but a faint shaft of yellow glow and a soft breath of heat and oily smell reaching out of the darkness. The light picked out a patch of wet deck, struggled as far as the rail to show water guttering in the scuppers and the rusty davits and snarled tackle of a lifeboat. Lightning-blazed fast, and the Arcturus, with its funnel and masts and impossible little knot of people hustling along the starboard rail, fought the China Sea's storm.

And then there was nothing but that little patch of deck with its phantom yellow hatchway, gushing scuppers, rusty davits and shadowy lifeboat leaning outboard on trumpeting wind. But there was more in that little area of light. Hague had just reached the hatchway with Blair close behind him, when Blair let out a yell.

"Look!" The cry brought the rest of us stumbling to a halt; and the Scotchman spun around on his heel. Blair was pointing.

You know how lifeboats are covered with a sheet of canvas to keep out the damp? Unshipped, the boat hangs in its davits with a tarpaulin covering stretched from gunwale to gunwale. Sometimes stowaways hide beneath this excellent shelter. But no stowaway leaves one hand hanging limp over the lifeboat's quarter and the canvas rumpled where he climbed under cover. And there *was* a hand reaching out from under the rumpled tarpaulin stretched over the stern of that lifeboat. A limp pale hand that reached over the lifeboat's side and wagged with the motion of the ship.

Only Blair's sharp eyes would have spied it. Only Hague could have grabbed at it with a shout. Whipping aside the tarpaulin, he reached over the lifeboat gunwale; tugged; gasped; and hauled down to the deck a sagging, crumpled body.

"Good Lord! It's—it's Sparks. It's Dunlop, the radio operator! He's been killed! Shot through the temple—"

8

BEHIND THE BULKHEAD

LOOKING BACK ON that night of stark terror when a fiend loosed scarlet fancies across that storm-lashed ship lost in wild Asian seas, I am always amazed at the brawn of the human mind. Torture and red terror ride gibbering through the dark, the breaking point is reached, yet the well of courage is deep; there is unknown steel to fend off the smash of calamity; a man fights on.

Scared? Wow! You bet we were scared. But we drew on unknown sources for courage, and we had our ways of relief. Mrs. Phillipots could faint her way through any crisis. We could open our mouths and shout oaths.

I had a girl's tight hand to hold, and if her grip could be strong so could mine. I wasn't brave, God knows; but when you've got something to fight for, you can fight. And if the strain was terrible on all of us, it was a thousand times worse on the man from Scotland Yard whose job was to shackle the fiend, and on the big Scotch mariner, commanded to fight the whole hurricane.

All the rest of us had to do was keep out of the way of that deadly sharpshooter's bullet. Responsibility hung on that man from the London Yard and the grizzled master of the ship. There was that demon's note of warning. Head the ship around for Cambodia Point, or somebody will die. And somebody, moreover, would continue to die until the order was obeyed. Norwood had died. The radio operator had died. It was up to Andrew Hague. Andrew Hague was a wall of Highland granite. The Arcturus would not alter her course.

As for Blair, he stood over the dead wireless man, and the glow from the engine room hatchway found his British face not nice to see. Suddenly the whole sky was stabbed through and through with swords of livid flame, the ship jumped out of the darkness; and I remembered how the after deck hung at a steep tilt aloft on a sledding avalanche of brilliant ebony water, the after house and mast and taffrail outlined against the blazing sky. Chain lightning played and whiplashed around the ship, bringing three seconds of dazzling day.

Crash! The automatic in Blair's fist jumped and spat. Thunder bawled, crackled, slammed like iron doors banging in the sky. But Blair's voice rose above the tumult as his gun crashed again and he bounded down the deck. "I saw him! There he goes! Quick! Behind the after house!"

The darkness roared and the world vanished to nothing but deafening sound. Lightning stabbed again, and we could see Blair racing up an iron hill, legging it for the after house at its top. The ship lurched and a sheet of water came speeding over the rail and Blair disappeared for an instant in the cataract. Then he was running down hill, a weird figure under the flaring sky. Darkness swept the ship out of sight, and I found myself running in the middle of a shouting pack, pounding the invisible, treacherous deck with heels that hoped it would be there.

THAT AFTER DECK! Water flying in gusts around iron corners. Deck-bitts to smash your shins against. Ventilators leaping up to crack you in the face. The roar of pounding waves. The bang of hidden steering chains. Gear and tackle clanking and rattling, and a big square box free of its moorings and hurtling back and forth across the deck like a catamaran.

Somehow we (I don't know just who, but I was there and so were the girl and Major Phillipots and Hague) got around the corner of the deck house, after a desperate obstacle race up the starboard side of the ship. Blair was nowhere to be seen. Lightning speared into the heaving ink beyond the taffrail; showed the after deck deserted to a cloud of spray.

"Below!" Hague screamed. "Down that hatch—"

And down the hatch we went, tumbling and grabbing, anxious only to aid, to get there in time, to get hands on the demon Blair had seen. I know I expected to find Blair at the foot of that companion-ladder, dead with a bullet in his head. And nothing was to be found. I discovered the very same baggage room I'd run into when (it seemed a million bad years ago) I'd boarded this floating Hades in the Pahang River.

Remembering the hold below, I kicked through the jumble of steamer-trunks, plunged down the second companion and once more came up against the closed iron bulkhead. I floundered about the dim-lit compartment. The storm had played havoc down there. Hawsers and hose strewed the floor in a writhing tangle. Paint cans had been tossed from their shelves, broken open, and flooded the floor with red lead. Nobody had gone through that bulk-head this time, or the paint would have marked the trail.

"No one down here!" I shrieked, grabbing for the topside ladder. I heard Hague's answering call; heard the others go thumping up the ladder from baggage room to deck. There was no one to see me when the flooring pitched out from under my feet. I skidded, tripped in a knot of rope and lost balance. Down I went, flat on my face, in a swish-ing mess of red paint; and when I finally got upright, curs-ing and sopping crimson goo, and plunked topside to the deck behind the after house, I found my companions gone!

Believe me, the after deck of the Arcturus, right then, heaving and yanking through Cimmerian gusts of thun-dering sky and water, was a mighty poor place to be linger-ing in solitude. Nor was I, with my mouth full of paint, the one to linger. Stubbing my shins, hanging on with raw hands, striving to see through the screeching dark, I edged around the corner of the after house; started a race up the deck. Somewhere amidships voices called, coming faint down the wind that was like the blast of a cold explosion. Every soul on the ship seemed to be forward of the bridge, and I wanted companionship.

I got it!

I'd not gone twenty feet before a burst of ocean founted over the deck, flung me hard against a ventilator. A vivid tongue of light split open the sky. The ocean was bright from horizon to horizon. The Arcturus tossed under the glare. And there in front of me, conjured by the glow of the storm, stood that loathsome creature in the cape.

ON MY WORD, I was turned into ice. You have heard of the undead dead? The bloodless were-folk who prowl down the cemetery roads and feast on the souls of the young? But they are the phantoms of fiction, and radiant angels compared to the living kobold that grimaced before me in the wizard storm-light on that swerving deck.

That South China Sea lightning was no alley lantern-gleam; and I got one good look at that face. Let me tell you, the steward had not lied. I've seen the death masks of Carrier and Marat in the chamber of horrors at Madame Tussaud's. They were beautiful cameos by comparison. For the eyes in this head were like little cups of blood. A map of purple veins laced the temples. The right cheek bulged out, and the left cheek caved in, and the lips, drawn back, showed barren gums. And crippled?

Twiglike, paralysis-knotted hands wagged at the ends of malformed arms. Corkscrew arms, bent as if broken at the elbow and boneless at the wrists. There seemed to be no left shoulder and the sopping cape twirled around disjointed legs. All this I saw in that furious flicker of lightning; and the hot glare flashed on a massive automatic clutched in the twisty fingers of one crooked hand.

To this day I think the thing that saved me was the coat of red paint on my face. That monster had been waiting for me there, but unprepared to see my crimson-splashed countenance and scarlet-spitting mouth. And the lightning had gone when the automatic flamed. The bullet tore through my hair as I sprang, screaming. At the same time the sky came together with a roar, the deck tilted steep, water streamed through the whale-hole dark.

Kicking and hammering, I lunged into a billow of cloth. My knuckles struck into hard flesh. A dream! But the smash of the gun was reality; hot flame searing my throat and sending me stumbling. A smell of blood and powder, paint and burned cloth. Red in the darkness. My fingers on a rubbery wrist. Blows. Oaths. A whistly grunt. Somehow I got hold of the gun, lifted a kick, sent the weapon flying.

Then I was rolling on the deck, cracking my skull on a stanchion, fighting an empty cape. A salvo of yells was coming toward me. Boots thumping a tattoo. A light dodging in and out of gloom. Voices. Hands yanking me to my feet. Watery faces weaving in lantern-light. Hague. De Stroon. Phillipots. Gorn. A sobbing that was Mrs. Phillipots. A squeaking that was Dr. Smartbeck. All kaleidoscoping around me as I wobbled on sick legs and bleated out the words:

"I had him! Bentfinger! Right in my hands!" I was flagging the cape. The faces waxed and waned, steadied, took definite form. Gorn had me by the shoulders.

"Steady, Benson! Where'd he go—"

"There's the cape—"

"Which way? Which way?"

"Oh my God, he's all blood—"

"*Help!*" The wail echoed out of a basso thunder-clap, frantic, high-keyed, coiling up out of the blackness somewhere amidships on the other side of the deck. "Quick! Help—"

"It's Blair!" Hague waved the lantern; yelled. Led by the big Scotchman we rushed down hill across the reeling deck, sprinted in wild chase for the bridge. The weak light flowed through the shadows ahead of us; found Blair kneeling against the rail under a bridge-wing, supporting in his arms some one who had fallen like a drunk in the scuppers. That some one was the steward with the big nose. And the steward with the big nose was dead.

BLAIR'S WRENCHED MOUTH barked, his voice husky as sandpaper. "I saw it! That devil! I lost him back there on the after deck; thought the rest of you were behind me and rushed back to the bridge here. The second mate yelled at me. I ran up to the wheelhouse. Then I heard screaming somewhere aft. A second later—this—this devil was coming down the deck. Could see him by the lightning. His cape was gone. He—he's the devil, himself.

"This steward was standing down here. I screamed. There was thunder and a blaze of light and here's this man shot through the head and—and I don't know where—where the killer's gone. 'Who's next?' he shrieked. Then—then vanished." Blair's face dripped. His eyes glared at Hague. He panted. "The steward's dead. My God, Hague, do you think—do you think we ought to turn the ship back— before some one else—"

I think it was Gorn who was hollering. I don't know. Everybody hollered. Waving arms and opening mouths and dancing around in the lantern-flicker. And then there was that fusillade. *Smash! Smash! Smash!* Thunder in the sky? It was not. Gunfire, it was, and it roared up from the bow beyond the bridge. Tongues of dull flame licked out of the dark. A wild racketing blew aft on the stinging wind. A gnome-like figure sped out of the gloom, bounding toward us. The bald-headed bo's'n with the ears!

"Mutiny! 'Elp! It's th' crew! They won't stay on this 'ell-ship no longer! They're gonna take off wiv th'boats—"

Boots banged on the bridge-wing overhead, and a bearded ghost looked down. From the beard came a foghorn bellow. "Mister Haaague! Word from below! Our wheel's gone, Mister Haaague, an' we're startin' to list! Pumps won't work! An' we're quarter point off course an' white water dead ahead—"

Bombshells! Bombshells in wild cannonade. Mutiny. Murder. Storm. But I wasn't hearing. Going from one white face to another, I was, and shrieking at the top of my lungs. Gorn, De Stroon, Smartbeck, screeching back. "Don't know!"—"Didn't see!"—But I had Major Phillipots by the collar and pounded a fist on his chest. *The girl! Where is she? Where's the girl—*"

"Not here?" he bawled. "Why, she went back after *you!* You didn't come out of that after deck hatch, an' she waited in th' hatchway for you—"

Waited on that after deck for me! How I yelled! Throwing the major to one side, I knocked over the cluttering dandelion, and bounded off down the black deck.

It wasn't forty yards to that after deck, but right then it was four thousand miles. Four thousand miles through the treacherous dark. Now the deck slid out from under my feet. Now it rose up to slug me in the face. I scrambled, skidded, sprawled, skipped, caromed off the rail. Wind snatched at my legs, water slashed at my face. A fine, gentle romp I had with that boat already beginning to tip, Hades's own symphony playing riot on the distant bow, the air full of spray and thunder and faint yells and the snapping of guns.

A wave of white lightning shivered across the horizon and showed me a crowd of greasy-faced men spilling up out of a companionway behind the tilted funnel. Bells were clamoring, the men were yowling; and I yowled like a fool at them. "Help! Help find a girl—"

What did they care about a girl, those ruffians? There was water on the fire-floor, and it was going to be every man for himself.

Try to fancy the situation. That raving, crazy-rolling Arcturus. Mutiny before the mast. No hands to help her below. Leaking like a sieve, powerless without her wheel, surf breaking directly ahead. Four dead men with bullets in their heads. A toothless fiend loose in the storming dark. And somewhere, alone on that perilous after deck, a girl who had waited for me.

IT WAS IN a daze, I can tell you, and the bang I got in the face as I skated around the after house through a Niagara of spray did little to clear my numbed brain. Crying her name, I flung down the ladder to the baggage room. Hope Brown was not there. I shin-banged down the second companion to hit that lower hold heels over head in a shower of oaths, water and paint tins.

Heaven knows why I expected to find her down there. I suppose I looked because the back of my squirrel-brained head kept believing that the girl hadn't seen me when I dashed topside in the pitch before, and had come below, herself, to locate me. She was not to be seen, of course. There was just that topsy-turvy hold with red paint swirling across its iron floor, cans and rubbish and my own anxious boots drifting wildly around in the paint. There was nothing but that blank iron bulkhead and the dim-glowing electric bulb swinging down from a stanchion.

Sick in my very veins, I grabbed at the ladder going topside; got one paint-plastered shoe on the bottom step.

The hold spun and lurched stifling with the stench of turpentine and tar, and for a moment I could do nothing but hang.

Exhaustion plays queer tricks with the mind. Funny how I could hear the girl's voice calling to me. Calling. Calling from far away, faint above the thousand dinnings of iron walls and straining stanchions, like an echo from another world.

"Hope!" I shrieked. "Hope! It's me—"

"In here!" The faint echo twisted the fizzing head on my neck and set me going like a jumping jack. *In here! Help me! I'm in here!*

Do you think I didn't get a noise out of my lungs? That girl's voice was coming from the other side of the locked bulkhead—that slab-iron partition through which Bentfinger had disappeared so many mad hours before. I pressed my shoulders against the barrier, and yelled. "It's bolted on your side! Throw the bolt—"

"There isn't any bolt!" she wailed. "I can't get out! I'm locked in—"

"How'd you get through?" I screeched, desperate. "Where?"

"I don't know!" Her voice just reached me. "I thought you were in here! I was shoving on the door. Suddenly it opened. I fell into this room. The door slammed behind me! I think I pushed on a knob—Find a knob—"

Find a knob! Good Lord above, that cursed bulkhead was covered over with knobs. Reënforced with iron bands riveted onto the massive slab with at least two thousand bolts. Every bolt-head was a knob, and I hammered on those bolt-heads till my fists were raw.

Maybe you think I had a lot of time to go punching at those unresisting bolts. I did not. The floor was tipping at an angle of twenty degrees, and instead of swinging back upright it was staying that way. Black water was squirting across the aft end of the hold and deepening in a well in the lowest corner. And I could not open that bulkhead. My knuckles were pulped and my toes kicked numb as I thumped, slugged and banged on row after row of bolts, hammered and tore at giant hinges and casing, and that iron gate never budged.

"THINK!" I SCREAMED. "What knob? Where?" And the eyes stuck out of my head, watching the water creep up that floor.

"I don't know!" her voice sobbed. "The door just opened. I'm in a little room. There's nothing on this side of the door, It's just—just flat. And there's no other way to get out!"

I'd have knocked the foundations out from under Gibraltar with that attack, but that bulkhead in the bowels of the foundering Arcturus was shut and shut to stay. Somewhere I'd missed the right knob. If I didn't find that knob I might as well be yelling "Open Sesame!" at the vault door of the United States Mint.

Once more I thumped over those bolts. To this day it makes me sick to hear a riveting-hammer or see girders laid on a bridge. For I pounded on those bolts till I founted sweat and blood, and the floor kept tipping steeper and steeper under my feet, water climbed to my heels, the voice through the iron slab weakened to a feeble echo, and the puzzle of the bulkhead's lock would not solve.

And then the preposterous occurred. There was a rending explosion. There was a *smash!* like the breaking of the

There was a stunning, ear-smashing roar

axle of the world. The floor sprang out from under me.
The walls bulged in and spat smoke. Tossed off my feet,
I whirled through a gyroscope swirl of flying water, rope,
paint and tin cans, went acrobating against the companion ladder, bounced back spinning like a top, and cracked
head-on against the bulkhead.

And I hit the right knob! The door shot open like the lid
of a Chinese trick-box. That partition yawned wide, and
I flew through the opening, and the bulkhead slammed
with a *wham!* And there I was, doubled against the wall
of a narrow metal compartment—the strangest room in
the world. The cave of Aladdin was an unfurnished hall
compared to that secret cabin.

The compartment was all angles because the Arcturus
was leaning on her beam, but even if set on a level that
cabin was a place for astonishment. Walls, floor and ceiling
of polished steel. A brilliant incandescent lamp glowing in

the ceiling. A metal desk screwed to the wall, and fastened atop the desk a portable typewriter!

Fresh air blew from a funnel set high in one wall and whispered across the ceiling with a hobgoblin sound. A queer buzzing came from what appeared to be an electric furnace built into one of the narrow corners. Metal shelves laden with queer instruments—shiny forceps, torches, hammers, pipes, mortars—were set in the wall above the furnace. And there was a switchboard boasting brass handles and little plungers and rows of punch-buttons and wire plugs. Imagine a compartment ten feet long, eight feet high and four broad, resembling a physics laboratory and the control room of a submarine combined, and you'll have a faint idea of that cubicle.

Stunned, I glared at the high-voltage oven, that elaborate switchboard, the rows of strange instruments, that metal desk with its typewriter. Cotton cleared from my head, and I saw the girl. She was standing against the steel casement of the bulkhead, her poppy robe clutched tight about her small figure, her dark bob tousled and falling in curly disarray before her wide gray eyes. A cold fear wrought its expression on the pale oval of her face; and the heart turned to water in my chest. Not till then did I realize that the bulkhead had slammed shut behind me. And there wasn't a hook, knob or latch on the polished-steel inner surface of that bulkhead. No key to that hidden spring-lock. We were fastened, the girl and I, in a steel vault at the bottom of a sinking ship.

YES, THE ARCTURUS was sinking! I could hear rushing water slap against the barrier shutting us in. Bubbles oozed through cracks in the metal casement. Somewhere beyond the walls of our steel prison things exploded with muffled thumps, echoed by a jarring bump that lifted me to my feet.

"How," I panted at the girl, "why—why'd you come in here?"

She reached out a hand. "I waited above for you. You must have passed me in the dark. I ran down into that hold—saw your tracks on the floor. I—I thought you'd gone through the bulkhead. When I pushed on it, it opened—" The whisper died on her lips with a strange sob. She wasn't reaching a hand. She was pointing. Pointing at my feet.

I suppose I jumped straight up in the air. For I was standing against that wall where the explosion had thrown me; and on somersaulting into that compartment, I'd landed atop a mound of little leather bags. One of the bags had split open; and was spilling something across my shoes that gave me a shock. My mouth unhinged with a snap! Like a dolt I stared, the eyes bulging out of my head. Do you know what was spilling from that bag?

"Emeralds!" Hope gasped.

Yes, emeralds! Emeralds as big as fat grapes. And diamonds and rubies and pearls! I moved my foot, and the leather bag emptied, and across the polished steel floor there scampered a glittering, twinkly cascade. I shouted; kicked at another bag, and the leather burst with a vivid flash. Ransom of forty kings scattered, twinkling, at my feet. A thousand rainbow-colored points of light danced, brilliant, across the floor; glittering, winkering, showering darts of red, green and blue fire that flamed in the mirroring steel walls like atoms escaped from the sun. You understand? There were those bags of fabled gems, there was that steel-bound room—and all *that* on a rotten tramp steamer going down in the South China Sea.

You wonder that I yowled like a maniac when I scooped up a handful of those livid little fires and found real jewels in my palm? It's no nice sensation—thinking you've gone raving mad. But the girl's arms were about me; I suddenly realized that tan-hued smoke was puffing out of the air-funnel overhead; dark water leaked across that incredible floor! There wasn't any time to waste for breath-taking. That bulkhead had to be opened. I hurled myself against the slab. The Bulkhead did not move.

But a portion of the wall behind me moved! Hidden bolts creaked and a spring-lock binged! I heard a frightened scream from the girl. A damp wind smote the back of my neck. Leaping around fast, I was just in time to see a square of the polished wall at the far end of the cubicle drop inward. A stooped, dark figure stepped from this astounding aperture. The figure raised its head. And I was glaring at the face of the English silk buyer, Gorn.

Struck to stone Gorn stood, and so did the girl and I; and the glow from a dozen emeralds on the floor near the silk buyer's boots shed a witchy green light on his face. I can tell you he looked mad enough as his black eyes roved the cubicle, knifed at us where we stood against the bulkhead, and finally fixed on that little pile of gem-spilling leather bags. That magician's apartment with its typewriter and switchboard, trick trapdoors, queer furnace, and gems! Madness, I promise you. Yet the maddest of all in that aberrant scene was Gorn stepping through the hole in that steel wall, and holding in one hand the little blue-leather notebook that Blair had lost.

Gorn's other fist clutched a gun.

"Pick up those bags, Benson!" he growled in his throat. "Come on, girl. Move fast. She's sinking and we've got to hurry. You're both coming with me—"

I made a jump for him, but he saw it coming. Up lashed the gun-barrel; and I caught it. Square on the tip of the chin I caught it, and I dived in a shower of stars.

9

BENTFINGER!

HANDCUFFS ON MY wrists, my pockets weighted with leather jewel-bags, my jaw swelling, and the muzzle of Gorn's automatic ice cold on the nape of my neck, there was nothing for me to do but climb the narrow companion leading topside from the door in the steel wall. The girl was ahead of me, shackled, too; and I ground my teeth, ill with rage. She had given Gorn a battle. I could tell by the fresh scratches bleeding on his chin.

And I hadn't even touched the man. Now the only thing to do was wait for another chance. He'd withheld the fire of his gun, and at least we were not to be drowned like rats in a box, fastened in that vault-like compartment. But my head was spinning like a top, as my brain, dulled by knock-outs and exhaustion, groped through the riddle.

That secret compartment. Trapdoors and a companion-way hidden in the hull of the ship. Those bags of gems. And the appearance of Gorn carrying in his fist the notebook that had so mysteriously disappeared from Blair's hand! Gorn! Cold sweat oozed out on my cheeks.

"Hurry up!" he prodded fiercely. "Any more tricks and I'll let you have it! Move fast, or we'll never get out of here alive."

That was one bad moment for me, let me tell you. For myself I cared little. But to see the girl—Hope—trapped in this miasmic nightmare! Clenching my teeth, I fumbled along behind her.

Now that companionway was dark, the ladder began to spiral upward, tunneling between narrow walls. Giant catamarans seemed to be hammering against the wall on my left side, and I guessed there was nothing between us and the ocean save that plate of iron.

The wall against which my shoulder was wedged gave off a feeling of heat, and vibrated to a grinding and pounding that came from its other side. A choky smoke swirled about me, and I heard the girl cough.

We seemed to be climbing a chimney that leaned away from its base. Pawing up that crazy ladder, I moved past a red eye set in the dark wall. Smoke curled out of the eye, and it proved to be a hole about the size of a saucer. That hole looked into the engine room, and I caught a brief picture of hot inferno—peeped into a red, black and brass cavern jumbled with steep stairways, iron gratings, pipes going every-which-way. Smoke wreathed the railings and polished bars, and in the middle of the weird scene a pair of huge brass shafts moved up and down like pump handles gone lunatic in a madhouse of machinery.

"Step on it!" Gorn shouted. "You'll be out of this in a minute!"

"There's a door!" the girl cried; and I saw her small shoulders outlined in a square of dim light six feet above me. Gorn rammed me with his automatic, and I clambered to reach the girl. The door opened into a cabinet. There was a second door, swung wide. A moment later I was standing with Hope on one side and Gorn on the other, in an up-ended passenger's stateroom. Fingers of smoke writhed up the tilted floor, and the cabin was suffocating with the stench of burning grease, hot oil and tar. The cabin door banged, swinging on its hinges. Gorn shouted.

"Come on!"

No gainsaying the blaze of his black, beady eyes and the mouth of that massive automatic. Keeping us covered, he forced us through the cabin door. The corridor was topsy-turvy and black with smoke-gusts. Trying to shield the girl, I fought along through the smoke and found the alley leading to the deck outside. God knows I couldn't think. I remember tottering around on a tipping, slippery deck, scrambling through a maze of tangled gear, deck-tackle and rubbish, edging along close to the girl and waiting without nerves for a bullet to punch out my brains.

THE ARCTURUS LAY groaning on her starboard beam in a battering, booming sea. Storming water blew over her port rail to sweep the deck with a screech. Red flares were flaming on her bow, shedding a crimson haze that tipped with queer light the wings and upper decks of the bridge and made blood-like the ocean that bounded over the fore deck. A score of ghostly figures dodged through the red and black maelstrom, chorusing faintly above the diabolical tumult.

But we were amidships, and my yells never traveled as far as the bridge.

Can you see me there, hanging to that shivery rail on that tipped-up deck, rattling the steel bracelets on my wrists, cursing, my face scarlet with welts and red paint and fire-glow, my pockets bulging with bags full of emeralds and diamonds and pearls?

Can you see the girl at my side,—shackled as I was, her face stricken with fear, her poppy robe blowing, water sluicing about her feet?

Can you see that hell-ship leaning over in the storming surf, waves sledging her windward beam, spray whizzing down her decks, water founting over bow and quarter, all black and banging and the moan of tortured metal save where that mushroom, maroon flare blossomed to make dim carnival in the blind and boiling night? And there was Gorn's dark figure jumping and dodging about us, wagging his gun, clawing through knots of gear, yanking at hawsers and iron bars.

Somehow or other there appeared a gap in the rail. Gorn dimmed out in a cloud of spray.

"Get your hands on this rope, you two! Quick! There's a boat below and we can make it! This way, Benson! Lively there! Give me a hand, or I'll shoot—"

Lord only knows how we managed to get ourselves in the boat and away. Vaguely I recall sliding, scrambling, inching down a wave-doused iron hill, Gorn's arm around my neck as I battled with manacled hands to keep a clutch on the girl. Nor do I know how Gorn contrived to keep his gun on my neck-nape, grapple with the snarled tackle, and, at the same time, cut the sea painter and set us adrift without capsizing.

There was one awful minute while Gorn fought with the steering oar, screeching at the girl and me to get our hands on oars and pull away, when that eggshell of a dory soared skyward on foaming water and threatened to drop

with a smash on the flooded after house of the ship. Say
this much for Gorn—he was a seaman. He got two hand-
cuffed captives into a lifeboat and clear in water that boiled
like a channel beneath Niagara.

And there I was, hauling on oar handles, square in the
teeth of the storm. A comber snatched the dory to its crest,
and we sped through the gale like a chip in a mill race.
The Arcturus drifted far astern, a crimson smear in the
shouting dark. Some time later the crimson smear faded
out. Chill, clammy moisture brushed at my face. A weird,
cottony, white smoke whisked and swirled through the
darkness. "Row!" Gorn screamed; and I rowed. Above the
drumming of blood in my ears I could hear the somber
roar of tumbling surf.

FOG. THERE MUST have been dawn-light somewhere
above, for the mist brightened and where our dory clove
whitecaps clean rainbows shimmered. But the mist was an
added terror. You could not see an oar's length off the bow.
The vapor poured like white steam off the heaving, dark
water, wreathing its clammy tentacles, puffing and blowing
and conjuring cloudy ghosts that were quick to dissolve
in gray spray. It was queer and terrifying. Three of us in a
wooden eggshell lunging through creaming water. Our
bobbing heads and struggling shoulders swimming a swirl
of cold steam. You've seen fog on tumbling surf? But you've
never seen fog such as smoked up that morning from the
surf of the South China Sea. And I hope you never do.

I suppose I'd been rowing for two thousand years. My
body had long since ceased to ache. My backbone was
nothing but a twinge somewhere, my hands chunks of
numbness on yanking oar-handles. The chill white vapor

had drifted into my head. By twisting my neck I could look over my shoulder and see a pale oval of face behind me. Otherwise I wouldn't have cared.

Dimly I was conscious of hating something. Sometimes I thought it was the steel bands that gleamed on my wrists. Diabolical, those handcuffs. Just strong enough to bind me helpless; just loose enough to let me row. Then I would raise my eyes and see the dim figure crouched in the stern, gleams that were two black eyes, a glitter of set white teeth, a glint that was a leveled gun. How I hated that poised shadow that was Gorn! Gorn! Gorn with his dark face and flickery eyes crouched there in the stern, fighting with the handle of the steering oar, grim and devilish and holding me captive to his will.

"Row!" he bawled; and I rowed. A thousand wild schemes chased themselves across my brain. Tip over the boat. Make a sudden leap for that gun. Smash that face with the iron on my wrists. But there was the girl behind me—there was nothing to do but row.

I can't tell you how he steered us into the lagoon. I suppose it was a lagoon, for instead of boiling and smashing, the water beneath the fog settled into long, undulant swells and the dory swung along like a hammock. A thin shaft of amber light lanced through a hole in the swirling mist and picked out a patch of green seaweed. A rainbow arched through the vapor, and bottle-green water shimmered. Moving my head, I saw the girl as a shadow of poppy-color bent over her oars. Her forehead rested on her hands and the oars did not move, the blades swishing and bobbing in the cutwater.

Yes, Gorn still crouched in the stern. Water wiggled

down his swarthy cheeks, dripped from the tip of his nose, pasted a sheaf of black hair across his forehead. A purple bruise swelled beneath his left eye and the daylight, struggling through the mist, gave a bluish tinge to his face. His white teeth grimaced, and a harsh whisper sawed out through his colorless lips.

"We're through—Lord knows how. There's—the fog lifting. There's a beach—a beach up ahead—"

His lips closed with a snap. He was balanced on his feet, hand upraised. From out of the wreathing vapor off our beam there stole a thin sound. A queer, squeaky chirping. A spectral mumbling. The creak of oarlocks and the echo of distant voices! The plash of a moving boat! Mouth open, I reared to my feet. Gorn whirled about with a throaty oath; stabbed out hard with the gun.

"Down, Benson!" he breathed fiercely. "Down on those oars, and row. One peep out of you, and you and the girl are done! Now, row like the devil! Row!"

A LUMINESCENT CURTAIN, the thinning mists rose on a crescent stage of rice-white sand across which foaming battalions of breakers charged and dropped back in retreat. A steep hill, bare as a brown wall, backed the beach and raised its forehead against a sweep of clean, cobalt sky. Green nipa palms leaned seaward in the wind at the hilltop, and sunshine flooding down the slope and flashing on puffs of spray was so much liquid gold.

Our boat sped out of the fog bank high on the crest of a comber. Like a surf-board the little dory raced in a cloud of spume toward the beach. Voices yelled out of the vapor astern and were drowned by the shout of collapsed waves.

I'll never forget Gorn balanced in the stern of that

speeding smallboat. Never. Like something of rock, he stood, feet braced on the heaving bottom-boards, his body bent into the wind. Sudden sunshine was white on his tense, corded face. His unkempt black hair was flying. The tails of his drill coat stood out stiff behind him as he clung to the steering oar, battling its blade through the foam. The eyes in his head were points of black agate, straining to catch the first break; and he took us into a burst of white spray with a triumphant yell.

One agonizing minute as the dory turned turtle in a thunderous watery cloud. One agonizing second while I somersaulted through a fountain of flying water and sand. Then I was floundering on hands and knees across the beach, spitting the tooth that an oar-handle had knocked out of my jaw, coughing up a lungful of salt water and watching, dim-eyed, as Gorn plunged out of the spume with the girl's limp figure in his arms. I shouted as I saw him make a staggery dash across the white sand and, still clutching her poppy-colored figure, start a run up that steepling hill. I squalled at him, and he squalled back at me, and somehow I got my legs under me and started after.

That impossible chase up the face of that sun-washed slope! Gorn legging it fast with a girl in his arms, sand scattering from his striving heels. I could see her limp arms; see the sunlight glinting on the metal that shackled her wrists. Holding my own manacled fists in front of me, I followed on legs of melting rubber, dazed, fighting for strength, fighting for a footing, fighting for every breath in my tortured lungs. Whence either of us drew the power to run the good Lord only can guess.

Do dead men run up steep hills? They do! Two dead

men once ran up a hill on a tropical island, and one of them carried a girl in a poppy-colored robe. The other one carried handcuffs on his wrists and bags of giant jewels in his pockets and in his head a tiny spark of life that made him want to fight for the saving of that girl. I know, because I was that one, and I fought, at the hilltop, for the girl.

I caught Gorn at the hilltop, you understand, and fought. I suppose it wasn't much of a fight. I struck out with hands of tissue paper, trying to jam my steel wristlets into his face. He struck back with fists of cotton, yelling things I couldn't hear; and I'd been slugged in the head so many times of late that I couldn't feel the blows.

But there was a massive granite wall leaning between two tall palm trees. I bumped into the wall and fell down. Gorn leaned over me, grabbed at my belt, and dragged me over the stones. It was cool behind the granite wall. I lay on a bed of cool flagstones. Then Hope's marble-white face looked down at me. Her cheeks were wet and her gray eyes glistened and her brown hair blew about her shoulders. Somehow or other, her hands seemed to be free, and when she placed a trembling palm against my cheek I strove like Atlas and got up on one elbow.

THE NEXT THING I saw was the cannon. An ancient, rusty cannon, mounted on slabs of basalt and poking its blunt, stub nose over the rim of the wall. A bizarre, dream-cannon it was, its barrel scribbled over with strange cornices and inscriptions, a brass two-headed-lion couchant on its breech. I'd seen such pieces before—corroded green relics—but I thought they were all in the British Museum. "Presented to Her Majesty the Queen by King Sisowath of Ohore—Dec., 1840." Only this wasn't the British

Museum. It was not. A ruined fort at the top of an island in Asia, it was; and there was Gorn, a black shadow dancing at the gun-breech.

"Powder!" He was panting to himself like a maniac; like a maniac clawing at the lid of an iron box that came from beneath the gun's grotesque breech. The lid unlatched, and a black trickle fell to the flagstones. *"Dry powder!"*

Unreal? Of course it was unreal. That massive granite fort wall crowning the hilltop. The sweep of unmarred blue sky, hot with early sunshine. The towering nipa palms standing sentinel against the blue. That ancient Siamese cannon that should have been moldering in a museum. And the grim, bedraggled jinni babbling at the cannon's breech. Unreal, febrile imaginings. The fag end of ululating nightmare.

And the worst thing about a nightmare is its seeming reality. Certainly I had scrabbled and yammered across the decks of a fearful tramp ship. There had been people, and some of them had been slain. There had been a crippled monstrosity with a toothless mouth, and fire and water and pain. Cards bearing a typed name. A man from Scotland Yard who wrote in a little blue leather notebook. A topsy-turvy hold and a bulkhead covered with bolts. A fantasy room with steel walls and a secret passage. A sinking ship and a lifeboat whirling through storm. Fog and a plunge through wild water. Now a hilltop and sunshine, an old fort and a relic cannon; and a goblin-creature who yelled about dry powder and waved a ragged arm.

I ticked the fancies off in my aching mind. Nightmares all. Only in nightmares do monsters vanish and appear, do you find strange bags of precious stones, do you fall through space, and strive for a girl, and groan in the power of a dark-faced wizard. In nightmares you try to yell, and can't. I tried to yell, and could not.

Then soft hands had captured my cheeks, and a girl's white face was real as the sunshine of day. Gorn was shouting and pounding on an old iron cannon; and I lay on my back behind a wall. Far-away voices chorused and called. Gorn was running up and down, stooped behind the stone barricade, cursing and croaking like a frightened crow.

The girl's face looked down at me, and hot tears fell on my cheek. Like a corpse come to life, I sprang to my feet. Gorn flung at me; caught me by the shoulders.

"Come out of it!" He shook me till the smashed clockwork in my head clanked. "Come out of it, Benson. You've got to help me! They've landed on the beach and they're coming up the hill! Wake up! Snap out of it! I tell you, you've got to help—"

White hands flew before my eyes and fastened in Gorn's wild hair. Have you ever heard a girl's voice low with fury? By Heaven, it pumped some blood back in my veins. "Leave him alone—he's hurt! I told you I'd stay quiet if you didn't harm him! Let him be. What are you trying to do—what are you going to do?"

"Get back!" Gorn snarled, and yanked her to one side. I stumbled over him, and he drove me to my knees. "They're coming up the hill, damn you. *He's* coming up the hill." He was shaking me again, and the teeth clattered in my jaw. "You understand? And I can't find a shot for that cannon!"

HE PANTED. SWEAT poured down his face. Dropping to one knee, he tore at a flagstone with bloodied finger nails. "No use! Dry powder! Nothing to shoot!" His head twisted, jerked; his birdlike eyes darted quick glances from one side to the other.

Leaping up, he made a bound for the stone wall; clawed at the granite chunks. "Can't loosen them! Not a cannon ball in the place. Nothing—nothing to stop that cursed—"

"What are you doing? What are you going to do—" Hope knelt beside me. Her arm was about my shoulder, and her wind-blown hair was soft perfume against my cheek. She sobbed at the wild man, and he answered her with a snarl.

"You'll find out!" Darting to the cannon, he craned his neck and peered over the wall. "They're coming on. He's in the lead. *He* knows I'm unarmed. He knows I've nothing but an empty gun—"

"Empty gun!" I was reeling on my feet again, laughing like a hyena. Empty gun! This dark-visaged devil had been holding me captive with an empty gun. Plunging across the flagstones with a wail, I brought my locked fists down on his black head. But Gorn was a goblin that would not die. He went to his knees, but his arms were traps on my sick legs and I flopped over backward with a crash.

No drinker of absinthe could imagine what happened then. Those little leather bags of gems! Those little bundles of fabulous stones that had dragged like ton-weights in my pockets! We'd forgotten those jewels, Gorn and I; now they blazed into memory. For one of the bags burst open under my fall, and a shower of rainbow colors scampered across the sunlit flagstones.

Hope screamed. Gorn flung her aside and was on me like a catamount. Smothering my face with one hand, he robbed my pockets with the other, grabbing out the stuffed leather pouches and flinging them against the granite wall.

I couldn't get to my feet. I swear I could not. The sight of Gorn with his dripping, twisted face and frenzied hands snatching up those jewel-bags one by one and stuffing them down the mouth of that green Siamese cannon impaled me gasping where I lay. He stuffed those sacks down the mouth of that cannon, I say, his arm pumping in and out of the iron maw like a ramrod.

You needn't believe me—yet. I did not believe my own eyes. I managed to stand upright in the yellow sunshine of that place; and diamonds, emeralds and pearls crunched under my drunken boots. Once more I heard clamorous voices—a weird, human baying that seemed to grow louder and louder above the chant of distant surf. Hope stood against the granite wall, hands groping for support on the stone. Somehow I got to her side.

And when I looked down the slant of that hill bowling down to the beach I let a whoop out of my lungs that you could have heard on the Bay of Bengal.

On the glistening sands far below two lifeboats were smashed to kindling in the foam. One of those boats had belonged to us. The other belonged to them. And they were coming up the hill, all right. Coming up the hill on a run, crying out, waving hands, calling. De Stroon and Dr. Smartbeck and the Phillipotses. The bo's'n with the bald head and fan ears, three sailors with gleaming rifles, Hague and Blair.

They were water-soaked, and wobbly, ragged and tattered and torn, but they came on through the sunshine like an army of the Lord. Blair ran in the lead, and how he ran. His garments showered water. His sandy hair blew! His face glistened bright in the sunlight. He was almost up the hill, and I yelled when I saw the pistol glint in his fist; saw the brave set of his jaw.

"Come on!" I screamed. "You'll catch him!" Waving like a lunatic I bounced atop the wall. "He isn't armed!" I screamed. "He hid the gems in the cannon and ran—"

BUT GORN HAD not run, as I, right then, discovered. He had made one tigerish leap to the breech of the cannon, and that was as far as he went. Nor had he tried to hide those gems! A small metal matchbox fell from his fingers, and a puff of fire flared in his cupped hand.

Things happened fast. Blair came over the hill-crest on a bound, sighted Gorn, and sprang forward with his pistol spitting flame. Gorn's hand flew to the cannon-breech and the flare in his fingers dropped through a hole in the tail of the two-headed lion. There was a stunning, ear-smashing roar. One terrific, world-quaking sound-clap. A blinding spout of flame burst brilliant from the mouth of that cannon; flashed incredible lightning through the sunshine. No gun in God's world ever fired such shrapnel. No gun ever will, again.

Pearls, diamonds and emeralds volcanoed from the maw of that preposterous piece of oriental ordnance, lashed through the sunlight and struck Blair square in the chest. Not three feet from that cannon-mouth Blair had stood, and he made a red hole in the glare.

The strange red hole was a red ball bouncing down the hill. Ghosts farther down that hill screamed and danced to get out of the way. I got my face off a flagstone; made an insane rush at Gorn. He never lifted a hand to stop me, but he stopped me anyway. Leaning across the barrel of the smoke-spewing cannon, Gorn was pointing down the hill. His hand was palsied, but his face was chopped out of oak.

"Look! By heaven, look!" His lips formed the words, and the voice echoed up from a deep, deep well. "By heaven, Benson, look!"

I looked. I looked down that hill. I believe Gorn fumbled a key out of his pocket, unlocked my wrists, the girl came to take me by the hand, and the three of us ran downhill side by side. There were strange ghosts peopling the white, fine crescent beach. De Stroon, Dr. Smartbeck, the Phillipotses. Hague and the sailors and something else. That "something else" was the queerest, strangest ghost of all. I don't know how the others felt about it. I could hear them gargling and gurgling. As for me, I had to yell out loud to keep from going to pieces.

For there on the sand with its chest shot to shards lay the creature of an opium-eater's dream. Face up in the sunshine it lay, sprawled flat at the end of a crooked crimson path that marked its course down the hill. There was Blair's pistol in the twisted hand! There was Blair's soaked suit of clothes! There was Blair's shot-smashed chest! But the rest was a black, monstrous magic. A devil's thaumaturgy. An awful legerdemain. Blair had died on that hilltop, I tell you. But this *thing* lying dead at the foot of the hill—Listen!

The legs were twisted like bed-springs! The arms were malformed, bent awry at the elbows, boneless at the wrists! The hands were twisty-fingered, crippled claws! I've seen the death masks of Carrier and Marat in the chamber of horrors at Madame Tussaud's—they were beautiful cameos compared to this one. For the eyes in this head were like little cups of blood. The right cheek bulged out. The left cheek caved in. And the lips, drawn back, grinned on barren gums!

There was more, I promise you. More! Embedded in that veined left temple was an emerald the size of a grape. Sunshine touched it and danced off, green and shocked. Green and shocked, too, Gorn stooped and plucked something from the scarlet that welled on the sand. A set of false teeth!

Gorn's whisper might have come from those teeth as they jiggled on his palm; the voice was by no chance human or his.

"Bentfinger!"

Mrs. Phillipots fainted at last.

10

UNTANGLED THREADS!

YOU SEE SOME odd numbers on the oriental seas, but you never saw an odder lot than the passenger list of the Madame Chrysanthème. I guess the skipper of that Messageries Maritimes mail packet thought so, too, for the eyes stuck out of his head when he saw us on the wharf of the little island town. He looked almost as winded as the village priest who first saw us come up the beach. I suspect when we boarded the French steamer we were the oddest crowd of passengers in the world.

As for that decrepit old French steamer—well, she was a pleasure yacht, you understand. What if the bread from her galley wore whiskers and her cabins weren't white as blown snow? Who cared? She got us away from that frowsty island with its ghastly crescent beach and muttering reef where the masts of a ship jutted, grisly, out of the foam. She hurried us off down a blue and gold bay, and left clean horizon behind. A fine boat, the Madame Chrysanthème.

Her captain was a first class fellow, too. Out at the elbows, perhaps, and his walrus mustache needed fumigating; but a ship's master he was, acquainted with the finer points of his job.

Dr. Ernest Wonger Smartbeck craned out of his chair

with a gulp. "I knew it!" The glasses waggled on his nose and he made a grandmotherish gesture. "I knew it all along, Mr. Gorn. I just knew *you* were a man from Scotland Yard!"

Major Phillipots withered the dandelion with a sneer and acid comment: "Rubbish!" and subsided, snorting through his nose.

Standing at the rail, Gorn soberly shook his dark head, his somber eyes studying the adhesive tape binding his wrist. "Shouldn't be surprised if you people had guessed it, at that," he mourned. "The mysterious way I tried to act. It might have been better if I'd owned up and clapped the lot of you in irons at the start. But I'd never have got *him*, if I had. And I had to get him at all costs. That's what the chief said. 'Get Bentfinger at all costs.' I might have saved Norwood and the steward. And, yet—" Gorn sighed and twisted a fist on the ship's rail.

"Well, poor blighters, it couldn't be helped. The others— the radio operator, Captain Lane, the French sailor on the Pahang wharf—I had no way of saving them. No means of knowing—"

De Stroon was munching a sandwich and for a moment there was no other sound. I fumbled at the tight bandage on my head; watched purple, glassy water slide by abeam. Andrew Hague halted an uneasy pacing of the deck, mopped his seamy forehead with a tattered sleeve, and groped for words. "But, Mr. Gorn. I—I can't believe it, that's all. None of it. There are so many—so many things. Every time I think of what happened back there on the beach, I—just can't understand how—"

"I know," Gorn said. "And that's why I called you all out on the deck this evening. I think I've got it figured. Want to check up for my reports, too. And I want you to know the how of it, and go over the affair with me. Suppose I go back to the day the chief called me on the case.

"It was the day after the Bentfinger murder in Marseilles. You'll recall that Bentfinger had previously made a diamond haul in New York City, stolen a ruby tiara and slain the watchman in a Regent Street shop, and murdered a Scotland Yard inspector in London. The Yard was at its wits' end. Efforts to trail the killer had proved fruitless. We knew we were pitted against a master mind; a criminal, deadly genius. A fiend who hid his trail in a confusion of false clews. A dead shot with a pistol. No ordinary criminal. The audacity of the little typed card told us that. The pearl robbery and murder in Marseilles proved it."

GORN NODDED, WENT on: "The chief sent for me. 'Inspector Gorn,' he said, 'it's up to you. Get Bentfinger. Go to world's end, if you must, but get Bentfinger at all costs!'

"I flew to Paris, grabbed the first train south, hit Marseilles thirty hours after the murder. Our lads on the job had found nothing. We combed the town. Hunting needles in haystacks. But I had one tiny clew. We were almost certain the killer had fled London on a boat. I'd studied the shipping reports. The sailing time of a steamer was found to check. The Arcturus, of the Champion Line had left London River and Marseilles Harbor within an hour of the Bentfinger killings."

Gorn waved a hand. "Not much to go on. But I had the Yard busy looking up the Arcturus. Meantime I juggled with the French police, following a lot of blind alleys. Finally the report on the Arcturus came in. The Champion Line had cabled from the States. The Arcturus had been leased to an American shipper on some sort of fishy deal whereby the line could not divulge the lessee's name, the boat was practically owned by said lessee, and carried tramp cargo for said lessee. This party had paid promptly on the contract and put the Arcturus into Liverpool for alterations, the nature of which the Champion office did not know, footing all bills.

"The boat had started on a vagabond trip to the Asiatics under the Champion Line flag. That was all the Yard could find out about the Arcturus, and there was no official way of digging further into the business. Still it sounded a bit funny."

"It was a bit funny," Hague offered. "I signed on the ship just after she came out of Liverpool dry dock. Captain Lane signed me on. We made a run or two into New York, loaded so light we had to carry sand ballast. Captain Lane told me he didn't know where we'd be heading next. Always seemed uneasy about his orders. Didn't quite know who he was working for, he said."

"That's because his sailing orders were sent by the lessee through the Champion Line offices," Gorn suggested. "And the lessee was—Bentfinger. Of course I knew nothing of all that. I only had a hunch that Bentfinger might have jumped London and Marseilles on the Arcturus.

"Then the news flashed that Bentfinger had struck in Cairo, and when I discovered the Arcturus had cleared Egypt for India the same day, I played a long chance and chased the boat. Speed boats, trains, liners, airplanes got me to Bombay, and I found the Arcturus in port. When I heard the ball in the Asian Queen Hotel was due that night, I played another weird hunch. Right. Bentfinger struck in Bombay—almost under my nose. In an effort to look over the Arcturus I'd booked passage on the boat. I sailed with her at midnight.

"You know how and why I had an eye on this poor girl, Miss Brown. While we cruised for Pahang I played in with the passengers, watched. Certainly the girl was suspicious. And then I spotted Norwood."

Everybody gasped. "Norwood!"

"I'LL TELL YOU about him," Gorn went on. "I knew him, but he never knew me. I've a memory for faces, and I'd seen his years before in the files. Planter named Woods. Escaped from a Singapore prison while waiting trial for a homicide in Trengganu. I suppose he went into the mission field to hide his past. A murder in Trengganu. And that's why he never went ashore in Bombay or Pahang; why he was beside himself when Mr. Hague turned the ship back for Trengganu. But I didn't let on I knew him. A chance he was Bentfinger. I wanted to make sure.

"Then we were in Pahang River. You recall how it rained? I had to go inshore, get word from Bombay and send cables to London. I'd cabled the chief from Bombay, asking for another man. I found a cable in Pahang. A week-old message from the London office, saying another operative would be on the boat and get in touch with me. I judged the chief was rushing a man to catch the Arcturus. I supposed he'd locate a lad in Bombay. I didn't think the operator would reach me till we made Shanghai. I was wrong.

"That second Scotland Yard man was right on hand the day the Arcturus was to leave Pahang. I think he was on his way to catch the ship while I scribbled cables in the

Pahang police headquarters. But Bentfinger met that man from the Yard, pierced his disguise somehow, and killed him on the water front."

Gorn nodded. "Yes, the French sailor was the Scotland Yard man sent to join me. I should have guessed from Benson's story. Would Bentfinger have bothered with the tracking and killing of a mere sailor? Would a French navy man be liable to recognize the fiend and speak his name? No. That sailor was an operative. Bentfinger killed him; robbed his official papers.

"But Benson happens to stumble across the murder; gives chase. Bentfinger makes a dash for the Arcturus, and leaves a trail that ends before a locked bulkhead in the ship's after hold. That bulkhead was actually the door to a secret compartment built between that hold aft and the engine room.

"I believe Bentfinger must have built that cubicle when the ship lay in drydock; built it in secret. An amazing compartment, contrived so that none would know of it, it served as his control room. I suppose the sailors thought the bulkhead was jammed shut and only led into the engine room. The engineers saw nothing but an ordinary partition—"

"Blimey! That's right!" The bo's'n with the bald head tugged at one of his ears. "I tries to open that bleedin' bulkhead, meself, once. I tells Cap'n Lane it's jammed shut, an' 'e says let it be."

"No doubt his orders from higher up," Gorn explained. "At any rate, there was that room where Bentfinger could store stolen booty. His typewriter. Electric ovens. A chemist's outfit. A switchboard. By manipulating plugs in that switchboard you could time a contrivance that would turn the ship's lighting plant on and off. Then a secret companionway built in the ship's hull led to a stateroom off the main deck corridor. The upper door of this secret companion opened into the cabin cupboard.

"That's how Bentfinger gets from the after hold to the main deck. He knows Benson is after him. Decides if trouble comes he will play the man from Scotland Yard; erases the real operative's name from the papers and writes in his own.

"Meantime, the ship has left Pahang. Bentfinger—as Blair—watches the deck; sees Benson go to the captain's cabin; overhears the captain saying he will have something to tell the passengers in the saloon at eleven o'clock. Captain Lane knows and suspects too much. Captain Lane must die. Bentfinger sets the switch on his control board, timing the ship's lights to go out at the proper moment.

"However, the wireless operator must be slain first, the radio put out of commission. While you, Benson, change your garments in the captain's cabin, while the rest of us chat in the dining saloon, Bentfinger murders the radio operator, smashes the wireless, hides the dead body in the lifeboat. Then, suave and smiling, he comes out of the darkness and rain as Blair, joins the passengers in the saloon.

"Now the stage is set, I'm busy studying Benson, the strange newcomer. Captain Lane makes his appearance; he is distraught. He has gone to the radio room, discovered the damaged outfit. His operator is gone. Bentfinger is somewhere on his boat. Perhaps he had guessed this before—we have no way of knowing. At any rate, he walks into the saloon, and is shot when the lights go out. And

Blair does the shooting. Grabs out his gun, leans across the table in the dark, fires, hurls the weapon through the porthole he has seen opened. The lights flash on."

GORN SHRUGGED. "I? I cannot tell who fired that shot. I tell you, that was one bad minute for me. But I decided to wait under cover and let the rest of you, if possible, betray yourselves. Bentfinger was right there in that room. There was his card. I picked it up to see. Yes, it matched the others I had seen. I was on the point of arresting Norwood and the girl, when Mr. Hague spied the yellow glove that had come from under Blair's chair. That glove was a hitch in Blair's plans, I believe. In yanking the gun from his pocket he had pulled the glove out by accident. Now he shows his ace card; claims himself a Scotland Yard man.

"How was I to know? Headquarters had told me a Scotland Yard man would be on the boat. There were the official papers. Blair's story about being sent to watch another party, then switching to the Bentfinger case, was plausible. For all I could tell, he might have been watching Norwood, you see.

"I tried like the devil to remember, if there'd been a new man on the force named Blair, but in the wild flurry I couldn't remember. I didn't like the looks of it, though; decided to play Gorn, the silk buyer, for a while longer. If Blair was from the Yard, all right. If not—

"But he played the part so skillfully, I thought he was. He did exactly as I'd have done with the investigation, skillfully hiding his real identity by the masquerade. Meantime he threw suspicion on everybody else. I believe he was on guard, too. If the Yard had sent a man to Pahang on his trail, perhaps there was another Yard man about.

"By taking our guns he drew the teeth of all of us. He could examine us, too. I think he was more than suspicious of me, especially when he found that French railway ticket among my faked-up business letters.

"Do you begin to see his game? It was he who set fire to the linen in the empty cabin after locking us in the staterooms. Dropped a match in the cabin door when none of us were looking, let us say. Then, in the smoke and alarm, when we ran for safety, Blair dashes into my cabin for a look. Thank God, he didn't find the handcuff sets concealed in my valise. At the same time, I, under cover of the confusion, went into his cabin. Took a look at Benson's stuff, too, by the way. Finding nothing in his hasty search of my effects, Blair runs to the bridge."

"That's right," Andrew Hague said. "After shutting you all in your staterooms that first time, Blair came to the bridge. Then he went back to the corridor. That's when he could have fired the linen. He was back on the bridge when the fire call blew. He fled off in the smoke; came back to meet me just as I was dashing off to round up these passengers."

"Exactly. And had you, Mr. Hague, decided to head the boat back to shore before you made this intention known to the passengers?"

"I had. And Blair had approved the idea. Even urged it."

"He never wished it, though. You see, he knew it was coming, prepared the warning, and pinned it on the door of the wheelhouse while the ship was in an uproar. Then he rejoined you and the rest of us. We returned to the corridor, went again to our respective cabins.

"Then you discovered the note of warning. Now he—

Blair—had wanted to head off for Cambodia, you see. To carry out the threat in his first Bentfinger note, he crawled through his porthole, sped around the storm-darkened deck, picked Norwood as his victim. How this was done he himself later explained. But—"

"But, great heavens, Mr. Gorn!" Major Phillipots cried. "How did Blair ever get through his stateroom porthole out to the deck—"

"You'll understand later. Now Blair, as Bentfinger, has killed Norwood, carried out the threat of the note. He gets back into his stateroom; Mr. Hague, having found the warning, calls everybody into the corridor; Blair, playing the Scotland Yard man, investigates. There we find Norwood slain by Bentfinger. And it was at that time I got a chance to do a little investigating of my own. You see, I'd come across something. That little leather notebook in which Blair had pretended to outline the incidents of his case."

A FAINT SMILE played about Gorn's lips. "Do you remember what happened? We were standing, terrified, in the corridor. Blair drew the notebook from his pocket. I was standing near him at the time, and I spied something he'd written in that notebook. In his effort to play the part of the Englishman from Scotland Yard, conducting a police record and keeping a case book and what not, he'd overplayed his hand.

"Oh, the notes he'd written looked genuine enough. But the date, you understand. The *date!* That's what I spotted. I must get a better look, make sure, get hold of that book. The ship rolled, we tumbled in a heap, and I snatched the notebook out of Blair's hand."

"But he said there was something important in that book," Hague recalled. "Was that just a stall? Just to make us think he was a real detective and—"

"Exactly," Gorn pointed out. "Blair had to play up his faked sleuthing; pretend he was getting somewhere. As a matter of fact, there *was* something important in that book, but *he* never knew it. Yes, he wanted to stall us there in the corridor. You see, the Arcturus had already turned back for Trengganu—the last place Blair himself wanted to go. Blair wanted to keep us out to sea, you understand. He must do this by terrorizing the crew.

"Now just after setting fire to that stateroom, Blair had crossed the deck, wearing his Bentfinger impersonation. Intentionally he showed himself to the steward. He knew the steward would spread the story. And he stalled us there in the corridor waiting for the new alarm. Meanwhile, the incident of the notebook took place. I suspect Blair was pretty puzzled, wondering why one of us would steal that book from him. No doubt he believed the thief feared the book held incriminating evidence. Never in the world did Blair suspect that he'd written something there among his trumped-up notes that showed he was *not* an Englishman from Scotland Yard!

"But then the steward appeared with his story; told of seeing that weird cripple in the dark. Obviously, none of us could be the deformed monstrosity. Apparently Bentfinger was at that moment skulking the storm-dark decks. Blair affects fear, pretends to go after our guns. Presumably to arm us, he runs to his stateroom.

"You remember how long it seemed before he came back? That was because he must have dashed down that secret companionway to his cubicle, typed the second warning, flung it through the peephole into the engine room, sped back to the corridor. He told us the guns had been stolen. Matter of fact, they were still in his stateroom cupboard where he locked them, unloaded.

"As for me, I'm stumped. I'm crazy to get a look at the notebook hidden in my pocket, and I'm nonplused by the steward's wild story. And Blair is hardly back among us before the engineer comes running to us with the second Bentfinger note.

"We rush out to the deck. Hague swears he won't turn the boat. Blair must keep good the Bentfinger threat, and thus he pretends to find the body of the radio operator which he has previously planted in that lifeboat amidships. Blair wants to keep that ship away from the shore. He wants to frighten Mr. Hague and the officers into turning about.

"Again, he pretends to catch sight of Bentfinger on the after deck. Leading a chase aft, he disappears. We think he has gone below, and while we hunt below decks Blair hides in the dark; assumes the mask of the killer. He sees us come topside again. But Mr. Benson and Miss Brown are still below somewhere. When the rest of us run forward the killer waits; he catches Benson off guard and attacks. But Benson fends off the murderer's bullet, gives fight, *gets the cape*. By the way, Benson, did you examine that cape?"

I confessed I did not. "I think I dropped it somewhere. In the excitement—"

GORN NODDED. "IT was lost. But I think if you'd look at it closely you'd have found it of very delicate weave and manufacture. A fine silk or mercerized cotton. The sort of cloth that folds into a very compact, small bundle and may be carried in a pocket. Blair could yank out that cloak the way you'd draw a handkerchief, and put it on in a trice.

"But he'd lost his cloak. In the darkness he made a dash for the bridge while the rest of us rush aft to answer Benson's outcry. And now the Arcturus is only a few miles offshore. Determined to further his terrorism scheme, Blair encounters the steward under the bridge and promptly shoots him dead.

"His cries bring us running; there we find him, as Blair of Scotland Yard, with the dead man in his arms. And now I'm certain that somehow or other Blair is Bentfinger, or at least an ally of the crippled monstrosity. I must get another look at the notebook and try to get my hands on a gun.

"And a lot of things happen, suddenly. Things Blair himself has not counted on.

"The Arcturus runs aground, battered by the storm. The crew forward of the bridge, terrified, out of control, mutinies. The sailors attack the bridge, and Blair finds himself caught in an unexpected battle.

"This gives me a chance I've been waiting for. While the rest of you, Blair included, are fighting on the bridge, I rush back to the deserted corridor. Another look at Blair's faked-up case book and I'm convinced. But how has he managed to escape his stateroom at various times, unseen?"

"I dash into his cabin. There's the cupboard where the guns had been stowed. Blair had said the lock was broken. It wasn't. I break it, and find the guns inside the cupboard. More. In the back of that cupboard is a little door. I smash through the door and discover the hidden companionway. Benson can tell you how I came down into the cubicle and found him locked in there with Miss Brown. And now I had to get the two of them out of there and away, for the ship was foundering. I saw what I'd have to do.

"Benson was almost out on his feet. He and the girl would think *me* a criminal, and give me a fight before I could explain. And I never had time to explain, you can see that. I had to knock out Benson, get handcuffs on him and the girl.

"Luckily, before exploring Blair's stateroom I'd gone to my own and armed myself with the cuffs. Now I could take care of Benson and the girl. It was a job, though. I had to bluff plenty with the empty gun to get them out of there. And there'd been an explosion in the engine room just as I was climbing down that companion. Gave me a fall and I'd sprained a wrist. It was touch and go with these two captives of mine. I had to make Benson carry the bags of jewels—"

"Those jewels!" Hope cried. She was reclining in the deck chair beside me, and she'd been listening to Gorn's recital with bated breath. (The rest of us had been listening, too, I can tell you!) Now Hope could not contain herself. "Those gems, Mr. Gorn. Where—"

THE DETECTIVE CHUCKLED. "Amazing, weren't they? Listen. It's the most astounding part of Blair's scheme. You see, it was his idea to travel the world and steal the world's most priceless gems. A perfect diamond. A perfect ruby—emeralds, pearls. Hidden, there, in the bottom of that dowdy old ship where no one would suspect, he would stow the booty. And at night, while the ship slept, he worked down there. Doing what?

"Why, the man was a master counterfeiter. He was

making paste copies of those stolen gems. Making untold fortunes, for he could keep the originals and sell the paste imitations to fences and go-betweens who would think themselves buying the original article. Why, he could make millions. Millions.

"The minute I saw those instruments, that electric oven—I knew. But the ship was sinking. No time to stand around, examining things. I got Benson and the girl topside and into a lifeboat somehow. I saw Blair and the others go overside on the bow. I thought they were done for. Heaven knows how the three of us in our boat ever got into that island lagoon. But we did. And when I heard the voices, heard the other boat in the fog, I knew I was up against it. If I was caught I'd be shot dead and Blair would get away with the goods. He'd then have properly murdered the rest of you, too.

"But I spotted that old fort atop the hill. And when I found the cannon—well, I guess we can all blow old Lady Luck a kiss, what? That old cache of dry gunpowder was her kindliest gift. But I want to tell you I was in a fix when I could find nothing to shoot."

Gorn mopped his face at the memory and smiled. "Benson was giving me plenty of trouble, too; plenty. But poor Benson was out on his feet. And lucky for all of us, too.

"At any rate, I remembered how those old Napoleon-type guns would shoot iron balls or stones or crushed rock or anything. And I couldn't find anything until Benson and I spilled the fake gems. Sardonic, isn't it?"

Gorn grinned. "Dashed trick of fate that Blair or Bent-finger or an American shipper, or whatever he was, should have been shot to death by the very gems for which he had ravaged and slain and terrorized society. Killed by priceless bullets of his own making—"

Gorn's voice drifted out behind a smile. How quiet, then, it was on that twilight-bathed deck of the Madame Chrysanthème. How like sticks we sat in our deck chairs; Hague and his sailors, the Phillipotses, De Stroon and Dr. Smartbeck, and Hope and I. On the forecastle calm bells tinkled to change the watch, and a lookout's voice hailed. My companions seemed unable to speak, and at last I had to ask the question for them.

"But, Mr. Gorn," I blurted, "how did you know? What *was* in that little notebook? How—how did that notebook give Blair away? A date or something, you said. And—and how—how *could* he"—I was remembering that horribly crippled monster who struck at me through a flash of lightning on a wild deck. "How could Blair have been Bentfinger? That face! Those twisted arms and—and legs like crooked sticks—and—and how—I mean like a Jekyll and Hyde transformation—" I was thinking of Blair coming over the hillcrest, a flash, then a red ball bounding down the slope, and that monstrous thing dead on the beach below. "How could it have happened, that's all?"

"I'LL TELL YOU," Gorn said quietly. "The date in the notebook? Well, Blair was pretending to be an inspector from Scotland Yard. An Englishman." Seeking in his coat, Gorn produced the little blue leather booklet. "Now, an Englishman writes a date a certain way. He writes the day first, then the month, then the year. Thirteenth July, Nineteen hundred and ten. Always in that order. An American writes the *month* first, then the day and year. July thirteenth. That's the way an American writes a date. That"—Gorn waved the notebook—"is the way Blair wrote it here. Master mind, master gunman and chemist, master of disguise, Blair had his British accent perfect—and slipped up on a tiny point of form. But the disguise—the Bentfinger monstrosity—

"Well, Benson, it *was* a real Dr. Jekyll and Mr. Hyde transfiguration. In Stevenson's marvelous tale, the handsome and kindly Dr. Jekyll turned himself into the ugly and malformed character, Hyde, by drinking a magic potion. And finally the Hyde character became so powerful that it would come out of Dr. Jekyll of its own accord.

"In Blair's case it was almost the same. But Blair didn't turn into Bentfinger by any fiction-book magic. You remember, Benson, the terrifying way he seemed to change, dwindle in size as he ran down that Pahang pier? And how Blair got out of his porthole?

"Listen. Once in a lifetime a freak is born. A double-jointed freak who can, by muscular control, contort his limbs, atrophy the muscles of his face, even stop the blood in his veins. In half a second he can bring on a self-induced partial paralysis, double his spine into a hunched twist, knot his hands, unjoint his shoulders, arms, legs, become a thing of rubber and bunched muscle. There you have your explanation.

"Blair could force himself, almost without shoulders, through a porthole, or spit out his false teeth—and how that will alter any face!—and make of his body a wretched thing. And when he died with his chest shot away, the freak muscles of his body assumed, in the cold of death, the contortions to which he had habituated them. Yes.

Blair—an India-rubber man. And he died in true character—Bentfinger—the fiend that he was."

Gorn sighed, moved through a silence of stone, eased
himself into a chair.

"That's all," he said cheerfully, "and I'm dashed glad of
it. I'm two hundred years old right now. My apologies to
those of you I suspected wrongly. Everybody told such
strange stories, gave such odd accounts of themselves and
all. What with alibis and aliases, I hardly know who's who.
I was sure Miss Brown had given a false name, for example. I wouldn't be surprised, Miss Brown, if that was not
your name at all—"

"It isn't," Hope laughed. And then, because a girl just
can't keep a secret: "Go ask the funny little captain of this
boat. He changed it for me this afternoon. I'm Mrs. Benson
now—"

I could hardly believe it yet, either, and thank Heaven
Mrs. Phillipots took her eyes from my blush.

"Oh, dear," she offered, "I think I'm going to faint from
the excitement—" And she did.

DIRGE OF THE NANCY D

*When the skipper boomed out that death march
on his piano, and the sailor honed his long sword,
they used to mutter weird stories in the fo'c's'le—
and make grim predictions about the future*

A SEA STORY? Well, then, here is one. The story of a ship's concert. Not the sort of concert where, last night out from port, the audience arrays itself in evening dress and the gentleman who has studied in Austria plays a Beethoven recital and other handy talents come forward to stifle the lounge room with impromptu acts.

Not that sort of concert, God knows, because the evening dress was lacking. But there was a piano recital, and there were impromptu acts. The most astonishing ship's concert ever played.

But anything can happen East of Suez, and the Nancy D was an astonishing boat. The wonder of her was that she could float out there on the Saigon water side, for ordinary iron sieves do not float. A shabbier, older, more raffish craft could not be imagined anywhere; and when I rounded the end of a jetty and first saw the dowdy harridan I dropped my duffel and my jaw.

Gaunt she was, with saggy well-decks and crippled bridge and a skinny funnel that sat her middle like a top hat tilted on the head of a blowzy drunkard. Smears of red lead had failed to heal the rusty blisters that festered on her hull and her bow listed portward, tired under mounds of spoiling gear. What a craft! With that unlovely face, what could her insides be? But I closed my jaw on an oath and stepped for the gangway. I'd have sailed a Roman galley to escape Saigon and even journalists, when begging, cannot choose.

"Hey!"

I turned to answer the hail and was awarded my first glimpse of Georgie. Santa Claus, grown lean and withered and brown and with a beard dyed crimson, was squatting in the shadow of the freighter's sorry prow. He halted the operation of paring callous from one heel, thrust knife into dungarees pocket, beckoned with his foot; and I strolled over to sit down. For a minute his blue eyes watched me. I was accepted by a chuckle and a nod; then he exhumed a corncob from his shirt, stuffed it with something that looked like elephant grass, and blew himself a dense fog of smoke. The beard was a masterpiece, screening his face save for apple-hued patches beneath each sparky eye. He would bury the corncob, yank it clear, and loose a shrapnel burst through the screen. I grinned and he chuckled and shot a question out with the smoke.

"You shippin' on her?" His thumb stabbed the freighter alongside with a force that threatened to stave in her plates. "You goin' on deck?"

I nodded. Smoke purled from his whiskers and his blue eyes blinkered. I could not tell him I was a stranded journalist, but he guessed as much.

"Takin' a berth back for home, eh? Where'd they tell you this craft was headin' for?" he wondered in a sober voice. "Tell you she's clearin' for Frisco?"

I explained that the American consulate was shipping me out on the first boat along, and the little sailor made doubtful comment.

He was a gaunt, crazed genius, waking ghosts

"This ain't the best way to go," he advised with a wag of the beard. "But she may be better'n stayin' in this Cambojan hole. Meself, I ain't been aboard 'er so long. I made Yoko on a rag wagon, an' thought I might try steamin' clothes for a while so I ships on this tub. A bleedin' go in some ways, friend. Carryin' tramp cargo. We goes here, there, everywhere. Bos'n just told me the skipper just charted us west through Suez. Can you figger that one? He's always chartin' a draft course like that. You can't never tell what the skipper'll 'ave in the back of his bonnet."

My sailor stopped to suck his corncob and watch his wriggling toes. When he looked up his eyes were bright; suddenly strange. I had a queer impression that they had changed into little blue pebbles.

"You ain't," he growled, "seen the Old Man yet? Huh! No. Well, the craft ain't so bad an' the work ain't so hard, but the skipper is different, friend. Different. Nor the boat ain't in the general run, neither, it ain't. There's some funny goin's-on aboard 'er, Yank. Some funny goin's-on—"

Something in the old salt's voice gave me an apprehensive twinge, and I looked at the ragged hull looming dark above me in sudden anxiety.

"What's funny?" I asked; and Georgie swept off his sea cap to wipe water from his brassy head, and his words were gruff through the smoke.

"Keep your ears open, lad, an' you'll hear soon enough. Aye, you'll *hear!*"

If I'd guessed the import of those words I'd have stayed on six years in Saigon, debts, fever and all. But I had no time for guessing. A throaty *whooo* escaped the steamer's siren and shook her from stem to stern. Catching up my duffel, I swung up the gangway to the sailor who beckoned above. And that's how I swung up the gangway into the astounding story—the story of a ship's concert aboard the Nancy D.

I SHALL NOT soon forget the first act played that afternoon when the Nancy D escaped from the muddy Donnai, was belching smoke plumes at a sky of blue and gold, and standing out to sea. I was on the bow with Georgie, working hard because we were short-handed. There were only three other hands besides Georgie and me—if I live to be a thousand I'll remember them. Artz the Frenchman, with his bulbous, bird's-egg eyes, scrawny throat and swooping walrus mustache. Ritter the Australian, a lank, unhurried individual with a secretive mien, long wrists and long feet, nose like a stunted vegetable grown into his face and a mouth painted scarlet by the juice of the betel-nut it habitually chewed. Aaron Holm the Finn, squinty and swart with a dimpled chin under flabby lips that ejected their cigarettes only to spout foul words. Three more criminal types could not have been found out of jail, and their meek obedience to the ship's officers could only be accounted for by the muscles on the bos'n's neck and the mate's weighted pistol belt.

Sconfetti, the Corsican bos'n, serving as a sort of third and second mate, was no Boston drawing-room product. Though his legs and middle were swathed in waddly fat, his arms were the arms of a world's champion wrestler. I watched the muscle-eggs grow under those olive-hued shoulders as the bos'n struggled to shift a deck boom. The deck boom shifted. Then I turned my attention to the bridge.

Mr. Christian Hansen on the bridge was a smiling Billikin, blond as a haystack, and almost as broad in the beam. It must have been no small task to command from the bridge by himself, but he could smile. One time a grin had found his face and settled there. Now he smiled at the laboring bos'n. He grinned at the Finn who climbed to the monkey bridge to take over the wheel. He grinned at the coastline that thinned on the horizon behind us.

"Georgie," I questioned. It was just before eight bells to start the dogs. "Georgie, where's the Old Man? This surely is a weird ship. I thought at least the skipper'd be on the bridge when we left Saigon. I haven't seen him at all."

The little red-beard who had taken me in tow was screwing his pipe into those gorgeous whiskers, and ramming tobacco. At my query he watched his bare toes, and shrugged.

"I told you this mornin' this craft is different. Sails an'

goes off course about as she pleases. The crew takes it easy.
You takes your trick at the wheel or watch on the bow—"

"Listen," I demanded in sudden suspicion; "is she smuggling?"

"Maybe, Yank. She may carry contraband stuff. Right
now she's got some bamboo in 'er 'old. Can't tell what's
under it. She picks up what she can get. Y'see, Yank, the
skipper just wanders 'ere an' yon. The big Greek engineer
keeps the fire room workin'. The Scowegian an' bos'n navi-
gates us along. Long as the boat goes an' the crew minds
its business I guess the Old Man don't care. 'E treats the
crew above-board long's they run the tub. A New Bedford
Yankee, they say the skipper is. But 'e ain't normal. A funny
un. Different, like I said."

HE TALKED WITH his eye on a jumble of fleece caravan-
ing down the horizon. His voice was pleasant. Suddenly
I was amused and content, warmly conscious of sunshine
and clean sky, liking the tilt of the deck, glad to be on the
water again—

We both spun around with the shriek in our ears. The
Australian bounced to his feet. The bos'n heaved his bulk
from the booby hatch. The Finn peered from behind his
wheel; and the mate leaned over the bridge wing. The
shrieks continued, coming from some troubled region
amidships, coiling shrill tentacles of sound through the
sunshine. And before any one could start toward the
soul-freezing clamor, its origin rounded the deck house.

I give you my word my feet were leaded with surprise;
my eyes wide on the astonishing man who stalked to the
fore deck with a hand fastened on the neck-scruff of the
terrified Frenchman, Artz, who was squealing and kicking

like a kitten held by a mastiff. An astonishing man; yes! A furious Hamlet with ember-like eyes sunk behind the stack of blue-black hair falling down a long, pale brow. A gaunt, dark Hamlet in loose white linen that flapped on lean limbs as he flung the Frenchman to his face, and raged.

"Rat! Bungler! Lout!" He glared at the quivering lump on the deck, at us on the forecastle head, at the men on the bridge. "Fools!" he squalled, waving fists. "Fools! I let you run this ship to suit yourselves. Run it to Hades and I don't bother you. Your pay and quarters are good. You never work. But then, by heaven, when I tell one of you to polish my instrument you do it lazily and badly. When I want that instrument polished, I want it *polished!* Carefully! Not smudged and gummed like a scupper plug! Polished, damn you! Get that right, lubbers! And you, you stupid French ass, don't ever come into my cabin again, or I'll kick your head from your neck! Understand? Bos'n, you send this fool to my cabin once more and I'll finish you, too. See? That goes for you, too, Hansen!"

The mate touched his cap and did not grin. The gaunt man's eyes dealt us all a contemptuous slap; then, drawing back his foot, he drove his toe hard into the Frenchman's spine—*crack!*—and turned on his heel to stalk aft and away. The Frenchman curled up moaning; lay coughing and sobbing before dragging himself into the booby hatch.

I found my hands made into cold fists. Hot-eyed I stared aft where the tall ruffian had gone. That brutal kick! Who was the devil? What could be done?

Nothing. Mate and bos'n were chatting on the bridge. The Australian was on his back, chawing again. Georgie was studying the cutwater. Be damned! Who was the tall dog who could kick a sailor when he was down? Kick him because he had failed to polish something—some instrument. What the devil had he meant?

Right then I found out, and as Georgie had promised, I heard! I heard, right then, a roar of wild music come smashing out into the sunshine; a flood of thunderous chords booming the morose cadence of a Russian melody; a mighty spate of sound that could have poured only from the keys of a piano! A piano! I stood sticklike in amazement. A piano thundering music aboard that dirty tramp freighter churning down the South China Sea! I could not believe it!

I stood the tipping deck; glared at an unpainted freighter's bridge—a castle behind a smudge of sun-tinted smoke—lifted against acres of blue sky; glared, and listened to Rachmaninoff played as I had never heard playing before, while the sea tilted about me and tar-smell was sharp in my nostrils. It was more than past belief!

And from Rachmaninoff the notes swung into the somber, tramping dirge, "Ase's Death," that marched with the roll of the water. You know the number? I am no musician, but I had heard that funeral march before, and I remembered it. Grieg, isn't it? It starts off with three slow, measured chords; lamenting chords that chill. *Thrumm— thum—thrumm-m!* it goes. And it paces weirdly away; a grim, cadent chant. As I listened to it, then, echoing across the deep, drowning the drone of the moving ship, I thought I would turn mad.

The last note slowly expired. All sound in the world seemed to have died. I heard a voice behind me; whirled around with a start. Georgie stood there, blue eyes twinkling, brow calm, pipe in fist, smoke gently leaking through his beard.

"That's the skipper," Georgie said.

CURIOUSLY ENOUGH, THE skipper's name was Peter Gynt. So the bos'n told me when he called me from the forecastle after mess, jabbed a rag into my fingers, and whispered in a gossipy sort of way that I was to finish the task so unhappily begun by the Frenchman, Artz.

"An' Saint Giuseppe!" he hissed anxiously. "Do it well, Yankee. The Ol' Man, he's at mess now. You should be fineesh' by time he gets back. It is ver' special job he give to a pick' man. Not every sailor can go to hees cabin. The job is not'ing. Only to polish so the salt air will not eat the wood. With this oily rag. Justa polish—" He dabbed in pantomime. "Justa polish. Like that—"

Was ever sailor sent on errand more bizarre? Sent amidships to burnish a piano! Desirous of seeing this skipper's cabin, and not a little apprehensive, I picked way across the darkened deck to the companion indicated by the bos'n. Ducking down a short ladder, I found myself at the door of the strangest cabin ever to grace a ship. Ali Baba admitted to the den of ten million thieves could scarcely have been as astounded.

At most I had expected to discover a battered upright piano, outcast of some harbor joint, banged up by life at sea. Instead I won a surprise. Wine-hued woodwork shining dull light under the tawny glow of a cabin lamp, a massive grand piano loomed tremendous in its corner; imposing and beautiful, its silent avenue of keys agleam, its strings humming faintly to the throb of ship's engines.

And the cabin! How I stared! Stared at the flocculent

black rug carpeting the floor, at the massive furniture pieces crowding the piano and its bench, at the table weighted with reams of music scores, at the stuffed music racks, the bookshelf bulging with tomes, the pair of enormous carved-wood Buddhist candlesticks guarding the clay bust of Wagner in the wall niche. I stared. A sailor with a polishing rag, naked but for dungarees and moccasins, I stood there staring.

On the walls hung faces which returned my stare. Rows of gentry, whiskered, fatuous, smirking, sad, grim. Bach I recognized, and Strauss, Beethoven, Brahms, Schumann. And there were twenty more, *maestri* all of them. I knew them all, save one hanging near the door. That I did not notice until later.

The creak of the depended cabin lamp reminded me of the ship; recalled me to my task. Awed and feeling not a little like the only man in tweeds at a full-dress dinner, I approached that magnificent piano. The piano bench, I found, was cleated to the floor; the piano being fastened to the wall. Impelled by curiosity, I sat down, tucked rag under bare arm, thrust foot on the soft-pedal, and struck a timorous chord.

"You play, do you?"

The words snatched my fingers from the keys; spun me on the bench. Like a boy caught pilfering, I blushed. There was the skipper, glaring in the hatchway.

"Do you play?" he demanded in a voice that came from a cavern. In the low-ceiled cabin he looked taller, more saturnine than ever. His face was waxen under raven-colored locks. "I asked you if you played?"

"No," I floundered. "That is, very little—"

"Play!" he ordered.

"I play badly," I insisted, wishing to heaven I was out of there. The hot cabin tilted slowly. The skipper's command drilled through set, china-white teeth.

AND SO I crouched on that piano bench, writhed under its owner's severe glance, and dropped a stiff hand on the keys. Years had slipped by since I had touched a piano, but from some cobwebby alcove of my brain I exhumed a minuet— one of those trifles played by giggly girls with an eye on the clock and a mind on games of skip-the-rope outdoors. Feeling like a tinkling idiot, I played the thing. Fatuously and wretchedly. While a thread of sweat leaked down my nose. Happily my efforts were interrupted.

"Rotten!" The skipper's snarl struck quiet the mincing notes. "That's simply rotten! It's a piano, not a typewriter. You're terrible!"

Of course I was, and I was furious. "Never said I could play!" I snapped. "Ordinarily I'm a journalist. On this— this ship I'm a sailor."

"Get off that bench!" he growled.

Angrily I sidled from the piano. A heavy rosewood candlestick hard in the face would suit this frowning Hamlet very well. But he was master. I was a deck hand. And I was glad I had quelled temper, for he brusquely waved me to a chair, dropped like a nervous animal on the piano bench, turned his back on me and struck a wild chord. From then on I was not in the cabin. Reality was not. The world was a rushing, bounding torrent of sound lashed from the keys by music-tortured hands. Echoes thunderclapped from wall to wall. Wagner rattled in his niche. The wooden candlesticks danced. The hanging portraits came to life. The cabin quivered.

Deafened, I sat my chair immersed in a storm of sound. I shall not soon forget that picture. The cabin, gray-shadowed, tilting, painted with queer paradigms of light shed from the swinging lamp. Me, half-naked—a sailor on a ship, remember!—sweating, stunned in my chair. The skipper, a gaunt electrified genius crazed before a monster piano—God knows where it could have come from—hairshocks tossing to brush water from his colorless forehead, his linen jacket wetting across the shoulder-blades, his inspired hands racing like butterflies up and down the keys…

The concert ended. The cabin was empty. Music had smoldered out in the processional dirge from "Peer Gynt." *Thrumm—thum—thrumm-m!* "Asa's Death." You know how it goes. Somber, mourning chords.

THE SKIPPER SWUNG on his bench. His face, under blue-black hair, was snowy, worn. Nervously he wiped his hands. His dark eyes burned into mine.

"Well," he snarled, "how did you like it?"

I don't know what I said. My hands were wet, too.

"That last is my favorite," he muttered. "It's simple. I like it. Do you know what it happens to be, sailor?"

"From Grieg, isn't it?"

His smile was wry. "You're the first sailor who ever knew a thing about it," he conceded dourly. "Quite a triumph for one of my crew to know anything. Well," he lampooned me with a piercing stare, "I play better than any one *you* ever heard before, I wager. Worth a life, my genius, don't you think?"

"Worth a what?" I faltered.

"A life! A life!" irritably. "My genius worth more than some silly butterfly life. Worth more than some weak intelligence that would have warped it. And because some fools don't agree with me I'm hounded into the middle of the ocean; forced to bury my genius and my priceless piano behind a wall of oblivious water. Bah! A devil's time I had buying a ship suitable and getting my piano aboard. Had to rebuild the ship to do it. But I'm snug now. Safe. My piano and I. And the fools ashore are the losers. They cannot hear me play." He laughed unpleasantly. "My piano for a life, do you see? And they all lose. Ha, ha!"

His chuckle hung little icicles in the stuffy cabin; and his words, as I fumbled with them, made a funny taste on my tongue. Suddenly I was ill. Hastily I said: "You have a fine set of portraits." Interest in things musical might be politic on this vessel.

The skipper's smile was grim. "Twelve years' collection."

"Who is the man over the piano?"

"Rossini. A gourmet and a dabbling fool. If he had spent less time gorging himself— But how many men ask more than the noble privilege to eat, sleep, and produce more fools?"

I hated him for his sneer. His previous words were tangling in my head, and the hatchway became inviting. I stepped toward the companion, and for the first time saw the picture hanging near the door. As I turned to go, this photograph arrested my glance. A girlish face it was, British and square, with jaw too firm to be beautiful and nose too short, but attractively featured, too.

"Who is this?" I asked, expecting the name of some feminine composer.

The skipper lurched to his feet. I was startled to see his face tinged angry scarlet, his sullen eyes light a vicious glow, his fists go clenched. More startled by the vehemence of his tone.

"A fool! Just another fool! Well, go on!" he rasped. "Don't stand there first on one foot and then on the other like a gawking boy. Afraid of me? Why, I wouldn't hurt you for the world! Get out."

His infuriating guffaw climbed the ladder behind me; left me hot-eyed on the shadowy deck. The night, up there, was clean.

UNDER A NIGHT sky sullen with moonlit clouds, the Nancy D was nosing along. A thick mist crept over the horizon dead ahead. Ritter, the lank Australian, stood lookout on the bow; and I could see the face of the Finn behind the wheel-spokes on the bridge. There was a breeze. I would get a blanket and lie on the fore deck. I wanted to think over some words; and I knew I would never sleep below.

I swung down the steep companion burrowing into the forecastle. Artz, the Frenchman, was a ghost in the galley, daubing together a sandwich. As I passed, he called:

"What watch you on, eh?"

"Graveyard," I explained.

He limped forward, waving his sandwich. His mouth was crammed, puffing crumbs, and I failed to catch his speech; though what he said I remembered as sounding— well, something like:

"*Sacré!* Maybe soon none of us will stand no damn' watch, *oui!*"

It did not impress me, then. I whistled my way into the forecastle. The lamp on the table smote me half blind for the moment, and I was only conscious that some one huddled on a stool before a bunk was engrossed in filing on something. The steely rasp got to my spine.

"Hello, the watch," I offered; and it was Georgie who looked up. He had not noticed my entry. On seeing me, he thrust something shiny behind his back with guilty haste. Then he laughed, scratched in his beard, touched his nose with a file, and drew from concealment a long, gleaming sword. A sword almost as long as he was tall. With a chuckle he exhibited the blade.

"In the name of heaven, Georgie!" The steel was a lightning-streak in my hand. "Where did you get this thing?"

It was one of those two-handed swords such as the Crusaders used for converting the Turks; savage to see, sharpened to the slimness of a rapier, edged like a razor. Like a giant needle it shimmered in the lamp-glow, sending wicked shafts of light against the wall. And its handle was a cross of dull silver inlaid with polished purple bone.

Taking it from me, Georgie ran a caressing thumb down the blade. A ruby drop grew glistening on his thumb as he drew it away. His blue eyes twinkled, peeping over the red whiskers.

"Sharp," he chuckled.

"But what the devil are you doing with it?" I exclaimed.

He tossed away the file, brushed steel dust from his knees, wagged his beard and fondly patted the cross-bar handle. The sword reflected cold flame. "I'm sharpenin' 'er," he chuckled. "I files 'er an' I whets 'er to keep 'er sharp. A tidy relic, Yank. Never can tell when she'll come in 'andy. Me and 'er are on a crusade, Yank."

STORM HIT US at dark daybreak. Shivering from stern to stem, the Nancy D toiled through plowing waters; cringed under wind-driven rain. Ordinarily when she was making eleven knots on clement seas she was having a happy day, and straining her insides out to have it. When she was making twelve she spouted smoke like an irate Stromboli, her engines threatening to pull apart. Now she boiled along smoking and reeling, straining like the devil to make five knots down the swollen ocean.

A burst of rain had chased me into the oven-hot forecastle, where I encountered the Finn "scoffing up" with coffee in his bunk. Wanting none of his slimy dialogue I dropped into my berth, face to wall. I wanted sleep, but the roll of the ship, the smash of drubbing water, the stifling air, held me wakeful. Pictures disturbed my mind. Perturbing words echoed through my thoughts. Hamlet belaboring an impossible piano. The raffish Frenchman squealing from a brutal kick. Georgie bent to the sharpening of a long sword that gleamed like a heated wire in the lamplight.

Words. "Never can tell when she'll come in 'andy. Me an' 'er are on a crusade—" "There's funny goin's-on aboard 'er, Yank. Funny goin's-on!" Pictures. The photograph of the girl near the cabin door. Words. "A fool!" "My genius worth more than a life—"

"Holm?" I turned to address the man across the room. "How long have you been aboard this freighter?"

He grunted, spat, and politely informed me he had been

with her long enough to leave a score of wives in twenty ports of call.

"I gets me a fresh one each time." His red tongue flickered over his lips. The man was a lizard. "You know how it is, Yank. An' I guess I shipped on this craft most a year. Come on her after two years on a lugger carry-in' lumber up the Western Ocean. This boat's soft. She ain't no starvation line like Bruckenbach or the French outfits—"

"What do you think of the Old Man?" I interrupted.

"Gynt? The skipper?" Holm thumbed his nose in the direction of the bridge. "Nuts! He's loco, he is. Don't do nothin' but slam that damn piana. We've had hell an' high water, an' it don't stir him outa his hole. Allus plays durin' a blow. An' yer limey watch-partner drags his anchor, too. Loony. Squats in here a-sharpenin' that blade of his, grinnin' to hisself like a monk. The limey needs chokin'. He allus files w'ile the Old Man plays. Me, I likes a knife, anyhow—Listen! I told yuh—there goes the Old Man!"

Faint above the clamor of the blow sounded the chanting funeral dirge, indescribably solemn as it beat at the storm. *Thrumm—thum—thrummm!* Even the Finn seemed deeply impressed.

"He allus plays that. Creepy."

Creepy. The Finn had described it. And rather terrible, intoning above the noise of angry water slamming iron. The skipper leering at the God who could only stir a feeble storm to drown his music.

We listened. A roll of the ship brought Georgie staggering into the forecastle.

"Ho, Finn!" he greeted cheerfully. Rain ran down his face and showered from his unquenched beard. Kicking out of his wet dungarees, he sat a bronzed dwarf in his bunk, and laughed. "Bit of a blow we're 'avin'. But she'll be quiet by four bells."

"How you know?" spat the Finn. "You think you're smart, limey!"

"I am smart compared to some as I know," chuckled Georgie. "Ain't shipped half my life for nothin', I ain't— Say! For once the bos'n 'ad the deck workin'. Ritter an' Frenchy was lashin' a loose boat. We're slipped off course, an' Bos' says we're makin' fer Bangkok up the Gulf of Siam. Bangkok! Can you tie that? Ain't far off the coast, now. Lord knows where th' bloody skipper'll end us up." Hand to ear, he listened. "Old Man is playin', ain't 'e? Well, I got things to do."

BELLS CLANGED AND the Finn departed, leaving blasphemy in the smoke behind him. I turned in my heaving bunk. Georgie was fumbling. Then a file rasp sent shivers down my back. Georgie had his sword between his knees; a whetstone in fist. Rearing on elbows, I watched him. He was whetting to the time of the music echoing above the blow.

He narrated. "Got me this sword fi' years ago in Constant. There ain't nowhere I go that she don't go. We're sort of pals."

"Queer sort of pal," I protested.

"Ain't so bad, Yank. May turn out a friend in need. Some beauty, wot?" He cut a stab through the air. Light flashed down the ceiling. "Cut through an iron spar, she would. Crusader's sword, Yank, from them as fought 'cause one says 'I'm God,' an' the other says 'I'm Allah.' Bleedin' nonsense, that. I'm for justice, Yank. My crusade is right."

I waited. He went on: "Crusadin' for justice, Yank. Was a girl I loved. Weren't none finer outa England, Yank. Went an' married a bleedin' rotter in Frisco. Years ago, it were. 'E robs 'er of 'er last farthin' an' leaves 'er flat in a hospital. She an' the baby dies, see?" His file snarled. "Dies 'eartbroken. That scum same as murdered 'er, 'e did. Leavin' 'er like that in a strange country. I loved 'er, Yank, an' I found out. Never seen the bloody scum who murdered 'er—he'd skipped out. But I got a feelin' I'll find 'im some day, an' when I see 'im I'll know 'im. Some'ow I've allus thought *she'd* tell me when I saw the right man. 'Er spirit…"

His voice ached. From above came haunting music. It was not pleasant to hear a man talk like Georgie had talked. I lay in discomfort; said, to change the subject:

"I saw the Old Man's piano."

"Yeah?" cheerfully. "I never been near 'is cabin. 'E picks special men fer 'is lackey work. I ain't no charwoman, I ain't. Wouldn't polish no bloody fool piana fer nobody. I'm a sailor. Royal Navy once—"

With that he set to whetting again. Bent head furbished with perspiration; a naked, bronze gnome with a tremendous red beard, sharpening a sword as long as himself. Sharpening to the time of somber music sounding above the storm.

AT FOUR BELLS, as Georgie had prophesied, the blow went breathless. By late afternoon the water might have been oiled. We steamed up the Gulf of Siam with following seas, raising the Cambodian coast off the starboard beam just at evening. Under alchemy of sunset the scarlet pennants floating across the western sky were altering to gold. Cambodia was a tenuous thread of mauve with a monumental crimson moon wheeling down its tip. The Nancy D plodded, breathing hard after her battle.

Thoughts calmed by a cigarette and the unruffled evening about me, I sat the capstan on the forecastle head and watched the feather of a liner's smoke vanish into the sundown. A symphony was playing abaft the bridge behind me. Hamlet at his piano, again. Throughout the day he had played. And often, on passing the booby hatch, I had caught the rasp of a file sawing to time.

A sense of things sinister stalking the vessel oppressed me. Georgie and his deadly sword. This unseamanlike tramp with her abnormal master taunting at the storm, sneering at mankind, leering at a picture.

I had seen that photograph again. Knowing the cabin deserted, I had sneaked in to see, again, the face. I had found the picture turned face to wall; studied it fascinated and sweating, fearful the skipper would find me there. Have you ever heard of a man growing sentimental over a picture? But she was vastly attractive, despite stubby nose and a square jaw protuberant beneath the ears. Blue eyes, no doubt, and gold hair. And a charming smile made doubly so by a tiny bump—a tear drop—quaint on the tip of her chin. A composer, perhaps, or a pianist of note. Or some one who had nicked the skipper's ego.

Preposterous man! What right had he to such a picture? Yes, I was sentimental about her. I learned her face well; and wondered about her as I sat lookout astride the capstan.

Night, toiling up out of the East, dissolved the coastline off the beam. The glow in the west had burned down. The moon was smaller in the sky; and a scatter of pale stars moved slowly back and forth above the foredeck mast as the boat's roll made it describe slow arcs against the heavens. Eight bells clanged. Georgie clambered to the wheel to relieve the Frenchman at the helm. The mate and the bos'n were settling their dinners, pacing the bridge below. Darkness had come so subtly that the deck was black shadow and running lights beaming soft mists of red and green before I realized it.

The Frenchman sped past me like a ghost, leaving a brief echo in the forecastle companion. Ritter and the Finn sent snatches of argument adrift from the shadows of the fore deck. "—Siamese gal, and pretty enough fer the Prince o' Wales. Buy one fer six *tikals*. No better wench anywhere!" The Finn's voice contradicting: "Better in Panama. You know Coconut Grove? An' there's the San Francisco Hotel in Jamaica—" "—How about Waterfront Willy's Starboard Light in Penang?' At's the place I mean. You talk about the Cannebière in Marseilles an' that place in Tampico—" "—In Galveston, I mean. Remember? Tilly the Toiler they calls her—"

Slam! Slam! The two explosions roared amidships and clamored off across the water. The Nancy D staggered and groaned. *Slam!* Like a cannon shot. *Slam!* again. Then yells—strident yells. A howl from the bridge. Shadows charging through the darkness. A scream. Holm and Ritter crying out. *Slam!*

SUDDENLY THE DARKNESS had gone. A flicker of blatant flame was spouting from the hatch below the bridge. Simultaneously the deck amidships sprouted crimson fire-flowers that lit the ship from stem to taffrail and enameled red the sea. Yellow whorls of fire licked at the sky. Planking snapped, crackled, smoked and blazed. Another detonation flung a geyser of fire aft. Then below decks was booming and banging a salvo and in three breaths of wind the Nancy D amidships was Inferno.

On the forecastle head we were stunned. Georgie and the bos'n tumbled down from the monkey bridge. The mate raced out of the chart house, squalling oaths; stood on a hatch-cover, cursing, while the fire made red apples of his cheeks. Amidships roared and flamed.

Georgie yelled: "It's them contraband explosives we was shippin' below. Petrol, too. An' lumber—"

Slam! Screaming pillars of fire climbing up the bridge. None of us could stir a finger. Not one of us stirred a finger when a bawling, gesturing figure charged out from under the bridge, flung a blazing torch at the moon, and vaulted over the rail.

"Artz!" panted Ritter. "Did you see him? 'At was the frawg!"

"He fired the cargo!" some one yelled. "To get the skipper—"

"Listen!" groaned the mate.

Huddled together with parching faces, we listened. Above the shout of the kindling holocaust, the clamor of sudden tumult aft, we heard! *Thrumm! Thum—thrumm-m!* The skipper! I tell you we could not move. I think the awful fascination of the thing robbed our minds of power. Like sticks we stood, and listened. How we listened! *Thrumm!— thum—thrumm-m!* You understand? The skipper. Trapped in the cabin of his blazing ship, he was standing by that piano to the last; playing. "Ase's Death." The march to his own funeral pyre.

It taunted the roaring flames. It taunted the fren-

zied uproar loosened aft—the black gang escaped from
below and fighting for the boats. Screens of leaping flame
curtained them from view—that Frenchman must have
fired the whole cargo in a horrid race from stern to bows—
but their lusty screeching trembled against the song of the
fire and the ghastly dirge.

A pungent bouquet of tan-colored smoke eddied up
the fore deck, sprinkling sparks and pretty brands. I was
not in the abrupt scramble for the davit on the port bow.
Gear squealed. The dory swung out of sight; and hot smoke
hemmed me in. When it cleared, I saw the dory swamped
to the gunwales; the mate and bos'n splashing desperately; Ritter and his pal, Holm, struggling for ahold on
the submerged craft. Just before they drifted into an unlit
patch of water I glimpsed a knife in the Finn's free fist; saw
it glint; saw Ritter's head, wearing a grinning false-face,
sink in colored foam. I could not summon the strength to
cry. I could not move.

Another boat, filled with a gibbering tangle of men,
slid by into darkness. Stoked by a steady breeze, the fire
sprang hot and high. Spark-fountains whirled skyward.
Embers hissed into metallic crests of water. The volcanic
glow made carnival in the night; the heat was a searing
blast; and still a piano intoned a dirge from the heart of
the furnace. And still I stood on the forecastle head. Do
you know what I was thinking? I could not think of that
man playing a funeral march in his cabin while the fires
ate in about him. A foolish doggerel was running through
my head. My mind recited: "The boy stood on the burning
deck—" While ribbons of sweat wiggled down my cheeks,

and I twisted at the bow rail with agonized hands. And then I remembered Georgie!

AS I DID so he stumbled from the forecastle companion, and skipped past me, wraith-like in the smoke. A shoddy lucky-bag bobbed on his shoulder and his long-sword made a whip of light hanging on his belt.

"The skipper!" he yelled, half turning. "We can't leave him play back there." He sent his bag whirling into the scuppers. "We gotta save him!"

With an arm across his face, he fled over the fore deck. I screamed his name at the top of my lungs. He sprinted. I swear I wanted to go with him, but before I could budge my feet he was gone. Gone down the blazing companion leading to the skipper's cabin. Plunged into the roaring yawn of that furnace. Smoke whisked in behind him. The fires squalled. The funeral dirge chanted on. *Thrumm—thum—thrumm-m!*

Sick to my heels I glared at the molten hole whence Georgie had disappeared. *Slam!* Another explosion smote the Nancy D to convulsive trembling. Black smoke sagged close to the water, hanging a shroud over the listing craft. The heat was torment. The blaze soared. The music, which had echoed from amidships, came to an abrupt stop. And Georgie was back.

Georgie came back! I never believed the miracle about the boys who strolled from the king's incinerator under the asbestos wing of a cool angel. I did not see that. But I did see Georgie plunge from that fire-wrapped companionway to stagger blindly up the fore deck toward me. Fumbling out with burned hands he came; reeling. Brisk little flames made red lace on the cuffs of his dungarees. His jacket smoldered and smoked. As he lurched to the rail I thought he was going to fall. But he hung there yelling; and his face was a sooty mask; and I saw that his beard was scorched to a black goatee. When he beat a fist on his chin the charred hair wiped off as if shaved. Witless, I glared like a mummy, wild-eyed. What was the little man crying out?

"I seen her!" he shrieked. *"Her!* I knew 'er spirit would come to tell me. Come out of the smoke behind 'im, she did. 'Er face in the smoke an' she smiled at me plain as day. Come to tell me so's I'd know. 'Er face in the smoke. *Her—*"

Her! His cry broke to a laugh, and he waved empty hands. From astern roared a crash that made the deck bound; and I saw him go over the rail as I spun off my footing. Desperate, I dived overside. It was touch and go after my stunning splash, all I could do to get clear; and I could not yell with water strangling in my mouth. The Nancy D. stole away, a drifting garden of flames. The moon sneaked into a nest of fat, pea-green clouds. Georgie was gone in the darkness.

HOT SUNSHINE BROUGHT me around, spraddled flat on a pleasant, white beach. The Gulf of Siam reeled away and away beneath unclouded skies and frisky little waves came bounding up the sandy apron to wet my sprawled boots. Digging a stiff spine out of the sand, I pushed up on groaning elbows and blinked. A squad of *krah* monkeys abused me, acrobating in a near-by pandanus grove. Behind the beach a green hill mounted into the blue. With all the clamor of the monkeys, I might have been alone in a quiet, unpeopled Eden.

It was not a bad place in which to find oneself. Southward the coast curved splendidly, a giant, white horseshoe rimmed with lush green. Northward a jungly headland cut off the view. And the next thing my aching eye discovered was a bony spar floating in the shallows, and—kindly providence—a rum bottle bobbing beside it. This was Eden, then. I rescued the bottle, swallowed a scorcher, and rounded the jutting headland. The bottle dropped from my fingers to empty itself in the sand.

For the headland made a fence for a tranquil and pool-like lagoon; and cradled in the lap of that sleepy backwater, her charred corpse sunk to the scuppers lay the Nancy D. I tell you it gave me a shock to see that dead hulk lolling there in the sunshine, her bulwarks barely washed by the clean, easy swells sweeping in from the Gulf, her blackened bridge and skinny, warped funnel ugly against green jungle, the water dark around her, the stench of her burned middle mingling with the perfume of tropic flowers. The sight of her gave me a shock. And was I mad? Or did I really hear muted music stealing into the morning quietude. There! There came the sound again. A chord! A chord struck from a piano!

I shall never know from what source I drew the courage to swim out to that fire-ravaged hulk. I remember very well how my knees went sick when I dragged myself up on the blistered fore deck and heard again that harmonious chord echo phantom-like from the midships abaft the bridge. I recall, too, how horrible were the pools of sunshine lying on burned timbers; how nauseating was the odor of charred, wet wood. But the ghostly music came once more to force my feet down the deck to the fire-twisted ladder dropping into a certain cabin; to force them down the ladder.

Then I was sweating and ill at the bottom of that

companion. Stifled with the stink of dead fire in my nose. Chilled by the evil water swirling about my loins. Frozen by the sight in the skipper's cabin.

A shaft of dull sunlight slanting through a smoke-dimmed port picked in outline the evil figure slumped on the piano bench. The back was toward me. The head dropped forward, chin on chest. Black water lapped the keyboard of the piano and the long row of ivories gleamed like teeth in the dusk. Books, paper, kindling floated about the submerged middle of the frowsty thing on the piano bench. It was the skipper, you understand. Seated at his piano—and playing it!

A MASSIVE ROSEWOOD Buddhist candlestick, wedged beneath his dead right arm, lifted it as water swelled into the cabin. And as the water spilled back in retreat the arm was dropped so that the rigid hand fell lightly on the piano keys to strike a solemn chord. The water rose and fell. The cabin was haunted with music. You will say I imagined it; say it was the din in my ears. But I swear to heaven the skipper struck the chords of that dirge of his—the somber chords of his funeral march. All right; perhaps I could imagine that. But I saw:

A vagrant swell surged through the cabin. The right arm rose and fell. The piano mourned. And as the water receded I saw the sword-handle jutting from the skipper's side. Of the blade that pinned him to the bench I could see nothing. Only the handle driven hard against the ribs. A handle of silver, wrought like a cross, and inlaid with purple bone.

Then I turned to flee and I saw something else. Some-where the cabin ceiling smoldered. A thin mist of smoke wandered down the wall near the cabin door. Out of that smoke a face appeared. Her face. Smiling charm and about to speak.

I had shin-banged, yelling, up the ladder, fled the deck, and thrashed across the lagoon before I remembered the photograph near the door. A photograph that made a face behind a wreath of smoke.

I wanted to go back after it, but I didn't. Beyond the nose of the headland a man was whistling. The sound coiled a thin, shrill tentacle of piping through the sunlight; started me on the run. I rounded the headland, charging, and saw Georgie. He stood where I had slept. He recognized me with a shout, and I rushed him with a yell.

"I thought I seen some one up here," he chuckled. "I was lyin' a mile away. There's a town at the end of that horse-shoe. Come on."

Arm in arm we walked away from the headland, and I made no offer to turn about. Georgie did not ask, and I did not tell him of the lagoon. The little sailor was gay, want-ing to whistle. I remember very well what he whistled. He whistled that merry and somewhat indecorous little tune that all good British mariners know, "Ho, ho, me lads, did you ever see the queen—"

The piping was so jaunty, the whistler's face so childish without a beard, that I might have laughed. But I never laughed. I could not so much as move my opened lips. I could only stare at Georgie's unmasked jaw, square and British and protuberant under the ears, with a tiny bump like a tear drop quaint on the tip of the chin. And I could only remember the photograph on the cabin wall—the face he had glimpsed in the smoke. The face of his twin sister!

Georgie did not hear it, he was whistling so loudly. But

I heard it. It came from the lagoon behind the headland, a faint, dying chord, like the somber echo of slow-treading feet, stealing on the wind. *Thrumm—thrum—thrumm-m!* The last piano recital I ever heard.

ANIMAL MAN

"Bring 'em back alive!" was John Stanley's slogan—but there were two denizens of India who didn't want to be brought back

YOU HAVE SEEN him—the likes of John Stanley—in ports wearing such names as Mombasa, Makassar, Negapatam, Kuala Lumpur; outstanding in whites amidst the colors of Joseph's Coat, gesturing a palm leaf fan and talking trade figures in whatever huggermugger dialect may come to hand, or grinning up at the big mail ship as she eases away from the bund, watching her departure without envy. You have seen him (if you venture that far from home) up on the border of Nepal, quietly bossing a batch of Ghurkas; or over in British East, breaking brush at the head of a licorice-hued *safari;* or in the Million Dollar at Shanghai, taking them straight and smiling in content amusement at nothing in particular on the table-top.

The pith helmet and that way of lighting a cigarette. The unhurried stride and leisurely gesture of command. A coppery tinge to the little creases on throat and neck-nape, burnt there by exposure, and swift blue eyes that are not nearsighted from close-hemmed city streets, but sharpened by sun and wind and the look of far places.

"How are things in New York?" he will ask you, friendly; but while you are telling him he is watching the mountain range pictured beyond the window's frame.

"Business in the States?"—but as you speak of the latest

in the news he has stooped to pet the gray barroom tabby against his legs.

Here is a man, you feel, who has not been lured by the satisfied pavement to the narrow fireplace, the easy cushion and the echolalia of ticker-tape. Here is a man whose roof is the sky, whose doorstep the horizon; who mines his gold in an Asian sunset, and who, hearing of the recovery of the dollar, had rather commune with a tabby. But you know he has had to prospect the gold of understanding. There is, for example, the scar on his left forearm, purple as a wound stripe, running from wrist to elbow.

WHEN JOHN STANLEY was just under thirty he was going somewhere. In the New England he had hailed from he would have been labeled "go-getter" or "boy making good." In India he had won for himself the title, *"pukka shikari,"* which loosely means "dam' fine big game hunter." John Stanley was all of those, if business acumen, determination, unbounded confidence and expert marksmanship mean anything.

He had been a hunter, a crack shot since boyhood. Military academy, shooting in Maine, rifle and pistol teams. His brown, lean frame, brought up on discipline and proverbs, was powered with the stamina of Puritan granite, as many a football enemy of college days could have mournfully testified. And he had taken the Orient, jungle, natives, hardships, heat, the same way he had swept through zoography and zoology majors in his scholastic career—that is to say, in one self-assured stride, best clubs, head of the class.

"I'll show them *how* to hunt wild animals."

He did. He had that make of chin. The term wasn't around in those days, but John Stanley was one of the

*"Think you can
get me! ME!"*

first to "bring them back alive." In a big way, that is. There
were naturalists and trappers in the hills (collectors with
butterfly nets, John called them), but they didn't get the
goods the way John Stanley did. Hunting was more than
a business, a sport to John Stanley. In a way, it was a challenge to his convictions.

He would have told you that progress came only through
struggle. That Divine Providence had scattered a lot of
stumbling blocks (tropic jungles, for example) in the path
of man, and every time man had the courage to eradicate
such obstacles, chalk up an extra cubit to the stature of his
soul. If, meanwhile, it chalked up an extra dollar to the bank
account, why that was only the Lord's practical way (this
was in 1906, and John was from New England) of reward-
ing virtue. Thus figuratively, John Stanley went after wild
animals in much the manner of St. George going after the
dragon or Tancred after the Turk.

"That boy's a winner. Tougher the order the better he likes it."

John Stanley to his toes. He went after them in droves, in flocks. He drove one of the first automobiles in the *terai,* and to speed up operations he fastened a circus cage to a trailer and dragged them out of the forest by the car-load. His reputation traveled the animal marts from Port Said to Singapore. Cobras, black leopards, buffalo, grist for his mill. He shipped monkeys by the crate, leopards in clawing dozens, elephants in herds.

Surmounting a whole pyramid of stumbling blocks, he captured the largest white rhino on record, tied it horn and hoof, and hustled it from Bhutan to the London Zoo. He won commissions from museums, circuses and societies all over Europe and America. His collection of skins and trophies was finest on the river, bar none. His bank account was a matter of pride. All this in a handful of years; and he could well afford to write Molly Breadon and her father, back in the States, inviting them for a season's shooting (and something more for Molly) at his place in the foot-hills.

JOHN STANLEY WAS not unaware of his own impressiveness, that day he went to meet Molly and her father at the riverfront landing in Indapur. Smart drill and spotless sun helmet, automatic loaning glamour to his belt, pipe in teeth, he swung up the wharf among the snarling specimen cages, giving low-voiced orders to salaaming coolies and tapping a leather crop on his polished riding boots. Brown and manly as the open could make a fellow. And wait till Molly saw the country estate he had carved for himself in this wilderness. Old Man Breadon (the Breadon Knitting Mills) would know big business when he saw it. And Molly, little Molly who had promised to wait—

Molly was something, too. Somehow she had kept her frock starchy on that mildewed jungle backwater; and the sight of her smiling down from the steamer's rail set John Stanley's pulses thumping.

The ride to the bungalow was a tremendous success. John and his guests in saddle on his best mounts; the house boys pattering along with the luggage, all wearing flowers behind their ears, in such a colorful procession as Aladdin might have commandeered; the jungle in its brightest hues. Molly must exclaim and pause and ask a thousand questions. Old Man Breadon nodded and said, "Well, well, Stanley, you've certainly made something here."

After a brief siesta and tea served as only a house boy named Wing could serve it, John led them in a tour of the grounds, the trophy and gun rooms, the animal house. The compound, massed with rhododendron and traveler's palm and azalea. The trophy room, a pageant of leopard skins, tiger robes, elephant tusks, buffalo horns and gavial heads. The gun room with its shining racks of Winchester 30-30s, Mannlichers, Enfield specials, .475 elephant guns. The garage with the car and the cage trailer, models of efficiency in the limberlost. Lastly, the animal house filled with beasts waiting shipment. The elephant that had nearly trampled John Stanley to a pulp, docile in chains and ticketed for Comstock's American Circus. Monkeys boxed up like chickens going to market. Panthers for Copenhagen and wild boar for Rio. A black leopard bound for the Antwerp Zoo.

Returned to the bungalow and changed for dinner, John

Stanley entertained with cocktails and stories of the East. Molly must clasp her hands and listen wide-eyed to tales of desperate encounters and last-second shots, told with proper modesty but desperate none the less.

"And the natives. Molly, you should have seen them when I first bought my car. The men are Bhils, some of the best trackers in the country, hired from across India. Brave as they come, but superstitious as children. When they heard the engine they were panic-stricken. Deodar, the old headman, is the only one I could ever persuade to ride."

"But a motor car hardly seems to belong in the jungle—" HE GRINNED AT the little pucker in her forehead. "Why not? Some day there won't be any jungle. There'll be highways and grain fields. Maybe factories."

"Oh, John—"

"Why, surely," John Stanley declared. "We whites, some day we'll reclaim the East. Won't be any more of these fool superstitions. These Bhils, frightened of the car, that's not half. Worship snakes and all sorts of outrageous things. Think tigers turn into men and men turn into tigers, all that sort of rot. But on the hunt—absolutely fearless."

"Trader on the boat coming up was telling Molly and me you were pretty fearless yourself," Breadon admired over a cigar. "Said you'd bagged as many as ten tigers in a single day."

John Stanley shrugged. "Woods are full of the devils. Speaking of tigers—I was going to save this for Molly—but I just got a wire yesterday morning, a commission to catch the biggest specimens I could lay hands on. The order is from Luckenback—"

"Luckenback?" Breadon's eyebrows went up.

John Stanley nodded, trying to keep elation out of his smile. Luckenback, of course, was known the world over. "Tigers for the Berlin Zoo., And yesterday afternoon my men found just the trail. Never saw such tracks. Monsters. Perfect pair. I've got to go after them tonight, and ought to be back in time to hunt with you tomorrow."

Molly turned from the window, eyes bright. "Where— where do they live, this pair?"

"Worst sort of jungle. Drive about fifty miles up the valley on an old plantation road. Then off to Nowhere. Only the Bhils could have found such a trail. Biggest tigers I ever heard of. Listen, Molly. If I get these brutes, Luckenback's promised me the rest of his orders, and he's king of the business. It'll mean a fortune for me, for us. Another five years out here, with me supplying the animal market—"

It should have been a gay evening, lovers reunited, beautiful girl and "boy who made good," prospect of hunting days in the hills, Luckenback's prize order—yet somehow it didn't get across. A little tug of disappointment somewhere in the atmosphere, somewhere John Stanley couldn't put his finger on. Surely Old Man Breadon was won over to a prospective son-in-law. John had the ring, a canary diamond fine enough to have once caparisoned the finger of a Punjabi princess; but he wouldn't ask Molly to wear it until Luckenback's order was filled and the future assured. Was she disappointed because he hadn't asked her yet? She ought to know how things stood between them. Or was she disturbed at his leaving on business the night of her arrival? But he had explained how Luckenback could not be kept waiting. She couldn't be offended at that.

HIS DEPARTURE THAT evening would be dramatic, John

Stanley admitted in secret pleasure—to drive off with guns and natives, car and cage-trailer under the moon. Breadon strolled across the compound to admire the outfit, leaving John and Molly in the garden. Molly fixed a silvered face to the jungle that rose like a whispering purple wall in the moonlight. Far beyond the jungle-top the mountains lifted in the silhouette of a caravan, mysterious and silent, trooping down the sky. The night breeze whispered of distances. That way was Nepal. Beyond was Tibet. Below swept India. For a moment the couple stood in silence. Vines made a nocturnal rustling, then distant, somewhere, echoed a soft, throaty cough, once repeated. From the animal house behind the bungalow came a faint reply of whines, a chorus of furry snufflings, uneasy little barks.

"Brutes are restless," John Stanley jerked a thumb. "Sounded like a tiger out there. Say, Molly, I'm sorry as anything I have to pull out tonight. If it was interesting I'd take you and your father in no time. But the traps are already laid, nothing to see at night and the dickens of a trail. When I get back we'll go after them on elephants; that's the sport. Tonight it's just business. Harness 'em out of the pit and lug 'em back in the cage." He grimaced, patting the automatic on his hip, the hunting knife on his belt.

"But, John." She looked up at him, then, brushing a wavy strand of chestnut hair from her temples. "John, it does seem cruel."

"Cruel?" He looked down at her, mouth open a little.

"To make a living by hunting those wild things. To capture and shut them up in cages."

"Those—those brutes?"

"I hadn't thought of it before, John. But those spotted cats down at the dock in your cages. There wasn't any water. And the elephant chained in your stall. He looked at me so—almost pleading. And that black leopard cooped up like a common hen—" She turned from him, absorbed in the crystalline distance of moon-painted peaks. "When I see their home, like this, away off here in the hills—those poor creatures—"

"Poor creatures?" John Stanley had to be amused. "Savage man-eaters, you mean. Ruthless jungle killers who'd tear you limb from limb."

"And wouldn't you be savage, John? Invited to a banquet only to find yourself in a trap. Torn away from your home and—and loved ones; sent like a slave to a foreign country to be stared at by strange foreign beings?"

John Stanley was frankly amazed. "Now, Molly, what in the *world!* You talk of those murderous brutes as if they were humans."

"But don't they have the same feelings, John? Hunger and thirst and pain—like we do. And hate and love and pride, too. We ought to know because we—after all, men are animals."

"Men are animals!"

Her warm blue eyes, seeking his, were more articulate. Her lips trembled. "Men wouldn't like it, either. How would *you* like to be in a cage?"

IT WAS TOO much for John Stanley's imagination. He was corseted in too much of that whale-boned New England Yankee work-and-win soundmindedness. Give an animal the attributes of a human? Put the two-legged Lords of the Universe on the same footing as sabre-clawed jungle quadrupeds? Cause for mirth. Cause for: "Molly, what *are* you talking about? Why, it's a blessing to rid humanity of these pests!"

"To lock them in cages and—tame them?"

"So must every irresponsible, wanton impulse in life be tamed, overcome. How can you worry about the capturing of some thieving, red-eyed, savage beast?"

She regarded him gravely, her face misty in the translucent night-shine. "These creatures, the tigers, the magnificent pair you want to imprison. John, it doesn't seem right, somehow. I wish you wouldn't."

"Wish I wouldn't?" he almost cried. "Why, it's my business!"

"That's just it," her low voice went on. "I don't like it because I know what it's like to be in a cage. Father's held me in one—all my life. Girls' schools. City apartments. Nasty little parties with people I didn't like. Everything schooled and trained. Traditions and prohibitions. A certain time when you must do this and a certain way you must do that. I thought out here with you, I—we'd be free to—"

"But we're going to be free as the wind," he told her in amused impatience. "Five years filling Luckenback's orders and I'll have an honest to goodness fortune. There's a mint in this business, Molly. Then we can live anywhere we like. Paris. London. New York. Anything you—"

"And we win this freedom by putting others in cages. By killing and stuffing and taming and—making slaves of something else that's free. Those little homesick monkeys, and that leopard—pacing, pacing the way he was. No, I couldn't feel right about it, John. I wish you'd give up this

Luckenback business. Couldn't you be a planter or—a grower? Create things instead of—of destroy? If you could put yourself in an animal's place—"

DRIVING OFF INTO the jungle's moonlight and black, John Stanley choked down his annoyance. What in the dickens had come over Molly back there in the garden? Where'd she get all this nonsense from, staring off at those confounded hills? Rather have him a dinky tea planter than a successful big game hunter; that, in effect, was what she had said. Give up his animal business, the contract of a lifetime, for some maidenish sentimental whim. Hardly the reception a chap had the right to expect for his manful achievements in a profession too venturesome for most.

And her admonition to put himself in an animal's place. Those brutes! As if there was anything in common between Man (well, to make it personal, a college-schooled sportsman and gentleman of tradition and breeding, like himself) and a snarling carnivore. It had come to that. "But don't you think a monkey could suffer the same heartache as a philosopher?" she had insisted to the last. "And the other way around, a scientist can be just as savage as—as a beast. We think we're so far above the other creatures—"

"Molly, you're tired," he had assured her in masculine tolerance. "Tomorrow you'll see things differently."

Hold on, it wasn't worth thinking about. She was all in from that river trip, of course. Ride across India excited her imagination. Girls were like that. Molly was, of course, a darling child. Feeling sympathy for a batch of wild beasts. Ho! After they were married he'd have to humor her out of such silly ideas. Perhaps with a bit of firmness.

Tooling the car down that ancient jungle roadway, John

Stanley chuckled and, because his was the nature of mind that pushes trivial harassments easily aside, turned his thoughts to the business at hand.

"The traps set out as I ordered?"

"As you ordered, Sahib." Deodar, jouncing on the seat beside him, touched his turban and made the lucky sign. "The pits are waiting, the goats staked out. It is a fine night, Sahib; the beasts are certain to take the bait."

John Stanley's pulses quickened at the mental picture. By the reported spoor, these tigers should be gigantic. He had sent his best men to lay the snares; now he found it difficult to stem impatience. Hauling a cage-trailer on so difficult a road slowed the car to twelve miles an hour, and the engine protested with heat. The naked Bhils, jogging along barefoot, ghosts in the dark and dust, began to lag. John Stanley read midnight on his watch, and there were yet twenty miles of journey.

"Tell the bearers to keep up," he snapped at the headman. "We want to get back by morning."

The road, however, took its own good time. It was not for hurried travel. A dim road, abandoned by forgotten colonists to dissolution; treacherously gone in places; its narrow corridor close-pressed by the vegetal walls on either side. Here it was tented over by skeletal arches of liana and leaf. There the sidewall had collapsed across the path, spilling a mound of brush and the wreckage of vines. The thickets looked tigerish in the moonlight. The chugging, clatter and squeal of car and trailer made a racket in the stillness that clung among the trees.

THEY CAME TO a bend where the corduroy planking gave way to the wheel-ruts of a bullock cart, a wagon track grassy under the headlamps. John Stanley saw his men were hanging back, heads together in whispered confab. He fumed at Deodar. "What now?"

Eyeballs rolled in the old man's parchment face. "Sahib, the tigers will be waiting, surely. And my brothers are reluctant to go thus far in the forest at night."

John Stanley growled in new irritation. "Why not?"

"It is the valley, Sahib. Natives, who know it better than we, have told us it is charmed. It is the home of the werewalker, Sahib. Man's soul, in death, becomes that of the beast. Tigers have been known to become as men. Must we proceed at night, Sahib?"

The hollow tone from the old Bhil's beard started to creep up John Stanley's spine. The jungle, black and silver, steeped in the moon's silence, could be uncanny. Shadows, exploring through the trees, sent back a leafy rustling; and there was a smell of roots and mold.

John Stanley would not permit himself nerves. "Are you low-caste pariah sweepers that you fear the forest dark? We must proceed at night because there are guests in my house and I wish the job over with. No more of this nonsense. *Jaldi karo!*"

Unfortunately he could not give orders which the old headman could translate to the car. Five miles farther in, the road made trouble. John Stanley struggled at wheel and gears, the car skidding and pounding over gravelly ruts. Leagues from Nowhere the front wheels swivelled over a rock, and the car stalled with a fractured steering rod. John Stanley's restraint came from years of self-imposed training, and was admirable. Unpacking a tool kit, he calculated a repair job that might take hours, and called to one of his bearers.

"Gungoo, take the trail back to my house. You should get there easily by morning. Tell the Memsahib and her father I am delayed, may be late in returning from this trip. They are to make themselves at home and under no circumstances are they to worry."

REPAIRS WERE FINISHED sooner than he had anticipated. But the moon was down, and he drove with wearisome caution, a drag of two more hours until car and trailer chugged from timber into an open glade hedged by night-blue cliffs. John Stanley braked down a steep descent of grass and rock. At the foot of the hill the road petered out, halted by a sere, bone-white peepul tree that blocked further progress like an uplifted hand. As if to say man could go no farther. Beyond belonged to the wilderness.

Old Deodar pointed. "The pits are there, Sahib."

And occupied, by the sound. John Stanley laughed an excited laugh when he heard the roars that came funneling through the starlit gloom. Parking the car under the ancient tree, he leapt from the seat, distributed rifles, started the processional through belt-high grass. The Bhils set up a cry. "Tiger! Tiger!"

There were the jungle cats sprawled in the deep-dug well, shattering, the night's hush with a din even Stanley found appalling. But he shouted when his carbide flares revealed the captives. Male and female, they were far away the biggest tigers he had ever seen. Yellow-eyed, orange and black monsters of muscled rage, each a good twelve feet long. Luckenback would pay a price for this couple. What a rumpus they were making in that pit-bottom!

What a fight John Stanley had on his hands, lassoing them out of the mine and across the field to the cage.

A battle of volcanic fury, roar and danger; the sweating Bhils hauling on nets and tackle, leaping to dodge lightning claws and snapping fangs. The darkness shaking with the squalls of men and animals. Dust boiling underfoot. But the tigers were no match for John Stanley's crafty harness and runways; and the stars were only beginning to pale when the cage door slammed on the raging pair.

Ordinarily the Bhils would have started a celebration, a whooping ring-around-the-rosy about the cage, but tonight they hovered in a wilted group near the tree, eyes averted. John Stanley was too occupied with his catch to notice. He mopped his face, drew an exultant breath.

"Man, what beauties! Wait till Luckenback sees 'em! Wail till Molly sees! Scare some of the nonsense out of her." He grinned, nursing a fingernail bashed in the struggle at the pit. "Some specimens! Nothing human about *them!*"

Time to be off. John Stanley lined up the natives and passed water canteens; collected and stowed the rifles in the front seat of the car; cooled his own throat with a long drink; cranked the engine. Deodar swung into the place beside him, and he let in the clutch for the pull uphill. At the sound of the exhaust, the tigers caged behind the automobile began a tremendous scrap. Lathering in fury. Leaping insanely at the bars. Bounding around and over each other; hurling their contorted bodies at the steel door. Dynamite bursting in a box. The trailer rocked on its wheels. The car panted, dragging the convulsed vehicle up the ruts.

Looking over his shoulder at the storming beasts, John Stanley laughed. Something like a Roman circus, this catch. When Molly saw this parade come across the compound—

THE LAUGH CURDLED in John Stanley's mouth. Turned to a yell. The car was nosing over the forehead of the rise. *Crrrang!* Metal tearing astern. Jolt-worn couplers parting with a gun-like report. Runaway! Trailer and circus cage rioting downhill.

He jammed the brakes, and was out in the road on the bound. Automatic in fist, he sped after the escaping cart.

"Stop it! Stop that cage!"

He never looked around to notice the exodus of his men. At the first clang of trouble from the car, the Bhils had scattered forty ways through the dark, Deodar taking the forty-first. They had never trusted that mechanical magic carpet for a minute, and it needed no Asian intuition to tell them something had wried with the magic. John Stanley, who knew it was nothing but a broken coupling, chased the cage downhill; sprinting in the dust-swirl to catch the wagon tongue where the hooks had snapped.

He never caught that wagon tongue. The whipping bar caught him instead. The cage reeled, bounced along the roadside, and the flailing draw-bar slapped John Stanley across the thigh to knock him flying. Pale stars pin-wheeled about his head as he spun and went flat. Struck from his hand, the automatic capered across gravel and vanished in dark grass. Tumbling breathless out of his somersault, his mouth jammed with dismay and dirt, John Stanley heard the crash. He never quite knew how it was. But the trailer smashed into the tree at road's end; he was empty-handed on his feet, yelling; there was a stunning concussion and just enough light to see the cage door, sprung wide by the shock, wham open.

Streaks of orange and black lightning exploded through the door; rocketed past John Stanley's head. The wind from those soaring animals almost threw him to the ground. And tigers are the world's fastest acrobats. The beasts revolved in mid-flight, the tigress going one way, the tiger going another, landing resilient as rubber balls not two yards from John Stanley and facing him. There was only one way for John Stanley to go, and he went. A spine-cracking leap, straight into the cage. *Smash*, the door slammed; *clack*, the lock held.

"Deodar! Mukerjee Lai! Putarb! Haaaaay! Here!"

No answer. The Bhils might have seen him in the cage, but the Bhils knew the country was bewitched. Tigers turned into men, and men turned into tigers. If any swung back to look, they gave no sign.

Rose streamers were igniting a puff of cloud behind the cliffs, and John Stanley saw the wilderness empty of men. He saw his car, his rifles, his lunch and water canteen at the top of a misty hill. He saw a red coin burn through the fired cloud, the sky take flame with a rush. He saw, in the grass beyond a pattern of bars, two tigers crawling belly to earth, ears pasted to their heads, fangs bared, eyes like yellow candles in the sun. Morning left him no doubt. They were the biggest tigers he had ever seen.

BY EVENING JOHN STANLEY could still laugh at the joke on himself, but the laugh hurt his throat a little. He shouldn't have shouted so insistently throughout the afternoon; it had started to swell his tongue. Happily the day's heat was waning; there were clouds rolled against the sunset, and a bit of rain wouldn't go so badly, because— well, he'd have all the water he wanted as soon as those tigers vamoosed and he reached the car. No denying the violence of that sunlight, though. A real blast. Those cliffs, blue at night, had turned to copper. Certainly was dry, all right.

John Stanley rubbed at soreness on his thigh and looked around. They were still there, confound them. When he lifted a hand the huge male sighed to its feet and made a lazy, circling turn around the tree. The female arched up in the grass and blinked. Then she ran a pink tongue, large as a ham, over her whiskers; swung to a stand and quietly sauntered off. He could see her path parting the tall stems. She faded without sound, although John Stanley knew she could not be a jump away. Those silent feet were uncanny, made a fellow feel as if someone were standing behind him.

"Go on!" John Stanley shouted at the male. "Follow her! Get along! Scat!" His voice was growing hoarse, he realized. Unconsciously he passed a hand across his forehead; then noticed the gesture. Come, come, man. No use fussing. Naturally the brute would sit there for a while, reasonably a few hours. Then the wretched beast would get hungry and sneak off. Then it was only a matter of picking the door-lock with the hunting knife and making a dash for the car up the hill. If only the animal would quit staring like that and turn its back.

The tiger refused to turn its back on John Stanley. Sitting by the tree, staring, he might have been a painting in the dry twilight. His eyes were motionless as those of a photo-graph. No hair stirred on the Queen Elizabeth ruff under his white throat, on the glossy striping of his coat, on his cream-colored vest and shaggy belly. Only the tip of his tail moved, curling and wagging in a secret movement independent of the body; a release for the high-strung nervous system in that taut frame. Or he might twitch one of the white horsehair whiskers to chase a teasing insect from his black leather nose.

The wagging tail-tip had fascinated John Stanley at first; and they used to say if you stared a beast in the eye it might scare him off. The biggest tiger John Stanley had ever seen didn't scare. He sat. John sat. After a while the game could become definitely tiresome. Mustn't let the thing prey on his nerves the slightest. Now if he edged up on the door and started his knife fiddling with the lock the tiger might stay where he was.

JOHN STANLEY CREPT toward the door. Slowly and more slowly. Ha, the cat wasn't going to move. With stealth, John Stanley drew the hunting knife from its sheath. The tiger yawned a mouth of scissors, and leaned toward the cage with a menacing *ffffggggh!*

John Stanley shrank back from the door, sat down, flushing angrily. Too early yet. All right, any day he couldn't outwait this devil. No use losing his temper. If his throat didn't feel like leather for lack of water—thirsty—wait, better keep his mind off that.

To keep his mind off that, he fumbled in his pocket for something to read, and found Luckenback's telegram. Hell, it was too dark to read, anyway. He'd get these tigers, yet; get the two of them. If those cowardly Bhils hadn't deserted like a batch of rats. If—but damn it! He'd sent a message to the bungalow and told them not to worry.

Molly and her father, probably sitting down to dinner right now. Molly all in white—

Woof! John Stanley whirled at the sound. The tigress was back, nosing around the cage wheels. The tiger had blinked and vanished. The landscape was blotting out in the thickest dark John Stanley had ever known. A moment's dusk, then the valley was invisible, swept away in a vanishment so complete that a man would wonder if he'd gone blind, had he not been able to see the glowing, disembodied, sulphur-yellow eyeballs watching from night outside a certain cage. John Stanley stared at the eyes to show himself he was calm, and the yellow bulbs circled the cage without sound.

"Beat it!" The cry soured foolishly in his throat. Another set of eyes appeared. All right, let them sit there. Might as well take it easy and they'd forget him. He found the center of the cage and lay on his side, gingerly, because the boards were not soft. Instantly a humming particle shot out of nowhere and drove a needle into his cheek. John Stanley clapped a mosquito. Now the blackness was alive with a bedeviling orchestration, a tuning-up of tiny wings. Hmmmmmmm! Zzzmmmmmm! The cage was like a hive. He batted and thwacked furiously while welts grew to bumps of fire on throat, wrists and forehead. He wrapped his head in his coat, fought against scratching and was, all at once, smotheringly thirsty. The floor ate into his hip. He dozed. He jumped awake. Every time he woke he saw the yellow eyeballs staring.

HE WANTED THE sleep he did not get that night, for the day broke hot as a morning on Mercury. Heat on his eyelids roused him from a doze to see daylight like white flame

and the big tiger sharpening its claws, cat-fashion, on the
tree. When the cat saw him stirring, it padded towards the
cage, making sounds in its throat. John Stanley sat up and
rubbed weary hands over his bitten face. His cheeks were
raw sandpaper. Dry dust smoked off his fingers. He yelled
at the tiger, "Get away!"

He had to laugh at that; a strangely uncontrollable chor-
tle that died for lack of merriment, tearing at the lining
of his windpipe. The tiger was laughing, too; sitting at the
cage door with a massive grin. The beast even covered its
mouth with a paw to hide amusement; then said, "Huff!"
and walked behind the tree. In a queer blaze of anger, John
Stanley jerked out his knife, jumped forward and dug the
blade at the spring lock. The scraping of metal brought the
tiger around the tree at a skipping gallop; and to John Stanley's fright the door lurched wide. With a croak of terror
he yanked the casement shut. That door wasn't locked.
Merely jammed.

Made the roots of his scalp ache to know the door was
unlocked, and at the same time it was a taunt. It was not the
cage, but the tiger which held him incarcerated as helpless
as if there were a thousand locks.

The tiger slid at the door, touched a bar with an inquis-
itive paw, then sprang backwards, snarling. John Stanley
had recoiled to the front of the cage; the clicking he heard
was the sound of his own teeth.

"Stop it!" he whispered at himself. "They can't get in.
You'll be all right. The Bhils will come back, or—"

Rustling in the grass, a breath among the stems, and
the tigress stepping into the road. John Stanley rubbed
his prickling eyes. A flurry of bright color in the female's

wake, and there were four striped, half-grown, clumsy cubs. Tiger, tigress and cubs ranged themselves in the shade of the peepul tree and proceeded to regard John Stanley. With an oath that got away before he could stop it, he saw by his watch it was only seven o'clock. He bent stiff legs, and sat down. He would have given a thousand pounds for his automatic, right then.

A trio of buzzards cruised up from the cliffs and loafed in the sky overhead, like airplanes observing. The glade was a well of heat. The only shade in the cage was made of narrow bars, shadow-striping John Stanley's legs. Far to the north the mountains looked blue and cool.

BY THAT SECOND afternoon John Stanley was really tired of the thing. Tired of sitting, standing, carving initials in the cage floor. Tired of scratching at lumps on his neck and the smarting sunlight and the unchanging landscape. Tired of the iron framework before his eyes and the dirt in his linen and all the things with which he tried to divert himself. That was when he took to darting at the bars, peering up the scorched hill to where his car sat burning in the sun; peering and squinting in a hope for help. His eyes were like little pins, seeking sight of rescuers who did not come. Desolation pressed silence on his eardrums until he thought they must burst of listening.

But when he did listen he heard nothing but the sound of soft pads in dust; the snuffles and coughing of cubs playing tag about the tree; the reproving snaps of the tigress. Wait, there was somebody! No, merely the shadow of a bird crossing the slope. Again! Merely baked earth cracking in the heat.

The tiger lay on its side in the grass, paws outsprawled,

ears alert, and considered John Stanley with heaving flanks. John Stanley tightened his belt and tried to spit. All at once he was cursing. "G'wan! Go away! By God, you dirty—" His voice was a caw in his own hearing; he stoppered the outburst of obscenity with a hand clapped over his mouth. The two great cats contemplated this gesture with grins that might have been scornful amusement but more probably were hunger.

John Stanley rubbed his wrists, and took a turn around the cage. The tigress, annoyed by the mauling of her litter, swatted the cubs and led them with dignity into the grass. Then she returned to sprawl beside her mate and pant up at the cage, her tongue lolling. How long had those two striped fiends been staring at him? Hours or years?

John Stanley's legs were suddenly trembling. When had he eaten last? If he could only wash that scum out of his mouth. He took another turn, watching the hilltop, the mountains, the sky, the hilltop again. He walked in a circle. The sun, the blazing green of this landscape was giving him a headache. God, why didn't somebody come? Molly. The Bhils. Take it easy, man. They'll come. Now there were fifteen steps around the cage, three steps across. One, two, three, four—

"Oh, my God!" John Stanley panted against the bars, an arm pressed over his blistered eyes. Two tears rolled down his cheeks. "Stanley! Stop it, man! Oh, my God! You're—you're *pacing*—"

That was the second afternoon.

THERE WERE MOMENTS that night when he ran up and down bawling hoarse imprecations. Other times he crouched in darkness against the iron palings, sick, drained of energy, shuddering from the emptiness under his belt, too weak to strike at insects clouding at his face. A time, during that rainshower in the dark of midnight, when he scrabbled on the floorboards, begging the drops to pelt his cheeks, mouth yawned wide in his uplifted face, hands frantically wringing the dribble from his cuffs into the upturned bowl of his sun helmet. The silence after that black rain was the hush at world's end. The night was a year.

But the third day was eternity. Eternity born on a pillar of fire. Sometimes John Stanley curled his fists around the cage bars, cursing them, shaking them until the whole wagon seemed to rattle. Sometimes he lay on the floor, turning, heaving with dry, uncontrollable sobs. Then it was the landscape he hated, the sameness, the bated quiet, the burning green, the white shine slanting off the dead tree. Again, the daggering dayshine blinding his eyes, he was filled with a craft that made him giddy, agile as a shadow, light-headed as a balloon, strong as a band of steel.

Hunting knife in fist, he would crawl to the door, fling it open, make as if to jump. But then, as always, as a thousand times before, omnipresent as fate, there were the tigers. Giant, twelve-foot cats waiting with grins and fixed yellow eyeballs. Then he was weak and sick and the knife was a trifle in his hand. Those fangs would devour him in half a crunch. They knew it. They sat. They watched his slightest move, studying his face, waiting him out in cocksure, famished confidence. They had him—

"You have not! Dirty, wretched brutes! Think you can get me! *Me!* Ha! Ha, ha, haaaa—

He spraddled on his hollow belly and grinned at the cats, cursed them in a whisper as fierce as their snarled replies.

"Waiting, are you? Hungry, are you?" But then his eye
could see the stalled car not fifty yards uphill, the car with
its lunch basket, guns, promise of freedom, water canteen.
There it was, just beyond the bars. Damn the bars!

There were intervals, in that intolerable third day, when
John Stanley ran at the bars, brandishing the knife, trying
to stab one of the beasts as it ambled past. Intervals of
whirlwind rage when he tottered about the cage calling
soundless cries, threatening in furious pantomime the
sentinels stationed at the door. Finally there were moments
of glass-like lucidity when he sprawled flat on his face,
breathing the hot dust, and knowing he could stand it no
longer.

Those tigers weren't going away, they were part of the
landscape like the dead tree and the green-blazing grass.
They were hungry and, like the silence, they knew how to
wait. Molly wasn't coming. Nobody was coming. And he
was thirsty, shriveling, going to rust. Going to rust in a trap
of shining bars that gave him no room to turn, to think, to
breathe. Better make the dash before sun and thirst robbed
the final will from his mind. Better make the break before
those shadow-bands pinned his legs for good, before the
framework fastened him in forever. They wanted him, those
rotten, murderous brutes. They had him. But they were
going to fight for the morsel. Time to go.

St. George was going after the dragon, now! John Stanley must have been pretty light-headed by that time, but
the weakness was his last bid for strength. He strapped his
belt until it was a vise that hoisted him to a stand. He disci-
plined his legs. The hunting knife did not tremble in his
first, nor did he waver at the door. He thought of water—

The barred gate swung and crashed. John Stanley's leap took him blowing across the ground. His visual impressions were not clear, but he knew the way. Sunlight sprang off the blade in his hand, and shadows orange and black reared like flame in the green before him. In that hazed second he saw the tigress tower on her haunches against the sun; saw the tiger fly sideways like a convulsion of colored light. Screaming, he struck with the bright knife.

"Fight then! Take it! Yaah!"

The knife cutting sunshine—a roaring snort in his ears. A great paw lashing past his nose, dragging ribbons of fire down his arm. John Stanley whirled under the sky, saw the cliffs go wheeling and the hill come into view, and sat up, *bump!* against the dead tree. He stopped his screaming with fingers in his mouth. The landscape was silent and empty. Far from the road two soundless furrows were racing like wind through the grass. The grass flowed together and the furrows were gone.

John Stanley went plunging up to his car. That was where Molly and Old Man Breadon and the house boy found him, unconscious.

I MET THIS man Stanley in Naini Tal. It was the year after the war, and business was bad in tea. Stanley, who owned a big plantation, had been hit particularly hard, I knew. But when I asked him how he was getting along, he told me he was rich.

"Always rich," he told me, "long as you're free."

Then he pointed to the scar on his left arm, and gave me this story. At the end, he laughed. "If you want your ego set straight just watch a jungle cat turn up his nose at your valuable self. Those tigers didn't want me for dinner. No!

They watched me because they were *curious!* Like visitors in any zoo. And were just as scared when I broke loose. The way they turned tail and made for home—"

He chuckled at the memory, and I saw he was watching the mountain pictured beyond the window's frame. "They have feelings, too."

It was some time later I asked him how his wife was.

"Hospital just at present," he told me quietly. "That's why we're up here. Molly was pretty badly mauled when she got in the way of a tiger in the hills last week." Then, seeing the shock on my face, he nodded expressionlessly and turned his glance into his glass. "But she's getting better, now," he said dryly. "And tigers don't know any better."

ON EVIL BEACH

"It was an island," the captain said, "populated by the foulest scum that ever went down the Devil's drain."

"The Wickeder The City, The Holier The People…"
—Old Moslem Proverb

WE WERE TALKING about religion and Crewe, the visiting poet, surprised me by saying religion had lost its power in the modern world and he couldn't understand how a man could become a missionary and set out to save the heathen. "Batch of hypocrites. Come out here to preach the Bible because no one home has time for it any more."

Garth, the army man who had been in the Philippines, surprised me more. "It's Faith," he fumbled to explain. "Maybe there is a lot of power in the Bible."

It was Lantern who surprised me most. The tall, gray-eyed sailor who knew the back entrances of Asia better than most Rotarians know Main Street, and whose wide, easy shoulders had never been bowed in a pew, shifted around in his chair.

"It's funny," he observed, "how everybody takes a poke at the poor missionary who comes out East." He pointed his whiskey swizzle at the scene below the hotel veranda—a palm-lined boulevard languorous with the blues of tropical dusk; pantalooned natives drifting in this scented twilight; fireflies swooping in the sleepy park beyond, and

the pineapple-shaped pagoda spires of Bangkok in the moon-drugged background.

"Seems to me," he went on, "that when these natives get ruined it's generally when the fleet's in or the oil company wants a grab. But don't get me wrong. I'm not going to take up a collection for the London Evangelical Society. As I see it, there's truth in all religions—Buddha, Mohammed, Confucius all saw part of the light. It's when a man doesn't have any religion at all that it's bad, and maybe a missionary can do some good for that kind. Maybe for that kind the Bible has more candle-power than you'd imagine. I've seen it do some strange things out here," he added thoughtfully. "Some mighty strange things."

Crewe smiled. "You sound as if you'd seen an Old Testament miracle out here, or something. Jonah and the Whale?"

The sailor pushed back his white officer's cap and eased back in his chair with folded arms. "Something just as miraculous," he said quietly. "Only in this case the whale

*"The treaure I seek, brother, is that of your soul," the
missionary said. "And the soul of that wicked woman"*

was an island—an island populated by the foulest scum
of humanity that ever went down the drains of the devil's
sink—and the Jonah, you might say, the biggest fortune
in rubies outside of a Kimberly mine. Did you ever hear
about the Thirty-Eight Rubies of Jihan Ji?"

A jaw-drop of incredulity lengthened the army man's
face.

Anyone who had lived in Asia long enough to take a
siesta knew about those fabulous gems. Thirty-eight priceless rubies, each one set in a gold medallion as big as a
butterdish, each one worth a king's fortune, each crimson
as the blood that had been spilled by the adventurers who
had died in Asia looking for them. And a lot of men had
died, looking for those thirty-eight rubies.

"Don't tell me," the army man gasped, "you know where
those gems are!"

"I know where they were," the sailor said huskily, "and

it has to do with what we were talking about—religion—
are missionaries hypocrites—Bible miracles and all that.
I had those rubies in the palm of my hand once, and I let
them go. Yes, I did.... Those gems turned up on that island
I told you about, and that island populace turned into a
brawl of fiends fighting to get those red stones. Talk about
a treasure hunt in Hell! Then a missionary walked into the
middle of it with a Bible under his arm. He was a little late
getting there, because a big fat Hindu idol had got there
first and Saint Nick was king of that place. But Jonah and
the Whale made a small miracle, I think, compared to what
happened on that hell-island, Evil Beach. That was the
island's name—Evil Beach. Did you ever hear of a missionary in the middle of a treasure hunt in Hell? Listen—"

1

I SAID EVIL BEACH was Hell (the sailor began) and even today, when it doesn't go by that name any more, you'd steer a wide course around that island. Ships coming up the Gulf of Siam keep away from it, and that's why you didn't see it coming in to Bangkok. But it's only a day sou' by west down the Gulf, a fly speck on the chart, just a mountain lumped up out of the sea and surrounded by a nasty snarl of reefs.

It's bad navigating today, but in those days—just after the War—it was a lot worse. All the riffraff in the world seemed to be drifting around these waters after the War, and most of it beached on that island. It was a tough place.

I was a smart young kid in those days—life on a submarine had left a bad taste in my mouth, and I'd quit the Asiatic Fleet to try a go at the China Coast—and I thought I was pretty tough, myself. Those were the days when I didn't believe in anything better than a bottle of Hollands on one knee and a singsong girl on the other. I'd have told you religion was so much seaweed, and I had about as much respect for missionaries. Siam seemed like a good place to live cheap and I drifted into Bangkok. Next thing I knew I was broke. So I got a job running the *Siamese Sister* between Bangkok and Kelantan for a hungry Dutch trader named Ledbetter. Evil Beach was first port of call, and I could whiff that island nosegay—perfume of leprosy, opium and corruption—almost before I started out. And its reputation smelled to the Pleiades.

It was supposed to belong to Siam, but the Siamese didn't want it. Most of the island had been leased to an Irish-Arabian pirate named Abdullah O'Rourke, a fiend kicked out of the Pit because the devil had found him too tough to manage. Abdullah ruled the town at the mountain's foot, and that port of derelicts was no Zion City. Drugs, deviltry and damnation prowled the mud-paved alleys; hardly a week went by but what some scum came to grief with a knife in his back; the only law there was administered by Abdullah, a dancing girl, a fiddler and this heathen idol. I'll never forget my first glimpse of those four, beginning with the heathen idol.

IT WAS THE first thing you saw on Evil Beach—the jungle-covered mountain—the town at the mountain's foot—and halfway up the mountain, grinning, sneering down at the sprawl of rooftops, that big brass god. Only place I'd ever seen one like it was in Hyderabad, way over in India. The thing was fairly lifelike for Hindu sculpture. Looked like a pot-bellied brass ogre bouncing a pot-bellied brass baby on its knee. Papa and baby were mounted in the middle of a marble tank, twenty feet square, about nine deep, open to the sky, A mountain river tumbled near by; there was a sort of spillway you could open to fill the tank; but the tank had never been filled, by the look, and the bald head and shoulders of the idol reared up out of the tank and grinned down at the town below—for all the world like some bloated idiot sitting in a dried-up Y.M.C.A. pool.

Sightless, thick-lipped, it was ugly as vice. It gave you

a creep to make port for the first time and see that giant brass head shining in the sun up there like the spirit of the town it watched over.

"Keepin' watch over me," Abdullah O'Rourke would chuckle, pointing a thumb up the mountain, copying the idol's grin.

Shake hands with the Devil—Abdullah O'Rourke! Half Irish, half Arab; combining the worst of both halves in four hundred pounds of stale fat under a little red head with black eyes. Well, you might have shaken hands with Abdullah, at that, but you'd have found out it didn't mean hello. Shaking hands with Abdullah meant goodbye. Those who knew about it, walking into the local dancehall and seeing the fat man saunter toward them with outstretched palm, turned pale. Next day they'd be found a whole lot paler— lying in some nook of the jungle, or floating out to the sharks with a blade in the spine. Island gossip whispered that this "glad hand" of Abdullah's was a signal to his lieutenant, Stradivarius, to play the executioner. But Abdullah would have told you he was a poor trader running a dance hall, and Stradivarius was only a sad man with a fiddle.

Personally I think that gloom-faced German musician would have played while his own mother burned. Lord knows what crime must have sent him from the Berlin Opera to Evil Beach. I know he could play a violin fashioned from a cigar box and fish-twine and make it sound like Fritz Kreisler, and I used to imagine him holding some victim spellbound with a serenade while Abdullah O'Rourke tiptoed up behind with a butcher-knife.

In case the victim was deaf, there was Cobra Mary.

Cobra Mary did the only dancing in Abdullah's Brass

Idol Dance Palace, and I'd give a lot to know where that girl hailed from. I'd quit the sea and go there to find her sister—against all my better instincts, I would! They called her Abdullah's girl, but I never believed that. Not for a minute. Wickedness has its class distinctions, too. Her wickedness was like a jeweled dagger or the poisoned ice of a di Medici. O'Rourke stabbed your body with a knife, but that girl's dance stabbed you in the soul.

Hair like copper flame. Skin the hue of frozen milk. Slanted topaz eyes. Figure to burn down the conscience of a saint. Wrap that up in a green silk *sarong* and set it writhing like a snake to a murderer's violin with Abdullah O'Rourke at the cash register wondering who he'd shake hands with next and up on the mountain that brass heathen idol grinning down—picture that, and you've got an idea of Evil Beach. Add a treasure hunt, and you wouldn't have bet a *tikal* on the chances of the Gospel in that place.

A TREASURE HUNT was all the island needed to turn it into a first class nightmare, and I'd been making port there for about a year when it began. It took a Hindu priest to stoke up the fire. The priest was a Brahmin untouchable who boarded the *Siamese Sister* at Bangkok with a batch of Chinamen and some Australian hoboes on their way down to Kelantan to work a tin mine. The *Siamese Sister* never got to Kelantan that trip. A typhoon hit her as she started down the Gulf, and she drowned with nearly all hands on one of those wicked reefs off Evil Beach.

I swam ashore somehow, and that night while I was toasting my luck in Abdullah's dance palace, I found there were two other survivors. Cobra Mary was going full blast inside, the storm full blast outside, when the door flapped open and one of those Australian miners staggered in with that Brahmin priest in his arms. The Aussie was a hardy, black-whiskered fellow, on his feet although three-quarters drowned; but the old Hindu, whose ribs had been stove in like my schooner's, was dying. The Aussie carried him into a back room of the dance hall and laid him on the floor to die; but that priest lived just long enough to touch off an earthquake.

"Quick! Quick!" the old Hindu panted, reaching up to wring a quart of water out of the Aussie's brine-soaked beard. "Look from the window, *sahib!* In a flash of lightning I thought I saw an image on the mountain. Can you see it?"

The miner stared out of the back window, and, after a vivid flash of lightning, told the dying Brahmin he could see the image.

"It is Vasuveda!" the waterlogged Hindu gurgled. He was an educated old scarecrow, and he spoke to his bearded rescuer in English. "It is Vasuveda with the infant god Krishna sitting on his knee. The image is supposed to represent Vasuveda crossing the River Yamuna to save the little Krishna from enemy demons. The demons made the river rise, but the infant god Krishna was greater than any river. Ahee! When the water reached the infant god's big toe it could rise no higher. No matter how deep the flood, the infant god Krishna can never drown. Krishna is the Hindu god who saves us from drowning—who saved me tonight so that I might die on land. Does that mean anything to you, *sahib?*"

The bearded Australian looked bored. He was wet and exhausted, and he suggested that a bottle of rum would interest him more than a Hindu legend. But the dying priest had him by the beard again; he couldn't get away.

"Wait!" the old priest gasped. "If the image up there is sitting in a tank, it is surely the one of which I speak. It is an old image, *sahib*. It was erected on this island five centuries ago by Jihan Ji. To praise the god who had saved him from drowning when his ship went down on those reefs out there as ours did tonight. Jihan Ji was on his way back to India from Siam, and he had with him the Thirty-Eight Rubies. The image marks this island, then, as the hiding-place of the thirty-eight gems."

"You mean the rubies are on this island?"

"You rescued me from the sea," the old Hindu moaned. "I try to repay. If the image is the one I believe it to be, the Thirty-Eight Rubies will be here. Buried in a vault thirty-eight feet underground."

"Thirty-eight feet underground where?"

"Somewhere deep in the jungle. Two miles north of the image as the crow flies you will come to a giant silk-cotton tree. Climb the tree. In the topmost limb you will find carved the directions of where to dig for the treasure. There you will unearth the Thirty-Eight Rubies of Jihan Ji."

Having delivered that little acrostic, the smashed-up old Hindu hemorrhaged and died. I guess the bearded Australian miner who had fetched him ashore almost had a hemorrhage, too. He had thought he was alone with the priest but he wasn't. He jumped to his feet and turned around, and he saw there were some other witnesses to that death-scene.

EVERY MAN JACK in the Brass Idol Dance Palace had his face in the doorway of that back room. His ears, anyway.

My own ears were there, and right in front of me were the ears of Stradivarius and Cobra Mary and Abdullah O'Rourke. I remember thinking how Abdullah's ears resembled the little ears of a hippopotamus, pricked up. Those ears had been drinking in the dying Brahmin's speech the way the man's thick throat had been guzzling grog a moment before. Only that dying speech was thirty times as intoxicating as any grog. Thirty-eight times as intoxicating.

The Thirty-Eight Rubies of Jihan Ji! You could have heard a spider's sigh in the back room of that dance hall when the water-soaked Australian tin-miner turned to stare at the mob in the doorway and the mob stared back at him. You knew what that tin-miner was thinking, and you could imagine what the mob was thinking, too.

"The old Hindu was crazy," he coughed at Abdullah O'Rourke. "He swallowed a lot of sea water and went off his nut. Give me some dry clothes and a room. I'm going to bed."

"Of course he was crazy," Abdullah agreed with a disinterested look at the body. "Goodnight, my friend, and sleep well." He held out his pudgy hand.

That night the Australian disappeared. He took his damp beard and the dungarees O'Rourke gave him, walked up the stairs to his room, and in the morning he wasn't there. In the morning there wasn't anybody in the Brass Idol Dance Palace. That was Abdullah's alibi afterward. How could he have murdered the Aussie, he would snarl, when he, like every other fool on the island, had left the dance hall to go look for that giant silk-cotton tree.

You can see how it was. Every scoundrel who'd heard the dying priest's story had lit out by midnight to find that tree. The Klondyke gold rush was nothing to the stampede to find the forest monarch that would mark the first step to locating the Thirty-Eight Rubies. I was in that race, myself, you can believe. Cross-country through storming dark, and no holds barred.

It was a job going through the jungle in the pitchy blackness, and the sun was just melting its way through the horizon when I found the tree. About fifty others found it at the same time, and a yell went up in the sunrise when we did. The storm had cleared away with the coming daylight, but it wasn't any shout of praise that went up that morning. Listen!

The silk-cotton tree had been smashed down. Literally. About five feet of trunk remained standing, a huge raw stump split in half like a monster tooth; and the rest of that jungle giant made a great stack of splinters as big as ten haymows. No mistake about it being the tree in question, for those vast silk-cottons are scarce out here, and that was the only one in the neighborhood. Try to imagine that tree reduced to matchwood, as if the fist of some tremendous Goliath had demolished it at one blow; and then try to imagine the fury of those frustrated treasure hunters, confronted by the sight.

"Hit by lightning!" Stradivarius was there—I remember him scuttling out of the jungle's wall and thrashing into the mass of broken lumber. His eyes were mournful. "About one o'clock this morning, it was. *Himmelkreuzedonnerwetter!* I told Abdullah there was one big explosion!"

There'd been a lot of thundering while I was clawing my way around the island in the dark, and one crash louder than the rest. But that was nothing compared to the explosion which came from Abdullah O'Rourke when he panted out of the jungle and saw that pulverized tree. He roared at the island riffraff to get out of his way, and went ripping into that jigsaw puzzle of timber like a human buzz-saw. Don't think that splintered tree wasn't a puzzle, either. The key to that jigsaw was the topmost limb, and there wasn't any topmost limb in that silk-cotton giant, now. Upper limbs, lower limbs, twigs and branches were scrambled in a hill of chips and slivers—any one of those shattered limbs might have been topmost.

"Find the limb with the carving on it!" That was Cobra Mary's suggestion. She was standing there in the dawn with her eyes as green as lust, her own limbs wrapped invitingly in that wonderful silk *sarong*. "You must find the carved limb, or you will never find the rubies."

I WISH YOU could have seen the way the population of Evil Beach, myself included, went tearing into that stack of kindling. Sorting those shattered branches. Grabbing at twigs, slivers, broken limbs. We didn't find any carved directions, though. By nightfall we were still clawing and pawing that mess of timber. Next sunrise we were at it again. Well, Evil Beach went into that contest with something more than enthusiasm; for a week every denizen of the island was up there picking over that tree, but the winning puzzle-piece remained unfound.

That put Abdullah O'Rourke in a temper. He was boss of the island; and there was the world's biggest treasure in his dooryard, so to speak, and he couldn't find the directions that would tell him where to look for it. Mad? He swore by his Irish saints and the three-fingered hand of Mohammed's wife to find those gems. While the rest of us were working on that tree-puzzle, Abdullah began to blast thirty-eight foot holes all over the mountain. In another week the island looked like No Man's Land after a barrage, but the rubies remained undiscovered. The puzzle-fans couldn't find the answer, either.

It never occurred to me that there might be a nigger in the woodpile—that someone might've been there ahead of the rush and made off with the solution. But it finally occurred to me that it might be a mighty dangerous bit of luck for the man who dug up the prize. Abdullah was hardly the type to let someone play "finders keepers" in his territory. Getting off that island with the Thirty-Eight Rubies might prove more of a problem than finding them.

A month went by, and the rubies were still underground. By that time the rush of treasure-hunters had started, and Ledbetter sent another schooner, saying he wanted me back in the passenger service. I'd like to know how word travels like that in the East. Anyway, news of the bonanza had reached the mainland, and every foot-loose fortune-hunter from Port Said to Shanghai was buying a ticket to Evil Beach. Ledbetter gave me command of my second excursion boat—the *Siamese Twin*—and I took her out of Bangkok loaded to the gunwales with the wildest crowd of villains you ever saw. Every one of those dogs had a shovel in one pocket, a knife in the other. It was all aboard for Evil Beach, and the devil take the hindmost.

That a missionary should have been aboard that excursion seemed as unlikely as a gambler on his way to the Golden Gates.

2

I STARED AT the man. First and last I'd seen some odd fish in the Gulf of Siam, but in that boatload of ruby hunters, he looked like a herring in a nest of sharks.

"And you're landing at Evil Beach?" I had to goggle at him.

The man astounded me by nodding. Having boarded ship at Bangkok, he'd reclined seasick in his cabin most of the trip, and the sight of him coming out on deck as we raised the island almost knocked me down. A soul-saver, you understand. A missionary! The part done almost to a caricature—high-topped sun helmet—inverted collar—frock coat—Testament in elbow—even to the Mother Goose umbrella the cartoons always have those fellows carrying. I can see his face now as I saw it then—the studious, shell-rimmed spectacles, the rosy cheeks, the chin carefully shaved and talcumed, the innocent, eager countenance of your theological boy of forty, ascetic and inexperienced and out to set the world on fire for a Cause.

"Yes, brother, I am landing here. I had intended going to Kelantan, but I was told this island was more in need. So I have decided to make my mission here. The darker the error, the more in want of light."

I tried to keep astonishment out of my voice. "They tell

me it's a tough place, parson." I went on to suggest he'd better go to Kelantan, and he smiled at me.

"I shall carry the light to this shore, brother. I shall show these people the error of their ways—build a church—"

"Build a church?" I wanted to laugh. "And have Sunday School picnics and Wednesday night prayer meetings and things like that?"

Exactly like that, the missionary told me. "I intend to gather my flock immediately. Build a congregation. Perhaps some day we may be able to afford an organ, but for the present I will rely on the spirit of song and the inspiration of the Word. The Siamese government has awarded me an acre of ground for building, and of course the church will have pews and a fine steeple, and I will teach a Bible class and—"

Lord! In that setting the thing was incredible. Steeple! Congregation! Bible class! Those were the man's exact words, and I want to tell you they sounded impossible in that latitude and longitude. Eh? I had to turn around to confirm our position. There was Evil Beach off the bow. We were close hauling under the crinkled, jungly flank of the mountain; smell of damp rot and corruption drifted at us through the tropic twilight, and there was a faint, thin echo of violin music on the wind to greet us. As the schooner slipped under the headland a moon as big as a Javanese hat came around the mountaintop, and its yellow dust fell on the head and shoulders of the big brass idol.

I thought of O'Rourke and Stradivarius and Cobra Mary. The Brass Idol Dance Palace. Not that I had any sentiment, but it made me a little uncomfortable to think of this lamb going innocently to a slaughter.

"You'd better go on to Kelantan," I repeated my advice. "There's a million-dollar fortune-hunt broke loose on this island, and that much money means blood anywhere." I pointed to a crowd of drunken beachcombers brawling on our foredeck. "They're worse than that ashore. A sermon around here will be wasted breath."

He smiled at me cheerfully. "My mission is not to save breath, but souls."

"The only thing that could save a soul on Evil Beach," I said, "would be a miracle."

The missionary didn't hear me. His eyes were on the island, and there was a shine to his glasses that let me know he was deaf to my kind of talk. Anyway, he went dreaming off down the deck to the fo'c'sle head where some cargo boxes were stowed. My Malay bos'n had charge of cargo, and when I went aft to take the wheel, he told me the boxes belonged to the missionary. Carpentry tools! Hammers and nails! Actually that soul-saver thought he could put up a church.

"Bats in the belfry," I scoffed; and then I forgot the man. My thoughts had been revolving around thirty-eight rubies from the moment of sighting Evil Beach, and I was wondering if I might not take another try at finding the location of those gems. It's hard to get over a treasure hunt once you've got the fever. My temperature went up fifty degrees when I went ashore that night and found the town booming like the Barbary Coast, the alleys jammed with excited bonanza-seekers, and the Brass Idol Dance Palace doing a land-office business.

Abdullah's place was roaring like a bonfire, and the trader swam at me through a whirlpool of smoke and din

to welcome me, florid and dimpling, his enormous bulk
tented in stained pongee, his black Arab eyes twinkling
in his Irish face.

"The top of th' mornin', and Allah's blessing. Come in,
Captain. Come in and have the first drink on the house."

He was fat and sweating and cordial, with the spuri-
ous cordiality of a tiger's grin. I had to ask about the thirty-eight rubies, and he became as jovial as a Christmas
pudding.

"Ha-ha-ha. The town is mobbed. All the idiots in the
world are here to find that Hindu treasure. *Bismillah!* Since
the map to the treasure can't be found, one mud-hole is as
good as another. Me, I haven't turned a spadeful of ground
in three weeks."

I looked at the trader. It wasn't like him to quit any proposition that had to do with a million dollars. He chuckled
at my surprise; waved a hand at the jam-packed room.

"You see those boys? I let them do the work. This island,
I hold a lease on most of the land. They ask me can they
dig on my territory. Why not? *Rahmet Allah!* all I ask is a
fifty-fifty share from the man who finds the treasure. The
more diggers, the better, I say. Nights they come to the
dance palace to see Cobra Mary's performance."

Well, what an Eldorado that was! I had to take my hat
off to Abdullah that night. He might have lost his fortune
temporarily; meantime he'd found another. This boom rush
to Evil Beach was ringing his cash register like a three-
alarm fire. Abdullah had jacked up the price of a drink to
a dollar a glass. Do you see how he had that island mob
coming and going? If they didn't find the treasure, they

put another into his coffers. And if they did find it, it was fifty-fifty.

The place was a furnace stoked with sailors, beachcombers, halfbreeds, all the ruck of Asia and backwash of the War, hot-eyed with hope for a ten-strike and thirsty for liquor and amusement. Abdullah was feeding them the liquor, and Cobra Mary was feeding them the amusement. That was the set-up on Evil Beach when the interruption arrived. Out of the night like a bolt from the black.

"Stop!"

THE COMMAND CAME banging into the scene like a gunshot to jump the customers out of their chairs, turn Abdullah O'Rourke to a wooden copy of the idol up the mountain, and stand the dancing girl on her platform like a pillar of salt. The missionary was standing in the doorway. Face bleached the color of rice-paper. Eyes bulging behind their glasses.

I imagined the man, fresh from theological school, had never guessed there was such a dive or such a dancing girl in all the world. In the silence that greeted his appearance, flush crawled like fever into the hollows of his sucked-in cheeks. Abdullah made an involuntary step forward, and the missionary swallowed this sight in a gulp, but he didn't run. His stare went back to Cobra Mary, and his goggles seemed to widen and grow.

"Blasphemous! Absolutely obscene and blasphemous!" You know how the man would have said it. With a horror-hollowed tone only matched by the hollow astonishment in Abdullah's.

"Well, who the devil are *you?*"

They looked at each other; the fat man in greasy pongee,

the missionary with his frock coat, umbrella and Testament. Then can you imagine how Saint George might have announced himself to the dragon?

"I am the Reverend T. Ulrich Christopher, come at the instigation of the Far-East Missionary Society with permission to practice my calling here from the Siamese government."

The dragon, in this case, was amazed. "A missionary, huh? Well, I'm damned. Come to Evil Beach to hunt the treasure, too!"

The Rev. T. Ulrich Christopher lifted a long, pale hand. "Treasure, brother? Ah, yes, I have come to seek a treasure."

The fat Arab's Irish face was incredulous. So were the other huggermugger faces in that gin-mill. Then a twinkle of cupidity overcome unbelief in O'Rourke's Oriental eyes. "The more the merrier, parson; the more the merrier. I don't know why you shouldn't look around if you want. Only I'm the trader on this island, see? It happens to be my land. Anything you get out of it, you divvy up. Fifty-fifty."

The missionary's pale hand remained aloft. "The treasure I seek, brother, is that of your soul. Your soul, brother and the souls of these benighted people, and the soul of that—that wicked woman there."

I don't think Abdullah understood that exactly, but Cobra Mary did. Perhaps somewhere in her past she'd been to Sunday school—sometimes I wonder. Anyway, she laughed. How she laughed! Fingers spread on hips, she stood there like Circe on that platform, threw back her fiery copper head and loosed a peal of mirth that took hold of missionaries and souls and shook them together in a trill of scorn, and flung them into the face of the pale man in the doorway. At the same moment Stradivarius loosed an offkey "hee-hee-hee" from the strings of his violin, and every scum in the room roared like Falstaff. Abdullah O'Rourke caught the joke, and guffawed like ten truck drivers at a burlesque show.

"So y're treasure-huntin' for souls, is that it? By the beard of th' Prophet, that's a new kind of bonanza for this beach. But we got all the religion we can use on this island, mister. Right out there."

He pointed to the window which framed a view of the mountainside and the brass heathen idol grinning down at the dance hall. When Abdullah copied the idol's grin. I thought of his homicidal handshake and the Australian who had disappeared that night the Brahmin told what the image stood for.

The Rev. T. Ulrich Christopher never flinched. He lifted his gaze to that nasty image squatting up there on the mountain, and then he glared at the smoke-filled room.

"Sinners, you shall repent your ways. The Siamese government has awarded me a grant of land on that mountaintop where I shall build my church. In this island of wickedness and debauch it shall stand as an outpost against sin, a lighthouse in this night of iniquity. I have been told that a treasure-hunt has infested this island. The captain of the ship which brought me here has said that only a miracle might bring salvation to this place. Sinners, give up this hunt for base riches and seek for yourselves the treasures of heaven. Search for the riches of the spirit. Take care, sinners, lest the miracle that comes be one of the Almighty's wrath—the fiery vengeance that once before fell flaming on the wicked cities of the East. Repent, I say. Repent, for the day is at hand—!"

His finger was Judgment quivering at the ceiling. The moonlight touched an eerie yellow shine to his glasses; then darkness drank him up, and he was gone.

3

NOW NOBODY COULD have been more immune to a sermon than I was in those rough-and-tumble days, but something about that missionary's first sermon in Evil Beach got under my skin. Under the skins of those other tough guys in that dance hall, too. Under every skin there, except the skin of the dancing girl on the platform. For a minute the only sound in the place was the buzz of bugs around the ceiling lamps. Every eye was on the doorway where the missionary had vanished like a portent. A couple of Spaniards at the bar crossed themselves. Even Abdullah lifted his eyes to Allah uneasily.

Then Cobra Mary laughed again. That girl had a pelt as wicked as a leopard's. She signaled Stradivarius to strike up his fiddle, and she started her muscle-dance going where she'd left it off. In a twinkling the Brass Idol Dance Palace was booming as before; in half an hour the missionary was not only gone, but forgotten.

I forgot him myself. Before the night was over I was up there on the mountain clawing through the wreckage of that blasted silk-cotton tree in the dim hope of finding the lucky carvings. When I shipped out next morning I could only think of getting back there to take another crack at the buried treasure. Two weeks later, returned to Evil

Beach with another cargo of ruby-hungry immigrants, I was surprised all over again to see the missionary.

He was down at the wharf where some tramp ship had just unloaded a pile of lumber, and he came aboard the *Siamese Twin* to tell me the lumber was his and he was holding the fort.

"You must come right up, Captain, and see what I'm doing."

The fellow seemed famished for someone to talk to. I was frantic to get back into the treasure hunt during shore leave, but I had to go along with the missionary. Perhaps it was his flattering me with "Captain." Perhaps it was a vague sort of pity for the chap. And there was a feverish enthusiasm in the man, something fierce and electric burning inside of him and illuminating his glasses—a magnetic insistence that wouldn't let me put him off.

"You must come up and see!"

I went.

Well, he'd certainly picked an out of the way spot for his "outpost against sin." The place was as hard of attainment as heaven, and if the path wasn't as straight it was every bit as narrow. We squeezed along a bushy ravine bending up the mountain in a westerly direction, four miles of the hardest going. At the summit I was a rash of jigger-bites and thorn-nips. Below I could see that Vasuveda idol glinting in the sun. The shoreline was dotted with lean-tos and tents numerous (this was the missionary's description) as the encampments of the Philistines. I could see men and mules crawling all over the lower trails like ants.

It was a grand view, but the Siamese officials who'd donated the Reverend Christopher that clifftop had surely stung him. It was too hard to reach to be worth anything. A tangle of brush and capsicum on a peak higher than a vulture's nest.

Then I wish you could have seen how that missionary rushed around that piece of mountainpeak. "I'll clear a wide compound. Make a park for picnics, camp-meetings. Look! There stands the church—!"

ALREADY HE'D HACKED a considerable clearing, and the framework of an unfinished building—raw timbers and scaffolding—looked strange against that jungle background. Come to think of it, it did look something like a fort—a square edifice like a blockhouse, stout enough to last a while. I sat on a nail keg, admiring the construction job, while Christopher showed me blueprints of his own design, and proudly told me the church was going to have a forty-foot steeple.

Then I got a real glimpse of the man's zeal. Staring at the clutter of saws, axes, shovels, paint-tins and ladders, I wondered aloud where he'd ever hired the workmen.

"Workmen?" He rubbed a mosquito-bite, staring at me.

"The carpenters who did this job. The—"

"But I did it all by myself."

I tell you, I sat there gawping. The fellow talked about putting up that church on that mountainpeak as if he'd done it by a wave of the hand. Workmen? He hadn't been able to hire any. The men on Evil Beach, it seemed, were more interested in digging for a million-dollar treasure than in laboring for the Lord. Not a man on the island had offered assistance. With the help of the Almighty, then, he'd started the job by himself, laid the cornerstone, raised the timbers. Yes, he had sweated. Daytimes the sun had been cruel. Nights there were mosquitoes. But he hadn't done it single-handed, either. There was the Almighty—

If you know anything about hard work in a tropic jungle, you'll know why I sat on that nail keg with my mouth open. It opened some more when my eye spotted a couple of twelve-gauge pump-guns propped against a sawhorse.

"You been bothered by wild animals, too?"

The missionary opened his frock coat to show me a Webley-Fosbery buckled against his ribs. "Not animals," he shook his head sadly. "Men. I am sorry to say there have been human prowlers robbing the Lord's vineyard. Last week there was an attempt to steal my tools. One night they raided my lumber. The trader's doing, I firmly believe."

Well, I don't know why, but I'd sort of come to like this high-pressured evangelist—maybe "respect" is more the word—and I had to put in my two cents' worth, again. "Christopher, take my advice and give up this business. If you've brushed with that trader, you're bound to hear from him again. That Arabian Mick has a way of making people he doesn't like vanish, and one of these days, if you don't clear out, he'll be up here to shake you by the hand. Beat it before he comes to wish you goodbye."

Do you know why I said that just then? I said it because I could have sworn there'd been someone spying from the capsicum bushes edging the compound a moment before. A rustle in the brush that had made my neck creep. If Abdullah's executioners were laying for this missionary, it would take a lot more than evangelical zeal and the help of the Almighty to save him.

But I might as well have held my tongue for the look on his Salvationist glasses when I turned to leave, and as

I stumbled down the jungle trail in the sunset, wondering what sniper had been up there in ambush, I could hear the man sawing and hammering.

ABDULLAH BAWLED A laugh that night when I stopped into the Brass Idol Dance Palace to hear the latest on the Thirty-Eight Rubies. Nobody'd found those stones as yet, and I was wondering about staking out a claim myself to dig, when talk turned to the missionary.

"Me bother that bird?" Abdullah O'Rourke guffawed amiably. "But the man's plain daffy. Religion ain't no competition to my business, fella. These beachcombers don't want no sermons; they want them gems, and when they don't find 'em, they want a peg of gin and Cobra Mary's jig. *Rahmet Allah,* let the man put up his church! He thinks he's the Angel Gabriel or somebody, an' I'm the Devil. Ha ha!"

O'Rourke was a whimsical scoundrel. He went on to say he rather enjoyed this contest between the Angel Gabriel and himself.

"Only you better lay off him," I suggested daringly. "He isn't somebody can just disappear and nobody worry about it afterward. You know how the governments are about mission people. Besides, he's armed."

"Don't I know it?" the trader complained. "That church, it's more of an arsenal. The guy can shoot, too." He made a Moslem gesture of respect, touching his red-cropped forehead with a finger. "Regular marksman, by Allah! Other day he let fly at Stradivarius who walked up there just to see how he was gettin' on, no harm intended. Say! This missionary pokes a bullet through Stradivarius's helmet from a quarter mile off. Afterward tells him it's a mistake, he thought the white hat was a bird. I'll keep my distance from that, my friend. *Nekaaf!* I don't want to go to Paradise that way."

He mopped his forehead in mock anxiety. Then he settled back in his chair, his black eyes grinning at the scene beyond the back window—the brass image up the mountain a-gleam in moonlight, and far on the summit the tiny, moon-lit framework of the missionary's outpost. He said a queer thing.

"He won't be able to beat that idol, either. That heathen god has been here too long. It belongs out here. I've seen these soul-savers before. Won't be long before the sun an' fever an' loneliness will eat him. He'll be out diggin' around for the rubies, tellin' himself it's just for something to do. Then when he don't find 'em, he'll come down to the dance hall for a drink and a look at Cobra Mary. Same old tropics after all. *Kismet!* He'll learn you got to give the devil his due."

Abdullah O'Rourke winked like the spider that is in no hurry, confident of his fly. "I can wait."

Don't get the idea I spent a lot of time speculating on this contest as it shaped up, so to speak, between Good and Evil. Not me. My mind was mainly occupied with wondering how I might locate those rubies—I planned to start doing some digging on my own hook the next time I made port on that island—and if it hadn't rained, I probably wouldn't have seen the Reverend Christopher again.

But the rainy season overtook my intentions. When next I landed on Evil Beach, the water was coming down. All the holes dug by those treasure-hunters had turned into wells, and for the time being the hunt was off.

I sat on the wheel-box cursing my luck, for I'd saved enough pennies from the last two runs to afford a lay-off and time out to seek my fortune, and now I was docked at Rainbow's End only to find it dissolved by a rainstorm. Hell! The whole island had been forced indoors—which meant inside the Brass Idol Dance Palace. My taste for rubies would have to wait.

IT WAS STRADIVARIUS, happening down to the schooner to see if I'd brought any cigarettes, who gave me the latest gossip. They were still picking over the ruins of that shattered silk-cotton tree to no avail. The island was too big for random digging—like looking for a needle in a haystack. A couple of crazy Frenchmen had argued with Abdullah over the fifty-fifty split, and both of them had accidentally fallen over a cliff. It had rained for ten days. Nobody had done any work in this downpour except the missionary.

"Christopher! He's still around?"

Stradivarius lifted a pointing finger. *"Donnerwetter!"*

The rain had let up for a moment, the clouds breaking up around the mountain into bunches of dirty gray wool. Rays of afternoon light slanted through. For the first time I noticed a peaked white triangle newly visible on the summit above the harbor.

"The church!" I blurted out. "The steeple! It's up!"

"Finished a week ago, *ja*. The missionary did it. Everybody driven in out of the rain, and that soul-saver putting up a steeple there."

A note of awe hollowed the musician's voice as he spoke of the feat. The missionary had labored day and night. Carried all the lumber, plank by plank, up the mountain on his own back. Sawed, pounded, hammered up there in the solitude of a Crusoe—and no man Friday.

"Herr Gott! he not only built the church all by himself, but he preaches in it all by himself! Do you think he could get a congregation? Last Sunday he came down to the dance hall, and announced the church was open for morning service. Nobody went near the place. The natives here are afraid of his very shadow and won't go within a mile of that church. The rest of us are too busy. Me, I got curious. So I stole up the path behind him, and what do you think? He held a service, anyway. Preached to an empty room. That evening I went again, and listened outside. Again he preached a sermon all by himself. Do you know what his text was, *mein Freund?* Wisdom is better than rubies! That is funny, *nicht?"*

Somehow to me it wasn't. Tacking up a building on that mountaintop would have been a job for six engineers, and the thought of that missionary doing it alone made me feel a little queer in the stomach. Those lonely sermons made me feel queerer. You see? That fellow must have really been possessed by something—some power-drive beyond the ordinary. That steeple was close to superhuman. After while, because I had nothing else to do that afternoon, I was trudging up the mountain for a closer view of the wonder.

It was a wonder, too. I've seen Christophe's Citadel on a mountaintop in Haiti, but that marvel was nothing compared to the Reverend Christopher's church on a mountaintop above Evil Beach. On that jungly summit, a square white edifice with a forty-foot wooden steeple over its front door, for all the world like a New England meeting house transported to that tropical island by magic. Abdullah had been right—it didn't belong there as that brass heathen idol did. This church aloft in the jungle was incredible. It looked new and clean. White-painted window shutters. Arched door.

"The text for today's sermon is, 'Lay not up for yourself treasures upon earth, where moth and rust doth corrupt and thieves break through and steal. But lay up for yourselves treasures in heaven—!'"

Do you wonder I gave a start? It was a minute before I realized that voice had not spoken from the wet dusk around me, but had come from the church window. The twilight answered with a rumble of thunder, followed by a glittering gush of blue rain. I went inside. On tiptoe through the door, so quietly the preacher didn't hear me. He appeared not to see me. He was standing on a platform beyond a shadowy platoon of rough-hewn wooden benches that were ranged like pews. Standing tall behind a home-made pulpit, hands gripping the edges of the pulpit, a big Bible open in front of him, his head thrown back, eyes fixed blindly on some invisible gallery that might have been above my head.

I wouldn't have recognized him. He was thin as a picked bone, his cheeks stretched tight across the framework of his undernourished face. So thin his black frock coat hung on him loose as the skin on an elephant. John the Baptist, just back from a six-months diet of locusts in the desert, couldn't have been thinner than that. He must have sweated off fifty pounds. His voice rang above the drum of outer downpour with a tone like triumph.

"Brethren, you have heard the Word. No man can serve

two masters. Some men worship riches. Others worship righteousness. The Good Book tells us plainly we cannot worship both. Ye cannot serve both God and mammon, Brethren—!"

Brethren? There weren't any "brethren" there! Just empty pews and bare walls and one astonished sailor listening from the doorway. And that sermon ringing across dim lamplight, echoing through a smell of paint, raw lumber and tropic jungle—ringing out in that lonely wilderness as if the missionary were talking to a packed auditorium.

The man could preach. His voice rolled out of his throat to fill the little church with tones that might have come from a pipe organ. Chanting, praying, singing!

Yes, singing! I tell you I stood rooted in that doorway, and the missionary conducted that service to an empty room from beginning to end. He finished his sermon with a prayer, and he drank a glass of water. He announced the chorus of a hymn, sang it by himself, then smiled beamingly on nobody and announced there would be two services next Sunday. It wasn't until he stepped down from his rostrum, sighing and wiping his glasses, standing there as if to receive a line of parishioners, that he saw me.

"Welcome, brother! Welcome! You came to evening service? My first attendant! A thousand welcomes!"

LONG-LEGGED HE CAME up the aisle to wring my wooden hand. His own hand was an iron gauntlet of callouses, steel-fingered with a strength that made me grit my teeth. I've mentioned the queer inner vitality of the man. Now his eyes were like electric lights; he seemed to be full of charged batteries inside. I felt as if I'd grabbed one of those live-wired gloves that pranksters used to wear.

"Do come right in, brother! Do! You're the only congregation I've had in—well, in two Sundays—since church opened—!"

"And you keep on preaching—?" I murmured.

"For practice," he nodded vigorously. "And who can tell where the good word may fall? Aye, brother, as tonight—are you, yourself, not here like an answer to my prayers? But how do you like the church?"

I couldn't bear the hopeful shine of his glasses, and I felt a little uncomfortable about being the answer to his prayers, so I was glad to look around. Inside, the little church was as marvelous as outside. A wonder of carpentry-work. How had one man ever put up those beams? What terrific energy had nailed together those benches? The door looked thick and nail-studded as old doors you see on cathedrals in Europe.

The missionary apologized for the tools heaped in a corner, and the lack of varnish on the pulpit. I stared at a rude cot behind a wooden screen, gourds of stale water and a box of tinned provisions on a table. I stared at the Rev. T. Ulrich Christopher.

"Some day I shall build the parsonage," he explained, "but until then I must live within my temple. Also I shall put a bell in the steeple, and order a stained glass window. If there was room for a choir loft—"

The thing was remarkable. Not the job so much as the enthusiasm. Worked to skin and bones, half starved, the man went on with the fierce energy of radium. I asked him how he'd ever put up those beams, and he pointed to block and tackle stowed with his tools. But at least the builders of the pyramids had had plenty of helpers.

I couldn't get over the marvel of it.

"The gospel," he was saying as if in answer to my thoughts, "knows no obstacles. Wickedness rules the island at present, but one day Evil Beach shall be as Paradise." He flung out a hand to indicate the town down the mountain. "Sin shall be defeated. Glory will come."

Outside there was a burst of thundering, and I thought I'd better be under way. I invited the missionary down to the schooner for a meal, but he refused, taking a Testament from his pocket and smiling at me.

"Until my work is finished I must remain here." He held up a Testament. "This is my food."

A thing like that can be scary, do you know it? He ducked behind his pulpit, fetched another Testament, pressed it into my hand. "Take it with you and read it some time. Visit me again when next you are in port."

I scrabbled down the path in the rain with a funny taste in my mouth, and that's the truth. I guess my nerves must have been unstrung, for, on dipping into the downhill jungle, I had that feeling again that some eavesdropper had been around. I made a side-jump into a thicket of *tapang*, without knowing why, and a second later a shadow came thefting down the trail from the church and melted away in the rain. In the muddy path, as I examined it with a cupped match, I saw the outline of a woman's sandal. Now what had Cobra Mary been doing up there, spying on that church?

It gave me a mystery to chew on as I stumbled down the mountain with night coming after me. A couple of mysteries. Lights were blazing in the Brass Idol Dance Palace when I reached the beach—the boys were whooping it up—and I couldn't help thinking of Abdullah and his mob in there, and that lonely missionary living on dried prunes and proverbs in his mountaintop church. And why should that snake dancer have been prowling around the church-yard? The puzzle was as tough to figure as the whereabouts to dig for the Thirty-Eight Rubies of Jihan Ji.

Then I ran into a mystery that made those other Evil Beach puzzles go out of my mind. A mystery that almost made *me* go out of my mind. I shipped out of the harbor that night on my return run to Bangkok, and that's where I ran into the bombshell.

In Bangkok I saw one of the Thirty-Eight Rubies of Jihan Ji!

4

———

I WAS WALKING in the Sisowath Bazaar, and that gem was in the window of a British jewel merchant's, with a price on it to make your head swim. My head swam, you can believe it, but not from the price. What made my head go swimming was the fact that those gold-framed rubies were supposed to lie buried on Evil Beach, a day away down the Gulf of Siam.

I stared at that ruby with my nose spread flat against the glass—no mistaking the item!—and you can bet I went charging into the shop to ask how it got there.

I said I was a gem collector just back from the Burmese border, and I was particularly fascinated by rubies. After a lot of chatter, he told me he'd bought the bauble that morning from a one-eyed Siamese trader who'd said he'd soon be back with another and left without giving his name or address.

To say I was sore about that ruby is to say the least of it. Sight of that trinket blazing in the jeweler's window filled me with a sickness of envy for the lucky treasure-hunter. All the way back to the ship I cursed myself for a fool. Some dog out there on Evil Beach had pawed up a million-dollar fortune, and I was bitter as quinine because I hadn't tried to dig up the bonanza myself.

Then a thought stopped my oaths of self-reproach. Huh!

A one-eyed Siamese trader had sold that ruby to the British gem merchant? But there wasn't any one-eyed Siamese trader on Evil Beach! Only trader out there was Abdullah O'Rourke. And as far as I could recall, there hadn't been a one-eyed man on that island!

Well, I combed my memory, trying to recollect one and I couldn't remember any. I asked my Malay bos'n about it, and he couldn't remember, either. That was funny. There must have been a couple of hundred fortune-diggers on the island, lusty ruffians with two eyes—both eyes fixed on Cobra Mary, as a rule. I'd seen the lot of them in Abdullah's dance hall, and not a single-eyed dog could I remember. And when I said the whole island crammed itself into the Brass Idol Dance Palace for its evening entertainment, I meant the whole island. That is to say, every man on the island except the missionary.

And that wasn't all. Hadn't Stradivarius told me the rubies hadn't been found? Certainly a ten-strike like that would make big news on the island; Abdullah's pet musician would have heard about it. And all those treasure-mad bums would be going home, instead of waiting for the rainy season to end so they could start digging again. Altogether, this ruby turning up in Bangkok was a poser. The more I thought about it, the nuttier it got. Either the rubies had been found in some place other than Evil Beach—which meant the Hindu priest's story had been a fraud—or someone on the island had found the treasure, sure enough, and was smuggling it off the island unbeknownst to Abdullah and his crowd. To save the fifty-fifty split with the trader? But it hardly seemed possible for someone to dig up those sparklers without that Irish-Arabian knowing it, much less sneak them off the island under his nose. Aside from my excursion boat, Abdullah owned the only craft around there—how had the gem reached Bangkok?

When I sailed from Bangkok a week later I was still spraining my brain on the mystery, and pretty sure the treasure hadn't been on Evil Beach to begin with.

That I, myself, might be the smuggler never occurred to me.

LUCKY FOR ME I didn't tell what I knew when I made port in that hell-island that next trip, or I'd never have lived to learn the answers. I lit out for the trader's dance palace the moment I stepped ashore, and it was the Irish-Arab who did the talking.

"Well, Captain?" Rain was slamming down, and the place was jammed as usual, and he had to yell at me to get his voice above the din of bottles, glasses and general uproar. "Come back to take another whack at the Thirty-Eight Rubies?"

I had to keep my face in order, I tell you. I said there wasn't much chance of digging in the rain.

His black eyes twinkled. "All th' boys have had to lay off. That mountain's too wet. Sink a hole and it fills with water. Too bad. A couple of the boys had got down about thirty feet with only eight more to go. Then they had to quit."

I was looking around for a one-eyed Siamese when he said that. There were plenty of yellow slants in that rat-nest, but nobody one-eyed. Then I had to look back at the trader.

"A couple got down to thirty feet?" I asked. "Do you make them all report on how far they've dug?"

He squinted. "Not that I mistrust anybody. By Allah, no! But that Hindu said the treasure was buried thirty-eight feet down, eh? So! But none of these ditch-diggers are down that far yet. Naturally with a half interest in the treasure, I keep watch on the diggings. *Nekaaf!* How do I know one of these fellows wouldn't turn up the rubies and scoot? I have watched them all very carefully."

Something about the fat man's avid squint told me he wasn't lying about having kept his eye on that crowd. But there was that Jihan Ji trinket in that gem merchant's window in Bangkok. I almost blurted out something about it, then I didn't. Why should I tell this big squid his prize was gone? Do you know what he said to me then?

"Everybody who has come to the island I watch. And everybody who leaves it. I will search those boys like they search the fellows who leave a diamond mine. Do you blame me where a million dollars is at stake? But so far, Captain, you are the only man who has left the island since the treasure-rush started. You have done no digging?"

Well, somebody somewhere had done some digging, and Abdullah hadn't heard about it, that much was plain. I hated to think of the tantrum the trader would go into when he learned he'd missed a share of those gems. That hand-clasp of his would go working overtime.

For once I didn't sit in that dive entranced by the charms of Cobra Mary. She was going full steam on her platform as I left, twisting and coiling in the smoke-drift as though her limbs were tangled in the tentacles of evil music that crawled out of Stradivarius' violin. I got out of there.

The rain had petered out to let a fine new moon cruise into view, and the mountain above the beach was etched in black and silver. I must have slogged around the muddy waterfront for about an hour, trying to puzzle that treasure-mystery out in my head. If the rubies weren't buried on this island, why had that dying Brahmin spun a fairy-tale to the Australian who'd tried to save his life? If they *were* buried on Evil Beach, how had one of them reached Bangkok without Abdullah O'Rourke knowing it?

I went over the Brahmin's story about the idol. Put up to mark the island where the treasure had been buried. It didn't seem likely there'd be two such idols way over in the Gulf of Siam.

Pretty soon my feet were following my thoughts up the mountainside, and I was coming alongside that ancient image. I'd never had a close look at the thing before, for my main concern with the Jihan Ji treasure had been with that silk-cotton tree. Now, washed and glistening, its ugly brass face grinning down at me, that idol looked wickeder than ever. It looked like Hell, and twice as old. But, sitting there in its marble swimming tank, the tank knee-deep with rainwater, it illustrated the Hindu legend all right. As I pushed through the underbrush and approached the tank, I could see the brass baby sitting on the idol's knee. I told you at the beginning of this story that I'd seen a simi-lar idol way over in India; now I remembered the lecture of the guide who'd showed me that India model. This Evil Beach set-up was the spitting image in every detail. Vasu-veda and the infant Krishna, no mistake.

So the Jihan Ji rubies *must* have been buried on Evil Beach. I got it, and the puzzle of it captured my imag-ination. Where did the one-eyed Siamese trader come in? Who was putting one over on Abdullah? Then I got something else.

I WAS STANDING on the edge of that marble tank star-

ing at Papa and Baby, with the jungle dripping quicksilver
in the background, when I caught the sound of someone
hurrying through the underbrush to starboard. Someone
going up the mountain, and going fast. Curiosity doesn't
kill only cats. I made a dive for the bushes and waited for
that traveler to take a lead, then I followed. We were a good
quarter mile from the path leading up to the church; figure
my surprise when the trail swung on a tangent, and after
a tough climb, I found myself crouching on the fringe of
Christopher's churchyard.

The party I had been trailing wasn't Christopher! That
exalted missionary was in his pulpit preaching. His voice
was echoing out through the window-shutters. The party
I'd followed was Cobra Mary!

She was standing in the shadow of a tapang not a dozen
feet to the left of me; posed and motionless as a statue. I
don't know what was queer about that pose. Perhaps it was
the way one hand was spread, tense, on her bosom; the tilt
of her head, listening. But I do know there was something
queer about her face that night—something very queer.
A few crumbs of moonlight scattered down through the
tapang fronds to touch up her expression with phosphorus.
Glowing—the word doesn't describe her eyes. Her eyes
were fixed on that dim white church as a cat's eyes might
have fixed on a birdcage. Her lips were parted.

"—once more I implore you, men and brethren, to
repent, confess your sins, heed the gospel. Give up your
lust for worldly treasure. Recall the teaching of the Word:
that it is harder for a rich man to get into heaven than it is
for a camel to go through a needle's eye—"

The sermon-toned voice rolled out across the black-

and-silver compound, and the dancing girl watched and listened. I didn't hear much of that night's sermon. That woman's expression made the blood thump in my ears. Anyway, the service didn't last long. A prayer at the end, and a closing hymn.

The light in the church window went out. The dancing girl watched the church, and I watched the dancing girl. Then she went away so suddenly I didn't see her go. No sound. Even the foliage stopped dripping. I couldn't stand that. I crept over to the spot where she'd been, and the weeds were all flattened out around the tree as if some watcher had been in the habit of standing there night after night.

It was foolhardy of me to strike a match. *Bang!* Fire flashed from the church window as if I'd touched off a fuse, and that missionary sniper's bullet went through my sea hat like a knife-stab.

Wow! My involuntary yell brought him out of the church door, apologizing. Gaunt as an undertaker in his shirt sleeves, rifle in one hand, hymnbook in the other, moonlight on his glasses, anxious and sorry.

"Holy smoke!" I panted. "Are you always that quick on the trigger? I lost my pocket compass just now, comin' up here to see you, an' only lit a match to look for it. You sit all night by that window with a gun?"

He sighed and wiped his glasses. There were times, he said, when the Almighty's workers had to give up the olive branch for the sword. The Lord's vineyard was still harried by the foxes. Prowlers from the wicked town below continued to trespass on sacred ground. If they would but come in the open, seeking salvation. But no, the wicked wished only to confound his good works. Just last night some vandal had tried to pry open a church window. The wicked must learn to respect righteousness.

"I am desolated, my dear Captain. Had you come in time for evening service this near tragedy would not have occurred. Wednesday night prayer-meeting. I held it alone."

Everything was funny that night. Seen in moonlight just then, there was something funny about the Reverend T. Ulrich Christopher. What? Afterward, trying to recall, I couldn't put my finger on it. One of those things like a man always wearing his hair parted in the middle, then one day parting it on the side. You notice something odd; can't quite place it. Too insignificant. At the time I was feeling too seasick from that bullet-hole in my cap to mark the reason for some current under the surface. Like everything else on Evil Beach that night, Christopher seemed funny, that was all.

"Thank God," he raised his eyes, "I didn't kill you. My nerves—it is something of a strain—living all by oneself. Brother, you are always welcome. Only next time come by the front path. And be sure to come again. It has been lonely here. Ah. There are only too few visitors to my little church."

Yet he didn't ask me in, and for some reason I had an idea he was anxious for me to leave. Not that I didn't want to go. I stuck my finger through the hole in my cap and mumbled some excuse for hurrying away. As I turned to walk off, he put the hymnbook in my hands.

"Take it with you, brother. The great revival songs of

Moody and Sankey. Cherish it with your Testament. God be with you, and good night."

I stuck the hymnal in my pocket—ungraciously, I have no doubt—and I think I said goodnight with considerable emphasis. I was glad to get my anchor out of the Evil Beach mud that trip—plenty glad! Have you ever smelled a storm beyond the horizon? Rain was blotting out the island at midnight when I shoved my schooner seaward, but the storm I smelled in the offing was a different kind. Something about everything on that island—had all the little nerve-ends under my skin flying danger signals. The great revival numbers of Moody and Sankey weren't much comfort in that sort of storm; I remember taking the hymnal out of my pocket and tossing it into my slop chest with the Testament. Going out on deck, I promised myself I'd steer clear of that island from then on.

The road to hell is paved with that type of intentions. I wasn't back in Bangkok a day before I was sick to reach Evil Beach. May I swallow the hook, if there wasn't another of those wonderful rubies in that Bangkok gem merchant's window.

THE SIGHT OF that second piece of jewelry in that city shop window almost drove me crazy. Honestly it did. That gem merchant must have thought me batty as a zebu from the way I capered into his shop to ask about it. He kept one hand on his burglar alarm and one eye on the corner policeman while he told me to get out of there and stay out. Unless, of course, I wished to buy the relic? Buy the relic? Not while there were thirty-six more of them kicking around somewhere. All I wanted to know was where they were coming from, and how. The jeweler shrugged. A one-eyed Siamese trader had brought in this second gem two hours ago. None of his business who the trader was or where he went, so long as the man could bring in bonanzas like these.

It was six in the evening when I spotted that second blazer in that Bangkok window, and I spent the rest of the night hunting a one-eyed Siamese trader who seemed to have the key to Ali Baba's cave. Listen to what set me off! I asked the corner cop if he'd seen such a man enter the gem shop—friend of mine, I said—and the policeman told me yes. A ragged Siamese coolie with one eye! The cop didn't know where he'd come from or where he'd gone, either, but that was fairly conclusive evidence there was such a man.

Start out to trail a one-eyed Siamese in the capital of Siam. Try it some evening. You'd be surprised. The minute I set out through the bazaars looking for that bird, I began to run into one one-eyed Siamese after another. Word of honor, now I wanted such a man, they came at a dollar a dozen. All these Orientals have eye trouble. Cataracts. Blindness. Squints. Every yellow coolie in Siam was ragged—now, as if some blight had overtaken the country, every third Siamese seemed to be half blind.

I was half blind, myself, by next morning. Half blind from peering into dark holes, black alleys and opium dens looking for that trader with one eye. Half blind from trying to see the answer on how he had those rubies in his possession.

And that wasn't all I wanted. I wanted a crack at the rest of that treasure. Just one of those blazers would have kept me in pocket money the rest of my life, and I wanted to get my hands around that Siamese trader's neck and wring

his secret out of him. I was convinced that treasure had
been unearthed on Evil Beach—the appearance of Ruby
Number Two convinced me of something else. Whoever
had dug up that batch of gems was smuggling them off
the island one at a time. One at a time because they were
easier to hide piecemeal, and if the smuggler were caught
he could bribe his life with the rest. Somebody on that
island was a hell of a lot smarter than Abdullah, for all his
spying. I couldn't figure how the rubies were reaching the
mainland, but that one-eyed Siamese go-between would
know. Wring his neck? I would have killed him to learn the
answer. There were thirty-six of those gold-plated rubies
left.

Another dose of treasure-fever had me. Worse than the
first. All my good intentions were burned up in that relapse.
I spent a week racing up and down the Bangkok alleys,
grabbing at one-eyed coolies and asking futile questions.
By the end of the week I'd discovered at least a hundred
Siamese mongrels who answered to the necessary description, and too many cooks had spoiled the broth. Why, my
Malay bos'n had even hired a one-eyed Siamese to load
cargo on the morning I'd made port.

Ledbetter, the Dutch ship-owner, hailed me into
his office. He said I'd been neglecting my work, and he
wanted to know what the devil. Twice he'd been down to
the schooner to see me, and I hadn't been on the job. I'd
forgotten to turn in my log. The decks wanted holy-ston-
ing. Maybe I didn't want to run *Siamese Twin* to Evil Beach
and Kelantan any more.

I told Ledbetter I'd been sick, and that was nearly the
fact. Sick to find the trail to those Thirty-Eight Rubies of

Jihan Ji. And if the trail ended in a gem shop in Bangkok, it began somewhere on that island. So it wasn't long before I was dropping the hook in that rain-gloomed harbor again; gazing hungrily at mountain and headland and the tin roof of the Brass Idol Dance Palace, the stench of tropic decay smothered by the smell of a million dollars in my nostrils.

That was how I figured in the final episode before the blow-off. The play just before the showdown in a million-dollar game that started with a mystery and ended in a miracle.

5

—

THE JOKER WAS that I didn't even know I figured in the
episode. Me? I was sick in every sense of the word when I
reached Evil Beach that trip. Playing hide-and-seek with a
one-eyed Siamese in the rainy season had given me something more than treasure-fever. Before I could step ashore
this time, I went down. Malaria. Knocked flat in my bunk,
too weak to lift a finger much less prowl that stinking
littoral.

I was out of quinine, and I sent my Malay bos'n to
Abdullah's after a box. Abdullah didn't have any. Neither
did anyone else on the beach. A lot of that huggermugger crowd were down with fever; no medicine in town. I
thought of the missionary.

I couldn't have walked up that mountain with a pair
of Seven League boots, so I sent the Malay boy. He was
back with the quinine in an hour, and a message from the
Reverend Christopher. The Reverend Christopher wished
me to know he would have come himself, but he was holding a vesper service that evening and he had to prepare a
sermon. I was welcome to the quinine; would I be sure to
attend church the next time I was in port? Meantime he
was sending with my bos'n some spiritual food that might
do me more good than medicine.

The spiritual food was a leatherbound copy of *The Life of*

John Wesley which my bos'n handed me with the message.
I wasn't in the mood for any sort of victual, spiritual or
otherwise, and the book went into the slop chest with the
hymnal and the Testament. Down with fever for a week in
that port, I lost my taste for rubies, too. The schedule called
for Kelantan, and three weeks later I was back in Bangkok
ready to resign for the third and last time.

I didn't resign for the third and last time because after
I'd been to see the company doctor, I couldn't help taking
a peek at that gem merchant's window in Sisowath Lane,
just in case. Do I have to tell you there was another one
of those rubies in that window? Do I have to tell you that
the minute I saw it I got infected with treasure-fever all
over again? All right. A third ruby was there, and according to the merchant, the same one-eyed Siamese had sold
it to him.

Again my impulse was to hunt for that treasure-hunter—a surge of wild envy that I hadn't found the cache
myself. Then I was plenty relieved I hadn't. I was heading
along the go-downs that night, with more Hollands aboard
than was good for me, when a shadow stepped away from
a wall and put a knife-blade against my throat.

"Cry out, an' by Allah! I'll slash your bloody head off!"

"Abdullah O'Rourke!" I whispered.

"Sure, it's me. Step over behind them hogsheads,
Captain, an' try no tricks if you like your windpipe healthy."

It was dark behind the hogshead. Only enough light
for me to see I was in a bad way. "Abdullah," I tried to be
casual with cold steel against my jugular vein, "what are
you doing in Bangkok?"

His eyes were black opals in the gloom. "*I* came with

Stradivarius to buy medicine. Tell me, Captain, what're *you* doing here? No! What are *they* doing here? Speak, or I'll knife out your tongue. How'd you find 'em?"

"Find what?"

"Ha-ha," his great stomach jiggled against mine. "Ha-ha-ha."

"Find what?" I managed again.

His stomach hardened to a boulder. "As if you don't know, you scut. I seen you come out of that gem merchant's shop. Three of them sparklin' in the window, an' you're the only man as has so far left Evil Beach—!"

"But it isn't me!" I groaned. "It's a one-eyed—"

"One-eyed my grandmother," the huge man growled softly. "You're a smart sailor, ain't you? Mighty smart to bring them gems over one at a time. Merciful Allah, ye knew if anyone seen you carryin' a bundle off th' island, they'd guess what it was. So you been bringin' 'em over in driblets, eh? In your mouth, maybe. Well, where is it?"

TRY ANSWERING A question like that with a knife as cold as the guillotine pushed against your windpipe. Besides, I couldn't answer. I didn't know. I couldn't so much as swallow. Abdullah was growing impatient. He whispered, "I got no time for bickering, Captain. There's thirty-five more. I don't know how you dug 'em up, but if you're wise, you'll hand over the rest. Do I get my cut fifty-fifty, or do I get it with the knife?"

I don't suppose I've ever been closer to the next world than I was right then. That big devil's reasoning was logical even if it wasn't the truth, and he'd have had out my tonsils at a flick if a figure hadn't sneaked out of the night behind him just in time to stay my execution.

"Abdullah! Wait! It ain't the man!"

Stradivarius! I was glad to see that sad-faced violinist for the first time since I'd met him. Very glad. A lank shade darker than the night itself, he gumshoed up to Abdullah and whispered in the fat man's hippopotamus ear. Three pounds dripped off me in ice water during that whispered conference. I might have cut and run for it, but that unexpected meeting with those Evil Beach boys in Bangkok had stunned my reflexes, and the glint of the trader's knife held me in paralysis.

The glint of the trader's knife? That was nothing compared to the glint in his Arab eyes as the German musician whispered on. I didn't dare catch what was said, but one phrase broke loose from the blurred undertone—a phrase my ears clung to as a drowning man clings to a straw.

"One-eyed Siamese rat—!"

The German's whisper broke off. Abdullah O'Rourke was an elephantine shadow, glaring. He gurgled as if he were drinking some kind of acid. "But how—?"

If I live to the millennium I'll never forget Stradivarius' answer to that. Spoken in the voice of a crow. Low and harsh, intended solely for the ear of that murderous Irish-Arabian, but audible to my own humming ears as the crash of an exploded bomb.

They didn't know I heard, that worthy pair. Or if they did, they never imagined I might get the drift. Abdullah O'Rourke bobbed his head at me and muttered: "It seems I made a mistake." Without further apology, they were gone—the fat man and his lieutenant—vanished off in the shadows of the go-down as if a waterfront breeze had blown them away.

I couldn't move. I stood rooted. After three minutes that seemed three years, I heard the trader's launch heading out down the Gulf of Siam.

I broke from my trance with a stifled shout; started a run for the wharf, full of gin and insanity if I ever was. Halfway down the jetty I stumbled over a body sprawled face-down on the planking. The native wasn't drunk. A leak of light from somewhere revealed the man's face, and that one-eyed Siamese scarecrow had died from something a whole lot worse than the D.T.'s.

It was a lonely quarter of the Bangkok waterfront, and more than one poor devil had been murdered there, I'll wager—but I'll stake you that's the first coolie ever left there strangled by a violin string. That G-string biting the throat of that dead man trademarked the job.

I suppose I should have yelled for the police, but I didn't. Not with what I had on my mind. Fast as my legs could go, I made for the jetty's end where Ledbetter kept a little pleasure launch—an expensive toy that was the pride of its owner's heart; reserved for week-end cruises and what Ledbetter called "fishing parties." No honest sailor would have crossed a millpond in such a tub. That night, if necessary, I would have set sail in a swan-boat.

A quarter mile out, the lights of Abdullah's putter were dwindling southward; I hadn't a moment to spare. Even so I had to stand there on the jetty's end, pop-eyed, staring at the horizon where the launch was heading—the direction of Evil Beach.

That German violinist's last speech! He hadn't said

much. Oh, no! Only enough to start me off for that hell-island in a stolen launch—mad with malaria, treasure-fever and curiosity.

What Stradivarius had said was: *"The steeple!"*

IT OCCURS TO me that you may have been wondering through all this yarn what in the devil it has to do with the original subject of discussion. Remember? We were talking about Faith. The power of the Bible. What inspires missionaries to go out in the jungle, preaching. We were talking about hypocrisy and miracles. Perhaps you think my yarn has drifted pretty far off course. A confusion of episodes and people all tangled together like the cordage on a Chinese junk.

Well, that was the way that Evil Beach business seemed to me, too. A jumble of happenings as meaningless as the flitty capers of a dream—the possible jumping overboard into impossibility—all very much like everything else in the East—everything confused as a granny's knot, yet somehow strung together on a vague thread of relationship.

Just how they might have been connected—Abdullah and missionary, dancing girl and sermons, mountaintop church and heathen idol, buried treasure and three Jihan Ji rubies in a jeweler's window in Bangkok, and that violinist's G-string around the neck of a one-eyed Siamese beggar—just what they might have to do with each other, I couldn't have told you.

That bombshell from Stradivarius. *"The steeple!"* That did it! Not that I had any answer, but it tied in somehow; strung all those puzzles together like the knots in a log-line. You'll see how a final yank on the string undid each knot along the line and ended with a miracle to make old Jonah's take a back seat.

"Good Lord! Good Lord, *no!*"

I remember saying that to myself all the way of that crazy chase back to Evil Beach. I must have been crazy, chasing Abdullah O'Rourke back to that island. I'm sure I was. But I had just sense enough not to let that fat killer know I was following him. Steering in a sou'westerly direction, I charted a course to give him a wide berth. I wanted to make the south side of the island—a cove hidden from the trader's town—and I drove that pleasure-tub to the last spark in her cylinders, sweating for fear I'd get there too late.

Too late for what? Sink me, if I knew! I couldn't believe the ideas that began to shape up in my head, but I did know Abdullah and his orchestra-leader were heading back home in a hurry, and that haste had something to do with the Thirty-Eight Rubies of Jihan Ji. That one-eyed Siamese must have told Stradivarius a mouthful before the German shut him up. That mouthful had something to do with those gems. Which was all I needed to keep me in the race. I was mad to get my hands on that treasure. Mad with a greed as big as Abdullah O'Rourke's.

My heart was pounding like the engine in Ledbetter's launch. And that engine was going some. I hate to think of how I bounced that expensive toy over the waves all night, into a dawn as flame-hued and hot as the gold-plated treasures in that Bangkok window. How I drove that borrowed craft roaring through a day of solid gold. The rains were over, and a big head sea came butting up the Gulf, filling the air with spray and flying fish. It was matchless weather, but the seas slowed me down, and it was sunset before I raised the island—crimson sunset that might have reflected the rays of those thirty-five remaining gems.

I wanted to shout when I saw that mountain come up out of the sea. The moon was a silver sickle slicing a silk evening sky; there was a smell like opium in the offshore breeze; and my first landmark was that white New England steeple like a monument on the mountaintop. I did shout when I saw that.

Abdullah's launch was nowhere in sight, and I almost tore my gaudy boat to pieces, jumping her over the reefs and into that sheltered cove. A few stars were already twinkling when I sprang ashore. Hot-footing it around the headland for the town, I was sure I was too late.

As a matter of fact, I'd beaten the trader to his port. He was only coming alongside his dock as I galloped around the mountain's foot; I heard him holler to his wharf-rats, and saw Stradivarius jump to the dock to help the fat man disembark. Knocking natives and beachcombers aside, the pair came scuttling up the wharf. Then I did some fast scuttling, myself. Behind a screen of nipa palms. Abdullah had his knife in his belt, and Stradivarius was carrying his violin, and it wasn't till then I realized I hadn't brought my gun.

6

IT WAS NO time to learn I'd forgotten my pistol, either. Let those two wolves see me on their heels, and they'd know I'd tailed them—my life wouldn't be worth a chew of cut-plug! I know the look of murder on a man's face, and I saw that look on Abdullah O'Rourke's face when he went by. Trader and violinist hustled past my hiding-place like two wolves on the scent of a meal. You can bet I kept my distance from that team!

I followed them, though. I followed them because the thought of the treasure they were after had me like the grip of a drug. When I saw them enter the trader's dance palace, I waited for the dark to blacken the veranda; then I had to creep around to that back window for a peek. From the babel inside I judged the place was jammed with its usual mob, the crowd all waiting for Cobra Mary to start her evening dance.

But Cobra Mary wasn't performing in the Brass Idol Dance Palace. Not that evening! I was almost under the window when a word—a throaty-whispered word—stopped my tracks at the corner of the building; held me breathless. You may have perceived there are whispers that come louder than a shout. The whispered word that stopped me was, "Rubies!" and it came from an unlighted window at the side.

"Rubies!" the whisper was repeated. "You mean they are in Bangkok? The Thirty-Eight Rubies of Jihan Ji?"

That was the dancing girl's voice, and it was followed by a German guttural. "Bangkok, hell! Only three of them's in Bangkok. This one-eyed Siamese was the fence for them, *verstehen-Sie?* I made the gem merchant tell me his name. I choked it out of him. Then I caught the Siamese, and made him tell me everything. *Ja!*"

"But there has been no one-eyed Siamese on Evil Beach?" that girl asked the same question I wanted to ask. "How—?"

"The gems were sent to him," was the answer. "One at a time. Mailed, *hein?* There is that schooner from Bangkok that takes mail. There is—"

Abdullah's harsh rasp cut in like a rusty blade on iron, "Allah's blood! who cares how the gems reached Bangkok. We want the rest of them, see? We want them tonight!" The trader's speech drifted off into a string of oaths. He could curse in Irish and Arabic, and he spent the next two minutes using up all his profanity.

There was a baited silence while I froze myself under the sill. Stradivarius, somewhere near the dark screen, was panting, and I could hear a faint jingle of bracelets as if the girl were walking up and down. Then her voice came with the vehemence of an exclamation, low but clear.

"Then that Siamese dog must have lied. What you say he told you is impossible. Impossible! Have I not been up there every night? And all of us? All of us have watched! He put up the church—we saw that. Then he went in—like a cuckoo in a clock. Since then he has not come out. I tell you, he stays all day in that church," the woman whispered. "I have watched."

"All of us have watched," Abdullah's snarl agreed. "That is it, you fool. All of us have watched, but we did not see! The jackal has been fooling us! Right before our eyes! Pretending he was too good for us. Too pious and good to associate with us down on the beach. So he stays all the time in his church and—"

"But the treasure," Cobra Mary's words made a sound like dark water slipping over mossy stones. "The treasure thirty-eight feet deep in the ground! One would see the pit! Piles of dirt—!"

"Huh?" the trader's snarl harshened. "Don't waste time asking questions. You'll see. You'll see tonight, by Allah! Trick me, will he? Trick Abdullah O'Rourke?" Passion threatened to strangle the fat man; he had to clear his throat of another slew of oaths. Fiercely, "But we can't rush the joint; it's built like a fort. And me wondering why he put up all those heavy timbers! Ha! The other night we could not even pry loose a shutter. By the Prophet's Holy Beard, he can lock himself in there like a guard in a bank!"

"That's right," Stradivarius put in gloomily. "He'd snipe us like rabbits if we tried to chop through that door. Keeps a watch from that steeple, he does. Like a hawk. He'd see us if we tried to cross the compound. I'm not forgettin' how that devil can shoot."

Abdullah snarled bitterly, "Neither am I. And that's what I'm talkin' about. We can't get *in!* That ain't the way. We got to get him *out!*"

Cobra Mary whispered, "Get him out?" and the trader's answer sent a tickle of icy sweat-beads down my spine.

"Yah, get him out. We gotta be careful about it, too. Remember, you can't kill a missionary. I don't want no warships pokin' their noses around here."

"*Aber* getting him out will be harder than getting him in," Stradivarius murmured hoarsely. "Do you think, Abdullah, you can go up there and offer to shake hands? I think not. A smarty like that is not so easy. *Nein.*"

"Well, think of something!" the trader's whisper raged. "We haven't got all night, you fools! I don't like to burn him out and bring all that mob running from the beach, but we could tell the police his little place caught fire, and—"

"Abdullah!" I wish you could have heard the dancing girl's voice as I heard it then. Frozen in the night outside that window, I could picture her lips smiling in the darkness, the gleam of her slanted green eyes as her brain conceived the scheme. "Abdullah, I can get him out!"

"You!"

"He is a man, is he not?"

"More like a devil, I'd say."

"Man or devil, he is lonely." If you'd heard the girl's voice as I heard it coming from that dark room, you'd know why she had that name. "Have you not often said the loneliness would eat him. Sooner or later, he—"

"Merciful Allah!" the trader gasped. "You mean—?"

"Suppose I go up there?" came the deep-throated whisper. "You and Stradivarius, you hide in the jungle by the compound. He is lonely, Abdullah. He has been shut in up there for a long time. He would not be liable to shoot a woman. When I get inside I will slip the latch on the door, and then—"

Her words broke off into meaningful silence. A silence

in which I was afraid my stifled lungs would burst. Then Stradivarius, the skeptic, gutturaled: "But suppose he don't open the door."

Cobra Mary laughed. Secretly. Almost soundlessly. A low-pitched, devilish mirth that seemed to come through the window on a ripple of sugary poison. The laugh with which she'd once slapped the missionary's face was nothing to that sound. Eve, handing out the first apple in Eden, knowing Adam could not help but take it, might have, laughed to herself like that.

"He will open the door."

I WISH I could describe to you my feelings as I followed those three Evil Beachers up to the Reverend Christopher's church. Oh, yes, I went along. Having dug up that much about the treasure, I wanted the rest of it—the treasure, itself, if I could somehow get my clutches on it. But talk about walking in a dream! Do you remember how the missionary had told us he'd come to Evil Beach to treasure-hunt for souls? Then picture those three treasure-hunters out to get the missionary's soul!

I don't think Satan, himself, could have planned such a raid. Certainly he couldn't have foreseen how it would end. I couldn't foresee how it would end, myself, as I followed that lovely trio up the night-swathed mountain.

The Irish-Arab, the dancing girl and Stradivarius were shadows mounting in the glooms ahead of me, and I was on their heels like a nervous jackal. White stars were ship-lights in the roadstead of the purple velvet sky; the sickle moon pruned the jungletops to shed ghostly ponds of light on the landscape where it wasn't blotted out. Striped pale-yellow and black, the three ahead of me moved like jungle cats, stopping only when the trader halted to take a nip from his bottle. That gave me a chance to catch up, and he halted often. Abdullah was one of those elephants who could walk without breaking a blade of grass, especially with a bucket of alcohol enlivening his brain.

By the time we reached the missionary's acre I was prepared for anything. To have found the clearing, church and steeple vanished away would not have surprised me. More surprising to find that jungle-hemmed compound, that white New England meeting house still there.

The three ahead of me melted in the soundless jungle-wall, and the little church, moon-washed, was like a house asleep, its arched door peaceful, shuttered windows dreaming, its face composed and prim under its prim peaked hat. I could imagine Abdullah's cunning bulk secreted like a rhino's in the underbrush at the side. Stradivarius, a lean panther, crouching. The girl gliding forward like her nickname. As I crept around to the other side of the church, making for a vantage point where I could see and not be seen, I could picture the Reverend Christopher snoring in his hermitage like a mole—wrapped in his righteous blankets atop a box of chance-found bonanzas.

How he might have stumbled on that treasure I still couldn't fathom, and I didn't dare think about it for fear my thoughts might make a noise. That night was silent as a growing hair. One sound on my part would have finished me. And then, when that dancing girl oozed out into the moonlight on that compound, I almost hollered.

Do you think she walked into that churchyard? Walk isn't the word. That girl was a dancer, remember, and she knew what to do with her figure and how to do it. She had that green silk *sarong* around her like a coating of absinthe, and the moonlight, when it touched her copper head, turned into curls of flame. Her walk was a come-on, if I ever saw one. Inviting? I tell you, every step the woman made was a coax. She moved slowly. Languorously. Hands on hips and eyes on that church-door, taking her own wicked time.

Then, when she almost reached the church, she stood off a little way and faced the silent door as if she wasn't sure whether she ought to go in or not. She walked back down the path, looking at the church door over her shoulder. Then she posed, one hand behind her head, looking up at the moon in thought.

Brazen? I suppose it was the church that made her the most brazen woman I'd ever beheld. The contrast. That little meeting-house with the steeple facing that *nautch* girl clothed with absinthe, flame and moon-silver.

You could almost hear her calling to the missionary to come on out of his church and play. Then how did she know he was awake in there and watching her? Don't ask me how women know such things! I'd have sworn she knew it, though. She knew his eye was on her out there, and she was posing for a minute, giving him a chance to drink her in.

Posturing and hesitating out there on the compound, she struck about six poses, like a model displaying garments in a Paris gown shop. Only she wasn't displaying garments. It was wonderful the way she put on that show, and the best piece of acting she saved for the end. A dozen paces from the church door, she stopped, bowed her head and turned her face aside, put an arm across her eyes and began

to weep. What a pantomime that was! As if she'd come to
that church with a trouble on her soul.

HE OPENED THE door. Do you wonder at it? I could see
the heavy portal move an inch on its hinges, the glitter of
a startled eyeball at the crack. Sound of that woman's low
sobbing; then a choky exclamation from that onlooker in
the church. *Thump!* That sound was evidence to all that
fellow's incredible will-power. Blow me down, if he didn't
shut the door!

That woman looked up with a face all silvery with tears.
Do you know she almost fooled me then? The woe on her
features might have been the sadness of all the remorseful
women in the world. Magdalen!

The door opened again. What man's door in this world
wouldn't have? Three inches this time. Eyes glaring out,
retreating, peering out once more like the fascinated optics
of a bass hanging back in marine shadows, hesitant, fighting to keep from charging the bright lure spinning at the
bottom of a lagoon.

Oh, she got her man. She got her man without even
knocking on his door. Not a word from her, and he opened
the door to let her in. In my mind's eye I can vision that
scene to every detail—that wicked temptress playing Peni-
tence before the white-steepled church—and that man in
the church doorway, gaunt, fish-eyed, that perfect cartoon
of a missionary in his frock coat.

And then? And then you couldn't have stunned me more
by a blow on the head with a belaying pin! That Circe
had her fish. You could see that from the haggard collapse
in his face. The white, winded trembling of his lips. That

dancing girl had her fish, hook, line and sinker—but she didn't go in!

"Your gun!" Facing that man in the church door, she was gesturing at him frantically—gesturing in a way that couldn't be seen by anyone hiding in the jungle-wall behind her near the path—her whisper low-pitched in panic, calculated only for the hearing of the missionary. "Get your gun! They've come for you—Adbullah and the German!—they're hiding back there! Get your gun—we must run for it—quick, or they'll kill you!"

"Gun? Run for it—?" The Reverend T. Ulrich Christopher didn't understand the woman. He was looking as stunned as I must have looked when I heard that whisper from where I was hiding.

"The rubies!" Cobra Mary panted at him. "They think you've found the treasure, can't you see? They'll kill you if you don't kill them first! I can help you get away. The trader's launch. I—"

"You came to help me get away?" How those goggles were staring at her then. "My dear girl, why in—but come in!"

"No, no!" I tell you, there was an agony to her whisper that you couldn't help but believe. "Don't let me in! Pretend to argue, send me away! I'm supposed to come in and keep you company while—"

The man gave a sort of low groan. "And you're telling me this? Warning me of your own free will?"

"Because I like you," the girl sobbed at him. "Every night since you been here I—they sent me up to keep watch. But I heard you talkin'—Sundays! Prayin' up here all alone—" She put a hand to her face; sobbed at him through her fingers. That Cobra Mary! That green-eyed dancing girl! "Won't you take me with you? We'll kill them—get the launch—make for some other place where I—"

"But I *did* find the rubies!" That missionary's whisper was like the cry of a lost soul. A lost soul way down somewhere inside of the man, locked up somewhere and crying to get out. I tell you, swaying there in that church door with his Bible hugged under his arm, he had the look of a man crucified. The girl was staring at him, wide-eyed, and his face was white and twisted as though he'd been stabbed. "I *did* find the rubies, don't you see? But I—"

"Then they'll kill you for sure. You've got to shoot them before—"

"The Bible," he whispered, "says: 'Thou shalt not kill—'"

"Then you got to run," she moaned, desperate-eyed. "Run—"

"I cannot abandon the treasure I have found. I cannot abandon the Lord's work." What was the man saying now? "If it has been given to me, through sin, to see the light, I must wash myself clean by continuing to labor in His vineyard. No, the gems are not the treasure that has come to me. The gems I will send to a mission hospital in Australia while I stay here in my church, praying, bringing others like myself to believe the Word—"

SHE DIDN'T FATHOM that look on his face, any more than he'd fathomed the look on hers. Tears gleamed on his glasses, and his words were incoherent, struggling; but I got something out of them, and I wanted to yell. What I got out of them was what had come to me on this last run to Evil Beach, and "Good Lord, no!" had changed to, "Good Lord, *yes!*" You remember how the chap had looked funny to me on that night he'd popped a shot through my sea cap? Just a glimpse—some quirk of his features that puzzled me? It was "mission hospital in Australia" that did the trick! But, my God! If he *was* that black-bearded Aussie who'd fetched the dying Brahmin ashore that night of the wreck—who'd listened to the treasure story, and disappeared—!

The glimpse I had of him, then, almost knocked me over backward!

All the dancing girl understood was that he'd found the treasure and wanted to stay in his church.

"No, no! You can't! They'd burn you out to get those rubies! You don't know Abdullah! He'll kill us both, now."

Her despairing cry echoed a crash in the jungle at her back. The trader and his pet musician. They'd seen there was something wrong with that little show in the church doorway.

I almost bit my tongue off to keep from yelling as those two devils charged out into view. With a stifled scream, the dancing girl rushed forward to seize the missionary's arm. "Quick! Quick! The back-trail! The ravine beyond the idol! Bring the rubies!"

The missionary dashed back into the church and out again with only two seconds to spare. I thought he'd gone back for his rifle, but he was still clutching his Bible when he came out. His hoarse gasp, "I've got the rubies!" was drowned out by a roar from Abdullah O'Rourke.

"Stop, you! We've got you at last!"

The trader was coming up the field like a maddened rhino, head down, knife in fist, Stradivarius loping at his heels.

Sweeping the girl along with him, the Reverend Christopher made a sprint for the nearest thicket. I was crouching there, and those two went by me like a flying wind—a flying wind followed by a tornado. And if you think Abdullah was not like a tornado you are wrong.

I waited, flat as a lizard, for the storm to whistle by; then I followed as though sucked along in the back-draught. Those four in front of me were moving, I can tell you. Tearing at top-speed through that down-the-mountain jungle. The girl knew the mountain, and she led way with the speed of a gazelle. Christopher had legs on him, too. It was all I could do to keep up with the chase. A million questions were spinning around in my brain as I raced down the mountain, and those questions made me want to stop and think. What in the world had come over that dance-hall vixen tonight? Was the Reverend Christopher that Australian miner with his beard shaved? And if he *was* the Australian, why the missionary outfit? The sermons? The church-building? How had he come on that treasure, anyway? And what the devil had come over *him?*

Those were questions that would have made that statue of The Thinker sit for another two thousand years. And I had no time to think them out. No, I didn't. That girl and missionary were taking a shortcut down the mountain, going like Olympic racers. I don't think those wolves at their heels would have caught them, the odds being even. **BUT THE GIRL** had forgotten the mountain river. Remember I spoke of a stream that flowed down the mountainside and elbowed near to that heathen image half way down? The river that had a little floodgate where water could be let into the idol's swimming tank?

Cobra Mary had forgotten it. But the rainy season hadn't forgotten it. In the weeks of rain that stream had become a plunging, thundering torrent. Black water crashing down through the jungle with a current no amount of inspiration could span.

That's where those two fugitives were caught. On the bank of that torrent right under the eye of that grinning heathen idol. It was like Fate, wasn't it? That the treasure-hunt which had started with that wicked image should end up there like that?

I got there too late to see the fight. I was pretty far in the rear of that downhill rush, and in my haste to catch up, I ran through a thorn-patch and fell down a fifteen-foot mine some treasure-hunter had dug in the jungle. That shook me up plenty; I was about twenty minutes clawing my way up out of that pit.

So I didn't see the scrap on the river bank, but I'll bet that missionary and that dancing girl put up a real one. Abdullah and that murderous musician looked like it afterwards. As if the girl and the missionary had fought like two furies backed to a wall. They weren't the kind to give up easily, understand?

Above the boom of the mountain river I could hear the fierce, faint yells. The yelling died out while I was still trying to scrabble out of that steep-banked mine. Ten minutes later when I did get out, I couldn't hear anything but the river. Can you guess why that put me in a sweat? I was in a sweat for fear I'd missed the showdown. I knew that girl and missionary wouldn't last long against the trader and his pal with their knives. I was afraid Abdullah had killed that pair and made off with the rubies.

Well, the missionary and Cobra Mary had been captured, all right, but Abdullah hadn't killed them, and he hadn't made off with the rubies. Not yet, he hadn't. Hustling to reach the river where I'd heard the yells, I caught the echo of voices starting up again. I ducked back on the trail and made a skirting sneak forward, careful to keep under cover. Then circling around some rocks, I came out on a ledge that was like a balcony overlooking jungle and river-bank. What I saw when I looked over that balcony-like ledge was a scene I'll never forget if I live for another million years!

7

I CAN SEE it all in memory as though I were looking at a scene on a stage—the river booming like a stampede on the sideline—jungle in background and wings—in the foreground that big marble swimming tank—and that monstrous Hindu idol with its ugly brass baby on its knee sitting there in the middle of the tank.

That idol wasn't the only thing in the tank, though. I can close my eyes and see that brass image grinning in the moonlight, and then I can see the missionary and the girl. They were there. In the tank with that idol, tied hand and foot so they couldn't move, and lashed upright to the stone pedestal at the base of that heathen shrine.

That missionary was clad in nothing but his shorts, and that dancing girl wore less—they were tied with strips of her green *sarong*—and they looked like sacrificial victims fastened to an altar, bloody and torn. They looked small and beaten under that vast, brass-bellied gorgon, their chins no higher than the feet of that hideous brass infant and their heads below the brim of that marble tank; small and beaten badly, but they weren't bowed. The Christians in the Roman Coliseum might have stood like that and had such faces.

"No!" the missionary's cry was hoarse. Hoarse and defiant as the cry of an old battle-horn. "No, I won't tell you where it is! The treasure is not yours, Abdullah! The treasure is God's!"

He was shouting up to the trader who was posed knife in fist on the rim of the swimming tank. O'Rourke screamed down, "I want those rubies, see? They ain't in your clothes!"

Frock coat, pants, shoes, the missionary's clothes were in a pile at the trader's feet. I saw the Bible lying in the weeds a little way off, and the cleric glasses shining on the ground like a pair of eyes. The trader dealt the frock coat a savage kick.

"Come across, you fathead!" he squalled down. "You dropped those rubies somewhere up the mountain, didn't you? Where? I'll have your life an' the girl's, too, if you don't tell where—!"

"The girl doesn't know! The girl doesn't know," the missionary cried back, "and I won't tell. You don't dare kill an innocent woman, O'Rourke! And those rubies are going to a mission hospital—"

I dug my nails into my palm, listening to that. Abdullah hadn't killed the missionary because he hadn't been able to find those gems on the man! And then I dug my nails a lot deeper, listening to something else.

The sound I heard was water. Water gurgling and bubbling and swashing through an inlet into the marble tank. I forgot to say the missionary and Cobra Mary were standing up to their knees in water when I caught first sight of them there. At first I'd thought it was the stagnant rainwater I'd seen in the tank before; now I saw the water wasn't stagnant. It was rushing in through that floodgate at the back, foaming and boiling in at about fifty gallons a minute.

Do you see what that trader was up to? Stradivarius was back there holding open that ancient floodgate like a canal tender working a lock. Abdullah signaled at him to shut off the water, and when the inflow stopped the trader yelled his question again. Again, when the missionary refused to answer, more water plunged in.

And each time the missionary refused to answer. The water boiled up over his kneecaps. He wouldn't tell where those rubies were. The water rose, swishing around his shanks. He wouldn't tell. When that swimming pool was up to his middle, his face took on a yellowish tinge, but he wouldn't give away the hiding-place of that treasure.

THAT THREW ABDULLAH into a blind rage. His temper had been rising with the water in the tank, and he screamed at the violinist to let it in faster. The flood came into the tank at an inch a minute, then. Up on my rock ledge, I was sick. That trader would drown those two without a quiver if they didn't give in. Give in? But the dancing girl's chin was like carved marble—probably she didn't know. As for Christopher, his jaw was granite.

"I won't tell you, O'Rourke! God help you, if you drown us! I appeal to you—for the sake of your soul—"

"My soul!" the trader screeched. "Devil take my soul!"

"Repent! Repent before it is too late!"

"It'll be too late for *you*—if you don't tell me!"

The missionary's answer was a groan. Water was swirling under his armpits just then, and his eyes were on the girl at his side. I wonder if he wasn't going to tell, but she shook her head at him, and the tank kept filling. It knotted my stomach under my belt to see the water up to the dancing girl's throat. I dug my nails to the quick in my palm.

Why didn't I help them, you ask? Well, I'll tell you why. I was thinking about those rubies right to the last. The missionary had told the girl he'd brought them along, and I was wondering where he had them. I'm not a bit proud of the way I hung up there like a vulture. It makes me sick to remember it. I thought the missionary would finally tell where he'd hidden those blazers, and somehow I might have a chance at them.

Do you believe the missionary told? His lips were moving when the water came as high as the dancing girl's throat. Only he wasn't telling. He was praying! Praying to God to forgive that halfbreed trader and the German for drowning them.

"The rubies!" Abdullah screamed at him. "Or I'll drown the both of you!"

"Repent, Abdullah O'Rourke! Seek forgiveness for your sins! The Bible—!"

"Yah!" Wheeling fiercely, the trader kicked at the Bible in the grass, sent it flying into the underbrush with an oath of Moslem contempt. "Drown 'em, then!"

NOW I'M COMING to the part of the story that has to do with something you skeptics may not believe in. Faith. The power of religious conviction. Miracles. Miracles? I give you this one! That missionary and that dancing girl in that heathen idol's tank with the water up to their chins. The girl with her face uplifted like the face in a picture I once saw of Saint Joan dying in the flames. The missionary with his eyes on the tropic Stars overhead, making his confessional.

"God have mercy on me, a sinner!"

Can you hear him crying that out above the boom of

the tide that was lapping around his chin? But you'd never guess his next speech, I promise you.

"I came here masked as a missionary to steal an earthly treasure! The church was to hide the mine! To hide my workings in the mine! Thou knowest how I dynamited the silk-cotton tree that night with explosives that floated ashore from the wreck. Thou knowest how I blasted the tree after climbing to the top to find the carved directions to the treasure. Filled with greed I returned to play a masquerade, hiding behind my disguise as Thy servant. The sermons to fool any watchers who might be hiding near the church. The false words to the schooner captain. The insincere pleas to make the others believe in my piety. The digging in secret—"

There they were—the puzzle-knots, untied one after the other. All the way down the line. The answers to all those strange mysteries—the unveiling of that treasure-hunter's whole nefarious scheme. How he'd hurried the church to get it up before the rainy season. How he'd worked day and night, digging the mine under the floor. How he'd carried the dirt, bucket-system, up into the steeple, so the islanders would see no evidence of the job. His voice went on, hoarsely, entreating forgiveness, praying for Divine grace and mercy.

I don't know how long that confession lasted. Listening to those words, I forgot the emergency. The water was roaring into the tank as the missionary's voice went on, flooding in gallon after gallon. I was too stunned to realize that something else beside that drowning man's confession was going on. I didn't see it, until Abdullah O'Rourke yelled.

"The water! Merciful Allah! The water's stopped rising!"

DO YOU UNDERSTAND what I'm telling you? The water was pouring through the floodgate into that tank, but it had stopped rising. A ton of it had gushed into the tank while the missionary talked—the water was still no higher than his chin! I can see it yet—the tank three-quarters filled—the girl standing on tiptoe to keep her mouth clear of the flood—the missionary praying with his face undrowned, uplifted—Stradivarius staring at the inlet, pop-eyed—Abdullah glaring white amazement at the flood that rushed in but rose no higher.

Another moment passed! Another!

"Thank God! Thank God!"

The man's voice from the swimming tank came clear. On the edge of the tank, Abdullah O'Rourke was sinking to his knees. I think the German musician put his hands to his forehead in fear. I know the water was still booming in when I finally got away from that ledge, and I could hear it pouring as into a giant bathtub when I stopped, breathless in downhill flight, some minutes later. I could see that brass idol's face leering down at me over the jungle-tops, and something about that image must have thrown an echo. Above the boom of river and tank, I could hear voices. The missionary's voice and the voice of the dancing girl. Abdullah O'Rourke's deep rumble, and the German accent of the musician.

I went on down the mountain in a mystery of Asian darkness. Behind me in the night, the missionary and his converts were praying. The missionary, after all, had had his miracle.

THE SAILOR STOPPED speaking with a gesture that let him lean back in his chair. For a while the only sound on the veranda where we sat was the drone of insects at the screen, moths trying to reach the lamp. Then Crewe, who had started the religious issue, reached over to the table and picked up glass and syphon. He squirted a moment, watching the soda fizz up in the glass.

He quirked an eyebrow at Captain Lantern. "Do you think you could stop that by Faith? The soda overflowing the glass? Really, now, Captain—"

Lantern shook his head.

"But the river, the marble tank!" Exasperation put an edge on Crewe's voice. "No different in principle! I mean, that miracle—!"

"If you mean the water going no higher in the tank," the sailor said slowly, "that wasn't any miracle. God works in a more mysterious way His wonders to perform. No cheap tricks like that. That was luck plus a perfectly natural explanation. I knew it, the minute I had a chance to get my wits about me. That Hindu tank wasn't what I meant by the miracle."

"Well, how—?"

"That tank," the sea captain offered bleakly, "is a trick as old as India. As I explained in the story, it was supposed to tell the legend of the god, Vasuveda, carrying the infant Krishna across the Yamuna River. The Brahmin priest spun the yarn. How the demons made the river rise, but the water never rose above the baby's big toe. And that's where the flood in that marble tank rose to. As high as the foot of that infernal baby and no higher. Lucky that wasn't above the missionary's or Cobra Mary's chin."

Crew insisted, "I still don't see."

"I should have," the narrator grunted. "I'd seen that

whole show before in a Vasuveda shrine in India. The guide there explained it to me, but it was a number of years before, and I'd forgotten. Trap outlet at the base of the idol, that's all. The trap gauged to open at a certain pressure. Water rises to a calculated height and the weight opens the trap. Secret drain. But the superstitious natives fall for it the way Abdullah did, and I suppose Christopher, himself, thought it was an answer to his prayers. But I think that's the miracle—Christopher's prayers."

Lantern gripped the wicker arms of his chair and leaned forward. "Think of it! That Australian miner snatching the carved directions to the treasure, blasting the tree, sneaking off the island to the mainland—I found out afterward he'd made Bangkok in a lifeboat from the wreck—plotting that scheme to dig up the thirty-eight rubies, then coming back and putting it across. Only he put across that missionary act too well. How's that for the power of the Bible! Up there alone in his church, nothing to do for relaxation but read the Scriptures and preach those fake sermons—well—the man converted himself! Imagine that for a treasure-hunting devil who'd risked his neck to put over that fraud, done all that cover-up work, and already had three of those priceless gems sold in Bangkok. A man like that converted by the religion he was pretending to preach. I think that's the miracle."

The speaker paused to gaze at moonlight ebbing across the deserted boulevard. He rubbed his chin self-consciously.

"Or maybe the miracle was me not snatching those rubies when I had the chance." He flushed. "I was a smart, tough kid in those days, I guess. I didn't believe in anything, either, until I saw that dancing girl risk her life to save the missionary's, and then heard that chap's confession. Well, I had a chance to get those stones, and I told you at the beginning there was a minute when I had them in my hand. That missionary's confession answered all the questions I'd wondered about except two. How he'd smuggled the blazers to that one-eyed Siamese in Bangkok, and where they were hidden when he fled the church. I got to thinking about it as I walked down the mountain. Abdullah had frisked his clothes. Nothing else he could hide them in. He'd carried nothing with him but his Bible—

"Then I had a flash. Every time one of those gems turned up in Bangkok, I'd just sailed over from Evil Beach. Same day. Suppose Christopher had written that one-eyed Siamese a letter telling him to look for something on my boat. What? A Testament? A hymnal? *The Life of John Wesley?* Sure, the missionary had given me those volumes, knowing I'd never read them, and if I did I'd never get to the chapters in back.

"Afterwards, on my return to Bangkok where Ledbetter fired me for stealing his launch, I found out those hunches were right. I got those books out of my slop chest, and the last hundred pages of each book were hollowed out and glued together—a little nest for a gold-plated ruby. Anyway, I crept back that night for a look at the missionary's Bible. I found it in the underbrush where the trader had kicked it. I picked it up out of the weeds, and it was heavy. Heavier than even a leather-bound Bible had a right to be. I was shifting it in my hand when I heard voices beginning a hymn. Peering from the brush, I saw the missionary and the others still kneeling by that unfilled marble tank. I put the Bible back in the bushes again."

The sailor rubbed his mouth with the back of his hand. "I don't know," he concluded quietly. "Maybe the biggest miracle is that island they called Evil Beach. No, it doesn't go by that name any more. First thing you see when you sail into harbor is the church at the top of the mountain. White. Like a monument. There isn't any dirt in that steeple. You climb the path on Sunday and you'll walk with a crowd. They say the Reverend T. Ulrich Christopher is still preaching. All the people from the town go up to hear him. Cobra Mary teaches a Bible class (Mrs. Christopher, I mean) and Stradivarius leads the choir. And I don't have to tell you who stands at the door to welcome strangers with an outstretched hand. Well, there's your miracle."